His attention slipped lower, to her lips.

"My obsession for you, it scares me. I don't want to lose my soul to a witch."

"I don't want your soul."

"You want my heart."

"I want to stay with you, here, in your bedchamber." Lucinda touched his hair, recklessly caressing him, tracing his ear with one finger.

"If we make love, honor and duty will force me to marry you, and neither of us are ready for marriage." Richard's voice was low, rough.

"Leave. Now. Before my resolve gives out entirely and we find ourselves leg-shackled to each other, until death do us part."

"Don't send me away." She pressed her face against his neck, breathing him in. "Show me, Richard. Show me what it means to love."

His eyes darkened and he seemed to wrestle with some inner demon. Knowing he teetered on the edge of surrender, she kissed him, her lips soft, teasing.

"Little witch," he murmured, and then he crushed her to his powerful form, deepening his kiss, bringing a part of her to life that no one else could. . . .

The critics adore Tracy Fobes and
TOUCH NOT THE CAT

Books by Tracy Fobes

Touch Not the Cat
Heart of the Dove

Published by POCKET BOOKS

TRACY FOBES

HEART of the DOVE

SONNET BOOKS

New York London Toronto Sydney Tokyo Singapore

This book is a work of fiction. Names, characters, places and incidents are products of the author's imagination or are used fictitiously. Any resemblance to actual events or locales or persons living or dead is entirely coincidental.

An *Original* Publication of POCKET BOOKS

 A Sonnet Book published by
POCKET BOOKS, a division of Simon & Schuster Inc.
1230 Avenue of the Americas, New York, NY 10020

ISBN 978-1-4516-4679-5

First Sonnet Books printing August 1999

10 9 8 7 6 5 4 3 2 1

SONNET BOOKS and colophon are trademarks of Simon & Schuster Inc.

Front cover illustration by Lisa Litwack

Printed in the U.S.A.

Prologue

The Village of Somerton
Bedfordshire, England

1593

Morgana Fey cried out as the coldness slammed into her and bent her double. It clawed its way through her skin, a numbing pain far more intense than she'd ever experienced.

Whimpering, she dropped the ladle she held into her cauldron of bubbling venison stew.

Staggered away from the hearth.

Collapsed against the wall, clutching her stomach.

The coldness burrowed deep into her midsection, squeezing, ripping, shredding. It expanded in her like some ice-baby, some deadly malignancy which fed on her and would soon be born.

She pressed her hands against her temples. Curled herself into a tight ball. Fear pulsed through her, leaving her breathless.

"No, please," she begged.

Without explanation, the pain vanished.

Morgana lay stunned. She felt boneless, her body naught but a mass of jelly. The pain was gone but the fear remained. What had happened? From the moment she'd awakened this morning, the hours had passed uneventfully. Christopher, her husband, had left near noon and was due back in an hour or so. She'd felt fine all day. And now this.

Shuddering, she uncurled herself and pushed onto one elbow. Her chin felt warm and moist. Blood. She'd bitten her lip. She wiped her chin with her sleeve and sat up. In the aftermath of the coldness her stomach felt abnormally heated, as though she'd just drunk a tankard of ale.

Her gaze flickered past the stone walls of her home, the timber-and-wattles framework upon which she'd hung a few old tapestries, the neatly mended cushions that lay sprawled upon the rushes. No demons hid among the shadows created by her candles.

The familiarity of the cottage soothed her. She began to wonder. *Ague, fever, apoplexy, palsy, the pox.* Had some chance disease gotten hold of her?

No, the attack was too severe. Too quick.

A spiritual attack, then.

But who?

She looked from left to right, searching this time for the witch who had battered her. Candlelight mixed with wisps of smoke from the hearth and filled the cottage with a soft, ambient glow. Bunches of bee balm hung from rafters darkened with soot, their fragrance spicing the air. Shutters blocked the autumn wind which moaned against the window panes.

Everything appeared normal.

She listened intently.

Heard nothing but the crackling fire.

Was her adversary outside?

She closed her eyes and pictured the yard around the cottage and the lane in front of her house. "Moon be full, make shadows flee," she whispered. "Show me what I do not see."

An image formed in her mind. A man. Cloaked.

He hadn't arrived. Not yet. But he was coming. She could feel it. Her talent told her so. The figure could be a warlock or even Satan himself. But it didn't really matter who he was, because in the end, Morgana knew his purpose would be the same.

Death.

She lurched to her feet. She hadn't much time to protect herself and prepare a defense. Silently she seethed over the unfairness of it all. How dare anyone threaten her after she'd worked so hard to find happiness!

At one-and-thirty, Morgana considered herself a respectable matron. She'd married a man who loved her. Together they'd settled in the village of Somerton and made their small home comfortable. Her skill as a seamstress contributed to the family coffers and her well-made dresses graced the backs of numerous ladies.

Granted, she owed a good deal of her success to witchcraft, her secret hobby. Love spells, charms to bind enemies, talismans for eternal beauty, and other assorted rituals had contributed to her current state of well-being. Sometimes, when she cast a particularly nasty spell, she wondered if God approved of her magic. Before she could think too deeply on it, however, memories of her childhood would overwhelm her and she'd decide she didn't really care if He approved or not.

Sudden heat seared through her white cotton gown. The fire in her hearth had begun to crackle and leap wildly. Morgana cried out. Trembling, she staggered to the closest window and tried to open the shutters. Even though they weren't latched, the wooden boards refused to move.

The door.

She ran to the front door and jiggled the latch. It moved freely, and yet she couldn't pull the door open. Magic had trapped her inside her own house.

Her enemy was strong.

Who was doing this to her? And why? Tears gathered in her eyes but she dashed them away. Aware every second counted, she grabbed her robe and shrugged it on. The black silk whispered as it settled over her dress, enfolding her in a familiar embrace.

Confidence flowed through her, as though she'd donned a suit of armor. The basic rituals of magic always made her feel that way. She swallowed her tears and fought for control. She'd made a life for herself as a faithful wife and seamstress of good quality, and wouldn't relinquish it easily.

Heat began to build within the cottage. The fire roared crazily, sucking at the air and threatening to spill into the kitchen. Morgana ran to a trunk pushed against the wall and lifted its lid. Inside, a small crystal dove lay nestled upon black velvet, its wings folded gently against its sides, head tucked toward the left. She sensed the power emanating from the statue, could feel the magic in her body jump in response.

She grasped the dove and brought it out. The statue refracted the firelight into a rainbow of colors. Deep in its core a ruby heart hung suspended, as

4

though the crystal dove had been poured around the heart.

The heart of the dove, Morgana knew, was the seat of the dove's power. Used in magical rituals for centuries, it had absorbed magic from each witch who called upon it. It was a warehouse of ancient power and Morgana was just beginning to learn how to unlock that power.

She slipped the dove into her pocket. She'd use it only as a last resort. Its magic was wild and unpredictable in the hands of anyone but a master, and her own status still fell short of that. Other spells, those of protection and binding, could very well prove adequate in dealing with the figure who wore the face of death.

Morgana pulled her grimoire from beneath the bed, turned its crinkled old pages in a frenzy, read for a minute, then gathered the items she'd need from her stock of supplies. That done, she pushed stools back, moved cushions, and swept away rushes until she had cleared a large space in the middle of the cottage. She grasped a sack of salt and poured a thin stream onto the floor, walking as she did so, creating a nine-foot circle of protection. Her cork-soled shoes whispered across stone as she jumped inside the circle and faced east.

"Great ruler of air, of whirlwind and tempest, guard me from he who comes from the east," she intoned, then turned south.

"Great ruler of fire, of sunlight and lightning, guard me from he who comes from the south."

West and north followed, and shortly she had completed the circle to the best of her ability. Next, she began her spell of binding.

She spread a small velvet cloth upon her palm. Gossamer spiderwebs covered the surface of the cloth and glistened in the candlelight. On top of the webs, she placed a butterfly, recently dead.

"With spiderwebs I bind him tight. I break his legs and stop his sight. He cannot hear or speak or fight."

She completed the spell by folding the cloth into quarters, forming a bag, and tying the top with a piece of cord. Her palms were sweating by the time she'd finished, but she noted with satisfaction that the fire in the hearth had resumed normal proportions.

It was too early to assume victory, but with time . . .

Morgana sat down and waited.

She listened to the wind blowing against the eaves, to the pops and spits from the fire. She examined every shadow in the cottage and found them all harmless. She sniffed the air and pictured the yard and lane in her mind. All seemed clear.

After an hour had passed without incident, she decided she'd routed her tormentor. She placed the binding-bag into her pocket, next to the dove, and silently vowed to discover his identity. He had made an enemy this eve, and Morgana would not rest until he threatened her and those she loved no longer.

She stepped outside her circle of protection.

A bolt of pure agony lanced through her, driving her to her knees. She screamed, but no sound emerged from her throat. A giant, invisible beast was savaging her, sinking its ice-cold claws into her guts and gnawing on her bones.

Gibbering, she clawed at the floor. Tried to drag herself back into the circle of protection. She couldn't move, the pain was too terrible. Her fingers hooked, she reached into her pocket, feeling for the dove. Where was it?

The door banged open. A chill autumn breeze ripped through the cottage. Blood streaming from her freshly bitten lip, Morgana raised herself on an elbow and stared at the cloaked figure in the doorway.

Edward Drakewyck. *The vicar, by God.*

And Henry Clairmont, his henchman. With a sack slung over his shoulder.

She held her hand out toward them. "Please," she choked. "Stop."

Edward Drakewyck waved negligent fingers through the air. The pain ceased immediately, leaving her breathless, her nerve endings overloaded. She stared at his harsh face, at the brown hair streaked with gray that shot back from his forehead, and the eyes lit with zealous fire. His lips were thin and cruel, and when he spoke, his voice had a righteous tone that made her want to scream again, this time with outrage.

"Your time has come, Morgana Fey."

She dragged herself to her feet. She would not crouch before him. "So, Vicar, you are also a warlock. You hid your magic well."

The vicar gestured to his companion, Henry Clairmont. For the first time she noticed the ancient tome beneath the vicar's arm. The leather-bound cover displayed the word *Goetia* in gold lettering. *He carries a spellbook,* Morgana thought, *rather than a Bible. Oh, this is rich.*

The younger man dropped the sack onto a pile of rushes and untied it. Fabric fell away, revealing the battered face of an unconscious man. *Her* Christopher.

Another sort of pain grabbed hold of her, this one of the spirit. Her heart began to beat with slow, hollow strokes. They were not just going to kill her. Christopher was going to pay for her sins, too. She caught sight of the crystal dove resting against the leg of a stool several feet away. With it she could blast them to Hell, but could she prevent them from hurting Christopher before the dove's magic took over?

No. She would risk her own life, but not her husband's.

Her shoulders caved inward. "What do you want?"

"Morgana Fey, you have become corrupt." Edward walked a tight circle around her. "Your vanity has led you to excesses that display a startling lack of morality. You represent the worst aspects of those with talent. You have maimed and will murder unless you are stopped now."

"Who gives you, a warlock, the right to pass judgement on me? You, too, cast spells."

"You and I are opposites. I provide. You devour." He paused for a moment, his gaze touching on her cooking fire, her bed, the cushions scattered about the floor. "I have come for the dove."

"Ah." Morgana forced a laugh. She should have known. Any witch or warlock within ten miles would have sensed the dove's presence and come investigating. "You covet the dove's magic and have decided to challenge me. Tell me, do you plan to use the dove in your rituals? You must be the first vicar to prefer a pagan statue over a crucifix."

"You've used its magic to devour people. I will ensure it never falls into the hands of the wicked again."

She clutched the locket which hung around her neck. Of gold filigree, it contained a portrait of her husband. "And after I give you the dove, will you arrest me and put me to the Question? I see you are carrying *Goetia*. Perhaps you have some spell in mind. Or will you simply slice me across the neck?"

"Give me the dove."

She tapped her chin, playing for time. She needed to *think*. "I'll wager, good vicar, that you haven't the slightest care for your god. You've adopted priestly robes because it is an excellent way to hide. Who would dare accuse a vicar of witchcraft?"

"Where is it, witch?"

"You hypocrite," she hissed. "*You* are Satan's spawn, not I." She slipped her free hand into her pocket and squeezed the binding-bag, hoping against reason that her spell might still have some effect on the vicar.

Edward Drakewyck blinked and took a step backward.

"With spiderwebs I bind him tight," she whispered, "I break his legs and stop his sight—"

"Stop it!" Henry Clairmont demanded. A knife in his hand, the younger man positioned the blade against her husband's throat and nicked the skin.

Blood ran down to Christopher's shirt and trickled over the matching locket she'd given him as a wedding present. Morgana wondered if his blood had seeped inside the locket to obscure her face.

Christopher opened his eyes and stared at her, bewildered. She released the binding-bag instantly. Even as her hand fell to her side, her urge to fight back shriveled. She wouldn't endanger him. She loved him too much.

Edward Drakewyck strode in front of her, glaring. "No more tricks, Morgana. Give me the dove. Now."

"Will you spare Christopher?"

The vicar nodded unwillingly. "To kill is to devour, and I do that only in the direst of circumstances. He will be spared."

"And I?"

"I won't stain my hands with your blood, either. It isn't necessary."

"So I'm to go to prison, then."

"You're far too dangerous to place in prison. You shall sleep, instead, for all eternity."

A sleeping spell, Morgana thought. She could ask for no more. If she wasn't dead, a chance for vengeance remained. "The dove is there. I give it to you of my free will."

The vicar followed her gaze and strode forward to scoop the dove off the floor. His eyes widened as he held it and a dreamy expression molded his countenance into something almost pleasant.

Morgana thought he looked drunk.

The vicar shook himself and opened *Goetia.* Its parchment pages rustled as he turned them. He found the page he was looking for, stared at it for a moment, and then closed the book.

"With the dove, I do not need *Goetia,*" he said to Henry. Then, frowning once again, Edward turned to her. The dove began to glow against his palm, washing his face with a rainbow of color. "Morgana Fey, I conjure thee," he intoned.

Beside him, his henchman tied three knots into a cord.

Morgana held tight to her locket. She could feel the magic flowing off the vicar in waves. It didn't bring pain this time, or cold, just numbness. She closed her eyes and imagined herself in Christopher's arms, warm and protected. "Moon be full, make shadows flee," she mumbled. "Show me what will come to be."

An image began to form in her mind. A man with a scarred hand. A woman with flowers in her hair. The dove. She watched, her eyebrows rising. She saw *herself*. So, it wouldn't end here.

"I dim your eyes with graveyard dirt and plug your ears with hardened clay," the vicar chanted and pulled a handful of earth from his pocket. He tossed it upon her.

Henry Clairmont tied three more knots into the cord.

Morgana smiled beneath the rain of dirt. Revenge *would* be hers. She focused upon Edward's righteous frown and gave in to the urge to tell him that the evil he'd done this day would be his family's undoing.

"When the world is older and you are dead," she sang, "and I am sleeping in my bed, a Drakewyck witch and Clairmont knave will awaken me from my lonely grave. They will love and the dove will be mine, and utter destruction will be thine."

Edward paused, his eyes wide. He looked at Henry, who seemed frozen. "When we are finished here," the vicar soothed, "I'll record her words as a warning to our families throughout the ages. Take heart, old friend. It will be over soon."

He turned back to Morgana and chanted faster. "I seal your mouth with cups of sand and bind your limbs with lengths of vine."

The vicar threw sand and a small piece of ivy upon her. Fingers trembling, the younger man tied a final three knots and passed the cord to Edward.

Edward gripped the cord in his hand. "Dirt, sand, vine, and clay, the Earth has bound you on this day. Fall to the ground, Morgana Fey! Not dead but asleep you'll forever stay."

The numbness had invaded every part of her body now, and as she collapsed to the floor she felt nothing. If not for her sight, which was fading fast, she wouldn't even have known she was lying prone. She caught Christopher's gaze and pleaded with him to forgive her, to never doubt her love.

He closed his eyes and turned away.

Morgana groaned. Edward Drakewyck had taken everything away from her. Even her husband's love. When she awoke as the vision had predicted, her fury would know no bounds. Hers was a thirst for revenge that could never be quenched.

"Ah nal nath rac, uth vas bethad, dochiel dienve."

She heard the words and knew Edward had continued his spell, but her vision was fading. Mist filled the room, mist that flowed from the vicar's mouth and wrapped around her like a spider's web. Smothering her. Binding her.

She couldn't feel her chest rise. She'd stopped breathing altogether. And the blood in her veins—it had stopped moving. Her very heart was still. But these things didn't pain her. A curious effect, she thought.

And knew no more.

1

Bedfordshire, England
1856

Water dripped in a steady cadence from birch leaves, soaking Lucinda Drakewyck as she walked through the Bedfordshire woodlands. The rain had stopped some time ago. But like miniature pitchers, the newly unfurled leaves had gathered water and emptied on her as she passed beneath.

Warm and dry beneath her velvet hood, Lucinda smiled. She was up to her ankles in mud and enjoying every moment of it. The winter, coldly persistent in its bid to ruin her days, had blanketed the town of Somerton with two surprise snowstorms well past the first of April. Rain hardly seemed dreary after months of being caged in Drakewyck Grange with Uncle George.

Besides, today was special. May Day had arrived, signaling the return of life and fertility to the world. Lucinda planned to celebrate the day with a Beltane

ritual totally unsuited to a lady of property and connections. She grinned at the thought of Uncle George's
expression should he discover what she was about.

Sunlight fought its way through the treetops and
glinted upon silver-limbed saplings, teasing the tulips
and forget-me-nots that peeked through the under-
growth with the promise of warmth. Calm permeated
the forest, a deep, humid peace that coaxed birds to
somnolence and encouraged butterflies to roost upon
warm boulders. Lucinda eased herself and her sack,
weighted down with a flask of May wine, around an
outcrop of rock.

Uncle George loved her dearly, of that she had no
doubt. Still, he disapproved of her magic-working and
insisted it would only bring heartache. "Find something else to do," he'd often told her. But what was
a lady to do with herself week after week?

Gentlemen had their pursuits, of course: hunting,
riding to the hounds, overseeing the estate, or even
collecting old books, Uncle George's favorite pastime.
And ladies? Well, true patricians didn't earn a living,
and Lucinda had an obligation to preserve the Drakewyck family name by avoiding both the trades and
manual labor. That ugly business was better left to
maidservants and farmer's daughters. Ladies devoted
themselves to embroidery and naught much else.

She shook her head as she hoisted herself, along
with her many petticoats, skirt, and cloak, over a decayed timber fence. In truth, she'd never cared much
for rank and connections. The higher a person's rank,
the more dependent on servants he or she became,
and hopelessly inadequate husks bored her silly. In
deference to Uncle George's nerves, however, she *did*
place boundaries on her behavior and tried to remain
respectable, at least in public.

Aged rocks, coated in yellow-green moss, tumbled in heaps, and violets peeped from beneath brown mulch. In the distance, she saw a stone retaining wall, a landmark which meant her glen, the place where she cast her spells, was nearby. She quickened her pace, not only eager to start the ceremony but to drop her sack to the ground. She'd tied a rope to the sack and slung the rope over her shoulder, and now the rope was cutting into her skin.

Beltane, she thought. A time when warmth imagined in winter becomes a reality, when the future becomes the present. What sort of future had she? She supposed she would spend her days caring for Uncle George and reading her books and poetry. Uncle George had told her on several occasions that he didn't need her and wouldn't mind marrying her off to some amiable lad, but Lucinda still preferred to fuss over him.

And books, unlike embroidery, were a worthwhile pursuit. Rank and connections did not make a person interesting, she'd decided. Books did. She'd always gravitated toward clever, well-informed people who gave all ideas equal consideration, and didn't listen to the gossip that called her a bluestocking. So she debated with Uncle George's cronies and quoted poetry and frightened away all the men who would court her.

And tried not to feel lonely.

Still, she wanted something more than amiability in a husband and was quite certain the local gentlemen would have left her dissatisfied. Would she die a spinster? Probably. She'd already turned twenty and hadn't a single prospect. Perhaps she'd even die a *poor* spinster. The good Lord knew she and Uncle George were having their monetary difficulties.

Lucinda stopped short. She'd reached the glen and, as usual, its beauty left her breathless. Spikes of strawberry foxglove had taken over the clearing, growing in clumps that hosted both bees and fluttering moths. A fallen tree lay upon the remnants of a cottage, evidence of a secret disaster that ivy would soon obliterate entirely. 'Twas a tranquil place—quiet, soothing— and as she waded through the flowers, pleasure filled her. But when she leaned down and plucked a piece of lavender, her smiled faltered. A bloated spider had attached itself to the flower and was spinning its web around a butterfly.

She dropped it. Something about the spider bothered her. It seemed to represent more than Nature at work. Indeed, her instinct suggested the spider was part of a larger pattern of corruption she hadn't yet discerned.

Evil had come to her small glen.

She forced a laugh. What fancy!

Her stone ring, used to keep fires within bounds, glinted dull gray in the sunlight. She walked toward it and dropped her sack. The smell of balsam and fresh earth filled the glen, reminding her of the reason she'd come. Determined not to ruin her celebration, she thrust the dark thoughts aside.

The ground appeared drier in the clearing. With a little sigh she flopped onto the grass, her sprigged muslin skirt and petticoats billowing around her. She was thin enough to forgo a corset—too thin, as Uncle George would have it. Lucinda, for her part, found her slenderness quite gratifying. Without the device she was able to sit and stand and stretch, impossible feats when properly rigged.

Her drawers began to feel damp. Perhaps the ground *wasn't* so dry. This little adventure might well

cost her one of her spring gowns, and she hadn't
many to spare. Still, fussing wouldn't dry her out. She
might as well enjoy herself, wet seat and all.

She removed a length of ivy from her sack, twined
it through her hair, and tucked a few violets behind
her ear. Next, she poured herself a glass of May wine,
spiced with woodruff, and sipped. It tasted as sweet
as spring itself but still retained the bite of winter.
Her stomach grew warm and she sipped again, chuck-
ling this time.

If Uncle George could see me now.

Abruptly she threw back her head and finished the
wine. Pshaw on Uncle George.

Humming Schubert's *Serenade,* she stood up, shook
her skirts, and began to gather bits of kindling. When
her arms were full she set the kindling into the fire
ring. After a few strikes on a flint and a bit of nurtur-
ing she had a fire that popped and spit at her. The
acrid scent of burning wood filled the glen, overpowering smells of wet earth and sunshine.

Her lips compressed into a moue of distaste. Burning wood, the essence of winter. Horrible! Quickly she
pulled a few hemlock cones—symbols of fertility—
from her sack and tossed them into the flames. Next,
she lit two wax candles, both blue, and arranged some
violets and lavender around them to create a make-
shift altar.

Softly she murmured the words of Beltane and
welcomed a new year of growth and prosperity.
"From frozen ground to soft, rich dirt; from dreary
skies to azure blue; from icy ponds to flowing
streams, the Earth will change from gray to green."

Lucinda closed her eyes and focused on the sunlight falling across her face, warming her skin. She
concentrated on the taste of May wine on her lips and

the smell of burning hemlock cones in the air. She opened herself to the magic in the trees around her and the promise of life in the mud that clung to her boots.

For one moment she was no longer a lady of property and connections. She was no longer a human being who lived with and talked to and loved others, but at the core, always remained alone. She became a part of a greater, timeless truth, a consciousness not bound by the physical limitations of the human body but universal, filled with thoughts of minds long dead and those yet to come, vibrating with the spirit of Nature.

Lucinda thought of the place she'd entered as a dark garden, where past and present swirled together and became a little of both. It echoed with mysteries and voices of old, and 'twas there that the source of her magic rested. Now, as she walked through that dark garden, its magic renewed her spirit just as winter passed and the Earth awoke from its long, cold sleep. Even thoughts of the spider who'd spun a web around a butterfly couldn't dampen the appreciation and gladness that buoyed her soul—

Heat invaded her chest without warning. It wrapped around her heart and sizzled its way across her lungs, leaving her gasping for air. Her eyes snapped open. The sunlight suddenly seemed too harsh, the trees dark and huddled together, menacing.

No, not again. Not today.

The heat crept up to her shoulder blades. It became a burning pain. Red dots swirled across her field of sight and she fell to her knees, her head clutched in her hands.

"No," she begged, but the vision cared not for her desires.

18

Somewhere in the distance, on the other side of the forest, a hound bayed. A hunting party, perhaps. Panic mixed with the fire slowly flooding her neck. If someone found her hunched over, wet, disarrayed, and in the throes of a vision, there'd be no end to the trouble. Still, as soon as the panic had come to her, infernal fire charred it to nothingness.

Heat blasted up past her mouth and nose to settle in her brain. She bit her lip. Pressed her fingernails into her palms, drawing blood. The months ahead coalesced into a single image and assaulted her senses until a moan of pure agony ripped from her.

The vision roared in her mind, beginning in its usual way. She saw a man who looked familiar but defied naming. Hazel eyes, strong nose, full lips, and a damaged hand where the first two fingers ended just past the knuckle. Whimpering, she tried to sort through her impressions of this man. Intense longing for him nearly drowned everything else out.

Who was he?

Handsome and strong at the core, yet damaged somehow, and vulnerable, he was her protector. Her "Lancelot." He would save her even if it meant sacrificing himself. She knew this with absolute certainty. At the same time, she understood that love between them, if it grew, would mean nothing but death. That knowledge was the source of her longing, for she wanted him terribly but could not have him.

Eyes squeezed shut, she gave herself over to the next portion of the vision, the part that reared its head in her nightmares. The woman came, just as she always did, her wheat-colored hair blowing in a crisp autumn breeze, her eyes blue and icy, and a gold filigree locket around her neck. Hers was not a mortal fury but something much stranger and deadlier.

When Lucinda met the woman's gaze she saw a soulless desire to inflict suffering of the worst kind.

A witch, Lucinda thought.

The witch turned and stretched out her hand, palm up, seeking something. Lucinda began to shudder. For a moment she was no longer hunched by her Beltane fire. Instead, she was *in* the vision, feeling the cold emptiness of the witch's stare and clutching a small, hard statue in her hands.

The witch wanted Lucinda's statue, some sort of bird. Lucinda held the bird tight, caught in indecision. The witch, she sensed, would become evil incarnate if she gained the statue. But Lancelot would die if Lucinda refused to relinquish it, even as he saved her life.

The heat and pain abruptly receded from her head, flowing downward before fizzling out entirely. Lucinda stood on trembling legs and looked around. Her sight cleared. Mist had invaded the glen, but otherwise, everything appeared unchanged. She wiped away the tears she hadn't even known she'd been crying and struggled to her feet. Despite the ferocity of the vision, her body remained unharmed.

Scowling, she kicked dirt onto the fire. That was the third time in as many months that the vision had ambushed one of her ceremonies. It always played out the same way and left her with a choice. She could choose the man and allow evil to go unchecked through the world, or she could sacrifice the man and prevent the witch from hurting others.

Heaven help her, was it true? Were these things that *might* happen, or were they already fated to occur? Despair settled into her like the chill of winter. Never before had she felt so alone and completely out of sorts.

Uncle George. The time had come to tell him about the vision. Granted, he didn't approve of magic and had forbidden her to practice it, but she was desperate and needed his wisdom. He would not turn her away, not when she suspected her life was about to go very wrong indeed.

Something rattled in the thicket to her right, where the edge of the forest met the clearing. Without warning, a barrel-chested dog jumped the bushes, bellowed a deep, throaty *woof*, and trotted up to her.

Lucinda stepped backward, hand pressed against her chest. "Upon my word, Samson, you startled me. I see you've sniffed me out. Where is your master?"

She scanned the trees, looking for Sir James Clairmont. They were neighbors, separated by miles of woodlands and fields that precluded close association. Even so, she and Sir James shared a love of nature that occasionally brought them together in the woods. Today, however, she would rather the baronet not see her in this condition. He'd ask questions she couldn't possibly answer.

The huge, slobbery hound wandered over to the embers in her fire ring and sniffed. Lucinda ran a hand along Samson's thick, black-and-white fur, noting that mud covered his withers. The dog was so large she didn't even have to lean over. "Playing hard, eh, Samson? Well, I don't know where Sir James has gotten to, but I believe I shall escape before he discovers me."

Samson trotted away to the far corner of the clearing. He snuffled in the leaves and sent a squirrel up a tree.

Hurriedly she gathered up her flask of May wine and dropped it into the sack. The sun drooped lower on the horizon, suggesting the hour had grown close to teatime, a perfect opportunity to corner her uncle and insist he listen to her story. Just as she snuffed her two candles and congratulated herself on her escape, a figure cloaked in black appeared at the edge of the woods.

Lucinda froze. "Sir James?"

The figure stood perfectly still while the mist ebbed and flowed around him, obscuring his features. She'd never seen Sir James in a black cloak. He preferred a red hunting jacket. She took a step backward and cast a wary glance toward Samson. The hound, unconcerned, was rooting around in a thicket.

"Sir?" she said again, and this time her voice quavered a little. She would give him exactly ten seconds to answer before she left the glen as swiftly as her feet would allow.

The man put one hand to his mouth and whistled, once, twice. Samson woofed in response and ran toward him. The man stepped forward to meet the hound. As he left the shelter of the trees, sunlight played upon his countenance.

Lucinda pressed her hand against her chest.

The world seemed to tilt on its axis.

Tall, one hand shoved into his cloak pocket, he pierced her with a brooding hazel gaze. Mud clung to his trousers and boots, and his shirt bagged where he'd tucked it into his waistband, suggesting he'd had a lengthy tramp in the woods. He sported perhaps a day's growth of beard, and he'd tied his black hair in a queue, much the way gentlemen had a century earlier.

She'd seen him mere minutes before.

In her vision.

Heat suffused her face as she stared up at him. Just as quickly it drained from her. Every nerve in her body began to sing with his nearness. *He's come*, she thought.

Silence stretched between them as he measured her with a single glance. Evidently he found her wanting, for he turned to go. Lucinda reached out to him, begging him to stay, to be the Lancelot she'd expected and rush to her side, offering aid.

He hesitated, lips compressed into thin lines. Even as she trembled beneath the intensity in his eyes, she wondered why he hadn't at least stepped forward to introduce himself.

Who *was* he?

His easy command of Sir James' hound suggested he knew the Clairmont family well. A friend of the family, perhaps? He might even be Richard Clairmont, Sir James' only son. The younger Clairmont had supposedly just returned from the Crimean War, but she didn't know what he looked like. Richard had left for boarding school while still a youth and had returned for a few brief holidays before attending Eton and joining the army.

Another question, one even more mysterious, nagged at her.

What had she done to offend him?

Before she could utter a word, he turned his back on her and slipped into the woodlands, Samson at his side. Open-mouthed, she watched him disappear from sight. Once he'd gone, outrage replaced the strange sense of connection she'd felt toward him.

If *he* was her Lancelot, then only God Himself could save her from the witch.

$\mathcal{G}$loom filled the drawing room, a murky oppression that settled against the tattered velvet drapes and stained the walnut furniture to mahogany. Tulips, arranged in a chipped vase, looked more gray than yellow, and a musty odor clung to the carpet that had cushioned too many feet. Even the fire in the hearth appeared subdued, licking hesitantly at the logs and doing little to warm the room.

Lucinda pulled her shawl closer against her shoulders. The darkness, she thought, was more a product of her own poor mood than of the dismal evening skies. She'd thought of the man in her vision as Lancelot, her white knight who would rescue her from death. And look who Fate had finally tossed her. Although he was handsome enough, the man had the manners of a toad. No kiss would transform him, not that one.

She took a sip of tea. Five o'clock had come and gone, and still Uncle George hadn't joined her. He'd probably found a book of particular interest and had lost himself in it. Well, she'd give him another five minutes before rousting him out of his library and insisting they talk about her vision.

Frowning, Lucinda stood up and began to pace. If she'd learned anything from her meeting with dear Lancelot, she knew he'd prove less than cooperative in any attempt to save her. And yet, the vision had seemed to suggest she'd need his help. Somehow, she had to discern his identity and then remain close to him, to give him a chance to rescue her.

Once she discovered who he was, what lure could she possibly use to draw him close?

He didn't seem inclined to become a besotted swain, and quite frankly, she didn't think she could play the coquette and flutter her lashes while murmuring compliments in his ear. She'd never met a man quite so taciturn as her Lancelot.

No, flirtation was not the answer.

Uncle George chose that moment to shuffle into the drawing room. He examined her with a mournful curve to his lips. "What are you doing, gel, pacing about like that?"

She rushed over to him and grasped his hands. His skin felt cool and dry, like parchment. "Much has happened today, Uncle. We must talk."

"Talk? Why do you women always want to talk?"

"I've had a vision," she announced.

A sour frown turned his mouth downward. He pulled his hands from hers.

"And I've met the man in my vision. Sort of."

Sighing, Uncle George flopped into a chair. " 'Tis time you married, gel. You're having visions, imagining strange men—it isn't right. You're rotting away in this old house of mine."

"Marriage? Who would have me?" Lucinda dismissed his comment and began pacing again. "We have other, more important matters which need airing."

"Marriage is a natural state for a gel your age," Uncle George persisted. "Squire Piggott is looking for a wife, and if you ask me, he's a fine catch."

"Squire Piggott is the last man on earth I'd marry. But I don't wish to discuss marriage. We must talk about my vision."

"You wouldn't be troubled by visions if you gave up witchcraft and closed your mind to them."

Lucinda winced. "You know I've been casting spells?"

"It may seem as though I've turned a blind eye to your magic, but I'm aware of what you've been doing. I, of all people, understand the lure of witchcraft. Experience has taught me it brings nothing but loneliness and heartache."

He poured himself a cup of tea from her teapot. When he tasted the liquid, he grimaced and set his cup down. Both eyebrows raised, he shook his head. "You're so enamored of witchcraft that you've begun drinking lukewarm bilge rather than tea."

With a snort Lucinda pulled the servant's bell. "I'll have Bess bring a new pot of tea. In the future, however, if you put your books aside and joined me at the proper time, we would both enjoy hot tea rather than lukewarm bilge."

Uncle George shook his head, evidently unconvinced. Before he could continue his harassment, however, their housekeeper breezed in with a fresh tea tray.

Lucinda smiled. "You've a bit of magic in you, Bess. How else could you know we'd want a new pot of tea?"

Her gray bombazine gown perfectly starched, and her mobcap artfully arranged on blonde-gray curls, Bess smiled. " 'Tis what sets me apart from the others."

She curtseyed and left as quietly as she'd come. Not for the first time Lucinda mused that their housekeeper must have been quite beautiful in her day. The good Lord only knew why she stayed on with Uncle George and herself.

Lucinda slipped a tea cozy over the teapot. "Why are you so determined to marry me off? Have our circumstances changed?"

The older Drakewyck shifted in his chair. His movement dislodged a pipe he'd shoved into his waistcoat pocket, revealing a small burning hole.

"Uncle George, you must snuff your pipe before putting it in your pocket."

Exasperated, she eyed his thin hands, the shock of gray hair that refused to lay tame, the glasses set askew on his nose, and knew an exquisite mixture of embarrassment and love. According to the matrons in Somerton, George Drakewyck was a gentleman of three outs: without money, without wit, and without manners. Still, he had a rare passion for books, and she thought passion one of the most important qualities anyone could possess.

"Hmm, ah, yes," he muttered, and pressed his palm against his pocket. Then, evidently gathering his wits, he focused upon her and frowned. "I've had a visit from our solicitor."

"And? What did he say?"

"My investment in India bonds has gone belly-up. The rest of our money is tied up in public funds, with a return rate so small that it won't save us in time."

"Can we not work out another arrangement with our creditors to forestall payment?"

"I have, Lucinda. The duns won't leave off forever. We must cut expenses."

"Cut expenses? Why, they're already at a bare minimum."

"Yet our debt continues to grow," Uncle George insisted. "The jacket I bought from the tailor last year cost only ten pounds, but with the constant renewals, the cost has grown to nearly fifty. Such is the case with all our debts."

"What about Lady Rothfield? She is my aunt, after all. Perhaps she would extend us credit."

"We've gone to that well too many times. It's dried up."

"How do we economize, then?"

"Perhaps the carriage—"

"I don't understand," Lucinda cut in. They had so many problems she hardly knew where to start. "We may not possess a title, but we've owned, for centuries, one of the larger estates in Bedfordshire. And yet we're bankrupt."

Uncle George directed his gaze toward the threadbare carpet. Moments passed, tense seconds while she waited for him to speak. She wondered why he sat there so silently and refused to look at her. Did he have gambling debts? A mistress stowed away in some cottage somewhere? Impossible. Not him.

"Uncle?"

"I am at fault," he suddenly admitted.

Startled, Lucinda dragged an ottoman over to his chair and sat down near his feet. "You? Uncle, I cannot believe it. How are you responsible?"

He looked her directly in the eye. "I refused to accept the vicariate of Somerton."

Lucinda hesitated. The parish vicar had almost always been a Drakewyck, as the Drakewyck family had owned the vicariate in Somerton for centuries. Traditionally, the eldest Drakewyck son inherited the estate, while the youngest inherited the vicarage. If there was only a single Drakewyck male in a generation, he gave the vicariate to a friend for "safekeeping" until a Drakewyck son was eligible to become vicar. As a consequence, Drakewycks always seemed to be in the thick of things, and they'd prospered because of it.

"But surely your refusal wasn't a crime," she finally said.

"No, it wasn't. But had I become vicar, we would still be receiving an annual tithe and collecting income from the lands surrounding the parish." He sighed deeply and took another sip of tea. "The income would have gone far to make up for the losses in investments. But I sold the vicariate off years ago. With hindsight, I see the decision was ill-considered."

"Is that why you wish to marry me off, Uncle? To preserve my standard of living?"

"Yes," he answered baldly. "Both in Somerton and in London you are accorded the deference of a Lady of Society. I wish to keep it that way."

"Well, in that case, let me tell you that I would rather scrub floors on my bare knees than marry a man I did not love."

Uncle George shook his head. "Nonsense. What is love when compared to an advantageous connection? You're a romantic, gel."

She jumped off the ottoman to face him. "One's place in Society holds little interest for me. I value the *mind*, not birth, or accomplishment, or even the cut of one's clothes."

"In such beliefs you secure your unhappiness."

Lucinda turned to stare out the window. Her uncle was obstinate, annoying, and firmly entrenched in his own beliefs. Still, if he was so determined to preserve their standard of living, why had he refused the vicariate? A vicar's obligations weren't many. He merely had to perform the Sunday sermon to collect tithes and farm the parish-owned land.

His hatred of religion and magic almost seemed reactionary. What had happened to him to sway him so?

She spun around to face him. "Why did you refuse the vicariate, Uncle? Had it to do with magic?"

Uncle George looked away. Silence stretched between them. Just as Lucinda began to think he hadn't heard her question, he turned back to stare at her with dark, haunted eyes.

"Do you remember your Drakewyck history, gel?"

"A little."

"My reasons for refusing the vicariate begin with Edward Drakewyck. He settled in Somerton late in the sixteenth century, just after a monastic order had purchased the village parish. The order appointed Edward their first vicar, and Edward performed the clerical duties of the parish."

"I remember him. Isn't there a portrait of him in the attic?"

"Perhaps." Uncle George shrugged. "Edward also was one of the first Drakewyck witches to display considerable talent."

"I have always considered it ironic that a witch would lead the local parish in Christian worship."

"Ah, yes, but to Edward, the vicariate was no less than atonement. You see, the talent we Drakewycks possess is considered a gift from Satan, not God. What better way for the Drakewyck witches to redeem themselves in the eyes of God than to use their talent for the good of the community?

"That is the Drakewyck charter, my dear. Expunge the evil blood by doing God's work rather than Satan's. And that is what we all have done, down through the centuries."

"Except for you," Lucinda pointed out.

"Ah, yes, except for me." Uncle George took off his glasses, rubbed them against the edge of his jacket, and placed them back upon his nose. "Your father and I grew up with magic all around us. Your grandfather encouraged us to learn all sorts of spells and groomed me, the youngest son, for the clergy.

"But then, one summer day, the unthinkable happened. We were in the middle of a drought, and Father encouraged me to bring rain to Somerton. I cast the spell, and it rained. It didn't stop raining for three days. The River Ouse quickly overflowed its banks. Fields flooded. Houses were swept away. People drowned. A winter of starvation followed, for all the grain and produce had been lost."

Lucinda swallowed. She'd heard stories about the terrible floods in 1816.

"And after it was all over, do you know what Father said to me? He told me to try again. He insisted all witches made mistakes and I shouldn't blame myself too harshly. He acted as though my learning to cast spells successfully was worth a few lives. In short, gel, he'd placed value on human life and found it lacking. He rationalized his decision, of course, by pointing out that a healing spell, if properly cast, could save hundreds of lives."

Uncle George trembled. "In my mind, he'd done terrible evil. He didn't recognize how he'd come to value magic over life, thinking witchcraft a *charter* that made him second only to God. I decided 'tis impossible to practice witchcraft without doing Satan's work. Even those with the best intentions are eventually seduced by their talent and the power it brings. And so, I refused the vicariate and refused to practice magic any further."

"And my father?"

"Daniel didn't worry about things as I did. He continued to learn and became quite accomplished. I always thought he would have made a good vicar. Magic didn't save him from the typhoid outbreak in 1841, though. Nor did it save your mother."

"I wish I had known them. I haven't a single memory of either of them. Sometimes I feel so . . . lonely."

"They died when you were but five years old, gel. You cannot expect to remember them. And I wish I could tell you your father lived a happy life. While he loved you, his dabbling in magic brought him much sorrow."

"Is this why you've tried to discourage me from using my talent? You feared I would give in to evil?"

He nodded. "I did not want you to suffer as I have suffered."

"You have very little confidence in me, Uncle. Please give me the freedom to make my own choice about magic."

"Haven't you already made your choice?"

Lucinda grew still. She had, in fact, embraced magic even in the face of his disapproval, going so far as to cast spells behind his back. Reluctantly she nodded.

He sighed, long and deep. "I fear for you, Lucinda."

"I chose magic because I could not do otherwise," she insisted. "I cast spells of all sorts: fertility and love, healing, spiritual renewal, any that are good and kind. I do this in secrecy, to protect the Drakewyck name, but I must admit that sometimes, when my spell produces the desired effect, I want to shout from the rooftops."

Uncle George nodded. "Magic has already seduced you."

Lucinda stood and clasped her arms against her chest. "Last month when I saw Mrs. Biddow in town with her infant, healthy and squalling, I began to cry. I'm quite certain she thought I wept over my lack of husband and family, for she patted my arm and told me I would marry someday. She doesn't know that the week before I had cast a spell on the babe, to cure her palsy and bring movement to her limbs again. I was overcome when I saw her happiness. How can my talent be evil when it brings such joy?"

"It brings joy now, but will it always? That is for you to discover." Uncle George rubbed his eyes behind his glasses. "You spoke of a vision and a man you'd met. Tell me about them."

She plopped down onto the ottoman again. "The vision frightened me. It's terrible."

"Ah, so already you begin to see the dark side of magic."

"Everything has a dark side. How can you value the warmth and brightness of daylight if you have not experienced a cold night?"

"Point taken. Tell me about your vision."

"I see a man," Lucinda said, the skin on the back of her neck prickling. "He is my protector, my Lancelot, but I know I must not love him, for to love him is to die. I also see a woman with blonde hair and ice-blue eyes. A gold filigree locket hangs around her neck. This may sound extreme, but I cannot dismiss the notion this woman means to see me dead."

Uncle George paled. He shot a penetrating glance her way. "Do you see a dove?"

"A dove?" Lucinda knitted her brows. "Well, I too am in the vision, and I'm holding some sort of statue, a bird—"

"Good God!" Uncle George heaved himself out of his chair. His expression registered somewhere between dread and wonder. "This man that you've met, your Lancelot. Is he connected in any way with the Clairmonts?"

"I don't know. He didn't say. But he was walking through the woods with Sir James' hound, so a connection is likely. 'Tis his face that I see in my vision."

Uncle George began to pace, his steps quick, unsuited to the slow-moving turtle she'd always thought him to be. "We are in trouble, Lucinda."

Lucinda stood, too. She clasped her hands. "I know we're in trouble. My vision has told me so. But I do not know what *sort* of trouble."

"Wait here. I must show you rather than tell you." With that cryptic remark he left the room.

Lucinda chewed her lower lip, wondering at this extraordinary turn of events. Her stomach churned with the certainty that her life was spinning out of control, that disastrous things would happen which she had not the slightest ability to change.

Uncle George returned with a large tome beneath his arm. He placed it on a side table and blew on its cover. A cloud of dust rose up, revealing gold lettering. *Goetia.* Lucinda had never heard the word before, but the look of the book—its leatherbound cover, coarsely cut parchment pages, and iron hasps—suggested great antiquity.

"A grimoire," Uncle George said, evidently reading her puzzled expression. "Once belonging to Edward Drakewyck."

Lucinda ran a finger over the cover. Something inside her stirred. How many witches had consulted this spellbook through the ages, looking for ways to heal mind and body? She suddenly felt a strange kinship with them, as if time had ceased to exist and they stood in the room with her, contemplating the unfathomable.

" 'Tis a family heirloom, passed down through the generations, to all who'd displayed talent." Uncle George picked the book up and placed it in her arms. "My father gave it to me, annoying your father to no end, for he felt himself the stronger of us two."

"What does it have to do with my vision?"

"Open the cover and read for yourself," he directed.

Chilled by his grim tone, she snapped the iron hasps apart and lifted the cover. On the first page, someone had scrawled several closely written lines in a rather stingy hand. She brought the book over to an oil lamp, turned up the wick, and began to read.

> *Somerton, the 31st of October, 1593*
> *Let this be a warning to all who will come.*
> *Herewith lies a record of Morgana Fey, witch unrepentant and bringer of evil to the village of Somerton. Let me not justify my actions here, for her crimes were many, but simply say I was persuaded there could be no other end for her.*
> *The events that occurred on the eve of Samhain, in the year of our Lord 1593, concern the safety of*

the Drakewyck and Clairmont families. I thought it my duty to acquaint all who will come with the particulars of her final moments.

Brow furrowed, Lucinda looked up from the spellbook. "This is not a document from a public witch trial. Indeed, it seems almost . . . furtive, buried in the spellbook like this."

Uncle George shrugged. "As far as I know, Somerton hasn't tried a single witch throughout its history. Given that the vicar of Somerton has always been a warlock, I would expect as much. The Drakewycks have been careful to protect themselves throughout the centuries."

Brow furrowed, Lucinda ran her finger over the first paragraph. "What does Edward mean by saying he would not 'justify his actions'? What sort of action did he take against Morgana?"

"I know not. He obviously put an end to her. Still, that doesn't necessarily mean he killed her. As you will see when you read on, Morgana promises she'll 'awaken from her lonely grave.' She may not be dead but sleeping somewhere."

A shiver raised bumps along Lucinda's arms. What a notion! "So Edward used his magic for evil purposes."

"Evidently. Magic has corrupted the Drakewyck family right from the start of its very existence."

Silently she vowed magic wouldn't corrupt *her*.

"This passage concerns the Clairmont family as well," she said. "I did not realize our two families had ever been anything but nodding acquaintances."

"I suspect Edward had more than a passing connection to the Clairmont family. Read on, gel."

HEART OF THE DOVE

Her confusion mounting, she returned her attention to *Goetia*.

> *As Morgana Fey was put to rest, she called upon witchcraft to curse our families and predict our end. "When the world is older and you are dead," sang she, "and I am sleeping in my bed, a Drakewyck witch and Clairmont knave will awaken me from my lonely grave. They will love and the dove will be mine, and utter destruction will be thine."*
>
> *You, my ancestor, will know her by her wheat-blonde hair, beautiful, lustrous, and begging for touch; by her ice-blue eyes whose shifting patterns conceal something darker, more fluid, and dangerous; by the gold filigree locket she wears around her neck. I pray to God she never appears, but if she does, only the dove can destroy her.*
>
> > *I am, with all duty and respect,*
> > *Your most humble servant*
> > *Edward Drakewyck*

Beneath his signature, Edward Drakewyck had drawn a picture of the dove and scribbled some gibberish.

Lucinda peered at the scrawl. "What does this mean, *ah nal nath rac, uth vas bethad, dochiel dienve*?"

"It doesn't sound familiar. Nonsense, likely."

She chewed her lower lip. "Do you think, Uncle, that I am the witch, and the man in the woods this Clairmont knave?"

"I don't know, but we'll find out tomorrow night. Richard Clairmont has just returned from the Crimea with the Victoria Cross gleaming upon his uniform. Squire Piggott is hosting a welcome-home party for him. If the man in your vision has any relation to the

Clairmonts, he will attend, and you must point him out to me."

The party. She'd completely forgotten about it. Normally she dreaded affairs such as those, but this time a thrill raced through her. She might meet Lancelot again. Still, was meeting that taciturn man anything to look forward to?

She closed *Goetia* with a snap. "I can tell you with some assurance, Uncle, that at least part of the prophecy is false. I could never love the man I met. And he could never love me."

"Evidently you didn't get along."

"Not at all. He glared at me and walked away without even bothering to introduce himself. I've never met a man with a more ill-tempered disposition."

"You speak rather vehemently against him."

"He is rude and outrageous and an utter bore."

Uncle George examined her, and unbidden, heat rose in her cheeks.

The elder Drakewyck shook his head. "I'm worried."

"Edward Drakewyck spoke of a dove in his entry," she soothed. "I've never seen it. Unless this dove surfaces, I suggest we put our worry aside."

His frown become more severe. "Hold out your hand, Lucinda."

She lifted her hand, palm upward.

Uncle George reached into his coat pocket and withdrew a small crystal statue. It was a dove, wings folded gently at its sides, head tucked to the left. He held it up to an oil lamp. The dove refracted the light and painted a dozen rainbows on the far wall. Deep inside the dove, a heart-shaped ruby glowed with dull fire.

She gasped. She'd seen the statue before, in her vision. "It's real."

"I'm afraid so." Without warning he dropped it into her hand.

Tingling immediately shot through her palm and wound its way up through her arm. Mouth dry, Lucinda examined the dove from every angle, trying to find words to describe its qualities. It lay against her skin, perfect, magnificent, cool to the touch, as crystal-clear as a running brook, its weight comforting like a quilt on a winter's eve.

But that did little to convey its lifelike character. It changed as she looked at it, its depths almost fluid as the light shone through, swirling in patterns she could barely perceive. The heart of the dove—ruby red, smooth as glass—seemed to throb in time with her own heart, and Lucinda was suddenly sure that this statue would shape her destiny.

Unable to stop herself, she curled her fingers around it. Power emanated from the dove, subtly calling to her on some deeper level, and the magic in her body jumped in response. She could lose herself in its depths if she wasn't careful.

With an effort she uncurled her fingers and dropped it into her dress pocket. "The dove has a most disconcerting effect. 'Tis no ordinary talisman."

"No. Most charms and spells are simply tools a witch uses to achieve the level of concentration necessary to call upon magic. They might even help focus magic in a special way," he said. "By themselves, they are nothing, mere conduits of power. But the dove is a true magical icon. It has been passed down through the centuries and has absorbed the power of those who used it. Did you see the heart in its center?"

Lucinda nodded.

"The heart of the dove is the seat of its power, or so I've been told."

"The dove has a strange sort of lure to it. I can almost feel it calling to me."

Uncle George huddled within his coat, as though an errant breeze had chilled him. "Talismans like the dove, if old and used frequently enough, amass a great deal of magic. And the witch who uses them commands almost limitless power. Still, the effect is short-lived, for with each spell cast, she loses her magic as the dove extracts its payment."

"So the stronger the spell—"

"The quicker the loss of magic. I suspect that if a strong enough spell were cast, the witch would lose every last bit of magic she possessed, becoming ordinary on the completion of the spell."

Lucinda shivered. She felt the weight of the dove against her skirts and wished, for one moment, that Uncle George hadn't given it to her.

"Keep it, gel. And *Goetia*. 'Tis my duty to pass these things on to you. I confess I delayed a bit, hoping you might tire of magic. Now, however, it seems you may need them."

Lucinda grasped his hands. "Tell me true, Uncle. Do you think Morgana Fey comes for me?"

He rubbed his face with one hand. "I don't know. I would prefer to believe Morgana is serving her time in Purgatory, or Hell even, but your vision . . . it worries me. 'Tis better you have the dove. According to Edward, only the dove will save you."

3

$\mathcal{S}$everal hours later, after dinner had passed and Lucinda was supposed to be sleeping, she dressed in her warmest woolen gown and drew thick stockings on. Forsaking petticoats and corset and all other devices that restricted movement, she shoved her feet into a pair of sturdy boots and pulled her brown serge cloak around her shoulders.

She had a spell to cast, a man to identify, a future to reveal.

A sack containing the crystal dove and *Goetia* sat near the kitchen door, just where she'd left it. Lucinda hoisted the sack, lifted a lantern to light the way, and crept out into the darkness.

The moon was absent this eve. Lucinda thought its timing providential. Waxing moons were good for bringing things into the world, while waning moons helped with banishing. A full moon was a fertile one, while the dark moon spoke of secrets and revelations.

Tonight she planned to find answers to a few secrets. During the last course of dinner, as she'd chewed on the overcooked flesh of a gamey old hen, she'd decided to cast a spell to see the future. She needed to know Lancelot's name and hoped the power in *Goetia* and the crystal dove would amplify her vision, clarifying points that still remained a mystery. Of course, the dove would absorb some of her own magic. Still, that notion didn't bother her nearly as much as the thought of being unprepared for whatever evil stalked her.

After picking her way around upthrust roots, thickets of briars, and tree trunks so dark she could barely see them, Lucinda emerged into the glen. She paused for a moment and looked around. The trees seemed so different at night, crowding close, creating an aura of oppression she hadn't noticed before. Like gaping spectators at a hanging, the oaks and pines remained utterly still, yet expectant, waiting to see her feet dangle upon the earth.

Something slithered beneath her feet.

She jumped to the side, abruptly wishing she had more than her lantern and a bonfire to light the glen. She'd never cast a spell at night, and the sky seemed far too dark. Coal-gray clouds churned across the sky, hiding the pallid glow from a spray of stars.

She forced herself to remain calm and wiped her damp palms on her skirt. The spell was one of divination, not necromancy. She had nothing to worry about.

Breathing slowly and evenly, she set the crystal dove on a tree stump, propped *Goetia* up next to it, and gathered wood. Not just any wood, but pine and oak for understanding and spiritual journeying. Soon she had a sizeable amount piled up in her fire ring. She used a twig to transfer fire from the lantern to the wood, setting it alight and fanning the flames until they flickered about knee-high.

Next, she began to pace around the fire, a flour-salt mixture dripping in a thin stream from her hand. Brow furrowed, she created a nine-foot ring of protection around the fire and then stood in the center of the circle, facing north.

"I call upon the powers of the north to bless and protect this glen," she murmured, and repeated the invocation for east, south, and west.

A fat raindrop splattered against her skin. She looked up. Clouds rushed across the heavens with extraordinary speed, a blunt warning that a storm approached. Rain would put the bonfire out more quickly than Uncle George running for his armchair after a walk in the woods. Her movements swift and efficient, she inscribed seven points on the ring of protection, each equidistant from the other.

Above the ring, she poured the word *Thetragrammaton.*

The temperature in the clearing dropped a few degrees.

The air always felt coolest, she reminded herself, just before a storm. Even so, the skin on the back of her neck tightened. She had the oddest notion that someone stood just beyond the gorse bushes. Watching her.

Utterly motionless, she stared into the trees.

Listened.

Waited.

Nothing.

This, she thought, *is absurd.* She refused to let her imagination paralyze her before she'd even begun the spell. With a little toss of her head, she squared her shoulders and leaned down to read *Goetia.* The book glowed white beneath the light of her lantern. Hieroglyphs in various circular shapes adorned the parchment.

The seven planets came next.

"Aratron," she intoned, and poured the hieroglyph for Saturn above the first spoke on the ring. She moved to the next spoke.

"Bethor." The hieroglyph for Jupiter—a hook that cut a circle in two—required a bit more concentration. Moisture beading on her forehead, she created the symbol.

Some of the flour mixture fell into the fire. Blue flames belched from the blaze and almost set her skirt on fire. She jumped back and rubbed her eyes. The flame had looked like a giant hand.

Don't be a fool, she chided herself. Flames don't grab people.

A weak chuckle emerged from her throat, but her eyes remained wide as she poured the words *Phaleg,* and *Och,* and *Hagith,* and *Ophiel,* and finally *Phuel,* for the moon.

When she'd finished, she took a step back to admire her handiwork. The flour-salt caught the light of the bonfire and sparkled with an unexpected radiance. She felt very medieval in that moment, experimenting with old magic. Nevertheless, she wondered if she weren't making a terrible blunder, using the dove and *Goetia* to cast this spell. She had an urge to run back to Drakewyck Grange.

The sense that someone watched her had intensified.

It wasn't a friendly stare.

Mouth dry, she closed her eyes. "Protect my spirit, Lord."

A caw echoed through the clearing. She opened her eyes and examined the treetops. Now she knew why she felt as though someone watched her. Another chuckle emerged from her throat, this one weaker than the last. At least twenty crows roosted among the branches.

"I don't scare easily," she told them.

Feathered heads bent downward, they stared at her with beady eyes. Dark, pregnant clouds lumbered beyond their black bodies. Another raindrop splashed against her hand. She hadn't much time to cast the spell.

Her gaze settled on the dove. For the first time, she planned to cast a spell without calling upon the magic in her dark garden. Would the dove's magic prove difficult to control? And how much of her own magic would the dove absorb? Lower lip caught between her teeth, she grasped the statue. Warmth invaded her fingers, calming her even as it persuaded her that the price it extracted was surely worth its wondrous power.

Certainty flowed through her. She was doing the right thing. The dove would help her avoid the fate she'd witnessed in her vision. With her free hand she turned *Goetia*'s pages until she found an appropriate spell.

"Mother, sister, daughter, wife," she recited, "Fate decides our path in life. Ancient ones, I call to thee. Show me now my destiny."

Breath caught in her throat, she held the dove tight and waited for something to happen. She glanced at *Goetia*, wondering if it would fly at her like a deranged bat and tangle itself in her hair. She inspected the treetops, looking for a demon's glint in the crows' red eyes.

Nothing happened.

Her throat eased.

"Ancient ones, I call to thee, show me now my destiny," she repeated.

Heart beating uncomfortably, she waited for heat to invade her midsection. When would the vision roar in her mind, and what would it show her?

Again, she felt and sensed nothing unusual.

No vision, no fanfare, no howls, no barking hellhounds.

A low rumble of thunder, but that had wholly natural origins.

She released the breath she hadn't realized she'd been holding. A half smile broke out on her lips. Perhaps the dove didn't like her and refused to give its magic up to her.

But wait. Those odd words scrawled beneath the sketch of the dove in *Goetia* might have some importance. Frowning, she tried to recall them. They hadn't the poetic beauty of most spells and evaded her. After a brief struggle with her memory, she turned *Goetia*'s pages until she'd reached the front of the book and Edward Drakewyck's scrawl.

Mere gibberish, she thought.

Large drops of rain began to fall on the bonfire with a soft hiss. Beyond the hills to the east, lightning split the ground in two. A threatening growl rolled through the heavens.

She hadn't much time.

"Ah nal nath rac, uth vas bethad, dochiel dienve," she murmured.

An unexpected flare of light from the dove drew her attention. Had the fire reflected against its flawed interior? Or had it responded to the runes? She repeated the gibberish again, her excitement growing.

This time, the dove remained colorless.

Deflated, she listened to cold, heavy rain rap against the forest canopy. She couldn't sense any difference in the glen. Her eerie words hadn't impressed the dove in the slightest.

Desperation grabbed hold of her. *"Ah nal nath rac, uth vas bethad, dochiel dienve!"*

The bonfire withered to glowing embers. Something, she thought, should have happened by now.

"Please, do something."

A small twig popped.

Smoke waltzed up from the embers.

She stared at the dove for several moments before slipping it into her pocket. She must have done something wrong. Why else would it stubbornly refuse to release its magic?

"Ah nal nath rac indeed."

Whoosh!

A sudden gush of heat pushed her a few steps. Crimson sparks lit the night sky as if shot from a geyser, scorching the grass and setting a few nearby branches on fire.

What in heaven?

The smells of hot pine sap and scorched wood stung her nose and settled into her lungs like tar. Eyes burning, she stared at the blaze.

Blood pumped thickly in her ears and temples.

Each breath became a battle.

Flames eight feet high coiled like incandescent snakes. Great streamers of smoke twisted through the clearing and wrapped the birches in a spider's web of gray. With a high moan she fell backward and scuttled away from the flames, her movements uncoordinated, crab-like. A thorn pierced her palm, but she scarcely noticed the pain.

She wanted only to escape the flames.

Something hard hit her spine and she collapsed, only to realize she'd backed into an oak. Blackness

47

crept along the edges of her vision. She fought to retain consciousness with every ounce of will she possessed. To faint, she thought, would be to die. And if she died, she'd spend eternity waist-deep in offal, running Satan's errands.

Witches, after all, went straight to Hell.

Uncle George! she tried to scream, but her throat had closed. She was on her own. Lips trembling, she gawked at her handiwork. Thick, heavy smoke curled in crazy patterns through tree limbs that had caught fire. Pine cones snapped in protest and bark peeled back from overheated trunks. She had a heart-stopping vision of the entire forest engulfed in flames.

Wasn't this what she had wanted? Hadn't she hoped for this very outcome?

Beware thy wishes, that they may be granted.

She'd read that in a book once. In a fairy tale. Well, the gods of the cosmos had just granted her wish. The spell had worked. But the victory was an empty one. Deep inside she sensed something had gone very wrong. The greedy fire, the suffocating smoke—somehow she had conjured demons.

She pressed harder into the tree, unable to move, every hair on her head vibrating. Sharp pains radiated through her palms. She unclenched her fists, noting the bloody half-moon marks that cut her skin.

Smoke continued to billow out from the conflagration, growing so dense she could see only a few feet before her. She choked, her nose and throat burning, smoke filling her lungs like ground glass, a shrill wheeze coming from her mouth. A feeling of dread overwhelmed her and she began to cry.

What had she done?

*   *   *

Richard Clairmont leaned against the doorjamb and stared out across the stone balcony. As in the rest of the north wing of Clairmont Hall, the terrace had been neglected for many years, perhaps even a century or more. Chipped stone littered the floor and knots of decayed leaves rustled uneasily in a brisk wind. Beyond, lightning turned the stream that ran through the property into a ribbon of silver and the very foundation of Clairmont Hall seemed to vibrate with thunder.

But Richard, lost deep in memory, heard only the strident call of the bugle, urging the Light Brigade to charge, exhorting them to show courage and discipline. He saw only the bores of those massive Russian cannons, firing balls of lead from their glowing cores, cutting his men and horses in half with a single blow. He felt only the horse's flanks bunching beneath his thighs, bringing him into the mouth of Hell.

Six hundred British soldiers had charged that day.

Twenty minutes later, only one hundred ninety-five had remained.

He shoved his damaged hand into his pocket. He couldn't bear to even think about the scars. They represented his inadequacies in the war, physical evidence of his own failure. His shame.

Something impinged on his awareness, some unusual happening that demanded his attention. Like a drowning man forcing his way to water's surface, he focused on the trees which twisted in the wind, then glanced higher. Clouds were racing across the sky. He'd never seen them move so fast. Their very speed put him on edge, for it seemed almost . . . preternatural. Like something from a dream. Or a nightmare.

Holed up in the north wing, Richard usually spent his evenings prowling the rooms that had fallen into disrepair and looking for a way to forget. Indeed, he preferred night to day. Sunshine had a way of throwing light on things better left in shadows.

Tonight, however, his restlessness had drawn him repeatedly to the terrace door. He wondered if it had something to do with the woman who had plagued his thoughts since the moment he'd seen her. The air smelled moist and rich with earth, the same as it had in the glen, reminding him of the strange reaction he'd experienced.

Hiding in the mist, she'd looked like a witch or a madwoman. Regardless, he'd felt an attraction for her that he simply couldn't rationalize away, like the pure, instinctual desire of a moth to dive into a flame. He'd seen her fire ring and wondered what the hell she'd been doing. After hours of conjecture he still hadn't a clue.

Even now, he chided himself for leaving her there, pale and swaying. He hadn't even introduced himself as a gentleman should. But damn it, he'd come to Somerton to avoid society and its reminders of war. He didn't want to be placed in a compromising position with an unchaperoned female who built bonfires in the woods. Baffled, wary of the notion that their meeting had been predestined and inescapable, he'd left the glen determined to put her from his thoughts.

And failed miserably.

All through the evening hours, he'd known a compulsion to return to the glen. He'd fought it vigorously. But now, as the night closed in around him and the clouds galloped across the heavens, he wondered if a walk to the glen *was* in order, despite the storm that threatened. He'd like to poke around and see if he could find some reason why the woman in the glen had affected him so. A wet jacket was a small price to pay for alleviating some of his uneasiness.

He scanned the woodlands one last time, began to turn away, and stopped short. For the first time he noticed a soft glow deep in the woodlands, so far away it was barely discernable from Clairmont Hall. Even so, the glow emanated from the general direction of the glen, and his unease became a sense of impending trouble.

Sudden certainty overtook him. The mystery woman, he knew, would lay at the heart of this latest calamity. She must have built a large bonfire, indeed, for him to see it from Clairmont Hall. Was she trying to burn the woods down? Satan only knew what she'd gotten herself into.

Pausing long enough to grab his cloak, he raced through the labyrinth of hallways, down the stairs to the main hall, and out the front doors. A few large raindrops pelted him as he raced down a gravel path toward the stable yard.

Attached to Clairmont Hall, the stables and their four coach houses nestled within a grove of birch trees. Snores echoed from within. Their old groom sprawled on a pile of straw, his mouth wide open, displaying gums rather than teeth. As if sensing Richard's presence, he opened one bleary eye. "Sir?"

"Mack! Look lively, man, and put the bridle on Webster." Richard did not wait for a response but fetched the horse and began to saddle him.

Mack jumped to his feet. "Aye. Right away, sir."

The old groom displayed not the slightest interest in the request, nor did he seem surprised to see Richard at two in the morning. He'd evidently grown used to Richard's need for isolation, which drove him to solitary walks in the woods and forced him to flee to the north wing, away from his high-spirited sister and disapproving father.

Within a minute they'd saddled the roan. Richard mounted in one jump and kicked Webster into an easy canter. The glow had disappeared now that he could no longer see over the treetops. His sense of disaster, however, had increased tenfold. He nudged Webster, urging him into a gallop.

They raced across the lawn and entered the woods. Whorls of gray smoke began to assault his nose. Richard directed the stallion through birches and oaks, jumping rotting tree trunks and skirting around mountains of boulders. Webster's huge hooves threw up clods of earth, showering Richard in the process.

In less than a minute the smoke became impenetrable and Webster too skittish to handle. Richard dismounted, tied the roan to a tree, and softly promised to return before fire could harm him.

Eyes watering, lungs burning, he searched the woods, hoping to find a fire small enough to contain. But before he could pinpoint the source of the smoke, the puffy clouds dwindled.

A low murmur drifted toward him. Someone was sobbing.

Confounded, he walked toward the sound.

The trees began to thin, exposing the same glen he'd visited earlier. The ferns and pink foxglove that teased the edge of the clearing, so bright and vivid a few hours ago, now looked tattered and ashen. Patches of strawberries dotting the ground were covered with soot, and the lower limbs of the trees had burned, adding to an aura of recent disaster.

In the middle of the clearing, a bonfire flickered hesitantly. Nearby, a woman sat against a tree trunk, her face cupped in her hands. He took in her brown curls streaked with cinnamon, her diminutive form, and a knot formed in his chest.

He edged around the glen, his gaze passing over the ruins of the bonfire and a few strange marks, drawn with a white substance, decorating the ground. *What the hell were they?* The marks reminded him of his classical studies at school. The Romans and Greeks had sometimes used symbols like these to designate the various beings in their mythology. And yet, these had an older, stranger look, almost Druidic in appearance, similar to the esoteric markings found in stone circles.

Runes, he suddenly realized.

Witchcraft!

Disdain twisted his lips into a frown. How could she believe in such nonsense and even put herself at risk over it? Only a fool would prowl around the woods in the middle of the night, setting fires and muttering gibberish and waving magic wands about.

Trying to swallow his outrage, he touched her shoulder. "Are you all right?"

She looked up at him. Black powder covered her face, reminding him of a chimney sweep. Streaks of tears ran through the soot, and burn marks dotted her ivory bodice. These things he noticed in passing, for her eyes—deep brown with glittering flecks of gold—captured his attention. They were the color of cognac, with an equally heady effect. Propriety dictated he stop staring, but he couldn't quite manage it.

"Lancelot. Thank God you've come," she said, her voice husky, her gaze slightly unfocused.

She'd expected him. He wasn't quite sure how he knew this. Perhaps the finality in her tone had given him the idea, but whatever its source, he didn't deny the impression. Still, he didn't know why she would call him Lancelot. Smoke from the fire must have addled her brains.

He pulled his cloak from his shoulders and wrapped it around hers. "What in God's name are you doing here?"

"Will you tell me your name first, sir, before you lecture me?"

"Richard Clairmont."

She nodded as though she'd expected as much and focused on his scarred hand.

Without thinking, he shoved his hand into his pocket. "And you?"

"Lucinda Drakewyck."

He examined her with narrowed eyes. What did he know about the Drakewycks? Little to nothing. Their estates made them neighbors, but their families had never been close. Indeed, he didn't think he'd ever met Lucinda. "Need I tell you, Miss Drakewyck, of the danger—"

"Don't go on so. I cannot withstand it."

"I saw your bonfire all the way from Clairmont Hall. You nearly burned the woods down!"

" 'Twas a mistake."

"A *mistake?*"

She put her palms against the ground and pushed, as though she wished to rise, cutting off the rest of his rebuke.

"One moment," he ordered. "We'd better determine the extent of your injuries. Does anything hurt?"

"My ankle. Only a bit, though."

He leaned over her and pushed the hem of her skirt up to examine her feet, a forbidden sight in ordinary circumstances. Sturdy brown boots encased ankles that rivaled the finest he'd seen in London.

Moments passed, uncomfortable seconds during which he felt an almost physical pull between them. It was the oddest damned sensation he'd known in a long time. Why did she affect him so? He had to admit she was quite handsome, her form petite yet voluptuous, her face heart-shaped, and her eyes—that fascinating mix of brown and gold. Her hair, a mass held in place by a tortoiseshell comb, had the luster of chocolate streaked with cinnamon. He'd wager each strand felt like silk.

He realized he was lingering over the examination and struggled to concentrate on the task at hand. "Which ankle?"

"The left."

He unbuttoned her left boot, wondered if he dared ask her to remove her stocking, and decided he'd better not. He didn't trust himself. Instead he pressed his fingers against her stocking, feeling for heat or swelling.

Her ankle felt fine. Too fine.

"Captain Clairmont?"

A small hand settled on his, her touch gentle and warm. He could imagine her fingers' insistent pressure as they coaxed pleasure out of his tired body.

"Sit down next to me," she murmured. "You've inhaled too much smoke."

He realized he'd been gaping and mentally shook himself. He buttoned her boot back up as quickly as his fingers would allow. "Your ankle doesn't feel swollen and your skin is cool. You're fine."

"Thank you." She hesitated, as if preparing to say something very difficult, and then focused on him, her eyes large and pleading. "I feel as though there is a connection between us."

"Why do you say that?"

"I don't know." She looked away, her voice full of frustration. "When we are near, I feel as though I've known you forever."

He considered confessing his own odd perceptions, but suddenly realized how foolish he would sound. He was acting like a superstitious old woman, ascribing significance to every word she said, seeing omens in her eyes and feeling magic in her touch. The tugging between them, he decided, more than likely resulted from his lack of female companionship. Months had passed since he'd last been with a woman.

"You're distressed," he suggested. "The fire—"

"I'm not distressed."

"What is between us, then? Magic? I saw your runes. Evidently you think you're some sort of witch. Magic doesn't exist, Miss Drakewyck. Humanity has no need of witchcraft, no need of spells to invoke the devil. Satan is already within each human soul, waiting to emerge."

He'd been to Hell, seen greed and corruption in the eyes of his commanders, men who had sent him into a death trap and then went home for a hot bath aboard their yachts.

Her lower lip trembled. "Just like love, magic exists. It heals."

"I don't believe in love, either," he stated emphatically.

Her eyes narrowed. "You don't believe in anything."

A sound that was not quite a laugh escaped him.

"What an odd man you are," she said, her voice soft, almost pitying.

He stiffened and almost walked away from her. Memories of his earlier poor performance as a gentleman held him in place. He would execute the duties required of his gender and then seek the solace of the north wing. "I'll see you home. I suggest you confine your spell-casting to daylight hours."

She stood, rejecting the hand he silently offered, and picked up an old tome he hadn't noticed before. "I'll need my spellbook if I'm to cast any more of my nasty spells."

He sighed impatiently. "Well, you've fetched it. Are you ready now?"

"No."

"Why not?"

"I need my dove, too."

"What dove?" He looked into the branches, searching for a small, whitish bird.

"Not a real dove," she said, her tone calling him a nitwit. "A crystal dove. It should be here somewhere."

He frowned. He should have known she'd be searching for a *magic* bird. "What does it look like?"

"I'll find it myself."

"If we both look we'll find it faster."

"I don't want your help." She began to comb through the weeds and dying embers. He noticed with satisfaction she hadn't a limp. She would recover quickly from her ordeal. He wished he could recover from his own strange malaise with equal speed.

"Why don't you want my help?" he asked.

"I don't want you to touch it."

"What will happen if I do?"

"Just don't touch it."

Eyes narrowed, he wondered what made her magic bird so special. At length he shrugged. It probably had something to do with her magic rituals. God save them *both* from her rituals. "I refuse to stand around waiting. I'll look as well."

Ignoring her quick frown, he joined in the search. Tense minutes passed during which he wondered if he'd gone completely mad, scouring the woods well past midnight for a magic bird. But then he saw it, glittering in the light from the lantern she held aloft.

"There it is," he said.

"Oh, thank goodness you've found it."

She followed his gaze and surged forward to scoop the statue up. At the same time he reached out, intrigued, wondering what the dove would do to him when he touched it, suspecting it would do nothing and eager to prove a point to her.

They both touched it at once.

Light shot out from the dove, a veritable kaleidoscope of colors that painted the trees. Richard felt a vibration beneath his palm. He yanked his arm away as though he'd been bitten.

Hand over her heart, Lucinda stepped backward.

The dove lay between them, dull once again.

He examined his hand. Small welts had begun to form on his palm.

Cursing silently, he grabbed Lucinda's hand. Similar welts crossed her hand. "The bonfire must have heated your magic bird. It's burned us."

Trembling, she picked the dove up and slipped it into her pocket. "It's cool now."

"Evidently it's not made of crystal but another substance that transfers heat quickly. Where did it come from?"

"It's an old family heirloom," she explained. "My uncle gave it to me just this evening."

He shook his head, remembering how she'd told him not to touch the dove. "How did you know it would be hot? Did you deliberately place it in the fire?"

"I came here this evening to see what the future holds for me." Her brown eyes were vulnerable, her tone soft. "As this was the first time I've used the dove, I knew not what to expect. I held it in my hand and cast the spell for sight. I don't know why, but the fire grew to incredible proportions. In my haste to escape the flames, I dropped the dove."

"So it may have fallen in the fire."

"It could have," she admitted. "I asked you not to touch it for your own protection."

He heard the accusation in her voice. With a nod he acknowledged it, rather than tell her to be a little more specific next time. There wasn't going to be a next time. "I should have heeded your warning."

She dismissed his apology with a gesture. She looked all around at the trees and sky, and shivered. "Do you feel it?"

"Feel what?"

"Eyes upon us."

Brow furrowed, he scanned the surrounding woodlands. "I see no one."

"Nevertheless, someone is here."

"Miss Drakewyck, you must allow me to escort you home."

She pulled his cloak more firmly about her shoulders. "I would very much like to return home."

"My horse is a little beyond those thickets," he said, pointing. "Perhaps he's the one who's watching us. Watching and no doubt wishing to return to his warm stall."

"Mock me all you'd like, sir," she said, her eyes dark. "I suspect that time will force you to reconsider your words."

The woman stirred in her grave, awakened from nightmares which had no end. Dirt pressed in on her from all sides. It weighted her eyelids and crept up her nose and caked in her hair. Things squiggled on top and below her but they didn't touch her.

The darkness was absolute.

Who was she? *What* was she?

She couldn't breathe.

A thought began to echo in her mind: *They've buried me deep to cover my sins.*

She moaned.

Fingers hooked, she clawed at the earth.

She remembered a face. A man with cruel lips.

They've buried me deep to cover my sins.

She screamed. Kicked and pounded. Dirt sifted around her, became mud. The mud began to give way. She thrust her hand upward. It broke through. Cool air washed across her fingers.

Urgency shot through her. Her lungs were beginning to burn. She needed air. Her eyes wanted to blink, her limbs ached. Who was she?

Morgana Fey.

With a dull thud her heart began to beat again. It had been frozen for so long. Why, why, why?

They've buried me deep to cover my sins.

The dirt, it was all around her, strangling her. What had she done? She began to choke and cough, the mud foul now, moldering and corrupt, clammy, like the embrace of Death.

Only she wasn't dead. She'd fallen from grace but someone had saved her, someone had awoken her.

Like a dark mermaid surging upward from a sea of madness, Morgana thrust herself out of the grave with a keening howl. Dirt showered around her. She flung her hair back.

Moist, clean air caressed her skin and filled her lungs. She took a convulsive breath and opened her eyes. Stared at her grave. A recent storm had washed away most of the dirt that had set atop her. She swiveled. Saw rocks and bushes, an old cottage. She knew this place. Above her, trees framed a circle of stars.

back on earth back on earth back on earth I live

She threw back her head and laughed. The sound echoed among the trees before dying down. Stillness settled over the forest. Nothing moved. Nothing made a noise.

Morgana forced herself to stand on shaky legs and look around. They'd buried her in the glen where she'd cast her spells. She sensed magic close by. The dove. She remembered now. Edward Drakewyck had taken everything from her. He'd buried her deep to cover her sins. *The Drakewyck witch and Clairmont knave,* she thought. At long last, the pair must have used the dove to break Edward's spell.

How many years had passed? At least fifty. The hunter's cottage she used to visit had collapsed beneath tendrils of ivy. One hundred, even? It didn't matter. Christopher was long dead. Her chance at happiness was gone forever.

It was time for reckoning.

She lifted her hand. Rubbed some of the dirt off and examined her skin. Still soft and young looking. Her dress had profited from Edward's spell, too. Although covered with dirt, the linen seemed untouched by time.

Edward and Henry were long dead. They couldn't pay for their sins. The Clairmont knave and Drakewyck witch would have to stand in their place. She would destroy them and retrieve her property. Her dove. From there, who knew? Times had changed, but she'd adapt quickly. The long sleep had given her a very special vision for the village of Somerton. She wanted to make that vision a reality.

Morgana tilted her head. Something nagged at her, hiding just beyond the bounds of her consciousness. A voice, speaking to her. But she simply couldn't bring the voice to the surface, so she couldn't tell who it was or what it was saying.

She swatted at the air as if bothered by a pesky fly. The voice died away.

Growing stronger by the second, she stood and gazed into the glen. An aura of magic clogged the place. She sensed the presence of the witch and knave even though they'd left. Both were so alive, so full of vigor that Morgana could almost feel the blood pumping through their veins. The witch and the knave, a pair fated to love.

Morgana smiled.

4

$\mathcal{M}$oonlight cast pewter shadows on the barouche that rumbled down Mill Lane, through the rows of cherry trees that had provided fruit for many a pie. Ensconced within the carriage's musty interior, Lucinda calculated she and her uncle would arrive at Squire Piggott's residence within ten minutes. He lived at the very center of Somerton, his home a disagreeable hub from which the spokes of town life radiated.

Squire Piggott, Lord Lieutenant of Bedfordshire and arguably the town's most prominent resident, was hosting this eve's welcome-home fete for Captain Clairmont. Only the wealthiest citizens, swathed in silk and ready to sip the finest champagne, would attend. She'd even heard the Squire had hired a five-piece ensemble out of London to provide the music. The party, she surmised, would be much more pretentious than a simple country dance; after all, they were celebrating the return of Somerton's greatest hero, Captain Clairmont. Only the best would do.

She took a deep breath and fought to compose herself. Things weren't going very well at all with Captain Clairmont. The first time they'd met he'd displayed not the slightest interest in her. The second time, he'd called her a witch and reprimanded her at every turn. What must he think of her?

And yet, she needed him. According to her vision, he could save her from the blonde witch and her evil ends if he wanted to. The question was, how did she convince him he wanted to save her? She had the feeling that he didn't want to save anyone, not even himself.

Uncle George sat across from her, his back sagging against the cracked leather squabs. Imprisoned by her voluminous skirt, nearly six feet around at the hem, he stared out the window, his gaze fixed on a point unseen.

"If ladies' skirts grow any wider," he remarked, "I fear we shall have to broaden public thoroughfares."

Pulled from her thoughts, she nodded absently.

Their carriage bumped over a pothole. Uncle George groaned and dabbed at his forehead with a square of linen. He examined Lucinda through watery eyes. "We had better reach Squire Piggott's soon, dear gel, or I fear I shall catch fire." Sweat ran down his temples, for the day's heat still filled the carriage, creating an oven on wheels.

She forced herself to focus on him. She hadn't the nerve to confess she'd tried to invoke the dove's power and had nearly burned the woods down. He would only launch into one of his lectures on the evils of magic, and she hadn't the heart to debate with him right now. She only wished she knew why the spell had gone so wrong, and how much of her own power she'd sacrificed. She didn't *feel* any differently after using the dove, but she hadn't tried to cast any more spells, either.

"I would much rather be sitting in the drawing room, reading Walpole's *The Castle of Otranto.*" She lifted her petticoats, attempting to release some of the heat building beneath them.

"Well, now that we are dressed in this uncomfortable attire, we might as well put it to good use." He took off his glasses and polished them against his lapel. "Please be nice to Squire Piggott, Lucinda. His regard for you could prove quite advantageous in the future."

Lucinda stiffened. "I had not realized the Squire regarded me in any way but casual."

The elder Drakewyck coughed and harrumphed for a moment before finding his voice. "Oh, well, he has expressed a certain interest to me—"

"What? When?"

"Two days ago, at Langford's Book Shop, he asked if he might pay his addresses to you."

Lucinda stilled. The Squire? Oh, no. "You *did* refuse him."

"I told him I would think on it. I thought you might consider him as a future husband."

"I have no wish to marry the Squire. Why, pray, would he wish to marry me? We are nearly bankrupt, our lands and home fallen into disrepair. What is the attraction?"

"Why, you are. He thinks you accomplished and a sweet-tempered gel," Uncle George said. "I, ah, also suspect he prizes our connection with Lady Rothfield."

"I see. His pretensions to grandeur have led him to my doorstep. Squire Piggott disgusts me," Lucinda said forcefully. An image formed in her mind of the Squire: short legs stuffed into breeches and stained with sweat near the groin; hands which sprouted so much hair he appeared to be wearing gloves; full lips habitually chapped from too much wiping.

Uncle George waved a negligent hand. "You're just being picky. You'd reject any man who presented himself to you because you don't want to marry. Since you won't select a husband, I thought I'd put a few men before you and see what happened."

Her eyes narrowed. "Have you encouraged the Squire, Uncle?"

"Well, ah . . . no, no, I wouldn't be so foolish. If you don't want to marry him, you can stay with me forever. As you well know, I have grown used to your company and would dearly miss you if you left."

Uncle George's tone was one of innocence, and yet, Lucinda thought it *forced* innocence. "Uncle George, if you've—"

"We're almost at the Squire's," he pointed out.

Lucinda snapped her mouth shut. Obviously she could expect the Squire's attentions this evening. She looked out the window, lower lip caught between her teeth, vexed beyond measure that he would meddle in her life so.

The large, arched entrance to the town of Somerton loomed ahead, a portal to the heart of Bedfordshire. As the Drakewycks' barouche shimmied its way under that age-old arch, Lucinda gazed at its inscription: "Fortress on the Ford."

Nearly fifty miles from London, Somerton housed some six thousand souls. On the whole, the town's inhabitants were a devout lot who thought the Cromwell days some of the best in English history. No less than seven houses of worship graced the town's cobblestone streets, St. Paul's by far the most popular, perhaps because of its graceful spire. On sunny days, the gold-plated spire shone like a finger of God.

Indeed, she mused, God had smiled on the town of Somerton.

For a small community, the residents lived extremely well, their cheeks plump with vigor and goodwill. The River Ouse gave them the edge they needed to prosper, and not a day went by without barges, loaded with corn, wheat, barley—even lace—floating from the docks toward London. The shouts of the riverboat captains mingled with low-toned haggling from the butter and meat markets, while the smells of bleaching powder, soap, and borax leaked from the House of Industry, overriding the sometimes rank odor of the Ouse.

Altogether, she decided, the townfolk hadn't much to complain about.

A few Somertonians didn't care two figs for the peerage, particularly after the fire of 1802, reputedly set by a visiting nobleman. Reactionary progressivism against the Crown had reached even into their small county. But Squire Piggott—ever the faithful defender of the *order* of things—visited frequently with the Drakewycks' very own Lady Rothfield, and used the connection to write the Queen and curry her favor, while tattling on the reactionaries.

Those who valued their position in town *agreed* with Squire Piggott. And now she feared the Squire would begin to press his suit on her. How much aggravation was he going to cause her when she rejected him? Even if she'd wanted to, she couldn't marry the Squire, for she had to focus on Richard Clairmont. She had to bring the good Captain around before Fate got the better of her.

She didn't have long to worry about it, for within minutes their barouche had rattled onto Squire Piggott's carriageway. Torchbearers ran forward to light their way to the townhouse proper, and soon she and Uncle George found themselves announced and nudged forward into the fete.

Chandeliers blazed, illuminating a colorful press of bodies buzzing with conversation. Servants had removed most of the furniture in Squire Piggott's central hall and living room, providing space for dancing. Somerton's gentry squashed together, a tangle of Hessians and Highlows and ladies' kid slippers; of silks, taffeta, moire, and black superfine; of whiskers and tall hats, ribbons and lace.

Uncle George patted her on the arm. "Remember, gel, point the man in your vision out to me if you see him."

She tried not to wince. "I will."

She already knew the identity of the man in her vision but didn't want to admit it, not yet. If she told him she knew the man's identity, then he'd want to know how she'd discovered it. That would only lead them into a distasteful discussion about her fiasco in the woods with the dove, a talk she wanted to avoid, at least until later.

She parted with her uncle and settled into a vacant chair, her dress of *mousseline de soie* floating around her in a mint-green cloud. Large bows caught the hem up at the sides and patterned ivy ran down the front of the skirt, lengthening her petite form, while the neckline *à la grecque* exposed a modest amount of bosom. She'd bought the gown only last year, so it was still in mode, the notion giving her a measure of confidence she sorely needed.

From her vantage point near the entrance, she watched for him as each guest entered. She nodded to acquaintances and even hugged Donald Mallory, one of her uncle's cronies, when that old gent appeared. Half an hour passed. As the new arrivals began to thin out, Lucinda wondered if Captain Clairmont planned to stand his own party up.

"Come, Lucinda, let us mingle with our host."

Lucinda jumped. Uncle George had crept up behind her. He had a rather foolish smile pasted on his face.

"You've been drinking," she whispered.

"Nonsense." He winked, startling her so that she allowed him to draw her from her perch and hustle her forward. At the same moment, Squire Piggott minced in her direction, his gold-buckled pumps flashing beneath the light of a crystal chandelier.

She had the unsettling feeling she'd taken center stage at Drury Lane, so well orchestrated did their moves appear.

"My dear Miss Drakewyck." The Squire met them halfway. He wore a very short blue jacket, black peg-top inexpressibles that stretched visibly at the thighs and calves, and a waistcoat striped in yellow and blue. His oiled brown hair fell forward, revealing a balding pate. "And Mr. Drakewyck, too. How kind of you both to attend my party."

Lucinda leaned backward ever so slightly.

His smile unctuous, the Squire clasped her hand and bowed low over it. Sweat dotted his upper lip and plastered a few lank strands of hair to his forehead. With his arrival, the air had gained an undertone of unwashed flesh.

"Squire Piggott," Lucinda tried on a smile. It faltered. "How kind of *you* to host such an elegant party for Captain Clairmont."

He bowed his head slowly in acknowledgement. "How do you like my new decor?"

"Quite beautiful," she answered truthfully, her gaze touching on the white marble mantelpiece, the gilt-framed mirrors, the dove-gray wallpaper covered with turquoise roses and ribbons.

"I wanted to make the rooms comfortable."

"Feathering the nest, eh, Squire?" Uncle George prodded.

Squire Piggott ignored him, his attention fixed on Lucinda. "Mrs. Grose helped a great deal in planning this fete." He gestured toward an etagere pushed against the far wall, displaying an arrangement of oranges, apples, grapes, and Naples biscuits. "Nevertheless, I plan to marry soon. My wife will assume such duties."

"Ah, yes, every man must marry," Uncle George said with a significant look at Lucinda. "Once you choose, a luckier gel won't exist."

Both men stared at her.

"I feel quite parched," she blurted. "Excuse me." She slipped past them and made for a rosewood table displaying crystal pitchers of ratafia, lemonade, brandy, and champagne. She gulped down a glass of lemonade and watched, stomach sinking, as the Squire and Uncle George threaded through the crowd after her. She turned to the left and right, searching for an avenue of escape. A wall of silk and wool-clad partygoers hemmed her in.

When the Squire reached her side again, he took her elbow and urged her away from the table. "I had hoped to show you my library, Miss Drakewyck. Could I possibly interest you—"

"No." Lucinda hung back even farther.

"Ahem. The library's a very fine place indeed," Uncle George smiled; still, his lips remained firm. "Just been there myself. Many books. Take a turn with the Squire, Lucinda." He widened his eyes and nodded toward the hallway.

"I—"

"Come." The Squire pulled harder, and she found herself taking small, unwilling steps with him.

A sudden flurry of activity near the entryway caught their attention.

The Squire's butler stood near the door. Behind him, hidden in the shadows of the entryway, two tall men waited with a black-haired girl. "Miss Carolly Clairmont, Sir James Clairmont, and Captain Richard Clairmont," the butler announced in sonorous tones.

Polite applause filled the room. Squire Piggott, not one to shrink from attention, excused himself and joined the threesome in the entryway. Lightheaded with relief, Lucinda grasped the back of a chair for support.

The Squire gestured to the musical ensemble. The notes of a kingly flourish filled the hall. Beaming, he grabbed the arm of the tallest man and drew him forward.

Captain Clairmont took two steps and surveyed the room with an imperious hazel gaze, his black hair smooth, brushed back, the ends curling up. He descended the stairs, his sister, Carolly, on his arm, charging the room with energy. His torso—broad and muscled—filled out his black tailcoat, the buttons left undone, sleeves wide at the shoulders and narrowed toward the wrist.

He wasn't wearing his uniform, she thought, or his Victoria Cross.

A white satin waistcoat sheltered one of his hands, while his other hand rested on Carolly's back as he guided her down the steps. Lucinda suspected he deliberately concealed his damaged hand and wondered if it still pained him.

And what scars did he hide on the inside? She cast her thoughts back over the stories in the *London Evening Star*. Bodies of dead men rising out of the Balaclava harbor, fouling anchor chains and cables. Piles of amputated arms and legs, some still covered with sleeves and trousers. The wounded, lying naked in military hospitals on rotting unwashed floors, so immersed in filth that they did not trouble with the lavatory chamber. Lice, vermin, rotting sheep carcasses everywhere.

A surge of compassion for the Captain took her by surprise. Obviously his uniform was a reminder of things he'd rather forget. On further reflection she'd convinced herself she'd been too hard on him. Of course the man was taciturn. Who wouldn't be after charging with the Light Brigade?

Carolly sailed at his side, garbed in a demure dress of white silk trimmed with rose ribbon. Lucinda thought the dress more suited to a girl of ten or twelve than a young lady who would soon be presented at court. But the devilish glint in the girl's eyes—hazel like her brother's—belied her angelic gown and boded ill for her family.

Richard and Carolly took the steps slowly, descending into the ballroom with infinite grace, Sir James following behind them. Just as they reached the bottom step Richard looked at her.

The dark intensity of his gaze sparked an answering flame within her. Immediate longing made her ache, even though she knew the attachment was utterly preposterous on such a short acquaintance. She hadn't kissed him or held him in her arms; neverthe-

less, she *knew* the taste of his full lips and the feel of
his muscles and sinews beneath her fingers.

They must have been lovers in the vision, she
thought. The intimate knowledge she'd had of him,
or would have of him, had somehow impressed itself
on her subconscious.

Her heart pounded with hard, quick beats. Every
breath of air became difficult. She yearned to go to
him, to place her hand in his and walk beside him,
breathing in his scent and watching the candlelight
play across his coal-black hair.

For one moment, his eyes seemed to flicker, their
hazel depths filled with similar knowledge, as though
he'd seen her undressed, thoroughly kissed, and
needing so much more. But then his gaze settled into
a calm, steady regard before he nodded politely and
looked elsewhere.

Lucinda's shoulders drooped. She must be mad,
thinking he felt attracted to her. At their previous two
meetings he'd made it painfully clear he thought her
a nodcock without a notion of propriety and intent
on causing mischief, if not disaster.

Squire Piggott hurried down the stairs after them.
"Excellent citizens of Somerton, and good friends," he
announced, "I welcome you to my home, and bid you
make merry."

Several gentlemen, already tipsy, shouted encouragement, while the rest of the audience clapped again.
Lucinda pressed her hands together, too nervous to
applaud.

Squire Piggott held one arm up, and the noise died
down. "As you know, we are here to celebrate the
bravery and fine horsemanship of one of our leading
citizens." He laid a hand on Richard's shoulder.

73

"Captain Richard Clairmont, of Her Majesty's Eleventh Hussars."

More applause broke out, several women tittering and fluttering their fans.

Richard seemed unaffected by the ruckus. After a brief "Thank you," he strode into the crowd, Carolly securely at his side. He walked by Lucinda, his gait pausing ever so slightly as he passed her, but he neither nodded nor glanced her way.

"Miss Drakewyck. Would you join me in the first dance?"

Lucinda spun around at the sound of that oily voice.

His eyes mere slits of black in a pink face, Squire Piggott bent slightly at the waist in the manner of a French courtier enticing his lady, and clasped her fingers.

Her gaze fell and she hesitated a moment before answering, her spirits sinking into the floor. "But what of Captain Clairmont?" She pulled her hand from his a bit too forcefully. "Should he not have the first dance?"

"Captain Clairmont has asked me to honor him by performing the first dance in his stead. He is still recovering from the war and indicated he would rather observe."

"I suppose we shall dance, then."

Pained, Lucinda allowed the Squire to take her hand again and lead her onto the dance floor. As soon as they'd taken their places, three other couples joined them and the orchestra promptly struck up a melody suited to a quadrille.

Several minutes of agony followed. The Squire smiled and simpered at every opportunity while Lucinda did her best to appear polite without giving him false hope. He danced like a clumsy popinjay, his every movement so exaggerated that he elbowed the lady nearest him and received an outraged glare. When he began to move forward with the ladies rather than the gentlemen, she gritted her teeth and corrected him.

On and on it went, his dancing so disastrous that she tried to distract herself by searching the crowd for Richard. She craned her neck over the Squire's shoulder, only to have him turn around and see what had attracted her attention.

They both ended up staring into Richard Clairmont's sardonic gaze. He nodded at them and glanced at his watch fob. Swallowing, her cheeks warm, Lucinda focused on the Squire again. At last, the dance ended. She broke away from her partner as soon as propriety allowed and moved to the garden doors.

Light, informal side chairs upholstered in turquoise damask stood near the doors, some of them supporting Somerton's most distinguished elders. The heavy damask drapes, also done in turquoise and held back with gold cord, revealed braziers in the garden beyond, spouting orange flame. Peacock blue carpeting, patterned with leafy beige scrollwork, cushioned her feet in sumptuous luxury. Wall-to-wall, she noted. Must have cost the Squire a fortune.

As if thinking his name had conjured him, Squire Piggott began to push his way through the crowd in her direction. That tight smile on his lips told her she wouldn't fob him off with polite conversation. She slipped out the garden doors and between a row of lilac bushes, their flowers so purple and heavy they resembled grapes. Ahead, orange braziers lined a garden path which disappeared into the woods, most likely leading to the Squire's dock on the River Ouse.

She cast a glance back into the ballroom. The Squire stood a few heartbeats away, his hand on a doorknob, his gaze directed back into the central hall. Her skirts rustling, she spun around and set off at a fast walk, down the path, her high heels clicking on flagstones. Stars dusted the purple-black heavens but provided no additional light as her distance from the townhouse increased.

What was she going to do? Her imagination might indicate otherwise, but judging by his actions, Richard couldn't give a fig whether she lived or died. On the other hand, Squire Piggott was bleating after her like a ram let loose among the ewes. Well, she supposed things could be worse. Squire Piggott could have been her promised hero, and Richard Clairmont, the distasteful swain . . . although she had to admit, the thought of kissing Richard wasn't distasteful at all.

Lucinda stopped and turned to gaze at the house, tall and imposing in the darkness, the chandelier glittering beyond the French doors. She remembered the beautifully appointed interior, Squire Piggott's fussy attention to detail—and a plan occurred to her. The Squire wanted her because of her "good breeding" and connections. Well, she would just have to convince him that a pedigree and connections didn't always produce a superior example of womanhood.

Nearby, a bush rustled. Sounds of giggling drifted around the corner of a hedgerow. Lucinda paused, her eyes wide. Unwilling to witness a furtive embrace, she turned and began to walk back toward the garden doors. But she took no more than a few steps when a black-haired girl in white stumbled onto the path before her.

The girl had her attention focused on the hedgerow, and without warning, a youth followed her into the open, his cravat askew. Lucinda recognized him as one of Somerton's young bloods, an unprincipled lad with too much money and too little maturity. Lucinda lowered her gaze and hurried past Carolly Clairmont, wondering if her brother knew how close the girl was coming to total ruin.

$\mathcal{T}$he smile had grown stiff on Richard's face. He shoved his scarred hand into his evening coat and took another sip of brandy. Although he appreciated Squire Piggott's effort to celebrate his part in the charge of the Light Brigade, the memories well-wishers had roused scraped away at the scabs which covered his sore spirit.

Beside him, the tall case clock chimed eleven. Many of the guests had just arrived. Nevertheless, he planned to make an exit within the hour. His temples throbbed with the stress of smiling and acting as though nothing bothered him. He wondered if anyone would remark on the fact that he hadn't worn his uniform or Cross. He simply hadn't the heart to put them on.

A woman moved toward him, twisting between the dancers in the central hall, her gown a giant black tent. Turkish tassels and a crescent brooch decorated her bodice, an overt show of sympathy for their "gallant ally" in the war. She even wore a fez atop her black curls. Indeed, the entire scene reminded him of a camp in Balaclava. He saw a number of rounded tents of different colors, the poles sustaining them poking out of the summit.

"Good evening, Captain Clairmont." Avid interest in her blue eyes, she fluttered her fan. Her black mourning gown proclaimed her as newly widowed.

He forced a smile to his lips. "I don't believe we've met."

"I don't believe in formal introductions," she countered, and held out a hand. "Letitia Grose. Congratulations on your safe return." Her voice had deepened to the tone of a practiced flirt.

Richard took her hand and nodded over it, his neck barely moving. He'd seen so much death of late he couldn't countenance the widow's desertion of her recently buried husband. "I was lucky. But good fortune's a poxed whore. She makes you pay for what you want and later makes you regret you even asked."

Mrs. Grose tittered, her bosom heaving against her low-cut neckline. "I had the privilege of meeting Lord Cardigan during my recent visit to London. He called you the finest cavalry officer he'd ever commanded."

"How delightful." Richard felt the pressure to say more, to compliment his commanding officer in kind, but he simply couldn't utter the words.

Lord Cardigan. That bastard.

In his usual insolent way, Lord Cardigan hadn't bothered to confirm vague orders, and heedless of the Cossacks and Russian battalions which clogged the valley, had directed the Light Brigade to charge the Russian guns. After the brigade had captured the guns—and three quarters of the men had died—their commander had returned to his yacht, had a glass of champagne and a bath, and went to bed.

Unlike Lord Cardigan, John Burke had never even answered muster. Richard had buried his best friend himself, digging into Russian soil with his bloodied, scarred hand.

He drew a deep breath and released it gradually.

"Captain Clairmont, I . . . I feel in need of a turn through the gardens. The heat, you know." Mrs. Grose's full, red lips curved in a slow smile. "If you would be so kind to escort me—"

"May I suggest a visit to the graveyard, instead? Perhaps a turn about your husband's burial site would cool your temperature." He knew he sounded like a self-righteous bastard, but for God's sake, did no one respect the dead anymore?

Paying little attention to the widow's gasp, he looked across the room and saw Carolly at the refreshment table, a glass of lemonade in her hand and two swains hanging on her arm. His father was deep in conversation with Squire Piggott and hadn't noticed Carolly's antics—or he perhaps didn't care. Lips tight, he bowed to Mrs. Grose, who now observed him with a narrowed gaze, and strode forward to corner Carolly.

"Hello, brother," Carolly said gaily as he approached.

Richard grabbed her arm and drew her into an alcove. "Your behavior is beyond reprehensible," he warned. "If you do not curb yourself, I shall personally see to it that you wait another year before your presentation at court."

The girl's eyes darkened. "I wish you were still in the Crimea," she hissed. "I don't care what happened to you in the war."

"That's enough, Carolly."

She ripped her arm from his grasp and backed away.

"I hope you heed my warning," he said. "I am perfectly ready to act upon it should I need to."

With a huffy sound she turned and made her way across the dance floor.

Richard sighed. His sister was naught but a hoyden and would spoil her character at her first opportunity if she thought it might provide a thrill. She had no sense, no appreciation for her family. To Carolly, life was a game that could be started over if she didn't like the cards she held.

His gaze traveled over the laughing, chattering people around him, dressed in silks and superfine, the finest foods slipping down their throats. They didn't realize how much they had to be thankful for. They hadn't seen the hospital in Scutari, hadn't felt the pain of amputation and cauterization. In a way, he resented them terribly. And he wished he were anywhere but here.

Why had he agreed to attend this party? What had possessed him? He must have been mad to expose himself to this type of puffery so soon after Balaclava. When Squire Piggott began to walk in his direction, he turned and went to the opposite side of the room. He felt several pats on the back, heard many compliments, but ignored one and all. He simply couldn't stand to utter one more word about the war, wouldn't accept another toast. The Squire's guests, he mused, probably thought him the most churlish man in the room.

Right now, he didn't give a goddamn.

With an oath he tugged at his cravat, his throat tight and burning. He couldn't free himself of the memories, couldn't stop them. Every second of that battle—every image, sound, and feeling—had burned indelibly into him, and now it crested the surface of his consciousness like a behemoth from the deep.

The pistol in his hand, cold metal, his finger on the trigger, aiming toward a Russian infantryman, pulling.

A muffled crack, as if a barrel of gunpowder had ignited deep beneath the earth.

Volcanic pain burying in his palm and radiating up his arm.

John Burke falling in a graceful pirouette.

Without thought he shoved his scarred hand deeper into his pocket. More images plunged in his head, coming faster, harder, and he muffled a groan.

Thick particles of gunpowder making his eyes feel like two small pieces of coal.

Lurching like a drunkard on the corner of Piccadilly Square, good hand outstretched, cannons booming around him, screams of pain, Cossack howls and garbled Russian shouts, swords clashing.

The large hole in John's back. His final words: "Tell my brother, Richard. Tell him I loved him."

The voices of the damned.

"Leave me alone," he whispered.

And knew they would not.

A loud tangle of voices drifted from the center of the dance floor. The music—a concerto—abruptly stopped and the crowd parted to reveal an unusual sight. A woman lay on her side, several layers of stiffened muslin petticoats remaining over her head. A pair of pretty white drawers encased a rather petite bottom and slender, silk-clad legs. Unskilled in the management of her draperies, she had obviously taken a wrong step and ended in disaster.

Next to her, Squire Piggott stood gasping and wringing his hands, his ample body corseted into the tightest of peg-top trousers and surtout.

"Far be it from me," the Squire huffed, "to criticize, but you have trod upon my toes innumerable times, Miss Drakewyck, so much so I fear I shall have trouble with my ankles on the morrow. Please right yourself at once. You're making a spectacle of yourself."

She kicked her legs. "I can't."

Richard shook the thoughts of war from his head. Here, he thought, was another hoyden, a witch who seemed to have cast a spell on him. Richard could think of no other way to describe the way she'd affected him. Even now he struggled against a powerful urge to push aside her drawers and touch the skin he'd expose with his lips.

Hiding his unruly emotions beneath a calm gaze, he strode to her side and fished through the petticoats and silk, anxious to hide her drawers from the interested stares of several gentlemen. Quite by accident he brushed her thigh, and beneath his fingertips he felt the warmth of her skin through lace. He withdrew as if he'd touched hot coals.

"Pardon—"

She gulped, and in her haste to move away from his hand pressed her bottom against his arm. That sweet, firm flesh added to the fire in his loins and he nearly groaned aloud. Good God, he'd meant to help her, and ended up fondling her before a crowd.

"I beg your pardon," he muttered, jaw stiff, hoping his involuntary response wouldn't show beneath his trousers.

A few titters stirred through the gathering. Richard stole a glance behind him and intercepted a bearded man's wink. His jaw tightened further as he realized more than one of the Squire's guests thought he was taking advantage of an unfortunate situation. "Miss Drakewyck, stop struggling."

She complied long enough to allow him to grasp the layers of white cotton around her. When he at last pushed the fabric away, he beheld a wealth of tumbled chocolate ringlets and saucy brown eyes.

Thoughts of war were far, far away.

"At last, a gentleman." Pink tinged her cheeks and a well-proportioned bosom, which looked in danger of spilling from her bodice. She lifted her chin. "These fools seem content to stare."

Feeling more like a blackguard than a gentleman, he lifted her and set her on her feet. He avoided her eyes, certain she would detect the lust he couldn't quite banish, and with a touch of alarm glanced at her bodice. Encased in mint silk, her breasts surged upward, as if daring him to touch, to taste.

He swallowed. "Shall I escort you to the ladies' cloakroom?"

"I don't believe it necessary." She brushed her petticoats and gown into place. "Perhaps a glass of lemonade instead."

"Of course." Aware of the snickers behind them, he offered her his good hand.

Unaccountably, she clutched his damaged hand instead, as if she must touch it. Breath caught in his throat, he waited for an exclamation of loathing, but none came.

"Your hand," she murmured. "How did you—"

"Again I find you in a compromising position," he cut in, his voice husky.

Her lips quirked in a half smile. "I am unused to dancing, as Squire Piggott will attest. I took a step too hastily, and my petticoat caught on the Squire's shoe buckle, and I fell . . ." She shrugged. "You know the rest."

Eyebrow arched, he drew her toward the refreshment table. Behind them, the gawkers dispersed. "I did not think you awkward, but merely purposeful. You meant to teach poor Squire Piggott a lesson."

"And what sort of lesson would I wish to teach him, sir?"

"I would wager the value of distance. The farther he stays away from you, the less he will suffer. Am I right?"

"I am not accustomed to making gentlemen suffer."

"You seem to have made a career out of it," he said, feeling the ache in his loins at her nearness.

She drew herself up. "I do not consider that a compliment, sir."

"It wasn't meant as one. 'Tis merely a truth."

"I see." She winced ever so slightly, her brown eyes darkening. A moment later she raised her chin. "If you'll excuse me, Captain, I shall go back to my task of making gentlemen suffer. Enjoy your party."

He gave her a sharp bow and stepped aside, trying to ignore the hurt in her gaze. Deliberately he conjured thoughts of John Burke and the other men who'd died in the charge. They weren't sipping fine wine and conversing with ladies. Instead, they rotted in cold Russian soil. How could he think about having the little witch in his bed every night, their laughter muffled between kisses, when widows wept for their dead husbands?

Squire Piggott intervened, his gaze darting from Richard to Lucinda. "Come in to dinner with me, Miss Drakewyck. You will sit on my right-hand side."

She took the Squire's proffered arm, and with a prolonged glance at Richard, drifted into the dining room. Over dinner, Richard watched her carefully, his amusement growing. He became convinced she

played the part of an oaf, knocking over the fruit basket, pulling the tablecloth off the table, depositing little cakes onto the carpet. He nearly laughed aloud
when she knocked her glass of lemonade over and it
poured down the front of her poor victim's waistcoat.

Always she apologized, her cheeks pinkening, her
mouth curved with chagrin. Still, the sparkle in her
gaze—apparent to him even from across the room—
gave her away. He thought it a unique if rather obvious way to discourage a suitor, and knew the chit
was enjoying herself immensely.

The Squire's complexion grew mottled as the minutes wore on. Clearly he preferred eating his food to
wearing it. At length, they finished, and after a brief
delay they all returned to the ballroom.

Dancing resumed and card playing began in earnest. From across the sea of merrymakers Richard
watched Squire Piggott and Lucinda Drakewyck step
around each other in a complicated dance of pursue-
and-reject. Squire Piggott, however, cut her from the
herd at last and guided her down the hall with as
much finesse as a seasoned drover.

Richard watched them go. He knew Squire Piggott
had taken her somewhere to woo her in private, and
suspected she would continue to reject him. What he
couldn't understand was why the idea of Squire Piggott wooing her sat so poorly with him. Why should
he care about Lucinda Drakewyck?

Love and magic, after all, had no place in his life.

Squire Piggott shepherded Lucinda down a hallway and into the library, a Greek affair done in
amber, with rows of ancient-looking tomes, urns,
vases, and statues of various gods. A candelabra sat

upon a desk, casting a faint radiance upon Squire Piggott's countenance. The obsequious smile still curved his lips, but beneath the piety in his eyes something darker, more vulgar lurked.

A tiny shudder rippled through her. "Squire Piggott, I cannot think why you've brought me here—"

"Surely you are not unaware of my intentions," he said. "Your delightful companionship and stimulating wit has captured my fancy. Miss Lucinda, please allow me the honor to pay you my addresses."

Her hand fluttered to her throat. "I thank you for the compliments, sir. You do me great honor—"

"I'm not without prospects," he continued, dabbing his lips with a square of linen. "As you know, I'm Lord Lieutenant of Bedfordshire, with three thousand five hundred acres under my management. I've more tenants on my tillage than any other Squire south of London."

"I am fully sensible of your situation—"

"I understand that your own fortune has suffered a reversal. Let me assure you, Miss Drakewyck, that I am indifferent to your circumstances. I seek not an income but an elegant female who will support me in all my endeavors."

"Squire Piggott," she said forcefully, "it is hopeless for me to accept your addresses when 'tis clear to me we would never suit. Please accept my gratitude for the honor you've done me this evening and my apologies for refusing, but it simply cannot be."

"Did I mention that Viscountess Rothfield has approved our match? Why, just last week when I called at her noble estate, she told me how much she looked forward to regarding me as a relation rather than an acquaintance with whom she visited and corresponded."

"We are *not* a match, sir."

The Squire shook his head, his smile growing wider. "Miss Lucinda, I think you refuse me this first time as any lady of quality would, to raise your estimation in my eyes. I suspect we shall soon be driving through the park together and, if I might say so, holding hands."

"My refusal is most earnest!"

The Squire seemed unmoved by her vehement tone. "I'm certain once I've had the chance to inform your uncle of my intentions, I shall be upon your doorstep."

"Pardon me, Squire," Lucinda said, furious. "I must find Sir James. I haven't had the chance to inquire after his health."

" 'Tis feminine humility that gives you pause, an admirable quality that more women would do well to imitate—"

Lucinda didn't hear the rest of his words. She hurried from the library and the Squire's grasping paws. Lord, what was it going to take to put the man off?

She melted into the ballroom crowd, looking for Sir James Clairmont's tall form. The Squire wouldn't dare take her away from that elderly gent, whose pedigree and wealth made him one of Somerton's most distinguished residents. She found him near the gaming tables, examining a watch fob that dangled from his snowy waistcoat. His black hair had gone almost completely gray, and he leaned on a cane; even so, his countenance held the regal expression of a man used to getting his own way.

"Good evening, Miss Drakewyck," he said when he saw her. He smiled with genuine pleasure. "How kind of you to attend my son's fete. A deadly bore, isn't it?"

"Now, Sir James," she chided, smiling, "gatherings such as these may be tiresome but they're necessary. We learn of our neighbors' problems, we discover the latest fashions"—she paused as her gaze settled over Squire Piggott—"and young ladies have a chance to troll the waters for potential suitors."

"Ah, yes, what more could a thinking person desire?"

They groaned in unison, then laughed at the coincidence.

"Oh, Sir James," Lucinda sighed, "I would rather be walking in the woods this moment."

The older man nodded in agreement.

Suddenly, loud giggling and hearty male laughter dampened conversation in the ballroom. Carolly danced by with an army officer, her arms wrapped around him far too tightly. "More champagne," she called out to no one in particular. "I'm positively parched."

"Lemonade, Carolly," Sir James ordered, his voice cutting through the conversation.

If she heard, the girl gave no indication.

Eyebrows drawn low, the older Clairmont frowned. "I've already warned her twice this evening. One more misstep and I'm going to have to take her home."

"A party always draws high spirits out of a young girl," Lucinda soothed.

"She is always high-spirited. I don't know what I'm going to do with her. She will be presented at court in one month and tour the Continent at the Season's end; and yet, she has the manners of a farmhand. Punishments don't seem to work. They only increase her determination to make a fool of herself." He frowned, his eyes becoming shadowed. "I wish to

God her mother had lived. Elizabeth was taken in the typhoid outbreak of 1841, you know."

Lucinda nodded. "I lost my parents to the outbreak, too."

Silence stretched between them. After a moment Sir James shook himself. "We've chosen a poor time to ruminate about the dead, dear girl. Instead, please give me your opinion on my daughter. What am I to do?"

"Does she have a governess?" Lucinda asked, her tone gentle.

"Carolly's sixteen. She'll turn seventeen by the end of this month. She feels she is too old for a governess, and unfortunately, I believe she's correct on that score."

"Perhaps a companion would help."

Sir James's eyebrows quirked. "Now there's an idea. But who would have her?"

Lucinda thought for a moment. Who indeed would have Carolly? Any association with the girl could prove problematic, especially since she seemed determined to find trouble. Wild, stubborn, and completely out of hand, Carolly could very well destroy not only her own character but the characters of those close to her.

"You see? I'm stuck," Sir James said dolefully.

Lucinda nodded, her attention straying to the knot of partygoers to her left. In its midst she espied two men and immediately stiffened. Ever since their first dance together, Squire Piggott had stalked her with all the skills of a master hunter. Once again, he'd rooted her out. He stood ten feet away with Uncle George, their heads together, both occasionally glancing in her direction.

Frowning, she looked away, only to collide with Richard Clairmont's gaze, his eyes fierce, full of a message she couldn't quite understand.

"Miss Drakewyck? You look quite pale. Are you all right?" Sir James grasped her arm.

"I'll be Carolly's companion," she heard herself say.

The older man's eyebrows shot upward. He released her arm. "Pardon?"

She turned to him, her voice strengthening. "I want to be Carolly's companion. Will you give me the post?"

Not only would she be helping Sir James, but she'd be earning an income to put off the duns; discouraging Squire Piggott, who'd never soil his bloodline with someone who collected wages; and most importantly, she'd be living right under Richard Clairmont's nose. Of course, by entering the trades she'd probably lose Lady Rothfield's regard, but that was a small price to pay for a solution which solved so many problems.

Eyes wide, Sir James stared at her for a moment. "If I could, I'd accept your offer in a second. Your steadying influence would go far toward making a lady of my daughter. But you know I can't employ you. Why, your uncle would never let you accept, and he wouldn't thank me for offering."

"We are in straightened circumstances," she said baldly. "An income wouldn't do us any wrong."

A slight flush crept into the older man's face. "I've heard of your monetary difficulties, but you can't become a servant. Your birth and property preclude such a notion."

"Pshaw on birth and property. What good are they when your larder is empty and your home fallen into disrepair? Please, will you not reconsider?"

He hesitated. "I should discuss this with your uncle. Perhaps if I put money into a trust for you, rather than pay you wages . . ."

"Discuss it with him if you must. If he agrees, is the position mine?"

"Of course it is. Indeed, when Carolly is presented at court, you may come to London with us and sample its pleasures as a friend of the family."

Lucinda felt her spirits rise for the first time that evening. She grasped the elder man's hands and squeezed. "Thank you, Sir James. You have put my mind to rest."

He smiled. " 'Tis my pleasure, Miss Drakewyck."

"I'm certain my uncle will agree," she said. "I'll talk to him myself, right now."

"Hadn't you better wait? We're in the middle of a party."

"Why put off till tomorrow what you can do today?" She returned his smile, and before he could offer any more unwanted advice, sailed in the direction of her uncle, who talked with his old friend Donald Mallory. Nearly deaf, Mr. Mallory's voice rang out across the ballroom.

Arguments had already begun to form in her mind. She *would* persuade him. A man was nothing against a determined female.

"Oh, sirs, I accept your challenge."

Lucinda stopped short, Carolly's voice grating on her ears. The girl was near the door, out of Sir James and Richard's earshot, and surrounded by two wild-eyed bloods.

"My carriage against the two of yours," Carolly said, breathing quickly. "We shall race down Covington Road, and whoever reaches the Ouse first wins."

"What prize do you offer?" one of the youths asked.

Carolly tossed her head. "If I win, you and Mr. Pierce must give me the trophy your team won last year at Eton, the one you received in the cricket championship."

"And if one of us wins?"

"I'll reward you with a kiss!"

Both youths nodded vigorously. "We'll call for the carriages at once."

Lucinda, struck by a sense of imminent disaster, hurried to Carolly's side. "Miss Clairmont," she began, "do you think this wise—"

"Oh, hullo, Miss Drakewyck," Carolly said.

"Miss Clairmont, you don't mean to go chasing down Covington Road at this hour—"

"Leave me to my amusements," the girl said.

"You'll ruin your reputation."

"You're just a dried-up old spinster who didn't allow herself any diversions and envies anyone else who tries to find pleasure."

Lucinda tightened her lips. "Your reckless behavior is already causing a stir. Do you have any hopes of marriage?"

"I am only sixteen. I care not about marriage. But I can see your point about causing a stir. Mrs. Grose has already marked me, and in another moment, Father will too. I had better go."

She raced out the door.

Lucinda followed. Cool air nipped at her skin. She shivered and rubbed her arms. "I won't allow you to do this."

"You can't stop me. Now get along, Miss Drakewyck, and go preach to someone else."

"Carolly!"

The girl paid her no attention. Lucinda stood on the front porch, caught in indecision. A carriage race at midnight! They'd be lucky if their carriages didn't careen off the road, and Lucinda didn't relish the thought of a few broken bones. At the same time, if she left Carolly to ruin, Sir James might not consider her tough enough to bring the girl into line and retract his offer.

Which was worse, a broken arm or fending off Squire Piggott's clumsy courtship?

"I'm going with you," Lucinda said.

Carolly's eyes widened. "You want to come? By all means. Perhaps we will shake you from your bookish ways."

"I'm coming because I hope to talk some sense into you," Lucinda said, scrambling after Carolly as they hopped aboard a high-sprung gig.

"Do you suppose Richard will mind me using his gig?" Carolly asked, her lips curved in a shameless smile.

Lucinda glanced into the ballroom. Mrs. Grose was motioning to Sir James and Richard.

Carolly followed Lucinda's gaze and squeaked. "We'd better be off, or I'll find out too soon what Richard thinks."

She snapped the reins on the horse and they trotted away from the Piggott residence. Two other carriages fell in beside them, one a chaise and the other a curricle, their wheels without the size of Richard's more sporting gig.

Their small parade trotted through Somerton, Lucinda trying to talk sense into Carolly the entire time and coming up short. When they reached Covington Road, which led out of town and toward Drakewyck Grange, they stopped and lined themselves up. The carriages' lanterns threw light onto the road, but not enough to ease Lucinda's nerves.

"Miss Drakewyck," one of the youths said, "may we ask you to drop a handkerchief? That will be our signal to go."

Lucinda glared at them through narrowed eyes. "I will not. I ask you to turn these carriages around before someone is hurt."

Carolly dismissed Lucinda with a languid wave. "I'll count three, and on three we go. One."

The horses, perhaps sensing their owners' tension, pawed nervously at the ground.

"Two."

Carolly's hands tightened on the reins until her knuckles turned white.

"Three!"

With explosive force the three carriages hurtled forward, the horses quickly getting into the spirit of things and putting on extra speed. Lucinda clutched the side of the gig, her heart beating wildly in her chest, desperately scanning the road for potholes that, if encountered, might send her sailing through the air. Crazy patterns of light bobbed on the road as the carriages and their lanterns jolted along.

Carolly began to pull ahead of the others. She screeched with pleasure while they hooted and caroused behind her. Cold air whipped Lucinda's hair from her chignon and dirt showered her as their horse charged onward, his hooves pounding against the road and throwing up clods of earth.

The farther they traveled from town, the darker the road became, until Lucinda could barely see ten feet before her despite the lantern's glow. Vague outlines of trees huddled on either side of them, their forms gray shadows against black velvet, but otherwise, the night was absolute. She couldn't even guess how the horse knew to stay on the road and didn't think Carolly could see any better than she. Blind luck, she concluded, had saved them from mishap so far, but luck didn't last forever, and—

"Carolly, watch out!" she shouted. She'd seen something flash in the darkness, a pale silhouette on the edge of the road and in their way—

Carolly saw the figure at the last second. She screamed and pulled the horse hard to the right. The gig bumped mightily before bounding over the edge of the road and lodging in a ditch. The horse came within inches of ramming into a tree.

Lucinda sat stunned. That bump. Had it been a hill on the edge of the road, or had they run the figure over? She scrambled out of the gig and raced to the side of the road. A dark lump, one that didn't fit in with the landscape, lay motionless in the ditch. Nearly wheezing with panic, Lucinda touched the lump. It was a body. A someone.

The other two carriages stopped several yards ahead. Shouts echoed through the darkness.

"Carolly, come down here and help me," Lucinda demanded.

Sobbing reached her ears. The girl was crying.

Lucinda glared at her. "Save your tears for later. Get down here now and help me."

Sniffling, Carolly stepped down from the carriage. Lucinda couldn't see her face but hoped it reflected remorse, not for the trouble she'd just brought herself but for the person she'd run over.

"Help me turn him over," Lucinda said, assuming that only a man would walk alone in the middle of the night. "We must see if you've killed him."

Carolly sobbed louder.

"Stop it!" Lucinda stood up and grasped the girl's shoulders. "Now is not the time to indulge in self-pity. We must provide what help we can to your victim."

The girl hiccuped a few times and then nodded.

Her lips pressed in a grim line, she grabbed Carolly's hand and drew her back over to the still form. "Pull easily on his shoulder. I'll support his head. Together will we turn him over and see if he lives."

As directed, Carolly grabbed the figure's shoulder, and Lucinda placed steadying hands on his head, noting as she did so that his skin felt warm. She thought she felt a pulse in the man's temple and some of her dismay lifted. Not dead, she thought, but most likely wounded, perhaps seriously.

Together they turned him over, only Lucinda discovered to her surprise that *he* was a *she*. Long blonde hair, skin as pale as moonlight, the woman was beautiful beyond compare. A gold filigreed locket hung from the woman's neck and a beauty mark graced the corner of her mouth. Her eyes were closed, but Lucinda didn't need to see their color. She already knew the woman's identity.

The witch in her vision had finally arrived in Somerton.

*R*ichard clung to his horse as they galloped through the night down Covington Road. His father rode several feet behind him, his bay's hooves thumping against the road in a quick staccato. They'd left the party so quickly that Sir James had lost his cane and they'd both taken the first horses they could find. Richard scanned the road, looking for his gig. Trees arched upward beside them, each trunk more than capable of reducing an out-of-control carriage to splinters.

He muttered a vicious curse. Carolly had outdone herself tonight. Selfish and without any regard for her reputation, she'd shamed the entire family and would probably live with the consequences of this foolish act for many weeks to come. He could only hope that people would make allowances for her age.

If she survived her wild carriage ride.

For the first time since he'd left the Crimea, fear nearly paralyzed him. Infuriated at the senselessness of it all, he leaned into his horse's mane and spurred him to greater speed.

Miss Drakewyck, he thought, hadn't the luxury of youth to excuse her. He couldn't think of words that condemned her thoroughly enough. How could she, a woman of marriageable age, encourage a girl to embark on such a stunt? Hadn't she the slightest bit of sense? Obviously not. He was the fool for even questioning it. Any woman who cast magic spells and routinely tried to set fire to the woods wouldn't blink an eye at a carriage race.

Up ahead, the gray silhouette of a carriage materialized out of the darkness. Richard pulled his horse up sharply, the momentum carrying him backward as he dismounted. He immediately recognized his gig, its lanterns casting a dim glow. When he saw the shape sprawled on the side of the road, and another form bent over it, his gut turned to ice.

Sir James pounded up behind him and jumped off the saddle. "Dear God. Is it Carolly or Miss Drakewyck?"

Without answering Richard rushed toward the huddled pair. When he reached them, Lucinda Drakewyck turned to look at him, her mouth pinched at the corners, her brown hair wild with tangles. Her green dress appeared almost gray in the darkness. "Captain Clairmont. Thank God you've come."

"Carolly?" he choked out.

"No," she said. "She's right there. She's shaken but all right."

His sister, Richard saw, stood pressed against the side of his ruined gig. He nearly sagged with relief. A thousand harsh reprimands crowded his throat. "We'll talk later," he growled at his sister.

Carolly shrank away from him.

Richard swung around toward the prone figure. If Carolly hadn't been injured, then who was lying on the side of the road?

Sir James limped over to Richard and Lucinda. His gaze roving over the prone figure, he seemed to crumple. "I had thought the worst."

Fearing the worst wasn't yet over, Richard knelt down and examined Carolly and Lucinda's victim. A woman, he saw, the tiny lines around her eyes placing her at about thirty years, his age. Her skin had a strange translucence, as if it hadn't been exposed to sunlight for many a month. Blonde hair tumbled out of the cloak she wore and her eyebrows were two pale slashes across an unlined forehead.

Attractive, Richard thought, in a cold way. Miss Drakewyck, he realized, had wrapped the woman in her own cloak. Urgently he felt for a pulse, afraid her neck would prove cold and lifeless, just like the necks of so many men who'd charged in the Light Brigade with him. Her pulse beat steadily beneath his fingers.

Sir James, his stiff-rumped limp expressing wrath better than any words, went to Carolly's side. The girl began to sob, her cries gathering volume with every passing moment.

"You're a foolish girl," Sir James hissed. "You almost killed yourself tonight and for that I may never forgive you."

Riotous weeping filled the night.

Mouth pressed in a grim line, Sir James rejoined Richard and they both focused on the prone figure.

"She lives," Richard said. "But for how long, I cannot tell. We must get her to a doctor immediately." He arranged Lucinda's cloak around the woman to ensure she'd retain as much heat as possible, and rolled up his own cloak to form a pillow for her head. "We can do nothing for her here."

Sir James turned his attention to the gig. He ran his hands along the axle, and then straightened, his voice tense. "The axle's snapped in two. We'll have to go for help."

In the distance, carriages rattled and voices spoke in a subdued tone. "The two young men who raced against Carolly and me should be returning in a moment," Lucinda offered.

Sir James removed his cloak and placed it around Lucinda's shoulders. "Tell us what happened, Miss Drakewyck, while we wait."

Trembling, she stared at the injured woman. Richard interpreted her look as fear, one he'd seen often enough on the faces of soldiers about to engage the enemy. And fear she should, he thought, for she and Carolly had nearly taken a life tonight.

"Miss Lucinda?" Sir James moved next to her and put an arm around her shoulders.

With an effort, she dragged her attention away from the blonde. "Carolly wanted to race down Covington Road. I tried to stop her. She wouldn't listen. We took Captain Clairmont's gig"—she winced and glanced at Richard—"and Carolly urged the team forward."

Richard listened with growing disbelief to her explanation. Miss Drakewyck would have them think her completely innocent, but he knew better. He'd seen her prancing through the woods after midnight twenty-four hours before. "Did Carolly corroborate her story?" he asked, his voice harsh.

His father looked at him, eyebrows raised. "I see no reason to doubt Miss Lucinda."

Richard snorted. His father didn't know about her penchant for bonfires and witchcraft.

The elder Clairmont narrowed his eyes at Richard, then refocused on Lucinda. His voice, when he spoke, was gentle. "And after Carolly urged the horse forward, you began to race down Covington Road."

She nodded. "Two other gentlemen in their own carriages raced against us, each hoping to win and receive a kiss from Carolly."

"Who were they?"

"Mr. Pierce and Mr. Whitney."

"I'll keep watch for them," Richard said. He positioned himself next to the road.

"What happened next?" Sir James asked.

"I saw a figure walking along the edge of the road. I cried out to Carolly, and she saw it too, but not in time. I'm afraid . . ."

Her hands twisting together, she looked at the ground.

"Go ahead," the elder Clairmont encouraged.

"The horse may have trampled the woman. I also suspect the gig . . . ran her over before bouncing into the ditch."

Sir James closed his eyes. "Good God."

"Damn," Richard said. Hands on his waist, lips compressed, he shook his head. Lucinda and Carolly were the very devil of irresponsibility.

Just then the two other miscreants pulled up in their carriages, their heads hanging low, their voices soft. Like whipped curs, Richard thought.

Sir James greeted them. "I hold both of you partly responsible for the debacle this evening. Like true villains you have encouraged my daughter to display reprehensible behavior matching your own." He waved toward the injured woman, his voice harsh. "This poor woman happened to be in the way and now pays for your recklessness. You had better hope she recovers."

Silence reigned. Even the horses seemed cowed before Sir James' wrath and stood utterly still.

"Mark me, sirs, your fathers shall hear of this."

The silence grew deeper, and the two bucks' heads hung even lower.

"I need a carriage," Sir James demanded. He jabbed a finger toward one of the youths. "You. Help me transport this woman to Clairmont Hall."

Lucinda stiffened. "You're bringing her to your home?"

"What choice have I?" Sir James asked. He pointed to the other youth. "You. Go and collect Dr. Bennet. Bring him to Clairmont Hall as fast as you're able."

"Right away," they both said. The second youth jumped in his chaise and set off for town at a fast clip. Richard moved to the injured woman's side, and with his father's and the youth's help lifted her. She didn't weigh much at all, Richard thought, as they maneuvered her onto the curricle's leather squabs.

"You're next, Carolly." Sir James hoisted his daughter into the curricle and told her to sit next to her victim. "Cushion her head so that she doesn't bump it even worse," he ordered.

Tears streaming down her face, Carolly placed the woman's head on her lap. Sir James climbed aboard and took the reins, while the youth sat upon the groom's perch.

Sir James turned to Richard. "Stay with Miss Drakewyck."

Without waiting to hear Richard's assent, he snapped the reins and rattled down Covington Road.

Lucinda and Richard stood near his ruined gig. He rubbed his eyes with one hand.

"I am so sorry, Captain Clairmont," she murmured. "I would have stopped Carolly if I could—"

"I don't know much about you, Miss Drakewyck, but judging by our previous two meetings, you seem the type to encourage this kind of behavior."

"I assure you, sir, I did not."

He heard the quaver in her voice and relented. "I'd best return you to Squire Piggott's. Your uncle is likely overset with worry for you."

"But the gig, it's broken."

"We have two horses. We'll ride." He walked to the horse still tethered to the gig, murmured soothing words as he unharnessed him, and led him over to Lucinda. Favoring his left front leg, the horse wobbled with each step.

"Damn, he's limping." Richard ran his hands along the horse's foreleg. "I can't feel any heat or swelling. Still, you can't ride him. We'll ride the horse I borrowed from the Squire."

"Both of us?"

"We have no choice." With a frown he surveyed her frilly party gown, at least six feet wide at the hem, and tried to imagine her sitting on a saddle. "I've neither a mounting block nor a sidesaddle, and your costume is far from appropriate for riding. I'm afraid you're going to have to take those petticoats off. At least then you'll be able to sit."

"Sir!"

"Would you prefer to walk?"

" 'Tis almost three miles to Squire Piggott's."

"I cannot ride if a giant tent is billowing in front of me, blocking my vision."

"Captain Clairmont, a lady does not undress anywhere but in her dressing room."

"All right then, wait here. I'll go and retrieve a carriage for you. I shouldn't be gone more than fifteen minutes."

"Do you mean to leave me here in the dark?"

He pointed to the lantern mounted on the gig. "You have some light."

"Won't the Squire send a carriage after us?"

"He didn't know where my father and I were going, and we didn't have time to tell him."

Lower lip caught between her teeth, she scanned the woodlands. "I don't want to be alone."

"Only last night I found you in the woodlands, casting your spells or whatever it is you do. Why would the trees bother you now?"

"Last night I hadn't seen . . . I didn't know . . ." She lowered her gaze. "Turn around, Captain Clairmont. I'll take the petticoats off."

He inclined his head, moved slightly, and contemplated the trees. She stood several feet away, but he was so overwhelmingly aware of her that she might have been pressed against him, her breath warm against his neck. Squaring his shoulders, he tried to stir up thoughts of war. An image of Lucinda formed in his mind, her full lips pouting for a kiss.

"Have you finished?" he asked, his voice rough.

"Not yet. I seem to have knotted the strings. I don't know that I can remove them."

"Good God, Lucinda, we won't find a lady's maid lurking in the trees. You must remove them yourself." He paused, warmth creeping into his face as he realized he'd used her first name. "My apologies. I didn't mean to sound so familiar."

"I prefer Lucinda," she said, after a slight pause. "After all we've been through together, a little familiarity is in order. But I'm afraid we're going to have

105

to become even more familiar. I can't get these petti-coats off. I can't even see the laces."

He thought of his missing two fingers. "I have no skill at knots—"

"Then cut the strings off. Do whatever you must, Richard."

He felt certain she'd used his name deliberately, and the way she'd said it, her voice so deep and husky, caressed his ears like a lover's warm breath. He swallowed hard and spun around to face her.

Hands wrapped around her chest and shivering slightly, she stood alone, her skin white, her neck and breasts far too bare. Hot blood he'd thought the war had cooled forever surged in his veins, making him forget everything but the woman near him. The night was a velvety backdrop that emphasized her allure just as a square of black silk brings out the highlights in a jewel. She sparkled in that dim light, her eyes wide and vulnerable, lips parted as she tilted her head to gaze up at him.

"Your hair," he murmured. A heavy mass of chocolate-brown curls, it tumbled in riotous disarray over her shoulders. He fought a desire to bury his fingers in it, to rub it against his cheek.

" 'Tis a sight," she admitted. Her arms pale and gleaming, she plucked two tortoiseshell picks from her hair. It fell in waves to her waist, setting his imag-ination afire. Images assaulted him, forbidden thoughts of that hair dragging across his skin, catch-ing him in a silken web of pleasure.

But she hadn't finished with him yet. She twisted her hair into a long rope, coiled it against her head, and fastened it with the two tortoiseshell picks, her gesture so feminine, so practiced, that it fascinated him. She was so different from him, so small and sweet-smelling that even as he appreciated her every little part he wanted to devour her.

Richard remembered to breathe. "Are you sure you want me to cut the petticoats off?"

She grasped her silk skirt and began to pull it up, her gaze never leaving his. "How am I to ride if you don't?"

Smothering a groan, he took the silk from her. Hands trembling ever so slightly, he slipped behind her and dragged her hem up around her waist. He wanted to touch his lips to the nape of her neck, run kisses along the sweet curve of her shoulder and down to her breasts, which from behind, rested more full and tempting than he'd ever guessed.

Without quite realizing it he bent his head toward her, his mouth hovering a hair's breadth from her neck.

"Richard?"

He swallowed and tried to remember that he'd been raised a gentleman, not a plunderer of innocent young women. "I've found the first set of strings," he said in an even tone. "Do you mind if I rip them? I haven't a knife handy."

"No, go ahead," she agreed.

He wrapped the two ends of fabric around his palms, pulled until a tearing noise filled the night, and tugged the petticoat from her waist.

The second layer was much softer and scarlet-colored, the hem embroidered with gold thread. He muffled an involuntary exclamation. Whorehouse red, he thought. He trailed his fingers down the fabric, from her waist to her thighs, but lightly, so she wouldn't notice. Savoring the feel of the garment beneath his fingertips, he imagined the luscious curve of her bottom beneath his palm, her flesh warm and yielding.

Not trusting himself to speak, he ripped the strings on the scarlet petticoat apart and yanked it from her. The next petticoat came off just as quickly, making a noise that sounded like a cry of protest. A flame scorched through him as he fumbled with the remaining strings around her waist, his scarred hand rendering the simple bows more difficult to untie than knots.

At last he had the final bow undone. As that length of cotton fell away, he drew in a ragged breath. There, to his delighted eyes, were her drawers, prettily embellished and clinging to her legs like a loving hand. He slipped one arm around her, his fingers skimming her breasts, and placed his other hand against her bottom. She jumped at the contact but he tightened his arm around her, holding her steady even as he pressed his palm into flesh that had tortured him with thoughts of yielding warmth. Rather than appease him, that hesitant touch only made him want more. He pressed his lips to her neck, breathing against her skin, drinking in her clean scent.

Her slender frame trembled, and with a sigh she leaned into him. He knew in that moment that the ache was alive in both of them. The tension in his loins tightening, he dragged his lips up to her ear and flicked his tongue against its curves.

She gasped.

"Lucinda . . ." He turned her around, gently, and gathered her in his arms.

Eyes closed, she fit herself against him and, her hands around his neck, pulled him down to her. He took what she so willingly offered and kissed her, opening her mouth with his and savoring the sweet, honeyed flavor of her. Like a pretty confection she teased his appetite, encouraging him to admire and taste, and he ran his tongue along the inside of her lip and then deeper, savoring her as fully as he could.

She began to make little noises in her throat, and at first he thought them sighs of pleasure, but quickly realized they were half-hearted protests. Indeed, her response to his kiss seemed untutored, almost shy, not at all the behavior of a hoyden.

He stilled, the notion reminding him of one very important fact. Lucinda Drakewyck was a lady of quality. If he pressed his advantage too much further, he'd find a wedding band on his finger in a fortnight. How would she feel when she discovered she'd married a man who lived like a hermit in the north wing, hiding from the sunlight, thoughts of war and death dogging his every step?

With a neat twist she moved away from him. "Captain Clairmont," she stuttered, formal once again, "I cannot think what came over me—"

"Hush," he said, instantly contrite. "I took advantage, Lucinda. I apologize. The fault is entirely mine." He stepped toward her, wanting to tell her that he, too, felt the connection she'd spoken of.

The words remained lodged in his throat. Now that the heat of their passion had died away, he wasn't so willing to bare his soul to her. His, after all, was an ugly soul, full of pain and remorse.

She looked at him, head tilted, evidently waiting for him to say more. When he didn't, her lips curved in a wan smile. "Well, at least the petticoats are routed."

He ducked his head. "I'll gather them up."

Richard spent the next few moments picking up pieces of torn cotton and trying to fold them up. The softer pieces made a neat square but the starched ones defied him. In the end he simply rolled them up and tied them to the saddle.

"Are you ready, Miss Drakewyck?"

Raising her chin, she nodded.

"I'll lift you up, then."

He grasped her around the waist and set her at the front of the saddle, her skirts billowing to the left. She held on to the horse's mane as he mounted behind her. Richard closed his eyes at the thought of her bottom pressed against him and resolved to keep a discreet inch between them. When the horse began to walk, however, its rolling gait forced her against him, and eventually he relented. He wasn't particularly fond of having his arse hang off the end of the saddle and decided to permit himself this final, forbidden pleasure before he returned her to George Drakewyck.

God willing, they would never meet again, never tempt fate again. He had no intentions of marrying, and she deserved more than a lurid affair.

"I'll keep the petticoats," he murmured, thinking of her reputation. Tongues would wag if anyone saw him handing her six ripped petticoats. Indeed, as soon as he arrived at the Squire's residence he would find George Drakewyck and hustle her into the Drakewycks' carriage without anyone the wiser. "I'll have them returned to you at a later date."

She shifted in the saddle, rubbing against him in a delicious way. Tormenting him, in fact. "Why not hold on to them until I arrive at Clairmont Hall?"

Brow furrowed, he tightened his grip on the reins. "Has Carolly invited you to visit?"

"Not quite. Your father has hired me as your sister's companion."

"He *what?*" Richard brought the horse to a standstill. "When?"

"Only this evening." She looked over her shoulder at him. A shy smile curved her lips. "I'm going to try to make a lady out of her before she is presented at court next month."

"You?" He stared back at her, aware that his shocked tone must have insulted her terribly, and yet unable to believe this turn of events.

He wouldn't be able to say goodbye to her for good when he dropped her off at Squire Piggott's. No, she'd be underfoot for a month, likely more. She might not be the hoyden he'd imagined, but she still had a penchant for disaster. He imagined her invading his home, casting spells on everyone, luring his sister into trouble, encroaching on his dreams, intruding in the north wing, even. His home would become a circus worthy of Astley's Ampitheater.

"Miss Drakewyck," he said, his tone forbidding, "I will not have you living in Clairmont Hall."

She stiffened as though he'd prodded her with a hot poker. "Exactly *what* is your objection?"

"You are hardly an appropriate role model for my sister."

"I know you think I've an utter lack of discretion and propriety, but I assure you, Captain, with Miss Clairmont I'll prove a veritable matron of good sense. Her best interests will always remain my top priority."

"I won't have you at Clairmont Hall," he repeated. "My position isn't up for negotiation."

"You," she said, her tone husky, "aren't in a position to negotiate. Sir James hired me, and for Sir James I work."

Richard said nothing. He trotted up Squire Piggott's carriageway, relieved to find George Drakewyck and a small knot of men near the front door.

The Drakewycks' barouche sat waiting near the townhouse.

The elder Drakewyck rushed forward when he saw him. "Is she all right? Was she hurt?"

Lucinda slid off the horse without waiting for Richard's assistance. She fell into her uncle's arms, her face white. "I'm fine, Uncle."

George Drakewyck patted her back. "There, there, gel. I'll get you home and safe into bed."

They walked toward the barouche and her uncle handed her in. Once Lucinda was safely stowed, he turned to Richard and eyed him carefully. "I'll have an account of what happened in the morning."

*L*ucinda slept until mid-afternoon, and when she awoke, her thoughts were filled with images of Richard Clairmont. She touched her lips, remembering the press of his mouth against hers and the feeling of absolute rightness of their kiss.

Sunlight streamed through the crocheted bedhangings and set upon her face as though trying to banish her gloomy dreams, nightmares which had also included the blonde-haired witch who would destroy her utterly. Rather than banish the shadows, they merely chided for letting so much of the day pass by without accomplishment. She threw the feather quilt to one side and jumped off the bed, knocking a bolster onto the floor in the process.

She traded her nightgown for a chemise and drawers and began to browse through her dresses, pushing past the ones that looked worn or bland. Someone knocked on the door just as Lucinda decided her wardrobe had quite gone to the dogs.

Their housekeeper, Bess, breezed in when Lucinda bade her enter, her blue eyes full of purpose. Tea tray balanced on her hip, she poured Lucinda a cup. "Mr. George sent me up here to see if you'd awakened. He wishes to speak to you in the study."

"What sort of mood is he in, Bess?"

"I'd recommend you wear petticoats."

Lucinda groaned. "Short-tempered, is he?"

"You might say that."

Today, of all days, she wished Uncle George felt in an accommodating mood. "I'll wear a corset too."

Eyebrows raised, Bess walked over to her wardrobe and pulled out a *corset amazone*. She began to fiddle with its knotted laces.

Lucinda watched her, her gaze growing unfocused as she remembered the events of the previous night. Had she and Carolly run over Morgana Fey, the ancient witch described in Edward Drakewyck's entry, or was their victim simply a look-alike? She hadn't seen the woman's eyes and couldn't know if they were ice-blue, as Edward Drakewyck described. Still, instinct told her that Morgana Fey had indeed returned to Somerton. Her stomach coiled at the thought.

Morgana would stop at nothing to ensure the Drakewycks' and Clairmonts' destruction. How would she, Lucinda, protect herself, Richard, Uncle George, and everyone else who was threatened?

Bess held out the corset and gestured for Lucinda to step forward. With a little grimace, Lucinda slid the device on. The housekeeper began to pull the laces, compressing Lucinda's chemise into a mass of wrinkles.

"I hate these infernal things," Lucinda complained.

"You must have quite a favor to ask of your uncle today." Lips quirked in a tiny smile, the housekeeper pulled on the corset's laces, reducing Lucinda's waist by several inches. She tied off the laces and shook out several petticoats. "We'll turn you out proper, Miss Lucinda. He'll have a hard time telling you no."

Lucinda tried to smile, but couldn't quite summon one.

"Now the petticoats. Will two do?" Bess shook out a book muslin crinoline and a length of embroidered longcloth.

"Admirably."

She wrapped the petticoats around Lucinda and tied them at the waist. The smell of starch filled the room, mingling with the lavender scent Lucinda had used in her bath. "By the way, I seem to have misplaced several of your petticoats."

Lucinda pulled at the armholes of her shift, drawn uncomfortably tight by the weight of her skirts, and muffled a groan. Captain Clairmont had her missing petticoats.

Oh, what a muddle she'd made of the night. She really couldn't blame Richard for thinking her completely impetuous. The few times they'd met she'd either been setting fires or joining in carriage races. Nevertheless, her blood heated over the way he'd refused her entrance to Clairmont Hall, pointing out her faults when his own were equally bad. She hadn't forced a kiss on him . . . he'd willingly joined in.

"Miss?" the housekeeper asked, her eyebrows drawn together. "You look flushed."

" 'Tis the heat, the unaccustomed dress." Lucinda mentally shook herself. She had to invent some story to keep the housekeeper from speculating about the petticoats. "You haven't misplaced my petticoats. Just yesterday I went through my petticoat drawer and removed the torn ones for repair."

Nodding, Bess gathered her day dress, of ivory muslin sprigged with violets, and directed Lucinda to hold her arms up. She lifted it over Lucinda's head and brought it downward, waiting for Lucinda to push her arms through the sleeves.

As Lucinda moved according to the housekeeper's directions, she remembered the pressure of his hand on her skin, gentle and insistent, the soft caress of his lips against hers. Mortified, she squeezed her eyes shut while her stomach did a slow roll. No doubt he thought her a complete wanton for responding to him when she should have slapped him silly. But she hadn't been prepared for the searing pleasure he roused, the aching need deep within her that struggled to escape.

And yet, her vision had warned her that love between them would bring only death. She knew so little of matters between men and women that she had no idea if the longing she felt for him was a prelude to love. What, indeed, was love? Could men and women share intimacy without loving each other? Some fatalistic part of her hoped the two could remain independent, for the shock of his lips against hers had been so powerful that she knew her next response would prove not only wanton but demanding.

"You look fine, Miss," Bess said, stepping back to view the results.

Lucinda assessed herself in a looking glass. The gown emphasized her trim figure. Without the customary large bows and flounces, its clean, classic lines gave her an air of sobriety that she desperately needed.

Her eyes bright, Bess tied a matching velvet band around Lucinda's neck. A small cameo dangled in the hollow of her throat, its pink and ivory tones complementing her pale complexion. Next, she began to fuss with Lucinda's hair, drawing a brown tendril back into the knot atop her head, twisting the ringlets which cascaded from the knot into obedience. "Let me fix a few ribbons through your hair, Miss, and then I'll send you down to Mr. George."

"Don't you think the ribbons will be doing it a bit too brown?"

"How badly do you want to convince him?"

"Quite badly."

"Let me do the ribbons, then."

Lucinda submitted to these final ministrations, thinking about the task ahead. Uncle George might prove obstinate, but in the end, she would convince him. She *had* to convince him. The alternative—leaving Richard alone in a house with Morgana Fey—was unthinkable.

Bess finished twining ribbons through her curls and stepped away, her eyes alight. "Your poor uncle hasn't a chance against you."

Lucinda smiled in gratitude and left the housekeeper for the library, where Uncle George lounged in an armchair. His eyes looked bloodshot and his dark-green smoking jacket dusty. The tobacco in the pipe clenched between his teeth burned bright red, as if it, too, were angry with her. A plate of scones, biscuits, and crumpets sat on a nearby side-table.

As she walked into the library he looked up, measured her with a glance, and closed the book with a snap. Pipe smoke combined with the smell of musty old books, making her want to sneeze. She sat across from him and selected a crumpet.

Uncle George, his gaze never quite leaving her, poured her a cup of tea. "You look well."

She smiled. "Thank you, Uncle."

Clearing his throat, he fixed her with a gimlet stare. "I've received a brief written account of last night's events from Captain Clairmont. He did not say so, but I gathered from his tone that he thinks you partially responsible for Carolly's misbehavior. Is this so?"

Lucinda dropped the crumpet onto the tray and jumped from her chair. The infernal man! She prayed he hadn't revealed her desire to become Carolly Clairmont's companion. Uncle George would prove easier to convince if he hadn't much time to think of arguments against it.

"Well? Did you join in Carolly Clairmont's antics last night?"

"I rode with her in the carriage, that's all."

"And did you encourage her to race against those young men?"

"Of course not!"

"Then why is Captain Clairmont convinced you did?"

She swung around to face him. "My relationship with Richard Clairmont has become terribly complicated, Uncle."

Uncle George studied her for a moment before pulling his watch fob out of his waistcoat. " 'Tis two o'clock. We have three hours until dinner. Why don't you start from the beginning? We'll hash through it and find some answers."

"All right, I'll try." She pulled in a deep breath and clasped her hands together. "Two nights ago, you gave me the spellbook and the crystal dove. That same night I took them to my glen in the woods and tried to cast a spell."

"With the dove?" he asked, his tone becoming urgent.

She nodded.

"Good God, Lucinda. You didn't even wait a day before trying the thing. You should have considered more and thought about the consequences."

"I know. I've discovered as much."

Uncle George grew a shade paler. "Tell me everything. Don't leave out the slightest detail."

Lucinda tilted her head back and closed her eyes. "I went to the glen and built a fire in the usual manner. The night was dark, and rain threatened, but otherwise, nothing seemed unusual." She paused, remembering her sense of being watched. "For a moment, I felt a presence nearby, but then I realized 'twas naught but a bunch of birds roosting on the branches above me."

He nodded. "Go on."

"I brought *Goetia* with me and found a spell for divination. I called upon the magic in the dove because I hoped to see more of this man who would protect me and the woman who threatened me. I needed to know who they were and where they'd come from. But something went terribly wrong."

She shuddered and opened her eyes, remembering the crazy flames of the fire, the heat that seared her right to her bones. "My bonfire grew to incredible proportions and nearly burned the trees down. Indeed, I barely escaped burning myself."

Eyes narrowed, Uncle George thought for a moment. "Did you call upon the powers to the south?"

"Those of fire? Only in creating my circle of protection."

"And the magic you called upon when you cast the divination spell . . . was it your own or solely the dove's?"

"Just the dove's," she admitted.

He shook his head. "The dove's power is extremely unpredictable in the hands of anyone but a master. And you, Lucinda, are not a master. Who knows what magic you unleashed?"

" 'Twas magic of the malignant variety, I can assure you."

Uncle George rubbed his chin. "You said you were trying to cast a spell of divination. Were you successful?"

"Not at all. The dove's magic affected the bonfire, but naught more, as far as I can tell."

"You can tell very little where the dove is concerned." He paused to take a sip of tea. "How did you put the bonfire out?"

"It went out on its own, just as Richard Clairmont appeared. He raced into the glen, claiming to have seen my bonfire from Clairmont Hall. Evidently he'd come to investigate. He *is* the man in my vision, Uncle."

"I don't like this, gel." He placed his teacup in its saucer and studied her with a solemn gaze. "The witch, Morgana Fey? Have you seen her?"

"No," she lied. She didn't dare tell him she suspected the witch was lying abed at Clairmont Hall. He'd never agree to her becoming Carolly's companion. She'd reveal the witch's presence to him *after* she'd joined the Clairmonts.

"And Captain Clairmont? What did he say upon finding you out in the woods after midnight, huddling around a bonfire?"

She swallowed. "He saw my runes and realized I'd been trying to cast a spell. He thinks I haven't an ounce of good sense and probably considers me even more of a hoyden than his sister."

"Understandable."

120

Her cheeks grew warm. Eager to finish this part of the tale, she forged ahead. "As Captain Clairmont and I left the glen, I again felt a presence nearby, almost as if someone were watching me. I admitted as much to Captain Clairmont, and he added idiocy to my list of faults."

Lucinda paused, her thoughts flying to the witch's curse—that she and Richard would love.

"Protect your heart," her uncle suddenly advised. Evidently his thoughts had led him in the same direction.

"I don't need to. Richard Clairmont thinks me a ridiculous female and rouses nothing but my irritation."

Uncle George didn't speak. He simply regarded her. Hot denials crowded her lips, but she refused to leap into the silence. They stared at one another until he finally spoke.

"Why did you wait so long to tell me this? We sat in the carriage for almost half an hour on the way to the Squire's, and you said not a word."

"I didn't want to argue with you, Uncle. I knew you'd use my experience to bolster your arguments against magic, and I hadn't the heart to debate."

"I'll tell you why you didn't want to debate. You knew you'd lose." He patted the chair next to him. "Come over here, gel, and sit down."

She perched on the edge of the chair he'd indicated, her fingers entwined in her lap.

He took her hands in his and held them tight. "You haven't the skill to call upon the dove's magic. Promise me you'll put it away and never use it again."

"According to Edward Drakewyck, only the dove can stop Morgana."

"Then keep the dove in your pocket. But don't use it for everyday magic. You'll only call upon powers you cannot control."

She nodded unwillingly, instinct telling her that in this circumstance, her uncle was right.

"Do you have any idea how much of your magic the dove absorbed?" he asked.

"None. I haven't tried to cast a spell yet."

He pressed his lips together. "God willing it absorbed every little bit you possessed."

"Uncle!"

"I wish we had never been born with the talent," he said, his tone bitter. After a slight pause, he continued. "So you met Richard Clairmont for a third time at Squire Piggott's."

"Yes. We talked. He made it clear he thought me a reprehensible jade. He isn't the most pleasant of men, you know."

"Fate has saddled you with a fine one, gel, although I still prefer Squire Piggott for you."

Lucinda ignored his comment. Instead, she gathered her courage. "After I talked to Captain Clairmont, I met up with Sir James. He lamented on Carolly Clairmont's lack of polish and wondered how to make a lady of her before she went to London for her court presentation. I suggested he hire a companion."

Uncle George shrugged. "Seems sensible to me."

"Indeed, I suggested he hire *me* as his daughter's companion."

His eyebrows climbed to his hairline. "What?"

"I offered to become Carolly's companion."

He pulled the pipe from his mouth and slapped it onto a side table. "Out of the question."

"Richard Clairmont is the only one who can rescue me," she pleaded. "How will he rescue me if he is at Clairmont Hall and I am here in Drakewyck Grange? I must stay close to him to let Fate do its work."

"We don't know how Fate intends to operate. You've already met Clairmont twice in the woods. Who knows what circumstances you will both find yourselves in when the final moment comes? Fate could throw you together again."

"I'm not willing to rely on Fate. I'd like to stack the cards in my favor."

"I want you here, where I can watch out for you."

"We're short on funds," she pressed. "Extra income would be welcome, no?"

"You are a Drakewyck, gel, a woman of property and connections. Why, your aunt would cut you off forever if she learned you'd gone into the trades. I won't have it."

"Sir James suggested putting my wages into a trust fund for me. No one need know I'm a paid companion. People would think me a gentlewoman helping a neighbor."

Even as she reasoned it out she realized one of her private arguments for becoming a companion—to put Squire Piggott off—no longer held weight. He wouldn't know she'd entered the trades and would likely continue his pursuit. Silently she cursed him.

"Is that it?" her uncle asked. "Do you have any more reasons why I should consider this scheme?"

She took a deep breath. Only one thing would persuade him. "In only a month, I'll be traveling to London with Carolly when she's presented at Court. Her debut into Society will throw me in the path of several eligible gentlemen."

"Now there's a good argument," he admitted. "But what if Sir James cancels her debut to punish the girl for her carriage race?"

"He has arranged for the Queen to meet Carolly. Such an engagement is extremely serious and not canceled lightly. Sir James would need a very good excuse to disappoint the Queen. More likely, he'll punish her in other ways."

Uncle George nodded his agreement.

"I have several pretty gowns only a few years old," she added, "that would look quite fashionable with a bit of sewing and a few bows."

"I do want you to be happy, gel."

"If you keep me from Clairmont Hall, Uncle, I will be anything but happy. Please let me go to London. I promise to consider all the men I meet with an eye for marriage."

"You haven't the fortune, but more than enough charm," he said, "and looks well beyond the adequate."

"Are you saying I'm pretty?"

He cleared his throat. "Indeed I am."

She hid a smile. "I'm not the only romantic in Drakewyck Grange."

His cheeks gained a slight flush. "All right, I'll let you join the Clairmonts, but I do have several conditions. One, you must not use the dove. Two, your wages will be placed into a trust fund to protect your reputation. And three, when you go to London, you must promise me you won't dismiss the men you meet out of hand."

"I'll promise anything, Uncle."

"That's what worries me. You're far too eager to place yourself near Richard Clairmont. I suspect you like him and are already beginning to fall in love with him, as the vision predicted. Think, gel. Didn't the witch's prediction hint that his love would first save you before leading to utter destruction?"

"Yes, it did, but we will not love. We cannot. We are such opposites that I doubt we'll ever hold an agreeable conversation."

"You seem quite confident. I'll respect your judgement." Uncle George stood, went to his desk, and began writing. "I'll write to Sir James this very moment with my terms along with my acceptance of his proposal. And while I'm writing, I'll tell you my fourth condition. While at Clairmont Hall you must nurture your dislike of Richard Clairmont. Any other course will lead to disaster."

"I don't have to nurture it. My dislike grows with every word he speaks," she said.

And knew she had lied.

Richard Clairmont sat in an armchair of jade velvet, his polished boots stretched before a hungry fire. He had dressed in black, the snowy folds of his necktie slightly looser than normal, providing him with a bit of space to breathe—something his father seemed determined to avoid.

He studied Sir James with narrowed eyes. "I think you are making a serious mistake."

The elder Clairmont dropped George Drakewyck's letter onto a silver tray, lifted his brandy snifter, and swirled the contents before taking a sip. "I think 'tis our good fortune that Lucinda Drakewyck is willing to take Carolly on. Even though I've punished Carolly by canceling her trip to the Continent this autumn, I still worry that she'll do something to endanger her reputation. Lucinda will keep your sister safe from her own childish impulses."

Richard snorted.

"Carolly celebrates her birthday at the end of May," Sir James added, "which, I might remind you, is only a month away. I've agreed to have her presented at Court on June seventh. What would happen if Carolly debuted with those manners of hers? The girl would ruin herself in a moment."

"That's just it. I don't believe Miss Drakewyck qualified to teach Carolly manners and common sense."

"Why? Because she joined Carolly on that wild carriage ride? I, for one, believe Miss Drakewyck when she says she joined Carolly to talk some sense into her. She and I had already spoken about her becoming Carolly's companion, and I'm quite certain she felt it her duty to prevent catastrophe." Sir James shook his head, an unwilling smile twitching his lips. "There aren't many women of my acquaintance who would have put their own safety at risk as Miss Drakewyck did. The girl's got fortitude."

He glanced at Richard, as though expecting him to agree. Or perhaps, Richard thought, he was pointing out that Lucinda Drakewyck possessed the courage that he, Richard, lacked.

"I think you overrate her."

"You are determined to think the worst of her, I see."

"What about George Drakewyck? I can't believe he's going to allow his niece to collect wages and join the trades. She'll ruin her marriage prospects for good."

"She's not going to join the trades. I'll set up a trust fund for her in lieu of wages. When she needs money, she'll draw from the trust."

Richard frowned. They seemed to have thought of every angle.

"If you're so worried about your sister," his father challenged, "come down from the north wing and supervise Miss Drakewyck's interaction with her."

"You want me to supervise the supervisor? Why not hire *me* as Carolly's companion?"

"Unless you can give me another reason for your opinion," his father said, "I'll assume it's based on unfounded dislike and ignore it utterly."

Cornered, he stared at his father. He'd prefer to avoid tattling about Lucinda's spell casting. Tales of witchcraft would only make him sound like a superstitious idiot.

Still, if he didn't explain, Sir James would assume his objections to Lucinda based on irrational prejudice, a far cry from the principles that every gentleman lived by: balance, grace, and manner. In short, he could lose his father's trust, if not his esteem.

A moment's consideration convinced him he'd rather seem superstitious than narrow-minded.

"How well do you know Lucinda Drakewyck?" Richard asked, trying to lead into the subject gradually.

"Well enough." Sir James slouched into a chair near Richard and extended his legs, his feet pointing toward the fireplace. "I've known her since childhood. She always has a kind word for the poor and a basket of supplies for the sick. Have you not noticed, Richard, how easily a smile rests upon her lips? She's a spirited little thing."

Richard preferred not to answer. He'd noticed her smile and more: the way she pouted at him, the way her lips parted when he said something that surprised her, tempting him to kiss, to taste. Instead he withdrew a cheroot from his jacket and leaned forward, his jacket straining as he placed the tip of the cigar into a candle flame. He puffed once, smoke encircling his head, and held it loosely between two fingers.

His father grew misty-eyed. "Even better, she's not frivolous or concerned about appearances, and evidently knows her way around a library. More than once we've met in the woodlands and had a rousing discussion on Plato's *Republic* even as we stood ankle-deep in mud."

"Why don't you marry her?"

"I'm far too old. I couldn't make her happy."

"Am I the only one who has reservations toward Miss Drakewyck?"

Sir James shrugged. "Samson likes her. She doesn't scold him when he shakes his fur off near her, and pets his scruffy hide afterward."

"A ringing endorsement, if ever I heard one." Richard rubbed his eyes with his free hand. He was going to sound like a complete fool, but he had no choice. "I'm sure she's as charming as you say, but there are other aspects to her personality which you know nothing about."

"Oh?" Sir James began to lift his snifter.

"I believe she thinks herself a witch."

The snifter paused halfway. His father stared at him with wide eyes. "A witch? As in 'Double, double, toil and trouble'?"

"In essence, yes," Richard began, but Sir James' sudden burst of laughter drowned the rest of his explanation out.

"A witch. You're priceless, Richard. Whatever gave you that idea?"

Richard groaned inwardly. This was going even worse than he'd feared. "I stumbled onto two of her ceremonies in the woodlands. The first time, I was out walking with Samson near teatime, and we came to a glen in the forest. Miss Drakewyck stood near a bonfire, with flowers in her hair and two candles nearby. Mud splotched her dress. She looked quite . . ."

"Desirable?"

"No, disreputable." Richard grunted. "Even so, she had the oddest damned effect on me. I felt like she'd known I would come. As if our meeting were fated."

Sir James smiled. "She must have cast a spell on you."

"You're making light of a serious situation."

"Let me see if I have this right. You left your north wing and discovered a beautiful young woman in the woodlands, with flowers in her hair and mud on her skirts. Your body stirred and you wanted her. How does that make her a witch? Indeed, I'm grateful to anyone who can pull you from thoughts of war."

"Her actions, in my opinion, speak of a certain carelessness. Not many women of good sense would go wandering through the woods, alone, unchaperoned, let alone build a fire."

"But that is her appeal, dear boy. She has a certain *joie de vivre* that makes her interesting, where other women are insipid." He shook his head. "There is something I must say to you, Richard. Hard words that you must hear. I believe you've created your own private hell in the north wing. 'Tis a place where you can surround yourself with memories of war and ease your guilt over surviving when most of your men died."

Richard flipped ash off the end of his cheroot into the fire. His jaw clenched. Only his father would dare dissect him in such a manner and trivialize his experiences in the Crimea.

"You don't want Lucinda Drakewyck around," Sir James continued relentlessly, "because you're afraid she will lure you out of the north wing and into sunlight. You don't think you deserve to live, so you object to anyone who makes you feel alive."

"It isn't that simple," Richard ground out. He flung the cheroot into the flames.

"My God, Richard, you received the Victoria Cross. Why do you blame yourself so?"

Richard looked at his scarred hand. He swallowed. How could he explain the torment he felt every time he thought of his friend John Burke, lying on cold Russian soil, a fist-size hole in his chest? How could he describe the nightmares, the images that assaulted him without warning? He could almost smell the sulfurous discharge from the cannons and rifles, a stink strong enough to please Satan himself. The Crimea had been hell. The north wing was simply purgatory.

A lengthy silence ensued. Richard felt his father's gaze on him, but he didn't look up. He felt vulnerable. Weak. And didn't want the older man to see it in his eyes.

"I'm going to bring Lucinda Drakewyck to Clairmont Hall as Carolly's companion," his father said gently.

Richard stood and walked to the window, which looked out onto the front lawn and the sloping parkland beyond. He saw trees, gardens, and the carriageway, all perfectly tended, the very epitome of an Englishman's uncompromising pride and civility. His father would never understand how the war had turned him inside out, tangled everything he'd ever believed in, and turned the parkland of his self-esteem and good taste into a jungle of inadequacy and remorse.

"Bring her if you want," Richard said. He refused to try to discredit her any further. His father would only think him desperate to continue flagellating himself like a medieval monk who'd committed some minor sin.

Sir James laid a hand on Richard's shoulder. "I'm sorry, son, but I had to say it. I worry about you. You aren't happy and it pains me."

Richard shrugged his hand off. "Has Carolly's victim come around yet?"

The elder man, evidently unwilling to change the subject, paused for several seconds before relenting. "Her eyelids fluttered sometime before noon. Otherwise, she remains the same."

"Have you discovered her identity yet?"

"I've been making inquiries in Somerton and at hostelries on the road from London. So far no one has claimed kinship or any knowledge of the woman. Don't you think it's odd, how she suddenly appeared on Covington Road?"

Richard nodded. "Where was her family? Her carriage? Perhaps she's a wandering madwoman."

His father's lips drooped in a frown. "I haven't heard of any relatives in these parts being locked in the back room or sent to Bedlam. Nevertheless, I'm making inquiries along that line, too."

"What about her clothes? Did they give you any clue as to her circumstances?"

"Not really. They were so covered in dirt I couldn't tell what she wore. Carolly must have sent her flying into a muddy ditch."

"So she could be a farmer's wife or a princess."

"Overall, I received the impression that her gown was made of rich fabric and superior tailoring." The older man tilted his head. "I'm no follower of ladies fashions, but I must admit, the style seemed a bit antiquated."

"You mean she might be a servant who received her mistress's castoffs."

Sir James narrowed his eyes. "The gown looked older than that, I think."

"What do you mean, older? A decade? Two decades?"

"I'd never seen a neckline like hers before. 'Twas almost as if she wore a lace-edged ruff. Otherwise, mud had obscured all but the plainest details."

"Where is the gown?"

"One of the maids cut it off her," his father said, "to avoid moving her any more than necessary. 'Tis probably rags by now, if not ashes."

"So we know nothing." Richard focused his attention on the fire. "This entire situation is damned odd."

"Whatever the case, we must extend her every courtesy possible," Sir James insisted. "After all, Carolly almost ran her over. If she wanted to, she could bring Carolly before the constable."

Richard winced. "I hadn't thought of that."

"I have." Sir James put his snifter down and walked toward the door. "I sincerely hope our patient isn't the sort to hold a grudge."

8

*C*lairmont Hall was perhaps the most aristocratic dwelling in Bedfordshire and certainly the grandest Lucinda had ever visited. She caught her breath as the matched bays pulled her through an iron palisade and down a long, tree-lined carriageway. The building looked large enough to house an entire village, let alone a baronet and his two children.

A day had passed since Uncle George had written to Sir James, giving his approval to their plan. Lucinda had spent Monday at Drakewyck Grange packing and worrying. Events had moved too quickly for her peace of mind. First she'd met Richard, and now Morgana Fey was residing at Clairmont Hall. Everyone in her vision was under one roof. She'd come to Clairmont Hall to be closer to Richard, but with the ancient witch around, she'd also come that much closer to her destiny.

She wondered if she was going to die soon.

Though they'd closed only half the distance down the carriageway, the house loomed before her, a massive block of smooth brick walls and windows stretching three floors up. Gentle hills, oaks, and willows surrounded its walls, their lazy disregard for geometry making the house appear rigid in comparison.

She thought its adherence to perfect rectangular form a sobering reminder of discipline and rationality. Clairmont Hall seemed to say that one's life should be simple, with emotions always under check; the path chosen straightforward, not curving. Swallowing against a tightness in her throat, she wondered how difficult it would prove to live here, knowing the witch in her vision was hidden within its walls, knowing the man who would be her lover slept in a bed not far from hers.

She tensed as the barouche stopped before the house and tried to ignore an urge to run home. With a footman's help she climbed down and paused for a moment on the stone carriageway. She stood in a courtyard, its perimeter marked by knee-high walls. Urns, small statues, and a few bushes cut into the shapes of dogs and rabbits formed orderly lines around her. Lucinda thought the rabbits, in particular, looked unhappy at being fenced in.

She focused on Clairmont Hall, her gaze taking in long, thin windows, divided into equal sets by square columns. The house seemed to be staring at her. Taking her measure. Would she be an asset to this family, or would she prove totally lacking in sensibility—a creature of emotion, of the heart?

Two of her bags in hand, the footman cleared his throat. Lucinda lifted her chin. Clairmont Hall could not fail to impress, but she wouldn't let it intimidate her. She marched up the steps to the front door and smiled at a second footman who opened the door for her.

She walked through the portal and paused, trying not to gape and appear the country bumpkin. A lofty room of immense proportions greeted her eyes. She suddenly understood why the home was known as Clairmont Hall. The entire house surrounded this great hall, a place designed for feasting, dancing, and ceremony, the kind celebrated in medieval times. She decided she could almost hear the snores of sleeping knights.

Knights like Lancelot, she thought. She wondered where Richard was, where he slept. Would they be near each other? Her head told her she ought to pray they were situated at different ends of the building. A more primitive desire hoped they might have adjoining bedchambers. They were, after all, destined to become lovers.

Hallways stretched off to the left and right, and in the far left corner, an imposing stone staircase, at least twenty feet wide at the lowest step, pulled her attention upward. Arched timber girders supported the stone ceiling like a giant corset. Oak paneling and cream-colored plaster covered the walls, and a ridiculously large fireplace, guarded by stone lions on either side, took up the back wall.

Mahogany tables and chairs done in crimson damask sat in perfect squares. Lucinda eyed the chairs and speculated if anyone ever sat in them. How could one relax in such a ponderous atmosphere? She considered the notion that Morgana Fey was reclining in a bedchamber above her and knew *she* wouldn't relax. Her vision was coming to pass at a breakneck pace. She tried to imagine their first meeting and wondered if Morgana would exact her revenge on first sight.

Lucinda slipped her hand in her pocket and touched the crystal dove. For courage.

A third man moved forward to meet her, bowed, and introduced himself as Hilton, the head butler. He offered to take her bonnet and shawl. She removed them and handed them over.

"Please tell Sir James that Lucinda Drakewyck has arrived," she said, but before Hilton could leave, Sir James emerged from the left hallway to greet her, cane in hand.

Lucinda thought he leaned on his cane more heavily than usual. She wondered if his gout was bothering him, or if the witch had already begun her effort to destroy them all. Lucinda scanned the room, concentrating, her senses open. She felt nothing untoward. If Sir James' affliction had its roots in magic, she concluded, Morgana had enough skill to cover her tracks.

"Miss Drakewyck," he said, smiling. "How wonderful that you've come. I've had rooms prepared for you. I hope you find them satisfactory."

She returned his smile. "I'm certain I'll be comfortable, thank you. Is Carolly about?"

"I haven't seen her." He turned to the butler. "Hilton, please find Carolly and tell her that Miss Drakewyck has arrived. I'll expect her in the library at—" He paused to look at his watch. "—five o'clock, where she and Miss Drakewyck can talk. Tell Cook to send tea and scones to the library."

Lucinda plucked a small strand of hair from Sir James' coat. Sir James didn't notice the gesture, for he had his attention fixed on Hilton. She hoped Hilton hadn't noticed either.

The butler bowed, his face emotionless. If he'd seen her furtive gesture, he didn't intend to give her away. He picked up her bags, two footmen lifted her trunk, and the threesome trundled off toward the staircase.

Sir James regarded her. " 'Tis two o'clock now, Miss Drakewyck. I'll show you to your bedchamber. Would you mind a five o'clock meeting with Carolly?"

"That would be perfect. Please, call me Lucinda." She nodded toward the stairs. "Shall we?"

Sir James took her arm and smiled. "I'm glad you're here."

He steered her across the hall. To her right, she saw another, smaller staircase, its stone chipped in places. Her steps slowed as she wondered at its veneer of shabbiness.

"That staircase leads into the north wing," Sir James informed her. "The north wing is the original Clairmont Hall, built in Elizabethan times. Early in the 1700s our ancestor added on to the house, building all the rooms to your left. We've closed the north wing off and allowed it to fall into disrepair. Too expensive to maintain, you know."

Lucinda nodded. "I can well believe it."

Sir James hesitated a moment, as if thinking something through. Evidently he came to a decision, for when he finally spoke, his voice was firm. "Richard has decided to make the north wing his home."

"Captain Clairmont lives up there?"

"He claims to find the north wing pleasant."

"So you've had to refurbish it after all."

"No, he prefers it as is."

Brow furrowed, Lucinda tried to imagine Richard roaming through disused rooms filled with dust and shrouds, a graveyard of old furniture and forgotten times. Why did he prefer ghosts and memories to his family's companionship?

"Does he stay there all day?" she asked.

137

"Other than an occasional walk in the woodlands with Samson, he remains in the north wing. 'Tis his . . . well, he likes it there," Sir James said.

'Tis his prison.

The words hung between them, unstated, but Lucinda heard them clearly enough. Abruptly she remembered the impressions she'd gained of Lancelot during her vision. Damaged. Vulnerable. Deeply hurt. Those scars on his hand, she thought, must reach far deeper than flesh. A little ache gathered near her heart. Richard, she knew, must have suffered terribly.

Silently she vowed she would make him well.

Sir James urged her past the small staircase and up the larger one. They walked through a warren of passages, all stone softened by an occasional tapestry or portrait. Candelabras sat in nooks in the wall, their candles real wax, not tallow. At last he stopped before an arched oak door which hung partially ajar. A suit of armor stood opposite the door, a battle-ax gripped in one iron glove.

The voices of the two footmen echoed from inside.

"Here we are. You can find your room by looking for your guardian." Sir James gestured toward the iron knight, smiling a little at his joke. "A maid will be up shortly to help you unpack."

"Thank you, but I'd prefer to unpack myself," she said, thinking of the herbs and other spell-casting supplies she'd stowed in her trunk.

"As you wish. Please ask if you need anything. Otherwise, I'll see you at five o'clock." With a nod, he disappeared down the hall.

A moment later, the footmen slid past her, bowing as they did so.

With a little sigh she entered her bedchamber and assessed its condition. Houses as old as Clairmont

Hall often sported drafty bedchambers with leaking ceilings and puddles of muck on the floor, but this one seemed in top shape. As she passed by her canopied bed, she touched the embroidered counterpane, the lacy bedhangings. Everywhere she sensed Elizabeth Clairmont's presence, her delicate taste.

If Lady Clairmont had died in the typhoid outbreak of 1841, Carolly must have been only a year old when she lost her mother. Lucinda felt a sudden kinship with the girl, having lost her own parents at the age of five. She wondered if Elizabeth Clairmont's death, in part, explained the girl's disagreeable attitude. Clairmont Hall, Lucinda mused, might imitate a bastion of discipline and rationality, but Sir James seemed the only one within its walls that lived a simple, balanced life.

Her feet sinking into a plush oriental carpet, she crossed the room to her trunk, which the footmen had pushed against the foot of her bed. She lifted the lid and dug through gowns which had already started to wrinkle and begged to be unpacked. *Let them wait,* she thought. She had a few spells to cast, even though they might not prove as strong as her previous spells.

Yesterday she'd discovered that the dove had indeed drained some of her magic. She'd tried to cast a spell of protection and had difficulty finding the dark garden, the wellspring of her magic, a place where past, present, and future mingled as one. Nevertheless, she'd decided to keep it upon her person, as Uncle George had suggested, just in case she needed to command a massive assault of magic. The dove nestled in a pocket of her dress, its weight somehow comforting as it pressed against her skirts.

First, she pulled *Goetia* out, lifted its cover, and paged through until she found a spell of protection.

Next, she selected a velvet bag which contained four porcelain ovals about the size of small stones. An inscription for the four great powers—north, east, south, and west—decorated each oval. She walked around the room, placing an oval in each corner, orienting herself to the sun as she did so.

"Four nooks in this room for powers of old," she whispered, "and a bed in its midst, upon which I rest. Air, water, fire, and earth; guard this room from perils that approach from north, south, east, and west."

She closed her eyes and concentrated. She imagined wind blowing in her face, water flowing in a steady stream across her feet, the warmth of a fire heating her skin, and the smell of damp earth filling the air. Reaching deep within herself, she called to the powers in her dark garden for help, and heard only soft murmurs in response, where once she'd heard clearly.

Shoulders drooping, she refocused on her bedchamber. She wished she'd never seen the crystal dove, this statue Morgana Fey coveted above all else. It had made her weak, and she didn't appreciate the feeling, not after years of casting spells and rejoicing in their positive effects. What would she do if her ability to help people had gone forever?

Sir James, she thought. Quickly she paged through *Goetia* until she found a healing spell. Next, she selected a red geranium and a pink anemone from her supplies, two flowers she'd dried over the previous year. She arranged them in a pleasing way and rounded the posy out with a few leaves of bay laurel.

"Straightness of stem, make his bones firm. Redness of petal, make his blood flow. Smoothness of leaf, let his limb bend easy, till his body stands straight and his heart is well."

She wound Sir James' hair through the stems and tied it with a red ribbon. Then, with a sigh, she placed it on her bureau. Later she'd give the posy to Sir James and ask him to wear it. As long as he kept it near, the posy would protect him from any stray magic in the house.

Lucinda sat down on her bed, but her thoughts soon had her up and pacing. Somehow she had to convince Richard of the danger they faced, so he would be ready to fight whatever threat Morgana sent his way. But how to convince him?

She paused by the window, not seeing the sunshine-dappled trees and grounds but the dark interior of a church. First she'd have to show him the entry in *Goetia,* and then prove Morgana's existence by finding records in the parish register or even in a book on Somerton history. She could even visit the graveyard and try to locate Morgana's grave.

Yes, there were quite a few ways to confirm Morgana once existed. But how to convince Richard their patient was indeed Morgana Fey, somehow surviving the centuries to have revenge on the descendents of her tormentors? Lucinda wrestled with the question as she paced the room, wearing a trail in the carpet but coming no closer to a solution.

At last, the hour approached five. She freshened her appearance with a pitcher of warm water upon the commode and left her bedchamber. She found the library after only two wrong turns. Sir James waited within, and when she entered he smiled and waved her toward a damask chair. She sat down, his vast selection of books impressing her, and silently she promised to award herself a cozy little read before she left Clairmont Hall for good.

Sir James limped to a nearby chair and fell into it.

"Sir James, are you all right?"

A pained smile turned his lips upward. "My gout's been bothering me. 'Tis nothing."

Lucinda took her posy from her dress pocket, leaned over, and pushed the stems into a pocket on his jacket. "These are from the woods," she said. "Wear them. According to folklore, they're supposed to dull pain."

His eyes sparkled and his smile became more genuine. "Thank you, Lucinda."

She dimpled in return. From there, they talked about nonsensical things to fill the time while waiting for Carolly. He glanced at his watch fob several times, a frown gathering on his lips. Just as he appeared ready to go in search of Carolly, she bounded through the door and skidded to a halt, her hair tangled and loose from its chignon, her gown a frilly pastel totally unsuited to her dark good looks.

"Hullo, Father, I'm sorry I'm late." She swiveled to face Lucinda. "Oh, I see my companion's arrived. How exciting."

Her tone suggested she felt anything but excitement.

" 'Tis good to see you again, Miss Clairmont," Lucinda said. "I'm looking forward to our time together."

Carolly raised one dark eyebrow. "Tell me, Miss Drakewyck, just what does a companion do?"

"Carolly—" Sir James warned.

"No, Father, I want to know. Why is Miss Drakewyck here?"

Lucinda swallowed. "You must call me Lucinda. As far as my purpose, I'm here to keep you company, and—"

"Don't you mean, 'keep watch over me'?" She flashed her father a defiant look before settling her attention on Lucinda again. "I know why you're here. Father wants you to turn me into his good little girl. I'm to become a perfectly behaved Englishwoman who knows how to take orders but not to give them. And until I learn my lesson, you're going to ensure I stay in this rotting old house. You're my *jailer*, not my companion."

Sir James drew himself up. "Carolly! I've canceled your trip to the Continent this fall. Must I cancel your Court presentation, too?"

Lucinda laid a restraining arm on the older man. "I have no intentions of restricting you from anything, Miss Clairmont. In fact, my presence may allow you even more freedom than before. Two women may go places where one cannot."

Carolly turned to her father. "I'm sorry if I offended you, and I apologize for offending Miss Drakewyck, but I don't know why Miss Drakewyck is here. Faye is a perfectly reasonable sort and I confess after only an hour of talking to her I find we have much in common. She would make a far better companion than Miss Drakewyck."

"Faye?" Sir James looked bewildered.

"Our patient. You know, the woman I . . . ran into."

Faye. Lucinda's heart skipped in her chest. She realized she'd been hoping deep inside that the injured woman would prove to be someone other than Morgana Fey. The name Faye put a serious dent in those hopes.

His eyebrows rose. "She's awake?"

"She's been awake for hours, Father." Carolly smiled gaily. "She says she forgives me for hurting her and wants to be my friend."

Sir James motioned to Lucinda. "We must talk to her immediately. Would you care to come along?"

She nodded. "Indeed I would."

Lucinda and Sir James followed behind Carolly as she led them through the grand hall and up the staircase to the second floor. The injured woman had been placed in the bedchamber nearest the stairs, apparently also one of the finest in Clairmont Hall. When she entered, the sheer splendor of the fittings left her dazzled. Delicate rococo ornamentation in a soft ivory complemented plaster walls of pale blue, while fanciful patterns abounded on the four-poster bed, chairs, and bureaus, all of which were framed in gilded bronze.

"The State Bedchamber," Sir James whispered, evidently sensing Lucinda's surprise. " 'Tis closest to the stairs. We wanted to move her as little as possible."

In the middle of the four-poster bed, amid piles of spotless white bolsters, pillows, sheets, and counterpane, a woman lay. The skin on the back of her neck prickling, Lucinda edged behind Carolly, almost afraid to meet the blonde's gaze. This, she thought, is the final confirmation.

Sir James, without her fears, strode forward to the woman's side. "Thank God, Miss, that you've come around. We've been so worried."

Lucinda saw Sir James clasp a slender white hand. She slipped around Carolly and looked into the woman's eyes.

The blonde stared back at her.

Lucinda sucked in a breath and grasped the bedpost. *Ice-blue*, she thought.

Sir James, unaware of Lucinda's alarm, patted the woman's hand. "Carolly tells me you are called Faye. What is your surname?"

Faye thought for a moment. Her lips twitched. "Morgan is my surname. I am Faye Morgan."

Faye Morgan! Lucinda's inner temperature plummeted a few degrees.

"I am Sir James Clairmont, and this is my daughter Carolly," he said. "Miss Drakewyck is Carolly's companion."

Faye glanced at each of them, her gaze lingering on Lucinda. Moments passed as Lucinda stared back, aware that propriety dictated she turn away. She couldn't seem to move. Faye's eyes held her fast—peculiar eyes that saw into her soul, ice-cold eyes that sized her up. And beneath their surface, something fluid and dark roiled.

Lucinda crossed her arms over her breasts, the patterns she perceived in that fluid darkness more menacing than an outright threat. Something very ugly, she thought, was concealed in the blonde's skin. Her heart thudding against her ribs, she slipped her fingers into her pocket and touched the dove, finding comfort in its cool crystal presence.

"And your family, Miss Morgan, where are they?" Sir James asked, releasing Faye's hand. "I'm certain they must be worrying about you. Whom should I contact?"

Faye squeezed her eyes shut. Her brow crinkled. Lucinda seized the opportunity to study her. Wheat-blonde hair fanned out across the pillows, each strand shining silk, and other than the beauty mark near her mouth, Faye's skin appeared milk-white, as though she walked around swathed in veils to block the sun. Her lips, Lucinda thought, were full and red, beautiful yet somehow too luscious, as if she used them to suck the life out of those who strayed in her path.

145

A vague feeling of disgust flickering in her midsection, Lucinda studied the gold filigree locket hanging from Faye's neck. Whose picture did it contain?

Faye abruptly opened her eyes. "Please, call me Faye. 'Miss' seems so formal, and in this situation, hardly appropriate. As far as my family is concerned, I cannot remember anything. I seem to know only my name. I am sorry, sir. The bump on my head has addled my brain."

Faye's speech, Lucinda mused, seemed oddly formal. Stilted, almost. *As though she came from an earlier time.*

The older Clairmont's countenance drooped. "Don't apologize. 'Tis our fault that you're in this terrible predicament." He eyed Carolly with a narrowed gaze.

Carolly hopped onto the edge of Faye's bed and smiled prettily. "But Faye has forgiven me, Father."

"How can I not forgive one so young and charming?" Faye returned Carolly's smile with a weak one of her own.

Lucinda could see only that odd darkness in Faye's eyes. Faye, she thought, will never forgive.

She'll never rest until she's destroyed every one of us.

Moments later, a knock sounded at the door. Lucinda grasped the handle and pulled it open.

"Good evening, Miss Drakewyck," Richard said, his tone formal. "I see you've joined us at Clairmont Hall."

"Just this afternoon, in fact."

"I'm certain you and Carolly will suit perfectly."

Lucinda narrowed her eyes, discerning a jibe, but he shrugged, and for harmony's sake she let it go. Instead, she studied him from the tips of his polished black shoes to the top of his head. He had dressed for dinner in a black jacket and matching trousers, the snowy folds of his neckcloth expertly tied. A day's growth of beard on his chin, however, gave the lie to his otherwise orderly appearance. While the clothes were in shape, the man was not, Lucinda thought.

Still, the luster of his black hair, the full curve to his lower lip, the way his powerful shoulders filled his jacket, the hint of anger in his hazel eyes . . . all combined to spark a gnawing in her insides, a yearning she knew must be sternly repressed.

He lifted one black eyebrow. "Do I pass inspection?"

She swallowed, her cheeks growing warm.

"Our patient is awake, I hear," he continued.

Lucinda nodded and lingered in the doorway, wanting to shield him from Faye's ice-blue gaze.

He smiled, a ghost of a smile that barely curved his lips. "May I see her?"

Frowning, Lucinda moved aside and followed him into the room.

Sir James looked up at Richard's entrance. "Ah, Richard. Our patient is awake. Her name is Faye Morgan."

Richard bowed slightly in Faye's direction. "A pleasure, Miss Morgan."

The older Clairmont chuckled. "Well, we aren't sure about the 'Miss' yet, Richard. It seems her memory is spotty. We're to call her Faye, instead."

Richard nodded, his gaze assessing Faye. Lucinda could see no spark of attraction in either his countenance or manner, and the knowledge relieved her mightily. Instead, he seemed to be sizing her up, and perhaps wondering how long she might stay in his home to disturb him.

"Well, Faye," he finally said, "I hope your recovery is expeditious."

"Faye and I are going to become good friends," Carolly chimed in. "I want her to stay on for a long time."

"You may stay with us as long as you need to." His tone pleasant, Sir James gestured toward Lucinda and Carolly. "I'm sure the ladies will keep you company. In the meanwhile, I've been conducting inquiries in town and on the road toward London. Someone will ask for you soon, and if not, you should recover your memory."

"Thank you, Sir James," Faye said. "I don't expect I'll need to stay here very long at all."

Morgana stretched on the bedcovers, luxuriating in the softness against her skin. A soft chuckle rippled through her body, a body that had been so abused, so tortured. Edward Drakewyck and Henry Clairmont had done their worst, she thought, and still she lived. She breathed. Her spirit had never let go.

She had returned.

The Clairmonts and the Drakewyck witch thought she'd slept all the week. They were wrong. They were fools. She'd already lain under the ground for two hundred years and would never sleep again. They'd buried her deep to cover her sins, she thought, and throughout the centuries she'd done her penance. She'd been redeemed of her sins. And now, it seemed she'd even been granted a reward. Her deprivation in the grave had purified her senses, made them stronger; her eyes saw more, her ears heard more, and when she touched, the sensations were so full and rich she nearly writhed with the pleasure of it.

She was *strong.*

She'd spent the last week lying in this grand bed, listening to the maids talk around her, trying to get a feel for this place, this time. Her speech patterns had to match. Her mannerisms had to fit. The things she said had to make sense.

Surprise, after all, had its advantages.

She'd concocted the story about losing her memory because it provided an excuse for her lack of clothes, family, and background. In truth she'd spent the past five days remembering every excruciating detail of the last days of her life. Edward Drakewyck attacking her with his magic. Henry Clairmont slicing his shiny blade across Christopher's throat. Christopher turning away, rejecting her.

Christopher.

God, how she missed him.

How had he died? Did he marry again?

Morgana turned her face against the pillow, her eyes drier than dust. She couldn't seem to cry anymore. Her long sleep in the grave had taken that ability away from her. She could only feel hatred burning through her veins. It kept her heart beating and heated her blood to a boiling point, until she wanted to scream with the pressure of it.

She was going to make them *suffer*.

Of her sojourn in the grave she remembered little. Worms, ants, *things* around her, mud, moist dampness, the heavy weight of dirt, of a hundred sins . . . every time she thought about it nausea overtook her and she nearly vomited.

So she tried not to think about it. She preferred to relive the moment she'd awoken, surging upward from her grave, breathing in clean air and seeing the stars sparkle above her.

149

And knowing her moment for revenge was at hand.

Luck, at least, seemed to be on her side, as if Fate itself agreed she'd been wronged and eagerly pursued restitution. She'd jumped in front of the Clairmont girl's carriage because she'd sensed the magic of the crystal dove somewhere on board. And how the gamble had payed off! Here she was, snug in her enemy's bed while they fussed over her, doing their utmost to ensure her comfort. She would continue to play upon the Clairmonts' guilt until her job was done.

She looked out the window. Twilight reigned in the sloping grounds the Clairmonts called home. Morgana thought about the magic she would unleash upon this place. About the spells to strike Sir James Clairmont and any living Drakewyck relatives with long, painful illnesses until they begged for death, choking on their breath as she'd choked on hers. About the way she'd lure the Clairmont girl into ruining herself forever. She wanted to laugh with glee as the plans swirled in her mind.

She was going to have such a romp.

Indeed, she had special designs for the witch and knave. She'd sensed the crystal dove on the witch's person and the magic within it had called to her, strengthening her purpose. Nothing less than perfect, equitable justice would suffice. Once she'd forced the witch and the knave into marriage, she would torture the witch's husband just as Edward Drakewyck had tortured Christopher. When the witch nearly crumbled with pain at watching her beloved suffer, she would demand the crystal dove, just as Edward had demanded it.

And then, if she remained in a good mood, she'd cast a spell of eternal sleep on both of them.

If she grew vexed, she'd kill them.

She clenched her hand around the string she'd pulled from the witch's gown and the piece of lint she'd plucked from the knave's jacket. They hadn't even seen her take them, which suggested the witch was quite weak. All the better, she thought.

Morgana tilted her head. A buzzing noise hid just beyond the bounds of her consciousness. A voice, she thought. The same one that had spoken to her before. This voice, it cried for release, but her mind turned away from it. She rubbed her face against the downy counterpane and banished the noise. She had no time for ghosts. Her business was with the living.

9

$\mathcal{L}$ucinda awoke to the sound of birds singing and flitting in the oak tree outside her bedchamber. Dawn had not yet lightened the horizon; the oak had that pale, twilight cast of neither darkness nor sunlight.

She pulled the counterpane over her head. She'd lain in bed for hours, replaying her first meeting with Faye over and over in her mind, thinking about Edward Drakewyck's warning, and remembering that strange burst of light from the crystal dove when she and Richard had touched it simultaneously. At three o'clock in the morning she'd despaired of ever falling asleep. Exhaustion had finally claimed her, however, and she'd dropped into a fitful doze, only to wake up now with burning eyes and a roiling stomach.

Her first full day at Clairmont Hall was going to begin very early, indeed. She knew it was useless to try to fall asleep again. Worries about Faye would leave her cold beneath even the warmest of counterpanes.

Frowning, she kicked the covers off. She may not have slept but she had reached a few conclusions. The witch Morgana Fey had awakened. And Lucinda was quite sure she and Richard had inadvertently roused her that night in the glen when she'd been trying to cast a spell of divination and had ended up with a raging bonfire instead. The moment she and Richard had touched the dove it had given off a burst of magic. Considering Morgana Fey's curse, that "the Drakewyck witch and Clairmont knave" would awaken her from her lonely grave, Lucinda could reach no other conclusion.

The first part of the curse had played itself out.

What was the next part?

She hurried to her trunk, lifted the lid, and pulled *Goetia* into the early morning twilight. Shivering, she turned up the wick on an oil lamp and brought it close to the book. She grew even colder as she reread Edward's warning and the last line of Morgana's prediction:

"They will love and the dove will be mine, and utter destruction will be thine."

Brows drawn together, she shook her head. She wasn't going to fall in love with Richard, but assuming she did, how would their love lead to Faye acquiring the dove? It made no sense, and yet, Lucinda remembered the impressions she'd received from her vision. If she refused to give the dove to the witch, Lancelot would die, but she would live. If she gave the dove to the witch, they'd both die.

The look in Faye's eyes, that fluid darkness that spoke of both relentless determination and a complete lack of compassion, had left a tightness in the pit of her stomach. In that instant she resolved to have a private word with Richard at the first opportunity. She would show him the entry in *Goetia*, point out

153

the various inconsistencies surrounding Faye, and urge him to tread cautiously. Her conscience demanded she make an attempt, however ineffectual.

Lucinda closed *Goetia* and buried it in her trunk beneath her dresses. She would have to pick her moment carefully. She couldn't waltz through Clairmont Hall all day, holding a big, heavy spellbook and hoping to run into Richard. No, she'd have to either lure him into her bedchamber or find him in his own. Today, however, was her first day as Carolly's companion. She had to find the girl and smooth things over between them before she began her campaign to convince Richard.

Having decided on a plan of action, however small, she pulled a few garments from the trunk and dressed quickly, shunning her corset and all but one petticoat. The yellow foulard gown she chose sported a minimum of buttons, and she managed to fasten most without help. Then, her feet encased in kid slippers and a shawl around her shoulders, she opened her bedroom door and slipped into the hallway. The iron knight opposite her door seemed to wink at her as the glow from an oil lamp inside her room shone on his helmet.

The passage had only a single window at one end, and although a candelabra sat nearby in a stone recess, its candles had burned nearly to stubs, leaving her enveloped in shadows. She squinted through the gloom and started off, confident the grand staircase lay just ahead.

Within five minutes of wandering through a maze of identical passageways, she admitted to herself that she'd become hopelessly lost. A window at the end of the hall she currently found herself in filtered less light than she'd expected, suggesting a western exposure. From what she could remember, the grand staircase was situated in the west of the building. So where was the grand staircase?

She turned the corner. Another set of doors confronted her. Her frustration mounting, she knocked on one of the doors. With any luck, someone inhabited the room and would point her in the proper direction.

No one answered.

She walked to the end of this latest passageway and stopped at another "T" with halls to the left and right. Totally disoriented, she shrugged and turned right, which led her to a dead end, without additional halls to the left and right.

A large oaken door faced her. Was this someone's bedchamber? If she opened the door, whom might she disturb? She glanced over her shoulder. The hallway, dark and uninviting, seemed to stretch into a mile. Clutching the door handle, she pulled.

Stone steps, surrounded by a square tower, led upward. Quite a bit more light illuminated the staircase, as though the first rays of dawn shone through a multitude of windows farther up. The light seemed much more friendly than the never-ending hallways. She decided to find those windows and orient herself by looking at the grounds.

She entered the staircase, closing the oak door behind her, and began the climb upward. Cobwebs festooned the iron railing that hugged the steps, but the light grew brighter, and by the time she reached a landing her mood had improved dramatically. Certain the landscape would at least give her a feel for the portion of the house she'd entered, she peered through a window.

Outside, woodlands surrounded the castle, their green depths thick with wildflowers. A fountain filled to overflowing splashed lazily in the morning sunlight. She recognized nothing.

"Hellfire!"

She muttered the oath without thinking, and then blushed a little. She usually didn't curse, but sometimes the situation simply demanded it.

Another oak door faced her. She grasped its latch and pulled. Beyond, a clutter of dust, broken furniture, and chipped stone greeted her eyes.

The north wing, she suddenly realized.

She'd stumbled upon Richard's hideout.

Quickly she spun around, not wanting to explore further in that strange place.

An anguished voice halted her retreat.

". . . close in to your center. Back the right flank!"

A man's voice, she thought, full of restless urgency and yet slightly garbled. Muffled by intervening walls and moth-eaten tapestries, it seemed to come from somewhere down the hall.

She turned back toward the north wing and paused.

Listening.

". . . keep up, Private Wellstone. Close in . . ."

There, she'd heard it again. Husky with distress. *Richard,* she thought. He was having a nightmare. About the war.

She clutched the doorjamb. One did not gain friends by peeping at them during private moments. And this place, it looked so forlorn. So abandoned. Dangerous, even.

Just like him.

Silently she berated herself. Where was her courage? Hadn't she promised herself that she'd try to help him? It seemed the least she could do, especially when she expected Richard to save her life.

She wouldn't abandon him to his demons.

Eyes wide, she entered the north wing and closed the door behind her. The gray stone looked older here. Foliate masks about waist-high decorated every other block, their grins leering. She walked past the leaf-faces and windows so thin they appeared mere slits in stone, following the sound of Richard's voice. Rotting drapes, partially torn from the wall, fluttered as she slipped by, giving off dust.

". . . the Brigade will advance. Walk, march, trot . . ."

His voice grew louder, seeping from beneath an oaken door at the end of the corridor. Lucinda hurried around a chair missing two legs and doors fitted out with iron hinges turned rusty brown. A cold draft rustled past her and raised gooseflesh on her arms. Her slippers crunched on pieces of glass, and as she passed by a broken mirror, she paused long enough to stare at her reflection. Frightened brown eyes gazed back at her.

". . . attack, sir? Attack what guns, sir?"

The shouts now sounded strangled. Eyebrows drawn together, she crossed the last few yards to the oaken door and pulled on the latch. Squeaking, the door opened.

Richard let out a threatening cry. Had Faye gotten to him already?

Her heart thudding against her ribs, she slipped into the room. A single candelabra, sporting several stubs, sat upon a table and provided the only illumination in the bedchamber. A small pile of clothes and black boots formed a crumpled heap on the floor. The drapes, although tattered, blocked enough of the early-morning sunshine to fill the room with shadows. Lucinda had to squint to make out details.

A movement caught her eye. She took a few more steps into the gloom and waited for her vision to adjust.

Richard writhed on a gigantic four-poster bed set in the middle of the chamber. Candlelight played upon his naked back and arms, revealing deep, muscular grooves and a light sheen of sweat. Black trousers encased his thighs like a sheath, revealing contours that suggested years of development. He had the body of an athlete: strong, beautiful, very masculine.

She drew in a sharp breath, wanting to touch him, knowing she shouldn't. Never before had she seen a man without clothes, not even Uncle George.

Feet bare, he kicked out, evidently in a vicious fight with an equally violent, yet transparent enemy.

". . . Lord Cardigan, you bastard . . ."

Husky yet melodious. Vibrating with anger.

She took an involuntary step backward. His half-naked body had raised some pressing doubts in her mind. She edged around his bed, wondering how he would react when he found her skulking around in his private sanctuary. Would she only confirm his opinion that she was a reprehensible jade without a jot of common sense or manners, who invaded men's bedchambers and spied upon their naked bodies? Suddenly the idea of escape seemed much more worthy than that of comforting him.

He abruptly slammed his fist into the mattress, shouted, and woke himself up.

Scowling, he sat straight up. A heavy lock of black hair fell over his brow, giving him a boyish look. He took a deep breath and let it out slowly, his attention wandering along the room's various furnishings. She could sense the tension in him, see the anger in the way he sat, feel the anxiety that radiated off of him in waves.

Without thought she scuttled behind a dilapidated armchair and wrapped her arms around her knees.

He shook his head, and yawning, stood. His feet were bare, and tanned, and somehow, his state of undress seemed fitting—primal, pagan, unquestionably dignified.

He hadn't seen her, thank goodness. But now she was hiding from him, making her intent appear criminal. Oh, what had possessed her to hide? She should have brazened it out instead. If he found her crouching behind the chair like a common sneak-thief, he'd certainly question her motives—and have every reason to.

Hand over her heart to better quell its thumping, she checked her skirts. She didn't want even a scrap of fabric to show from behind the chair. If he caught her, he'd likely strangle her . . . that is, if she didn't swoon first.

Silence filled the bedchamber.

What was he doing?

Lower lip caught between her teeth, she peeked around the back of the chair. He stood by a set of drapes, his gaze unfocused, brow furrowed, as if he were trying to recall the details of his nightmare.

Her unease reached new heights as she remembered Uncle George's admonishments about the behavior of proper ladies. She was breaking every rule he'd bothered to teach her. And yet, she simply couldn't muster the will to move. Richard's clenched jaw and dark eyes reminded her of a coiled spring near to release.

With a violent expletive, he suddenly leaned down and grabbed a boot, his buttocks flexing beneath those black trousers. Balanced on one foot, he shoved his foot into the boot and tugged until the thing slid on. The other boot followed just as quickly. Then he stretched, full of flexibility and strength, a prime example of masculine vigor.

She pressed against the chair and swallowed. Hand fluttering to her throat, she remembered how he'd held her the night of Carolly's wild carriage ride, holding back all of that magnificent energy, his caress firm yet intoxicating, the lips he pressed against her neck warm, compelling, undeniably sensual.

"God damn those bastards," he muttered, startling her from her thoughts. His chest heaved with the force of the sentiment.

Lucinda suddenly felt about two inches tall. Now she wasn't just spying on his naked body, but also listening to his private thoughts. The longer she huddled here, the more culpable she became.

"Fire, blood, smoke, I'm sick to death of it." He spoke in a ragged whisper now. "Why didn't I save him?"

Seconds passed.

Lucinda's nerves coiled tight. *Save who?* she wondered. Part of her demanded she reveal herself immediately and end the suspense . . . while another part insisted she stay hidden. And pray he didn't find her.

"Bloody, miserable hand." His voice suddenly broke. He strode over to the drapes, and with one yank he opened them, flooding the room with sunlight, revealing every little aspect of the utter desolation he'd surrounded himself in. Dirt-covered windows. Motes of dust dancing in the air. Cobwebs. Pieces of furniture, destroyed for firewood. A statue, fallen from its pedestal, eyes looking to the ceiling, arms outstretched, silently begging for assistance. Mold, must, and mildew everywhere.

On the floor in the corner, his Victoria Cross lay abandoned.

She smothered a gasp.

He spun around, his gaze dark, haunted.

An urge to turn and run almost overwhelmed her. Common sense told her to stay, for surely he could, and would, overtake her within seconds. Her heart nearly bursting from her chest, she left the safety of her chair.

"Lucinda!"

"I should have made my presence known. I apologize," she said quickly, hoping he wouldn't hear the quiver in her voice. "I heard you cry out, and I found myself unable to turn away . . ." She trailed off, the feebleness of her explanation robbing the rest of the words from her lips.

He grabbed his shirt off the carpet and shrugged it on. "What are you *really* doing here?"

" 'Tis as I've said. I heard you cry out—"

"From where? Your bedchamber? I didn't know my father placed you in the north wing."

"I became lost, and somehow wandered up here."

He fumbled with the last few buttons on his shirt, his damaged hand giving him some trouble. After he'd finished, he focused upon her with glittering hazel eyes, their depths intelligent, harsh, eyes that could glow with desire or flash with hatred. He was an intimidating stranger, icy and reserved; and yet, she sensed a potent sensuality in him, boiling far beneath the surface, made more interesting by the tight control he exercised.

161

"Only a complete fool would believe your explanation," he said. "I want to know why you're here. What did you hope to accomplish?"

Lucinda couldn't seem to draw a breath, not when he stared at her like that. She wanted to squirm but forced herself to remain still. She *wouldn't* run. He wasn't going to intimidate her.

"I'm telling the truth. I wandered into the north wing by accident. I would have turned around at once and left, but I heard your voice. I heard your pain, Richard. I wanted to help."

"So you invaded my bedchamber."

Warmth invaded her face. "Yes."

"To *help* me."

She nodded.

"And you watched me while I slept."

She had no answer for him this time.

Slowly he rubbed his full lower lip with the ball of his thumb, his gaze assessing her from the hem of her dress to the curls that sat atop her head. His eyes blazed with male appreciation before he dropped his lids half-way. He wasn't so very handsome, she observed; his cheeks were too angular, his nose strong, and his chin far too square. But somehow, on him, they weren't faults at all. They combined to give him a very masculine appeal, one that could change from gentle to harsh given his mood.

Right now, he appeared quite inflexible.

"No one comes into the north wing." A glint in his eyes, he jabbed his shirttails into his waistband. "Not even you."

"Why do you stay up here?" she asked, slipping behind a chair. "What are you hiding from?"

"I'm not hiding. I prefer my own company. *You* were hiding."

162

"The war has turned you into a hermit, Richard."

His scowl deepened as he drew on a waistcoat. "Call me what you like."

She glanced toward his medal. "Why is your Victoria Cross on the floor?"

With quick, angry movements he strode to the medal, picked it up, and thrust it at her. "Here, take it."

"No, Richard, it's yours. For valor during the war."

"Keep it, I say! And stay out of my way from now on."

"That's not possible," she said quickly, dropping the bronze cross into her dress pocket. Too late she realized she couldn't give him an explanation of *why* it wasn't possible to stay away from him without describing her vision and the role Fate had deemed he'd play.

"Why not?"

"I've many reasons, but I don't think you're ready to hear them."

"I don't like mysteries."

"I can tell you nothing more. Please try to understand."

"Understand what? You haven't explained anything." Nostrils flaring, he circled around the chair toward her. "Let us examine the evidence more closely. You've crept into the north wing at daybreak, sneaked into my bedchamber, and concealed yourself behind an armchair with all the stealth of a thief. When I ask why, you say you want to help me. That we must remain close. And yet, you refuse to give a reason for it."

Lucinda trembled. He had her trapped. Right now he thought her a thief. If she explained her vision, he'd think her mad. She couldn't decide which was worse. A sudden wave of disgust washed over her. "Oh, why did Fate link me with you, of all men."

His eyes widened as if she'd slapped him. "Would you rather have encountered someone else?"

"At the moment, yes."

He gripped the chair next to them with one large hand, his fingers curled into the decaying upholstery. "Do you have any idea what could happen to a young woman who makes a habit of sneaking into men's bedchambers?"

"If the man was a gentleman, he'd let her go. Unscathed."

"Not all men are gentlemen."

She glared at him, heat inflaming her cheeks. "If you want, turn me over to Sir James. Or let me go. But please, stop badgering me."

His shirt bagging carelessly beneath his waistcoat, he shrugged into a jacket. "You belong at Drakewyck Grange, in your own bed."

She didn't like the inflection he used on the words *own bed*. In fact, she found his entire demeanor vexing. Lancelot indeed. "And you, like most men of your ilk, take great delight in telling me what to do. I'm not interested in your advice, *Captain*."

"This isn't a game." He caught her arm and held it tightly. "The dangers are very real. Allow me to demonstrate."

In one brisk move he grabbed her shoulders and yanked her against him. He slipped his hands beneath her shawl and eased it downward, the tie at her breasts loosening in response to his gentle pressure. Soon it had pooled in layers of crocheted lace at her feet, exposing her arms and the tops of her breasts to the morning air.

His palms were hot against her as he ran his hands down her back, along the yellow foulard to her bottom, kneading her flesh all the while, his thumbs rubbing hard enough to remind her she was utterly helpless, that he could do as he wished with the smallest effort. She froze at the intimacy, unprepared for the sweet tremors that chased through her limbs, for the delicious vulnerability he roused in her.

"Have you any idea what you do to a man with that defiant mouth?"

She twisted against him, to no avail. "Release me this instant."

" 'Tis too late for second thoughts." His lips thinned to a hard line. He tightened the embrace to one of bruising force, trapping her with arms so strong they could crush her in an instant. He traced her spine, touched the nape of her neck, fondled the sides of her breasts, each intimate caress awakening her to a new kind of sensation, one that flooded the secret place between her thighs with heat.

"I didn't come here to kiss you," she said, striving for an imperious tone but failing miserably. She could see nothing but his face, harsh yet unreadable; could smell nothing but the clean male scent of him, soap and bay rum. Drowning, she levered her foot back, ready to kick anything solid, desperately trying to ignore the feel of his heart beating against hers, the practiced vitality of his touch.

He sensed her intention and trapped her with one rock-hard thigh, his gaze resting on the soft folds of yellow foulard which framed her breasts. "You are so very beautiful, with your white skin and pert nose and soft brown hair which sweeps your shoulders. You tempt me to touch, to taste."

165

His voice was a throaty purr, deep, musical, almost as mesmerizing as the dark glow of desire that had replaced the harshness in his eyes.

"I don't want to kiss you," she insisted, knowing she'd lied as another pleasurable jolt weakened her. He moistened his lips with his tongue, his gaze never leaving hers. Slowly, still stroking her bottom, he lowered his head and covered her mouth with his own, his kiss gentle at first, drawing her will from her body.

She tried to hold back. Effortlessly he shattered her resolve, his tongue and mouth tormenting her so thoroughly that her legs buckled. He pulled her even closer, so close she nearly straddled him, her breasts crushed against his chest.

Abruptly he broke the contact between them, lifting his head to stare at her with eyes both harsh and full of longing, anger and desire at war. "Is this what you sought?"

"You've misjudged me," she said, her voice wavering. She knew her defense was half-hearted at best. Heaven help her, she didn't want to end the intimacy, the excitement, the rapture he promised her with one burning gaze. She clung to him, begging him with her eyes to kiss her again, to bring his plunder to its conclusion. He brought a part of her to life that no one else could, and she gasped at the potency of her own desire.

With a ragged sigh he bent his mouth to hers and claimed her a second time, thrusting his tongue forward, filling her mouth, robbing the breath from her lungs. Reluctantly she surrendered to that strong male form, that even stronger will, to the pure magic his lips wrought inside her. He deepened the kiss but she didn't stop him, didn't protest; he assaulted her every

sense until she could think of nothing but him. She
sank against him, loving the feel of his hard, unyield-
ing chest, and wrapped her arms around his waist,
her fingers slipping beneath his waistcoat and shirt to
touch the heated skin beneath.

At her caress, he smiled, curving deep lines into
his cheeks and at the corners of his eyes. A little jolt
shot through her at that smile. It was the smile of a
marksman—one filled with hunger, and triumph, and
just a touch of remorse.

"Richard," she whispered, suddenly unsure.

He pressed his mouth against hers, crushing her
denial, urging her lips wide as he tasted each recess,
his tongue like hot silk. The room pinwheeled around
her, stone and sunlight combining in a wild gray and
white shower, and she clutched his waist, the denial
becoming a moan of delight. He tightened his arms
and lifted her slippered feet from the ground until
she dangled, caught in a sticky web of pleasure. Her
reservations faded away as she, too, teased him with
her tongue, claiming him with her own untutored
response.

In one supple movement he scooped her into his
arms and laid her down on his bed. Almost dizzy,
she stared at him as he leaned over her, the pupils of
his eyes expanded, his features sharp, dark curls of
hair revealed in the vee at his throat. She knew he
waited for some sort of protest. She also realized if
she told him to stop, he would.

Another denial formed on her lips. This time she
hadn't the strength to utter it. Instead, she lifted one
shaking hand to his hair and brushed it back from his
forehead. Her arm scratched against the stubble on
his chin, and he nuzzled her flesh, his lips warm, in-

sistent. At the thought of those lips on her breasts, and even lower, tremors shot through her.

He joined her on the bed and threw one strong thigh over her skirts. Still, he waited, his eyes heavy-lidded, his mouth a sensuous curve promising even more pleasure.

The gesture hesitant, she slipped a hand behind his neck and drew his lips back down to hers, the bedcovers soft behind her back, the first rays of dawn painting them with splashes of pink.

A chuckle rumbled deep in his chest as he kissed her again, thoroughly, his mouth hard and possessive, driving thoughts of propriety from her mind and making the core of her slick with heat and moisture and pure need.

Hands shaking, she popped the buttons on his waistcoat, then his shirt, and traced each ridge on his bare chest and ribs. Everything else—the growing sunshine, the bedchamber, the counterpane beneath her—faded away as she concentrated on the dangerous contours of his body, and the feel of his hands exploring her in an equally bold manner.

With practiced ease he slipped her pearl buttons from their loops and loosened her bodice until she felt the morning air skim her chemise. His hand warm, he reached inside her neckline to cup one of her breasts, and she sucked in a breath, unprepared for the feel of his fingers dipping into her cleavage. He leaned down to drag his tongue across her skin, shattering her senses with the heat of him, the sight of his head against her naked flesh.

"I want to see more of you," he murmured, and she couldn't form a single protest; rather, she moaned, low in her throat, totally given over to the pleasure she sensed he could bring her.

At the sound, he smiled and planted a swift kiss against her lips before pulling her gown down around her shoulders and slipping her arms from the sleeves. Her chemise gained his attention next; he tugged on the little ribbon that encircled the bodice until the tissue-thin fabric loosened. Breathing more quickly, he pushed the chemise down until he had bared her from the waist up.

She felt nakedly vulnerable but forced herself to remain still as he stared at her breasts, then lifted them in his palms, his attention fastening on her nipples. With each second of his intimate examination, her heart seemed to beat faster, and the air in her lungs drained away, until finally she thought she'd swoon.

"You are beautiful, Lucinda," he breathed.

The warm throb between her thighs tormented her. When he touched her nipples with gentle fingers, circling them and rubbing their swollen tips, they hardened like small, pink stones and the throb became a nearly unbearable ache. Her cheeks flamed. She'd never guessed that such delight could exist between men and women.

Murmuring encouragement, he took her hand and pressed it against the heated fabric at his groin. She felt the outline of him, its tantalizing hardness bulging against her palm, and suddenly she wanted to open his trousers and see what they concealed, to touch him and taste him, even though the impulse shocked her. She rubbed that heated fabric and felt him grow even larger and knew that she'd pleasured him.

Hot, feverish longing to see him naked swept through her, mounting and mounting as he swooped down toward her breasts and locked his mouth around one tender, swollen nipple. He pulled at it with his lips, drawing waves of pleasure through her until she gasped aloud. She was utterly wicked, yet utterly ensnared, and when he nudged her fabric-clad thighs apart with a knee, she wished her gown completely gone.

Abruptly he froze, his hand fumbling at her waist.

"What the deuce," he mumbled, lifting his head. He drew something from her gown, and lifted his head to see what he'd discovered.

The crystal dove.

He threw it aside and fastened his mouth on her other nipple, making her groan in both pleasure and torment. She clutched his hair, wanting more, yet wanting to pull him away. The dove had reminded her of how much she risked with this intimacy between them.

Intimacy could lead to love.

And love, to death.

"Richard . . ." Her voice was husky, yet full of remorse. "We mustn't."

Even as she spoke, she flung her arms over her head and thrust her breasts against his face, arching her back, her passion rising, knowing she would only inflame him further.

Her hand bumped against cool crystal.

The dove.

She wrapped her fingers around it.

"We mustn't," she repeated, and twisted away.

"Lucinda, I cannot stop, not now." He pulled her back into his arms and rubbed his stubbled chin against the sensitive tip of her breast.

A little moan escaped her. "No. No more."

"Ah, God, you're right." He sighed, released her, and lay on his back, one arm resting over his eyes.

She gathered her crumpled bodice to her breasts. Silence grew between them and to her it seemed deafening. She noted the frown curving his mouth and knew she'd angered him.

"Richard?"

He sighed noisily and sat up. "So, you carry your magic bird around with you. Why? Have you been casting spells here in Clairmont Hall?"

His voice, she thought, held contempt.

"Right underneath your nose," she agreed, hurt that he would make love to her and then speak so scornfully. Evidently their kiss had cheapened her in his eyes.

"Don't toy with me, Lucinda."

"I believe you have just toyed with me." She pulled her chemise on, slipped her arms through the dress sleeves, and rearranged her bodice, forgoing the pearl buttons. She'd be damned before she'd ask for his help.

The lines in his face drawn tight, he leaned behind her and buttoned every one. Then he stood, took her hand, and drew her to her feet.

"I'm taking you back downstairs." He picked up her shawl and wrapped it around her shoulders.

She began to knot the shawl over her breasts, but he pushed her hands away and tied the ends himself, quickly.

"I don't need a nursemaid, but I can see you are determined to act like one." She tilted her chin up.

"You, Miss Drakewyck, need a husband."

"What do you know of responsibility?"

"Nothing," he growled.

Amidst the silence that settled between them, he buttoned his shirt, shrugged into his jacket and waistcoat, and escorted her downstairs to the second floor.

All the while she fought the appeal he exuded from every pore. If a heart beat somewhere beneath his surly exterior, she had yet to find evidence of it.

They emerged near the grand staircase.

"Where is your bedchamber?" He barked the question with such an air of command that she turned on her heel and pointed to the left.

"That way, Captain."

Lips twisted in an irritable frown, he regarded her closely. "Go to your bedchamber, Lucinda. I'll wait here until I'm certain you've followed my instruction. And see that you stay out of the north wing from now on. The next time I find you in my bedchamber, nothing will save you, your reputation be damned."

10

"*D*amn me all you want, but I'm not going to my room," Lucinda informed him. "I'm going to breakfast." She turned on her heel and walked away.

Richard followed her. "You're a defiant chit, Lucinda."

"And you think you are still on a battlefield commanding soldiers. *I* am not one of your men. Nor will I be treated shabbily."

"You invaded my private rooms. I'll not apologize for what happened between us."

"I'm not looking for an apology." She breezed down the staircase and into the great hall, aware he remained a few paces behind her. "I'm equally at fault. 'Tis your scornful attitude that I find objectionable. First you kiss me, and then you look down your nose at me as though by kissing you, I've cheapened myself."

She threw him a glance over her shoulder and realized he'd had the grace to blush.

"You haven't any respect for me, sir," she pressed, "and I don't like it."

"I have all the respect in the world for you."

"Then why did you treat me with such contempt?"

He dropped his voice to a whisper. "I felt frustration, not contempt. 'Tis clear to me you know little about men, Lucinda. When a man makes love to a woman, the need to possess her drives out all other thought. It becomes a physical pain that only she can assuage. After you broke away, I responded instinctually with anger, for the woman I desired most had been taken away from me. I apologize for my reaction. 'Tis not easy to control, not when I want you as much as I do."

She lowered her lashes. "I see."

"If I join you at breakfast, will you tell me why you insist we must 'remain close,' as you put it?"

"Only if you tell me how your hand became scarred."

"We'll eat in silence, then."

Together, they entered the dining room. Lucinda glanced around her, overwhelmed by the impression of opulence. Ivory-framed fanlights allowed the first rays of the sun to bathe the room in pink, while intricate papier-mâché scrolls and fruits danced around the ceiling. Marble Corinthian pillars, fine mahogany furniture, and a gold-rimmed Wedgwood dinner service all coordinated in color and theme. Even the ivory handles of the knives and forks were stained green.

A fine repast of cold and smoked meats, cheeses, omelets, porridge, Bath cakes, and biscuits cluttered the sideboard. Steam billowed from a bowl of porridge, mingling with the scents of cinnamon and coffee.

Lucinda poured herself a cup of tea, selected a scone, and buttered it with strawberry jam. She settled herself into a comfortable damask chair and watched as he piled his plate high. Whenever she glanced at him, he seemed to be looking at her.

"I don't believe I can eat in silence, Richard, especially after . . . this morning. A little conversation is called for. I might remark upon the weather, and you upon your plans for the day."

"What purpose would such idle conversation serve?"

"It would aid in digestion. If you stare at me throughout breakfast I fear my stomach will become quite upset."

Lips twitching, he nodded. "All right. I'll start. Do you predict sunshine or rain for today?"

She glanced at the window and scrunched her forehead in mock concentration. "Sunshine."

"And tomorrow?"

"Clouds."

"You're rather good at making predictions."

"Sometimes I even see into the future," she said, forcing a smile.

"What do you see in my future?"

A rush of explanations and warnings hovered on her lips. She bit them back, loath to break the lightness that grew between them. She was seeing a new Richard, one she liked very much. "A rather dense fog."

"Should I tell you what I see in your future?" He smiled, evidently full of masculine provocation.

"If you must."

"A rainbow, leprechauns, and a pot of gold."

She drew in a breath, several choice retorts coming to mind, but none seemed likely to shake his equanimity. She rarely lost in a game of words, but this time, she decided she'd have to yield. The devil now

175

seemed completely at ease, his brow unlined, his posture a casual slouch.

Never before, she suddenly realized, had she seen him so cheerful. He looked different, the harsh angles softened, the currents in his gaze now those of a clear pond. But he didn't have a boyish charm—no, his was a man's appeal, a rugged virility that hid a playful heart.

Her heart flip-flopped in her chest. "Very amusing."

Without sparing her a glance, he took a seat next to her. The mahogany table stretched out on either side, enhancing the intimacy between them. A moment later he'd harnessed that infernal smile, forcing it beneath a serious expression.

"And how have you come by such a detailed knowledge of the weather?" he asked, between mouthfuls of omelet.

"Through long, devoted observance of nature."

Shaking his head, he buttered a scone. "Oh, that's right. You're a witch. Why do I keep forgetting that fact?"

"I don't like the word *witch*. It's ugly and totally unsuited. Whenever I think of a witch, I imagine a little old crone with a hunched back and red eyes who eats children for dinner."

"What would you prefer? Spell-caster? I like 'charmer,' myself."

"Why must we put a name to it? 'Tis simply a talent, nothing more. Are people who take especially well to the hounds called hound-riders?"

He threw her a curious glance. "I don't understand why you bother to practice magic at all."

"Practicing magic is similar to flexing a muscle. We all have this muscle, but only a few of us choose to exercise it."

"I don't think it sounds like flexing a muscle at all. In fact, I would call it avoidance. Rather than facing up to your problems and trying to solve them through hard thought and even harder work, you simply wave your magic wand about and expect problems to go away."

"I prefer to think of myself as resourceful, not lazy. To 'solve my problems,' as you put it, I use every means at my disposal."

He inclined his head in acknowledgement of her point. "So, what sort of spells are you casting 'beneath my nose'?"

"Those that bring healing and protection. I never use my magic for anything but good."

"Who around here needs healing?"

"Everyone, from what I can see."

An unwilling smile twitched his lips. "Twice now I've seen you in the woods with a bonfire. The second time you damned near burned the woods down. I assume fire is involved."

"Fires are important," she admitted. "Indeed, they're central to most rituals. Fires help focus the mind."

"Do you worship the devil, then? Hell is considered 'The Inferno.' And in your own words you're practicing rituals."

She laughed. "No, I don't worship Satan. I don't even believe in him."

A strange recognition shadowed his eyes. "Neither do I." He studied his damaged hand for an instant before shoving it into a pocket. "You ought to turn away from these notions of magic. You cannot change your destiny, no matter how much you might wish to."

In that moment she knew his scars from the war went much deeper than mere flesh. She wished she

177

knew how to convince him that the souls of the men who'd died in the war were wandering in the dark garden. They were happy and didn't give a fig for Richard and his suffering.

Funerals, after all, were for the living, not the dead. The dead didn't care anymore.

"Still," she insisted, her voice gentle, "that doesn't mean that I believe in nothing at all."

"What do you believe in?"

"I think everyone has a soul, and on some level all our souls exist as one, without beginning, without end. I call that place where our souls are one 'the dark garden,' and my rituals celebrate the dark garden, or the unity of all living beings."

"And this talent you speak of? How does it relate?"

She took a sip of tea and spread strawberry jam on a biscuit. "My talent does not break any of nature's laws. 'Tis one we all possess, but few of us ever use. On occasion, I am able to visit the dark garden. I learn things. I see things. Sometimes I can even take some of its magic back with me."

"What *is* magic?"

She noticed the slight narrowing of his eyes, but forged on anyway. "In the traditional sense, magic is the power that makes something happen without apparent physical cause. When we see an event or action we can't explain, we blame it on magic. If the event occurs within a religious context, we even call it a miracle. In either case, 'tis simply the power of the dark garden spewing forth into our world, usually directed by one who has learned to tap into it."

Head cocked, he crossed his legs at the ankles and slouched in his chair. He was listening, yes, but he hadn't put the slightest credence in her explanation. "But how does magic *work?*"

"I don't know. There are a lot of things I don't understand, but that doesn't mean there aren't explanations for them. We still haven't discovered many of the natural laws at work in our world. Someday, we may be able to describe in a scientific, quantifiable manner how the dark garden operates, and things that are mysteries to us today will become clear."

He threw her a curious glance before returning to his omelet. "Does your uncle know about your hobby?"

"Yes. No. Well, ah, he didn't for quite a while, but he finally found out. He doesn't approve of magic."

"I heartily agree with him. You risk more than discovery by walking through the woods alone, even if you are courting your 'dark garden.' "

"Thank you for your concern, but I assure you I'm quite safe."

"You aren't going to encourage Carolly to start casting spells, are you?"

"Not if you promise to keep your knowledge about my 'hobby' to yourself," she countered. "When people hear the word *witchcraft*, they think of evil spells and devil worship. I assure you nothing could be further from the truth, but old prejudices die hard."

"I'll keep your confidence, although I suggest you learn to stand on your own, without this crutch you call magic." Sighing, he uncrossed his legs and sat up. "Tell me about your childhood."

"There isn't much to tell. My parents died in the typhoid outbreak years ago, the same one that took your mother."

"George Drakewyck raised you, then."

She nodded.

"I've heard it's difficult for a girl to grow up without her mother. Was it for you?"

"Yes, but Uncle George kept me very busy with book learning. At first I found it terribly boring and I hated him for constantly forcing me to work, but with time I discovered that a reasonable amount of fleas on a dog keeps him from brooding about being a dog. I had little time to feel sorry for myself."

He rubbed his brow. "Fleas on a dog."

She glanced at his damaged hand. Richard Clairmont, she thought, had his own set of fleas to deal with. She pulled in a deep breath, remembering the way he'd blushed while telling her he wouldn't apologize for his behavior. She'd lay odds that he felt at least a little guilty for kissing her as he did. She decided to take a chance and ask him a few questions that had long been bothering her, and hope his guilt forced him into answering.

She gestured toward his damaged hand. "Richard, how did you receive your wounds?"

"My scars aren't relevant."

"May I touch them?"

He shoved his damaged hand into his pocket. "Why this sudden interest in my scars?"

"Every time I mention them or glance at them, you hide your hand. And yet, my own eyes tell me they are far from terrible and do not require constant concealment."

Abruptly she grasped his wrist and pulled his hand from his pocket. Unresisting, he allowed her to touch his strong, lined palm and fingers. Two of his fingers—the index and middle—stopped at the knuckle, their ends a mass of scar tissue. She drew in a quick breath. How he must have suffered.

He stiffened. "Lucinda—"

"I don't find your scars ugly," she managed, and turned his hand over. Black curls covered the back of his hand to his wrist. She ran her finger from his wrist to his thumb in one delicate stroke.

"I'll sleep better knowing you approve." His voice had grown husky, and a slight flush colored his neck.

"Why *do* you hide your scars?" Her fingers trembling, she explored the bumps and ridges on his damaged knuckles. "Are you afraid people might find them disturbing?"

" 'Tis not how ugly the scars appear, but what they stand for."

She heard the pain in his voice, and felt the slight tremor in his fingers, and her heart squeezed as though held in a vise. "What do they stand for? Tell me."

He simply lifted his head and stared at her, eyes expressionless, but the tiny lines in his forehead and around his mouth gave him away.

"A good friend of mine died in the war," he said suddenly. He looked down at his plate and hesitated for several moments, clearly searching for words. "You would have me believe he's walking in this dark garden of yours, maybe even singing a little tune. I would like to, but I cannot believe in it."

Lucinda winced. Years had passed before she'd accepted her own parents' death, to wake in the morning without crying out, without longing to see their gentle smiles.

He raised his head, his gaze shuttered. "John stood not ten feet away from me, a Cossack with a loaded pistol pressed against his midsection. I had my own pistol, one I'd picked off the ground, aimed at the Cossack. But I couldn't fire at him, for he had a pistol trained on John, and he couldn't fire at me because he knew that as soon as he twitched his trigger finger, I'd blow him to Hell.

"A cannon blast to the left of us distracted the Cossack, and I pulled the trigger, but instead of killing the Cossack my pistol exploded and blew off two of my fingers. A moment later the Cossack had opened up John's midsection with a single shot. Another British cavalry officer opened fire on the Cossack, but he was too late."

In a flash she understood his obsession with the scars on his hand. "I'm so sorry for your loss," she said, all too aware of the ineptitude of her words. Surely he'd heard them a hundred times before, if not a thousand, and his reaction was just as predictable.

From the slight strain around his mouth, the spasm of pain in his gaze, she knew the wound from his friend's death was still fresh.

"Thank you." He brought the napkin to his lips with his free hand, wiped the corners of his mouth. Though he was there in body, she sensed in mind he roamed far away, in the past again. In his eyes she saw vulnerability and couldn't bear to have him think he was all alone in his pain. She shoved all disagreements aside, and without thinking further, laid both her hands on his damaged one. Smooth skin, warmth, the hard ridges of his knuckles . . . she clasped them beneath her palm and wished she could do more.

At that moment, the sun crested the window sash and sent a ray of light into the room, turning the green drapes to sea foam and gilding their hands. Its warmth felt like a benediction, a sign of blessing from above, and the solid knowledge came to her that she'd been right to come to Clairmont Hall. He needed her.

They needed each other.

He removed the last of her doubts by tucking a stray tendril of her hair behind her ear. Though pain still hid among the currents in his hazel gaze, it wasn't as strong now.

"Thank you," he said again.

"You've already thanked me."

"This time my thanks were not for your condolences, but for what you *didn't* say. I almost thought you were going to mouth one of those worn old phrases that illustrate how little a person understands."

" 'Time heals all wounds' is my favorite," she offered.

"Precisely." He let out a low, irreverent chuckle, thoroughly shocking in light of their topic. "I always fear my tongue will twist and I will instead say, 'Time wounds all heels.' "

He laughed aloud then, the sound one of the most beguiling she'd ever heard. Seconds stretched between them. He regarded her with an easy smile, one that asked nothing of her, yet offered her everything. "You make me feel good, Lucinda, and precious few people can do that these days."

Confusion made a jumble of her thoughts. A knot within her coiled tight, pulling at her thighs, flooding her limbs with heat, and she jerked her hands away.

"I've gone on far too long," she blurted. "You must think me a regular chatterbox."

"Perhaps, as you say, I've misjudged you."

"Then you *do* think I'm a chatterbox?"

"No, I think you're worth some thought." His mouth grew somber, and his eyes . . . they burned with hidden emotion, one she didn't dare name. "More thought, in fact, than I'd ever expected."

Seconds later Sir James entered. Richard's face drooped almost comically. Lucinda, too, felt the loss of intimacy keenly. She forced a smile to her lips, noting as she did so that the elder Clairmont limped a bit less.

"Sir James, has your leg improved?"

"It feels much better," he agreed, smiling. "Must have been the healing properties of that posy you gave me."

She felt rather than saw Richard's intrigued stare.

The elder Clairmont, evidently unaware of the currents running through the room, regarded his son. "I see you've decided to join us for breakfast. Good. I'd like to talk to you about a few estate matters."

Richard winked at her and hid a yawn behind his hand.

Lucinda muffled a giggle with her napkin.

Sir James eyed Richard with a wondering expression before gathering his breakfast from the sideboard. By the time he'd returned to his seat, however, he'd schooled his features into seriousness. He launched into a discussion of the Clairmont tenants and their various problems, one Richard paid complete attention to, and soon Lucinda felt forgotten.

She finished her breakfast quietly, left the dining room, and climbed the grand staircase. Once on the second floor, she studied the hallways before selecting the one she thought would lead to her bedchamber.

For once she'd chosen correctly. In under a minute she'd located her bedchamber door, which sat directly across from the iron knight. The door, she noticed, stood slightly ajar. Had she left it that way? She couldn't remember. Her heart quickened at the thought of an intruder.

She crept to the doorway and peered inside. A girl stood near her wardrobe, a hanger in her hands. Several of Lucinda's gowns already hung inside the wardrobe.

"Carolly." Lucinda crossed the room to stop at the girl's side. Annoyance surged through her at the thought of Carolly pawing through her private things. Just as quickly, warmth heated her cheeks. She had just done the same thing to Richard. Indeed, his Victoria Cross still lay in her pocket next to the dove.

"You're back from breakfast." Carolly hung a green gown in the wardrobe.

Lucinda tried not to scowl. "I see you've decided to unpack for me."

Her dark eyes giving up nothing, Carolly flashed her an easy smile. "You need to unpack, you know, or your gowns will become wrinkled."

A rebuke hovered on the tip of Lucinda's tongue. She didn't want the girl pawing through her trunk, particularly when she could run across her supplies and *Goetia*. Still, she remained quiet, unwilling to damage even further a tenuous relationship.

"I'll finish the rest of the trunk," Lucinda said, moving to the foot of her bed. She lifted the lid and saw her undergarments, neatly folded and apparently undisturbed. She took a quick inventory of her supplies. Her pouch of saltpeter looked depleted, but otherwise, everything appeared untouched. She couldn't remember if she'd brought an entire pouch of saltpeter and decided she hadn't. Some of her angst evaporated. "What would you like to do today?"

"You're supposed to teach me how to be a proper Englishwoman, right? Well, why don't we start by concentrating on our painting? All proper Englishwomen paint, or so I've been told."

"Told by whom?"

"Faye, of course. She's going to meet us in the salon with a few easels."

Her every sense alert, Lucinda stacked her chemises in a bureau. "I didn't realize Faye was up and out of bed."

"Just this morning she announced she'd done enough lounging for a lifetime, and wished to engage in activities which wouldn't tax her strength. We both thought painting a perfect answer to her requirements."

"Our day sounds well planned."

"You act as though Faye and I are conspiring against you, Lucinda. We're simply trying to satisfy both you and Father." Carolly's tone held contempt.

"I'm not your governess. I'm your companion. A friend."

"Faye is my friend."

"I'd like to be one, too."

The girl closed the wardrobe door and shrugged. "Let's go down to the salon, then. We'll paint and exchange confidences as friends should."

Without waiting for Lucinda, Carolly left the bedchamber and made for the grand staircase. Lucinda hurried to keep up. Her instinct told her Carolly was manipulating her, but for what purpose, she couldn't guess. Even so, her palms began to sweat at the thought of facing Faye in the salon with only Carolly for company. She slipped her hand into her pocket and touched the crystal dove.

She had nothing to fear, she told herself.

Faye wouldn't threaten her as long as she had the dove.

Carolly hastened through the great hall and angled into the lower floor of the Elizabethan wing, which housed Richard's apartments upstairs. The older portion of Clairmont Hall, on the lowest floor at least, looked well mended and comfortable. When Lucinda entered the salon, she immediately noticed a well-tended fire and pale blue walls that comforted the eye. The salon had an extensive selection of sofas and chairs, tea tables and small work tables. Two flower pedestals and a pianoforte dominated one corner of the room.

The salon appeared deserted.

"Where is Faye?" Lucinda asked.

Without warning Faye appeared from behind a secretary which was angled slightly to conceal the corner of the room. She kicked a dead mouse with her kid slipper, until it rested near the middle of the room. A trap squashed the mouse's body and had broken its back in two.

Faye's lips twisted in a mock frown. "Another curious mouse, caught in a trap. Clairmont Hall is full of them."

She sized Lucinda up with a casual examination. "Are you here to paint with us?"

Chin held high, Lucinda nodded. "I'm not much with a paintbrush, but I'll try. I also wanted to see how you were doing, and congratulate you on your miraculous recovery."

One blonde eyebrow arched, Faye took a step closer to her and spoke in low tones. "You are naught but a mouse, Lucinda, sniffing around for the scent of discarded table scraps. Eventually you will catch yourself in a trap."

Head tilted sideways, Carolly tried to follow the conversation, but she stood too far away to overhear Faye's murmur.

Lucinda shuddered at the thought of the mouse's small body crushed in two. "I prefer to consider the mouse that found the scraps and avoided the trap. A hearty meal, won through wit and knowledge, can bring a great deal of satisfaction."

Faye merely smiled. "And has seeing me awarded you any satisfaction?"

"Confusion is more appropriate." Lucinda swallowed. She'd never been fond of gaming, but this situation called for a risk. She had to do something to shake the woman's confidence. "I still don't understand how you recovered so quickly, but I can imagine such an extended rest must have been difficult to bear. Sleeping for all those hours! I think I'd be out of bed, too, regardless of my health."

A chuckle erupted from Faye. "All of that sleep has made me determined to sleep no more. Indeed, my health is nearly perfect and my appetite ravenous. Carolly, would you ask Hilton to retrieve us a plate of scones? Upon my word, I'm nearly *faint* with hunger."

"Of course." Her head tilted, as if she sensed the undercurrents in the salon but could not fathom them, Carolly left to find the butler.

Faye's features suddenly grew hard. She walked a tight circle around Lucinda. "Don't toy with me, witch. I'm far stronger than you. If I wanted to, I could send you to Hell in an instant."

"Then why don't you?"

"I don't wish to hurt you, dear."

Brows drawn together, Lucinda tried to gauge the truthfulness of Faye's statement. She touched the crystal dove in her pocket, wondering if the time had come to withdraw it. According to Edward Drakewyck's entry, the witch had planned their utter destruction.

Still, Faye might have reconsidered. And if she, Lucinda, used the dove against Faye, she could be condemning her needlessly, just as Edward Drakewyck had condemned her. God knew she didn't want to follow his example.

Even worse, if she blasted Faye with the dove's magic right here in the salon, she could release forces that would jeopardize all their lives, not just Faye's. Now was simply not the time for a confrontation with Faye.

She withdrew her hand from her pocket, leaving the dove inside. "Stop setting illnesses on Sir James," she demanded.

Faye's lips twisted. " 'Tis terrible, indeed, to watch those you love in pain."

"Will you stop?"

"I'm not responsible for his illnesses."

"I don't believe you."

Faye shrugged. "I suppose you're going to blame me for every misfortune in this household."

A cold draft whispered along the ceiling. Drapes fluttered against the windows. The door behind her swung shut, slowly, as if pushed by the draft. Her eyes blazing, Faye fixed her attention on a sofa near the window. "Oh, look at that."

Seconds later, a large spider scurried across the floor. Its body resembled a ripe grape, black and juicy. Lucinda had always hated spiders, especially the bloated ones; she imagined them ready to burst with skin-searing venom. This was perhaps the largest and ugliest spider she'd ever seen. And its eyes—black, fathomless—they seemed to follow her around, as though it were sizing her up.

Her skin began to crawl.

Faye scrunched her nose, as though in disgust.

The spider raced toward Lucinda, its legs working. Lucinda gasped and stepped backward, arms crossed over her breasts. She could actually see tiny fangs on the thing. Undeterred, it crossed the remaining space between them and scuttled onto her dress.

Lucinda flailed at it, a low moan building in her throat. She tried to keep it from slipping beneath her skirt. But it didn't desire her petticoats; it hurried up her skirt and advanced to the edge of her bodice, its eyes a murky black in the candlelight. She clawed at it, but the bloated body adhered to her dress like a button.

Revulsion tightened her skin. Finally, she managed to dislodge it, and it fell to the floor. One of its legs remained on her bodice. She tried to kick it away but it scrambled out of reach, toward Faye.

As soon as it drew near, Faye smashed the spider with her kid slipper. A pus-like substance spattered the floor.

Her gorge rising, Lucinda clapped a hand over her mouth. She couldn't quite prevent a low groan.

The door opened behind them and Carolly entered, followed by Hilton, his white-gloved hands carrying a tray of scones and a pitcher of lemonade. He placed the tray on a side table, picked up the dead mouse by the tail, and with a little bow exited the room.

"What was that sound?" Carolly asked.

Faye raised an eyebrow. "A spider frightened Lucinda. I killed it." Her voice had a devious finality.

"Oh." Carolly gave Lucinda a disgusted look, as though she felt certain Lucinda had cabbage rather than brains in her head.

Lucinda tried not to shiver.

"Shall we paint?" Faye asked.

"I'd love to." Lucinda walked to the easels, her defiant tone at odds with the sick feeling in the pit of her stomach.

Carolly looked from Faye to Lucinda. "Who will model for us, and who will paint?"

Faye nodded. "I'll model." She walked to the window and drew the drapes to the side, flooding the room with light. Her face expressionless, she then settled herself onto a sofa.

Carolly threw Faye a private little smile before handing Lucinda a dish of water and a box of watercolors. "Here you are, Lucinda. We'll paint side by side and see who does better."

"I can tell you who'll do better," Lucinda insisted. She glanced at the blonde witch and swallowed. An ache formed behind her temples and began to throb.

Sighing loudly, Carolly positioned herself before her easel and, paintbrush in hand, began to dab color onto paper. Lucinda did the same, noting how well Faye looked in this room, her ice-blue eyes matching the pale blue walls almost perfectly. The blonde witch, she admitted, was quite beautiful.

And yet, her watercolor of Faye looked awful. Blacks and reds combined to create a witch-like image that Lucinda hadn't even realized she'd been painting. What would Carolly say when she saw this picture? Suddenly panicked, Lucinda ripped the paper from the easel and wadded it into a ball. She gave the other two women an apologetic shrug and tried again.

All morning they painted, Lucinda's headache reaching unimaginable heights of pain until finally she could take no more. She gathered up her discarded paintings and excused herself, intercepting a significant glance between Faye and Carolly, and shuddered when they invited her back down after lunch to practice embroidery.

The pair, Lucinda thought, were deliberately trying to get rid of her. At least for the moment, they'd succeeded.

"'*T*is May eleventh. You've been at Clairmont Hall for about a week now. How are you enjoying your stay?" Sir James lifted a piece of sausage to his mouth and paused to cough, the sound dry and hacking, alarming Lucinda with its intensity before he gained control of himself and wiped his eyes.

Brow furrowed, Lucinda pushed her cup of tea and scone aside. "Carolly is most entertaining, sir. We draw, we paint, we embroider, and once she's quite exhausted me with feminine pursuits she slips away with Faye."

"No doubt they are working on Carolly's new gowns. I had planned to have my daughter fitted out with a new wardrobe when we arrived in London, delaying her Court presentation at least a week, but Faye has offered to sew gowns for Carolly. Carolly is thrilled; she will be able to dive right into her parties as soon as she arrives in London. They've been spending their afternoons deciding upon fabrics and styles."

"Faye is a dressmaker?"

"Evidently."

"And you trust her to design gowns appropriate for Carolly?"

Sir James shrugged. "I've seen some sketches. They seem perfectly appropriate."

"What a happy piece of news. What else has Faye remembered of her former life?"

"Nothing, I'm afraid."

"Oh? How odd that she could remember she's a seamstress but not who her family is."

His tone grew confidential. "Privately, I suspect our Faye remembers all too well who her family is. She's a runaway, I'll wager."

"You mean, her husband or family beats her and she doesn't want to return to them?"

He nodded. "Indeed."

"And she may stay here as long as she likes," Lucinda said.

"Well, I don't envision her as a permanent houseguest. I've been generous toward her because she damned near died beneath Carolly's wheel, but I have no desire to adopt another daughter. She may stay until she 'remembers' her past or until I can find a convenient situation for her. 'Tis fortunate she recalls a trade. That should make my task of settling her somewhere with an income much easier."

"I'm glad for her that she's up and out of bed so quickly," Lucinda said.

"Another piece of good luck," he agreed. "Most people, after suffering a bump like that, would have been abed for months." He began to choke again, his breath coming in quick gasps until the attack subsided.

Lucinda placed her hand on his arm. "That cough—"

"Sounds horrible, I know," Sir James finished for her. The redness in his face slowly leaked away. "It set upon me a few days ago. Dr. Bennet thinks I have a touch of pleurisy and plans to stop by on his rounds later today. Old age must be creeping up on me. No sooner does my gout clear up than my lungs start to object."

"Thank goodness you're going to see Dr. Bennet," she remarked.

Silently she decided that Faye had fed her nothing but lies in the salon. The witch had attacked his leg, and as soon as Lucinda had healed him with a spell, Faye must have shifted her attack to his lungs. Why else would such a dry, hacking cough come on so suddenly, with no other symptoms?

Lucinda knew she had to perform another spell of healing for Sir James, and watch carefully for an opportunity to use the crystal dove against Faye. "Too many men think they're made of iron and refuse to see a physician."

"I have no time for illness." He wiped his lips with a square of linen and shoved it into his jacket before she could check it for signs of blood. "How do you plan to spend your time today?"

"I haven't seen Carolly this morning," Lucinda admitted. "We'd an outing planned for this afternoon. Are she and Faye working on her wardrobe today?"

"I believe they took a trip to the draper's to select fabrics, and then plan to stop at Langford's Book Shop. They said they'd return by noon. Still, if you'd like to join them, I'm certain they'd appreciate another opinion. I'll bring you there myself."

"I'll take her," Richard said, entering the breakfast room. "I have business in town."

Lucinda stilled. She abruptly wished she'd worn a dress other than her white muslin and soldier blue paisley, an old favorite that showed its age. They hadn't seen each other much over the last week, other than an occasional meeting in the hall and a few words exchanged over breakfast. She guessed Richard was trying to fight the attraction between them, just as she fought it. His presence this morning, and his offer, suggested he'd lost.

Heat flushed through her at the notion.

He served himself from the sideboard, his gaze straying to her. Damp black curls clung to his neck, suggesting he'd recently bathed, and he'd loosened his cravat, the linen pale against his tanned skin. His navy blue surtout and fawn trousers, both expertly tailored, emphasized the graceful build of his powerful body.

"What sort of business?" Sir James asked with widened eyes.

"I'm thinking about renovating the north wing. I'd like to browse some of the stores in town to see if I can find anything appropriate for the rooms." Richard sat between Sir James and Lucinda and attacked his food.

Lucinda felt a bit giddy. The north wing, so broken and desolate, had come to represent Richard in her mind. When she heard him say he wanted to renovate it, she couldn't help but hope it reflected a rise in his spirits, as well.

"Upon my word, Lucinda," Sir James said, his voice lowered in mock confidentiality, "you've worked magic on my son."

Richard choked, then covered his mouth with a napkin.

"For the third time this week," the elder Clairmont continued, "he joins us for breakfast, and even states a desire to go into town. And why, you ask? Because he wants to renovate the north wing. How truly amazing."

Lucinda looked at Richard from beneath her lashes. "Thank you for offering to take me to town."

"I would do nothing to suspend a lady's pleasure."

Aware that Sir James watched both her and Richard far too closely, she drank her tea and waited for Richard to complete his breakfast as well. Once they'd finished, she sent for her shawl and they both stood.

He offered her an arm, which she took with a confident gesture at odds with her thudding heart. She felt the fine texture of his jacket beneath her fingers, breathed his heated male scent—linen and wool, a hint of eucalyptus. Beneath that civilized layer she detected the firmness of his muscles, smelled an earthiness that reminded her of the woods after a thunderstorm. For one dangerous moment, she imagined herself stripping away those cultured aspects of his character to reveal the warrior, the savage, the sensualist she fancied him to be.

Trembling, she put a few additional inches between them. The effect he had on her unnerved her. He wouldn't permit her withdrawal, however, and pulled her back with a flex of his arm. Held close to his side, they walked through the great hall and paused at the front door while Richard had a gig brought around and Lucinda collected her shawl from a maidservant. Silently Lucinda wished *Goetia* was small enough to tuck into her pocket, so when opportunities like this arose she could pull the spellbook out and show him Edward Drakewyck's entry.

At last, they settled into a phaeton, an old and crusty groomsman seated on the driver's bench before them. Clouds had gathered and blocked the sun's rays, promising a wet afternoon. Lucinda pulled her shawl closer around her shoulders as they trotted through an apple orchard, a thousand apple blossoms thrilling her with their sight and smell. The carriage stirred up a breeze that encouraged a few petals to drift down onto her hair. She looked at Richard, delighted, not bothering to brush them off.

"Have you ever seen such a beautiful place?"

He didn't answer. Indeed, he looked at her in such an odd manner that her heart began to trip in her chest. She quickly slid her gaze elsewhere.

"We made a bargain last week," he said, his voice husky, far too low for their driver to overhear. "You promised to tell me why we had to remain close if I told you how my hand became scarred."

She kept her attention on the rolling hills and patches of wildflowers which hugged the road. They'd almost reached Mill Lane, which would lead them directly into Somerton. The conversation couldn't continue for too long. Maybe she should stall him rather than blurting out what he would consider more sheer nonsense.

"You know how my hand became scarred. Now you must reciprocate. Tell me, Lucinda," he urged, a strange intensity coloring his words. "I remember you said once you felt a strange connection to me. You often mention Fate. How does it all fit in?"

"I . . . feel as though we were destined to meet," she hedged.

"I feel that too," he said.

"You're going to think me mad if I tell you why Fate has drawn us together."

"Try me."

"You don't believe in magic. You've said so yourself. Why should I bother trying to convince you of something when I know it's a hopeless task?"

"I'm sorry. I wish I could tell you I believed. But that doesn't mean I don't want to hear what you think, and consider carefully what you say."

"Why?"

"Because you're a very sensitive woman with a unique ability to see things that others don't and make connections where others can't. You've admitted to making a long, devoted study of nature. I suspect your study of people, even if unintentional, has been equally devoted. Your unconscious mind has evidently assimilated a series of impressions which have you convinced we must remain together."

" 'Tis more than intuition, Richard."

"How so?"

"Do you remember my description of my dark garden? How sometimes it shows me things?"

"I do."

"Well, several times when I called upon the magic in my dark garden, I saw you. Before we'd even met, in fact."

"What was I doing?"

"Nothing. I just saw your face. But I felt as though I knew every line in your face, the timber of your voice, your likes and dislikes, even the way you'd hold me. I had a sense that what I felt would come to be."

"We were lovers," he said, his voice taut with reckless longing. It gnawed on her, too, and she looked down at her hands, wondering how they could talk so generally about something that rocked them both to the core.

Before them, the groom cleared his throat and made a study of concentrating on his driving.

"Is that why we have to remain close? Because Fate had decreed we would become lovers?" he asked.

"That, and more. In my vision, I also had a sense you'll save me from disaster."

"I've already saved you from disaster."

"I know." Lashes lowered, she pleated her gown with her fingers. "But I think you might actually save my life at some point. We must stay close so I might avoid death."

Eyes narrowed, Richard shook his head. "Sounds like rubbish to me. But let's assume for a moment 'tis true. Do you mean to say that the only reason we must remain close is so I might have a chance to rescue you?"

"I know it sounds like I'm using you, and perhaps at first, I had been. But something has changed for me since I've come to Clairmont Hall." Her voice grew soft. "I've learned more about you, Richard. I've seen your suffering and playfulness. I sense a good heart within you and I've decided I'm not going to allow you to risk yourself for me."

Instead, she silently reasoned, she would rely on herself and the magic in the dove, and do her level best to keep him out of it. *If* Fate allowed her to.

Lucinda stared into hazel eyes softened with an emotion she couldn't identify.

"And what if I wish to risk myself for you?" he asked.

"I'll see that you don't."

The phaeton passed beneath the arch that read, "Fortress on the Ford" and entered Somerton. They turned left at the butter market and continued down High Street past the Old Guildhall. Painted signs hung over the storefronts, their colors bright, the lettering crisp. Beneath the roof of a red barn, a blacksmith pounded away on an anvil, his arms glowing with sweat, his face set. Sparks flew and the sound of a hammer striking metal underscored the occasional raucous laugh from the Tempest Tavern.

In the distance, she espied St. Paul's arched windows and spire. Determination stiffened her posture.

She would start to convince Richard of the peril they faced here and now.

She placed a hand on Richard's arm. "May we visit St. Paul's Church?"

"It's a dusty old building with little to recommend it," he said. "Why would you want to stop there?"

"I'm curious. The Drakewycks possess a very old book, a family heirloom passed down through the generations. This book mentions a woman who died in Somerton centuries ago, and I want to confirm her existence. Since we are passing by St. Paul's, I thought now a good time to check the parish register—unless you are pressed for time, of course."

"What is this book, a Bible?"

" 'Tis a spellbook called *Goetia*."

Shaking his head, Richard tapped their driver on the shoulder and asked him to pull the carriage to a halt outside St. Paul's. Once they'd stopped, he slipped out of the carriage and handed Lucinda down. Together they entered the church.

Candles, fixed in sconces, threw diffused light into the cavernous interior and brought a glow to the jeweled windows. Up in the balcony, the lugubrious tones of Bach's Toccata and Fugue in D Minor burst from a pipe organ. Other than the organist, the church appeared empty.

Lucinda and Richard walked toward the stairs to the left of a velvet-draped lectern. Incense spouted from a silver brazier, tickling her nose. Just as they reached the stairs, Bach's masterpiece died away, replaced by the reverent silence common to houses of worship.

"Who is this person you wish to investigate?" Richard murmured.

Before Lucinda could reply, Reverend Wood hurried down to greet them, a skeletal man whose simply cut black attire emphasized his bony physique. "Captain Clairmont. And Miss Drakewyck, too. I spied you from the balcony. What brings you to St. Paul's so early in the day?" A deep basso, his voice erupted from his thin throat.

" 'Tis not a matter of faith, but one of scholarly interest," she said, smiling to ease his worry. "I was hoping I might examine the parish register. I read a strange story and my curiosity has gotten the better of me. I simply must learn if it's fact or fiction."

"What an odd coincidence. You are the second person within the space of a week who wished to look at the parish register."

"Oh?" Lucinda tried not to look concerned.

"Why, yes. Miss Morgan visited not three days ago and descended into the cellar to view its entries. She emerged looking quite pale, I must say." Reverend Wood's eyebrows drew together. "What is your strange story about?"

"A woman named Morgana Fey," Lucinda said, surprise resonating in the pit of her stomach. Faye was one step ahead of her, and Lucinda didn't find the knowledge comforting. "She lived in the sixteenth century. 'Tis said she was a witch, and yet, I understand not a single witch trial was ever held in Somerton. I must find out if she really existed."

The clergyman nodded reluctantly. "Where did you read this story?"

"In our family Bible," she said, feeling Richard stiffen beside her. "It contains an entry penned by Edward Drakewyck that concerns Morgana Fey."

"How interesting. Was Edward not the first vicar of Somerton?"

"Yes, he was."

"I would enjoy looking at the entry, Miss Drake-wyck, should you find the time to share it with me."

"I will at first opportunity," she promised.

He responded with a generous smile. "The staircase to the right will take you to the cellar. Call if you need assistance."

Lucinda thanked the man and pulled Richard down a series of musty stone steps. Sconces lit their passage, throwing just enough light to reveal spiders in the eaves.

"Your family Bible, hmm?" he remarked as they stopped in a dusty room which harbored a number of bookshelves and a glowing lantern hanging from a hook in the ceiling. "You Drakewycks are an odd lot."

A spare wooden table and chair sat in the corner, and atop the table, a large, handwritten book lay open. Ignoring him, she grabbed the lantern from the hook and placed it next to the parish register.

She turned the wick up and began to page through the register.

> Emmylou Peters b. Sept. 1854
> father—Colin Peters b. 1832
> mother—Rose Peters (nee Williams) b. 1836
> Daniel Osier m. Beatrice White Jan. 1855

The entries continued down both sides of the paper, recording Somerton's most recent births, deaths, marriages, and baptisms.

Richard peered at the scrawling print. "If this Morgana Fey lived in the sixteen hundreds, you ought to turn to the beginning of the register."

She started to turn the pages backward, sifting through the years. "Isn't it unusual, Richard, how the names Morgana Fey and Faye Morgan sound so alike?"

He shrugged. "I knew a Joseph Warren in the Army. He could have easily passed as Warren Joseph."

"Has Faye remembered anything of her past?"

"Not yet." Eyebrows drawn together, Richard examined the page she'd paused on. "You're still in the mid-eighteenth century."

She pushed a stray tendril of hair away from her face and continued to turn pages, inching toward the front of the book. For several minutes they pored over the scrawling ink, finding nothing of value.

"Didn't you think Faye's speech strangely antiquated when she first awoke from the bump on her head?" Lucinda asked, trying for a casual note.

"Hmm?"

"Faye's speech," she pressed. "I thought she sounded rather antiquated when she first began to speak."

"I didn't notice. Oddly enough, my father said he thought her dress looked antiquated, too."

"Does he still have the dress?" she asked quickly, and realized she sounded too eager. Giving him an easy smile, she hefted a substantial chunk of pages, moving toward Somerton's earliest entries.

"I imagine the servants burned it. Mud had ruined the dress."

She stopped turning in midstream and stared at him. "Mud, did you say?"

"From the accident," he added.

The smell of mud, Lucinda thought, seemed to cling to Faye, as though she wore it as perfume. "Why do you suppose Faye came here to read the parish register, and then grew pale?"

"You're asking a lot of questions about Faye. What's wrong?"

She shrugged. "Nothing in particular."

He didn't look convinced. "Perhaps she was hoping to jog her memory by looking through family names, but on finding nothing, grew discouraged."

"No doubt you're right." Lips pursed, she reached the front of the register. One of the very first entries listed a man bearing the last name Fey.

Christopher Fey. b. Sept. 1563

"I wonder if he's related," Lucinda said.

"What does it matter? If this Morgana Fey existed, we would have found an entry for her. I think we can assume Edward Drakewyck's tale is fiction." He stood up and squared his shoulders in the manner of a man ready to move on.

"One moment, Richard. I may have discovered her," she said, the name Morgana catching her eye.

Christopher Fey m. Morgana Duchard Sept. 1583

Lucinda tapped the book with one finger. "Interesting. This could be her. Edward's entry in our Bible was dated 1593. This entry is in the right range. She might have married someone who lived in Somerton."

"What exactly did Edward write that aroused your interest so?"

"Only that she was a witch and he had put an end to her. He considered his entry a warning to those who would come. He was afraid Morgana might rise again to hurt his descendents."

"Are you serious?" Richard raised his gaze heavenward. "Another crackbrain. I don't think this is worth pursuing further."

She glanced at him from beneath her lashes. "Edward Drakewyck's warning encompassed the Clairmont family too."

"My family?" Richard shook his head. "The Drakewycks and the Clairmonts have never been more than acquaintances."

Lucinda shrugged. "That's another reason why I'm here. To find out why the Drakewycks *and* the Clairmonts felt so threatened by Morgana that Edward 'put an end to her.' "

"Let's find the record of Morgana's death," Richard said. He paged forward, stopping some ten years later, when the dates started showing 1593. They found her entry rather quickly.

Morgana Fey d. 1593
Under suspicious circumstances.

And below, a wide, looping signature:

— Edward Drakewyck, Vicar of Somerton

"Now that's rather unusual." Richard murmured. "If Edward admitted to putting an end to her for practicing witchcraft, doesn't list a trial in the parish register, and describes her death as suspicious, we can only assume one thing."

"That he murdered her," Lucinda whispered.

Richard nodded. "And concealed his deed to avoid prosecution."

"How ghastly."

"Indeed. But why did he risk himself? He could have tried her as a witch and had the law on his side."

"He may have had a good reason to avoid the subject of witchcraft and its trials."

Head tilted, Richard examined her.

"Perhaps," she ventured, "Edward Drakewyck practiced magic himself."

"But Edward Drakewyck was the vicar, for God's sake."

"Maybe he practiced good magic."

"Regardless of his magical orientation, what reason could he have for wanting to murder Morgana Fey?"

Lucinda shrugged. "Morgana may have practiced bad magic."

"This is nonsense." Richard stood up and ran a hand through his hair.

"Remember, the warning included the Clairmont family. To me, that suggests your ancestors were involved, too." Lucinda began turning pages again, moving to the following year. She pointed triumphantly to the page. "Look at this."

Christopher Fey d. 1594
Confessed to heresy, was relapsed, and was also
impenitent.
Convicted of murdering Morgana, his wife.
Sentenced to purging by fire.

And below the entry, Edward Drakewyck's signature.

Richard whistled, low and long. "If Edward admitted to putting an end to Morgana, he must have accused her husband of murdering her to save his own skin. And if he worried that Morgana would want revenge on the Clairmonts, then my ancestors must have been connected to this medieval mayhem in some manner. I'd say an innocent man died, all due to the machinations of our venerable great-great-great-grandpas."

"Magic corrupts," she whispered.

Richard leaned toward her. "Pardon?"

"I wonder why Christopher's witch trial wasn't made a part of Somerton history. Of legend."

"The vicar must have kept the trial secret." Richard put a hand on her arm, his touch warm and soothing. "You look pale, Lucinda. I think we should go."

She stared at the register, her gaze unfocused. A bizarre sense of ancestral responsibility washed over her and weakened her hatred for Morgana Fey. She tried to put herself in Morgana's position. The woman had been silenced through witchcraft and her husband executed after being accused of her murder. The murderers had not only walked away free but had hidden the deed from the public eye and had gone down in history as pious men.

No wonder Morgana had left this world cursing the Drakewycks and Clairmonts and promising revenge.

"I'm through here," she murmured.

"Your curiosity is satisfied at last?"

"Satisfied far too well."

12

Rain pattered softly against the glazed window-panes of Langford's Book Shop, muting conversation and deepening the gloom between the rows of book-shelves. Richard idly selected a volume entitled *History of England* and thumbed through the pages, more interested in the woman two aisles away than the failings of Elizabeth I.

She had paused by the works of Henry Fielding, her brown hair slipping from its hasty chignon to tease the back of her neck. Not a bow or flounce adorned her blue paisley dress, which hung limply from her waist, as if she'd forgotten petticoats. Her only frivolity—a scrap of lace nestled in the silken space between her breasts—seemed almost an after-thought, a hurried attempt to bring her appearance to order.

Eyebrows drawn together, she ran one slender hand across the books, her fingers long and delicate. When one of Langford's spiders spun its way down from the dusty eaves and landed on her sleeve, she set it gently on a bookshelf. It seemed even insects were deserving of Lucinda's compassion.

Richard felt worry gnaw at him. The shock she'd received in St. Paul's an hour earlier—that their ancestors had murdered and covered it up—seemed to have done her in, although why, he couldn't quite fathom. After all, it had happened centuries earlier. She acted as if it had happened yesterday. And where had she been leading him with those questions about Faye Morgan?

Head tilted, she examined the titles on the shelf, and suddenly gripped a burgundy edition, a playful smile curving her lips. Even from his distant position, he read the words *Tom Jones* on the binding, in gold leaf. Wincing, he recalled Fielding's bawdy tale about a young lad who couldn't quite keep his trousers on.

He closed *History of England* with a snap. He had a lot in common with Tom Jones lately. She'd turned him inside out with her smiles and talk about magic and Fate. Indeed, with Lucinda around, he forgot the war and lost all restraint. He told himself he was naught but a helpless male presented with glowing white flesh he knew would fit perfectly into his palm, and lips whose laughter promised an adventurous spirit and blissful hours of exploration.

And yet, some deeper, more instinctual part of him realized that Lucinda was different from other women. Every time they met he felt an aching awareness that escape was impossible, that he would never rest until he'd claimed her and made her his. Forever.

The door to Langford's creaked open and a wrought-iron bell tinkled. A blast of moist air cooled the shop down. Squire Piggott, as sour as a month-old pudding, with pursed lips and low brows maneuvered his bulk between the narrow doorjamb and held

it open. Carolly, smiling at the Squire, walked in behind him. She caught sight of Richard and Lucinda
and frowned.

Faye brought up the rear, dressed in a brand-new
yellow damask gown she must have sewn for herself.
Her gaze flickered over him as she adjusted her
shawl. Disquiet formed a knot in his gut. For a second, he'd caught a glimpse of diamond-hard eyes in
a granite face.

Squire Piggott allowed the door to swing shut.
" 'Tis my pleasure, ladies, to escort you to Langford's.
I shall see you at dinner over the weekend."

Carolly nodded and turned her back on him, her
gaze on the ceiling. She mouthed something Richard
knew was less than complimentary. Faye, for her part,
had not the slightest interest in the Squire. Instead,
she looked around the bookstore with an intensity
Richard thought rather odd, her regard finally settling
on Lucinda.

Squire Piggott divested himself of his black cloak.
Amid greetings from the nearby patrons, he removed
his hat, his brown hair thinning and pasted to his
scalp with a wealth of oil. He preened for a moment,
the way a man does when he desires every eye to
settle on his person, and cast a leisurely glance at
Richard.

Richard nodded.

The Squire smiled and bowed, his knees bending
in what looked like a lady's curtsey. When he straightened, his movements were so stiff he might have had
a rake attached to his hindquarters. He nodded at
Richard in an excess of flattery and then assessed the
rest of the bookstore's occupants.

Each step reluctant, Carolly joined her brother.
"Richard, how kind of you to bring Lucinda to Lang-

ford's to meet us." She turned toward Faye, who was hanging her umbrella on Langford's umbrella stand. "Faye, look. Richard brought Lucinda to Langford's."

Faye showed no change in expression. "Oh, what luck for us."

"Lucinda would like to assist in selecting styles and fabrics for Carolly's wardrobe," he said, struggling against the knot in his gut.

Why should Faye make him feel so uncomfortable? She'd clearly forgiven Carolly for the carriage accident. As soon as she regained her memory, she'd be on her way; and if she never regained it, Sir James would find her a situation as a dressmaker. Nevertheless, some lost part of him, shoved deep into the recesses of his mind, cried out at the strangeness of Faye, though he couldn't quite grasp what that strangeness might be.

"We could always use another opinion," Faye said, moving to join them. Her lips parted and curved in a half smile.

Her smile, Richard thought, didn't quite reach her eyes. Again that sense of peculiarity assailed him. What was it about her that set his instinct on edge?

Carolly tapped his arm. "Did you know Father invited Squire Piggott over to dine with us on Saturday? The Squire's threatened to entertain us afterward with passages from the Bible."

"Father didn't mention it."

They both studied the Squire. Mincing down the aisle, he extended a hand toward the Bibles near the window. "Ah, Langford, a wonderful selection."

His comment elicited a grunt from the bookstore owner, who was replacing books on a nearby bookshelf. "Your devotion to the Lord speaks well for you."

His eyes much like raisins in an unbaked biscuit, the Squire surveyed the room and eventually settled on Lucinda. A smile quivering on his lips, he began to ramble in her direction.

"Richard," Carolly breathed, "I do believe Squire Piggott has formed a tendre for Lucinda. Maybe that's why Father invited him to dinner. He's playing matchmaker."

Richard frowned. Sir James had overstepped his bounds if he thought to marry Lucinda off. Wasn't that George Drakewyck's obligation? In any case, the girl had a perfectly sound mind and was capable of choosing her own husband. He was going to have a talk with his father about this as soon as an opportunity presented itself.

His thoughts charged onward, growing more heated as he considered his father's interference in Lucinda's life when suddenly he felt Faye's gaze on him, seeking, questioning.

He returned her stare, seeing only emptiness in her ice-blue eyes. And yet, he had a hunch that a fire burned within her, one so hot it might melt them all.

He mentally shook himself. Lucinda and her magic talk were getting to him.

Carolly pouted. "It isn't fair that we should all suffer so Lucinda might catch a husband."

"I doubt Lucinda would have him," Richard offered.

Faye nodded in agreement. "I think Miss Drakewyck has tendencies in another direction."

Carolly's eyes widened. "How do you know? *What* do you know? Come, Faye, tell us."

"I know nothing, but my intuition tells me her heart is already taken." The blonde swiveled to look at Richard.

He cleared his throat, her intense, ice-blue stare piercing him. Suddenly he realized what it was about Faye that bothered him most.

She never seemed to blink.

"I think Lucinda is in need of rescuing," Richard said, nodding in her direction. She'd nearly bent backward in her effort to avoid Squire Piggott, who pressed far too close.

Carolly sighed impatiently. "I suppose we must rescue her, then."

With Carolly and Faye on either side of him, Richard walked to the Squire's side. "Squire, I understand you're to dine with us on the weekend."

"Yes, I am, and a great honor I consider it. Please tell your noble father that I've been looking forward to our dinner with unsurpassed happiness and anticipation, even though I had to cancel an afternoon visit with Lady Rothfield at her estate."

The Squire focused on Lucinda. "I'm pleased to tell you, Miss Lucinda, that your aunt is in the most excellent of health, and gives her blessings to our—"

"Oh, Squire Piggott," Lucinda exclaimed, "I'm feeling faint and in need of something cool. Please, fetch me a glass of water."

"At once, Miss Lucinda." The Squire, his brow drawn with lines of concern, charged off in search of a glass.

Carolly succumbed to a fit of giggles. "Better you than me, Lucinda."

Even as she fanned herself, Lucinda eyed Carolly with a raised eyebrow. "Take care, Carolly, for once he realizes I am unavailable, he may turn toward you."

"Oh, Lord, no."

Lucinda focused on their blonde houseguest. "Hello, Faye."

Faye nodded. "Lucinda."

Richard heard the enmity in their voices and wondered if the carriage accident still stood between them. He observed the two women for a moment and studied their differences. Faye's gown of yellow damask far outshone any other woman's attire, including Lucinda's, and attracted the attention of every male in the vicinity. He seemed the only one unable to feel the pull of her earthy beauty.

Far more to his taste, Lucinda was simplicity itself, with neither silk nor paint to enhance her demeanor. Candlelight from a sconce—lit in deference to the gloomy day—sparked molten highlights in her cinnamon brown hair, while her soft, full lips pouted at him, as if begging for a kiss. And those eyes held a golden promise of passion amidst brown innocence— a combination irresistible to any man.

He felt an ache in the back of his throat and swallowed.

Faye eyed Lucinda with a narrow stare. "Captain Clairmont tells me you wish to help with Carolly's wardrobe. We don't really need another set of hands, but if you're determined, you may join us this afternoon in the salon. We're embroidering the edges of Carolly's new petticoats."

"Embroidery? What a happy thought." Lucinda took a deep breath and let it out slowly. "Shall we convene directly after lunch?"

"The sooner we begin, the sooner we'll finish," Faye said. She touched Carolly's arm. "Carolly and I have had a busy morning and need to rest before lunch. We should go. Good day."

Carolly allowed Faye to lead her to the entrance, where Faye collected her umbrella and Carolly her shawl. Sunlight, Richard saw, had broken through the clouds and banished the rain. Faye and Carolly's imminent departure had a similar effect on his mood. A great sense of relief washed over him.

The little bell above the door tinkled and a young matron hustled in, an infant dressed in a lacy white gown held in her arms. Richard recognized her as one of George Drakewyck's tenants.

Carolly paused in putting on her shawl and cooed in delight. "Good day, Mrs. Biddow." She tickled the infant under the chin. "And you too, little one."

Mrs. Biddow, a smile wreathing her plain face, hugged her baby closer. The women exchanged pleasantries for a moment, Faye offering a few brief words, and when Carolly nodded toward Richard and Lucinda, Mrs. Biddow brightened even further and hastened to their side.

Lucinda's lips curved in a generous smile. She smoothed the infant's gown. "I'm so pleased to see Sarah's feeling well. I was quite worried, you know."

"I lost at least a week's sleep when she grew ill. Dr. Bennet had given up on her. To this day, he doesn't understand why she recovered. 'Twas like magic, he said."

A tremor ran through Lucinda and her eyes moistened. Richard studied her, wondering at her reaction. Some deep emotion had evidently grabbed hold of her.

"I am overjoyed for you," she said, and Richard knew without a doubt she'd spoken from her soul. And yet, the glint in her eye suggested a certain . . . satisfaction.

A wild idea nudged at him. Had Lucinda cast some sort of magic spell over the infant, and when by coincidence the infant healed, did she consider her magic responsible? Indeed, his father had jested about Lucinda's posy healing his gout just the other morning at breakfast. He found himself smiling. He thought it rather charming, if a bit naive, that she would cast magic spells to heal those she cared for, and then take credit for their recovery, when clearly they owed their good health to Dr. Bennet.

"May I hold her?" Lucinda asked.

"Of course." Mrs. Biddow placed her infant into Lucinda's outstretched arms. She watched with a contented smile as Lucinda cuddled the babe into her breasts.

"You have a fine touch, Miss Drakewyck," the matron said.

Lucinda's cheeks grew pink.

The infant yawned once, stretched one delicate-looking arm, and fell back to sleep with a sigh. Lucinda cooed softly to her, the baby's fuzzy head nestled beneath her chin, her slender arms protecting that small body, her face glowing with such gentleness of spirit that Richard felt his throat dry up and chest tighten with some unnamed emotion. He longed to enfold them both in his arms and bury his nose in Lucinda's hair, breathing her scent in.

She looked up at him and caught his glance. Her eyes grew soft. "Would you care to hold Sarah?"

"No, I—"

Before he could complete his denial she'd placed the child in his arms.

Richard held himself perfectly still. Warmth emanated from the tiny bundle, reminding him that the miniature face he gazed down at was human, despite its perfection and delicacy. He'd never held something so fragile before and didn't know what to do. He began to perspire, aware that Mrs. Biddow was assessing them with a knowing look on her face.

Lucinda moved next to him and arranged the baby's skirts so they cascaded over his arm. Richard allowed her to fuss, feeling inept and damned uncomfortable, too.

He glanced toward the door, wishing he might escape. Carolly had already stepped outside, but Faye had paused in the doorway to look back at them. A frown pulled her mouth downward, but it didn't hold any of the annoyance which so marked her attitude earlier.

She looked sad, he thought. Ineffably so.

Lucinda, too, glanced toward Faye, her eyes growing shadowed.

"You three look well thus," Mrs. Biddow said, breaking the spell. Faye spun around and left the bookshop while Lucinda returned her attention to Richard and the baby.

Richard handed the baby back to her mother with alacrity.

"She won't bite you," Lucinda teased.

"I'm unfamiliar with infants."

"Have you no babies in the Clairmont family?"

"None at all."

As Mrs. Biddow watched this exchange, her smile grew wider. "You will soon," she predicted. Before either he or Lucinda could react, the matron curtseyed to them both. " 'Tis good to see you in town again, Captain Clairmont. Good day, Miss Drakewyck."

Richard nodded while Lucinda smoothed the baby's skirt one last time. The matron moved off with her small charge, leaving him alone with Lucinda.

They faced each other. Lucinda's lips twitched and her eyes gleamed as she regarded him, the look faintly challenging. He cleared his throat, unable to find anything sensible to say though feeling the pressure to do so. The moment stretched uncomfortably until Richard remembered that she'd said she wanted to find a certain book.

He gestured toward the bookshelves. "What book were you looking for?"

She blinked with the air of someone jolted from a daydream. "Anything on Somerton history. We know now that Christopher Fey, Morgana's husband, was accused of witchcraft. I want to see if I can find mention of his execution elsewhere."

"Why don't we ask Langford? He might know." Richard noted the Squire heading in their direction, a glass of water in his hand. He clasped Lucinda's arm and drew her through the aisles, earning a wide-eyed stare from her.

"Squire Piggott has tracked you down again," he murmured.

She pressed a hand against her mouth to stifle her laughter. When she could speak, she lowered her voice to a whisper. "The Squire is persistent."

"To a fault."

They wound their way through dusty old tomes and back to the front of the store and Langford. The bookstore owner, his blue eyes faded and hair gone almost completely gray, engaged in idle chitchat until Lucinda finally brought him around to the purpose of her visit.

"Mr. Langford, do you have any books on Somerton history?"

"Plenty of them. You'll find them two aisles back from where you were standing with Mrs. Biddow. Let me show you." He took her arm, but Lucinda hung back.

"I'm looking for books that describe Somerton's history in the sixteenth century," she qualified.

"Oh." The old man released her and, arms clasped behind his back, rocked back and forth on his heels. After several moments of rocking he settled down and regarded her dolefully. "That will prove more difficult, Miss Drakewyck. Somerton was founded in the mid-fifteen hundreds. I don't believe anyone thought of it as a town until 1650 or later. Can you be more specific? Perhaps another book . . ."

"I understand Christopher Fey was prosecuted in a witch trial in 1594. I find it unusual that after living my entire life in this town I've discovered this fact only now. Have you heard of Christopher Fey's trial, Mr. Langford?"

"Indeed I have. But you're correct, it wasn't a well-known event. The monastery who owned the parish at the time tried and executed him quietly. I don't know why, and I suspect time has erased most of the details. Even so, Donald Mallory thinks the church had something to hide."

"Donald Mallory? Why, he's an old friend of my uncle's."

Langford nodded. "He's also related to the Feys. He traced his ancestry all the way back to Christopher Fey's sister and made a study of the trial. If you want to know about Christopher Fey, he'd be the best one to ask."

Lucinda turned to Richard. "Do you have time? Shall we go visit him now?"

Something about her attitude seemed too eager for him. "Lucinda, I think it best I take you home. It's been an eventful morning."

"You're right." Her shoulders drooped. "I've done enough for one day. Donald Mallory will have to wait."

Richard couldn't prevent a sigh of relief. She'd gone pale at their discoveries in the parish register. What would additional revelations through Donald Mallory do to her? "I'll take you home."

$\mathscr{13}$

$\mathcal{L}$ucinda fluffed her skirts of violet *crêpe de chine* and examined her reflection in the looking glass. Hair neatly coiled, neck and throat bare, she looked rather . . . bland. With a sigh she turned from the glass and headed toward her bedchamber door. Why should she care? Indeed, she ought to feel happy she looked less than attractive. Squire Piggott was coming to dinner tonight, and heaven knew she didn't want to excite his attentions. Their other guest—her own dear uncle George—didn't care a fig for style and would be happy to see her no matter what she wore.

Try as she might, this line of reasoning did little to improve her mood.

She entered the hallway and wound her way through the passages toward the great staircase, her thoughts lingering on style, or the lack of it. Designs didn't filter down from London very quickly, and her gown, made in Somerton some four years ago, had the dropped sleeves and flounces of a decade earlier.

Her involvement in Carolly's wardrobe had convinced her she'd become hopelessly out of date. While embroidering petticoats with Carolly and Faye, she'd occasionally picked up the *Journal des Demoiselles*, a Parisian guide to current fashion which Faye used to help design Carolly's gowns. Each sketch had underscored her own gauche appearance.

She and the Clairmont family were scheduled to leave for London in two weeks—the Monday after Carolly's birthday party. What would Society make of her gowns?

Lucinda chewed her lower lip.

Would she even see two weeks?

Faye had been very quiet, very subdued, not at all what Lucinda had feared. She'd expected Faye to try to send them all straight to Hell at the first opportunity, but other than a few illnesses, the witch seemed to have done nothing untoward. After learning about Edward Drakewyck's perfidy in the parish register, she wondered if Faye was going to draw out this process of revenge, to make them suffer as she'd evidently suffered.

Still, tonight was the first time they'd all be in the house together—the last remaining Clairmonts and Drakewycks. If Faye wanted to take them out in one big magical explosion of revenge, this evening would be the perfect time to do it.

She reached the grand staircase and descended, wanting very much to return to her room. Ahead, Sir James stood at the door to the dining room, her uncle at his side.

Uncle George rushed forward to embrace her. He wrapped her in his arms and gave her a quick squeeze before he released her. " 'Tis good to see you, gel."

"And you, Uncle George." To her embarrassment, tears pooled in her eyes.

"None of that, now," he said, his own eyes suspiciously moist. They both took out handkerchiefs and dabbed the moisture away, then laughed.

Lucinda stepped back and studied her uncle carefully. He looked pale, she thought. She picked a strand of gray hair off his jacket, smoothed his lapels, and slipped the strand into her pocket. "Uncle, are you feeling all right?"

"I have a touch of pleurisy. Makes breathing a bit difficult, but 'tis nothing serious." Eyes narrowed, he spoke quickly, his voice so low only she could hear. "By the way, I met the poor woman you and Carolly ran over several days ago. Gave me quite a start, she did. You could have warned me, gel. Indeed, you could have told me that Morgana Fey was recuperating in Clairmont Hall *before* you sought my permission to become Carolly's companion."

"I knew you'd never let me go if I told you about Faye," she whispered and started to turn toward Sir James.

Uncle George gripped her arm. " 'Twas poorly done, gel. I've half a mind to bring you home with me tonight."

"No, I won't go. Faye and I haven't clashed yet, and I can watch her more closely from here. We have to stop whispering," she hissed, then smiled at Sir James, who regarded them with a raised eyebrow. "Sir James, haven't you been suffering from pleurisy too?"

Sir James' mouth curved in a weak smile. "For a week now."

Faye, Lucinda thought. She tried to summon the same sort of anger toward Faye she'd felt before the trip to St. Paul's Church, but she understood the witch too well, now. Even so, her blood grew cold at the thought of losing Uncle George to Faye's illness. She silently vowed to cast another spell on both Sir James' and Uncle George's behalf at her first opportunity.

Sir James took her arm. "I feared you weren't coming. We've already sat down to dinner."

"I'm sorry, Sir James. I overslept." Heat flooded her cheeks at this tiny lie, for in truth she'd rustled through her gowns, hoping that one might prove satisfactory. She'd ended up disappointed and late.

He waved her apology aside and led her into the dining room, Uncle George firmly attached to her other arm. They stopped before the mahogany table that ran the length of the room. Fruits tumbled in studied disarray from a centerpiece which dominated the table, and fine bone china glittered beneath a wealth of candles glowing in a chandelier.

Squire Piggott and Richard stood as soon as she entered, both dressed in almost identical evening attire. Nevertheless, they looked quite different. While Richard's cravat was snowy white and perfectly tied, Squire Piggott's sat askew on his neck. Where Richard's jacket hugged his broad shoulders, Squire Piggott's hemmed his spare flesh in. Richard nodded briefly in her direction, and the Squire bowed at the waist and knees, in an excessive display of courtliness.

She sensed interest in both their gazes and froze for a moment, first wishing she had a new dress, then feeling glad she didn't, and finally settling on a smile of amusement at herself.

Faye and Carolly sat on either side of the table. They both wore pleasant expressions, but Lucinda thought she detected a shadow in Carolly's gaze. She glanced lower, noting her tidy hair and tailored gown and felt a surge of satisfaction. At least she'd talked the girl into taking more care of her appearance.

Concern replaced her satisfaction when she noticed that the girl had her hands twined so tightly her knuckles showed white.

Eyebrow raised, Lucinda took a seat as far from Squire Piggott as she could manage. The men sat down afterward: Sir James at the head of the table, Richard at the foot, Uncle George at her left, and Squire Piggott across from Lucinda and to the right.

Sir James glanced around the room and ended up pouring himself a glance of wine. Lucinda wondered where all the servants had gone. Usually they had at least one footman in the room with them before dinner started, pouring wine, pushing in chairs, and arranging napkins.

"My dear Miss Lucinda," Squire Piggott said in loud tones, "how delightful you look tonight."

"Thank you, Squire."

Carolly muffled a groan.

Sir James took a sip from his wineglass and grunted, evidently satisfied with the wine's bouquet. He rang a small bell. Carolly took a sip from her own wineglass—to steady her nerves, Lucinda guessed.

A clock on the side table ticked off a minute.

Sir James gave the bell another spirited ring and regarded the servants' door. Lucinda, intercepting a look between Carolly and Faye, also glanced at the door. A sense of foreboding grabbed hold of her. Richard, she noticed, studied his sister carefully.

"Miss Lucinda, I must say, I've discovered the most interesting little waterfall on my lands, and I'd be obliged if you'd come look at it, and give me your opinion," the Squire said.

Uncle George elbowed her discreetly.

Lucinda pressed a hand against her temple. "I don't know, Squire; Carolly and I have several outings planned—"

225

"Why, you must bring Miss Clairmont, and Miss Morgan too," Squire Piggott demanded, with an unctuous smile toward Faye.

Faye just stared at him.

Carolly muffled an even louder groan.

Desperation tinged the Squire's tone. "I find the thought of your company tomorrow afternoon a happy one, Miss Lucinda, and if your noble uncle and Sir James will give their consent, I'll pick all three of you young ladies up at, say, two o'clock? We can repair to my townhouse afterward for tea, and—"

"We cannot tomorrow," Carolly interrupted, her voice shrill. "Faye and I . . . that is, Faye, Lucinda, and I had planned a trip to . . ."

"The milliner's shop," Faye supplied.

"I'll join you, then." The Squire beamed at them. "I would very much enjoy a walk about town."

"But we're going to a lady's establishment." Carolly implored Sir James with her eyes. The elder Clairmont merely shrugged.

Richard, for his part, was pressing a napkin to his mouth, no doubt hiding an impudent grin, Lucinda thought.

The room grew quiet. Carolly replaced her wine goblet on the table with a clink and folded her hands.

Lucinda felt she must fill the silence before the Squire threatened them with another outing. She glanced sidelong at Faye, then turned to Sir James. "I must say, our two families get along quite happily. 'Tis a pity that we've allowed so many years to pass without becoming more than acquaintants."

"Indeed." Sir James smiled benevolently at her.

"How can it be, that we've lived side by side for almost two hundred years and we've never done much more than nod to each other?"

Faye leaned forward, tense, but then she slouched, in the manner of someone who wanted to say something but had thought the better of it.

"I believe our families were fast friends at one time," the elder Clairmont said. "When I was a boy, I found a portrait of my ancestor, Henry Clairmont, and his wife. According to the scrawl on the back of the portrait, Edward Drakewyck had the portrait commissioned for the newly married couple as a wedding present. To me, such a present is indicative of a deep friendship."

Lucinda nodded, Sir James' explanation confirming her earlier theory in St. Paul's. When Edward put an end to Morgana Fey, he'd had Henry Clairmont's help. Both families had earned Morgana's enmity.

She glanced at Richard. He nodded briefly, indicating that he'd come to the same conclusions.

"I'd like to see this portrait, if I may," Faye said, her vehemence surprising them all. Uncle George started in his chair while Sir James observed her with widened eyes. Lucinda felt a chill creep over her while Richard's gaze grew sharp.

"I haven't seen the portrait for many years. It might have been discarded. I'll check for you after dinner," Sir James said. "If we *have* dinner." He pulled out his watch fob. "Whatever could have happened to the servants? I haven't seen Hilton for at least an hour."

"Perhaps Cook is about," Carolly offered, a tremble in her voice.

Sir James dropped the watch, letting it dangle from his waistcoat, and shook the bell back and forth.

Lucinda felt her insides tighten with alarm.

Without warning, the servants' door burst open and a small, round woman rushed through, her white mobcap askew on gray curls, her generous bosom heaving with strong emotion. "Oh, sir," she panted, wringing her hands, "I fear an illness has struck the staff."

"An illness?" The elder Clairmont's lips parted. "Speak plainly, Liz. What has happened?"

"I'm afraid I've no one to serve you but myself," she revealed. "A peculiar indigestion has felled all who took tea at four o'clock."

Lucinda shot a glance toward Carolly. The girl shifted in her chair as though someone had filled the cushion with nettles. The feeling of foreboding clutching at Lucinda mounted to one of horror. She remembered her missing supply of saltpeter.

No. Carolly couldn't have.

"Over sixty servants work for me, Liz. Every single one is ill?"

Liz visibly swallowed. " 'Tis the truth, sir. Only the stable hands escaped, but they never drink tea."

He stood. "I'll send for the physician."

"No, no, sir, sit down. Dr. Bennet has already come and gone. He prescribed an evening's rest."

"Already gone?" Sir James plopped down into his chair. "God willing, something like this will never happen again. But if it does, see that I am the first to know."

Liz nodded, her jowls trembling. "Yes, sir." She hustled back through the servants' door.

Carolly sighed, her manner one of studied remorse. "Well, I suppose we shall have to cancel dinner for the evening, and sup in our rooms."

"Outrageous," Sir James declared.

The Squire shook his head. "Upon my word, I've never heard the like of it. I invite all of you back to my own townhouse for a quick repast."

Carolly shook her head. "No, we couldn't intrude with such little notice."

Nodding, Sir James removed his napkin from his lap. "I hope you'll forgive us for inviting you over to dinner and then sending you home with an empty stomach."

"Miss Lucinda, you and your uncle must come back to my townhouse with me." The Squire bowed his head and smiled. "Indeed, my door is open to you at all times. 'Tis my fondest wish that soon you will call my humble abode home. You lend such an air of feminine elegance to those plain walls that I scarce know how I will wait until we are—"

"I'll help Cook," Lucinda blurted out. She pulled her napkin from her lap, threw it onto the table, and jumped to her feet. "We will all eat here. Now."

She felt Richard's regard on her, his lips curled at the corners, eyes sparkling. Lucinda realized that he knew exactly what had prompted her offer and the knowledge afforded him endless amusement.

Sir James was on his feet in an instant. "Miss Lucinda. You'll do no such thing. Yours is not a servant's place here."

"Lucinda *is* my paid companion," Carolly offered, wide-eyed.

Squire Piggott drew in a sharp breath. He dropped the glass of wine he'd been holding in his left hand. The glass thumped harmlessly against the table but created a blood-red stain on the cloth.

Scowling, her father spoke through clenched teeth. "That was poor of you, Carolly."

Carolly shrugged. "But she is."

"Miss Drakewyck," the Squire whispered. "I had no idea."

Uncle George cleared his throat. "Now, Squire Piggott, she's not collecting wages. Instead Sir James has created a trust fund for her—"

"A paid companion," the Squire breathed.

Lucinda lifted her chin. "I'm going to help Cook."

Richard stood as well. "Sit down, Lucinda. I'll help Cook. I also suggest we have the pots left from the afternoon tea examined. We need to find the cause of this illness."

Carolly turned a shade paler.

Lucinda stepped away from the table. Under no circumstance would she sit there and suffer beneath Squire Piggott's shocked and accusing glares. "I want to help."

"All right, we'll both serve dinner."

Sir James leaned back in his chair. "Now this should prove interesting."

Lucinda turned and made for the servants' door, reserving a smile for Richard, one only he could see.

He winked back.

Feeling the weight of several stares, she made her way into the kitchen at Richard's side.

A large pine worktable dominated the kitchen, bearing a mess of vegetables, cuts of meat, bowls filled with sauces, a basket of eggs, and covered silver platters. An open range took up one wall, complete with a drip pan, cauldron, and kettle, while a shelf of copper pots and molds covered most of another. Liz, bent over a plate warmer stationed near the range, looked up when they entered.

"Mr. Richard! And Miss Lucinda." Liz wiped her forehead with a corner of her apron. "I'll have your dinner out to you shortly. There's much to do and I must watch the oven for the moment."

"We're here to help," Richard said. "Direct me to the dishes, and I'll bring them into the dining room."

Liz rocked back on her heels. "I've never heard the like."

"We do it gladly," Lucinda insisted. "We'll get through this night. You'll see."

"And when will you two eat?"

"Afterward. We'll sup right here," Lucinda said, indicating the pine worktable.

Liz shook her head slowly. "All right. I'll not turn away help. We'll begin with the pheasant consommé. If you start to feel tired, Miss, please tell me. I'll not have you dumping food into the master's lap."

"Give me the heavy dishes." Richard surveyed the covered platters on the pine worktable. "Which one is the pheasant consommé?"

"This one, Mr. Richard." A tentative smile curving her plump lips, the cook pointed to a platter, then skirted around Lucinda and began arranging silverware.

Lucinda selected an apron from the back of a chair while Richard draped a white towel over his arm. She grinned at him, feeling like a child playing dress-up. His own smile lit up his entire face. Co-conspirators they were, and she wanted to laugh aloud at the pleasure of it.

His grin judiciously restrained, Richard carted a tureen filled with pheasant consommé into the dining room. Lucinda followed behind him. As he stopped at each person's plate, Lucinda used a ladle to scoop consommé into his or her bowl. The room remained solemn as they made their rounds, while Sir James looked thoughtful. Squire Piggott, for his part, averted his gaze when Lucinda reached his side, his jowls quivering, likely with outrage. No doubt he was congratulating himself on avoiding a match with such an undesirable person as she.

The thought left her positively giddy.

When they paused near Uncle George, he examined her with narrowed eyes, then leaned close to her ear. "You're very clever. I hope your cleverness doesn't catch you up."

The tureen wobbled in Richard's grip.

Lucinda smothered a giggle.

At last they'd finished and made their way back into the kitchen.

Liz leaned against the table, her entire body vibrating. "How did you do?"

Richard set the tureen on the table and dropped his towel on the bench. "Wonderfully. We spilled not a single drop."

"We'll give them ten minutes, then." The cook turned over an hourglass.

"They get five." Richard fetched a glass of water for Lucinda and himself. They sat on the bench, drank their water, and laughed a little at the look on Squire Piggott's face as he'd watched Somerton's finest cart soup around the dining room and ladle it into bowls.

Too quickly their respite was over.

"What comes next?" Richard asked.

Liz scanned numerous platters, her attention settling on a smaller tureen. "Cauliflower puree."

Surveying the table with growing dismay, Lucinda frowned. "And after that?"

"Cod with egg sauce, trout, ham mousse with cucumbers, chicken, roast beef, a sorbet to clean the palate, then braised cauliflower, roast turkey, and spitchcocked eels. For dessert we're having Loundes Pudding and lemon patties."

"Good God!" Richard shook his head. "Do we eat that much every night?"

Liz looked at him with raised eyebrows and lowered chin, as if she might appeal to his common sense. "Only on nights when we're serving guests."

"Perhaps we can serve two courses at a time," Lucinda suggested. "That will certainly move the dinner along."

"The plates are very heavy," Richard said.

"You're just a little thing," Liz chimed in. "One needs a special knack—and a bit of muscle—to serve the master's dinner."

Eyes narrowed, Lucinda seized the tureen of cauliflower puree. "Let's see if you can keep up," she said to Richard as she marched into the dining room.

He quickly followed behind her with a platter of cod. Tureen balanced on one arm, Lucinda ladled puree into a fresh bowl while Richard slapped cod down onto their plates. They made their way around the table and then repaired to the kitchen. Sir James had to wipe a piece of stray cod from his sleeve, but otherwise, they'd made it through that course without mishap.

As soon as Lucinda and Richard had laid the platter and tureen on the counter near the sink, Liz sent them back into the dining room to collect the used plates and bring out fresh ones. Lucinda had to admit her arms were beginning to quiver from the strain but she'd be damned before she'd show it.

Lucinda took a deep breath. "They're ready for the next course. What do I serve?"

"Ham mousse with cucumbers," Liz informed her. "Mr. Richard can take the roast beef and chicken out. Then we bring out the sorbet and clean their palates."

Liz began to fan herself with her hand. "Can you manage it?"

"To hell with their palates," Richard said. "I'm getting hungry myself. This is the last course, Liz. Lucinda and I will bring it out and be done with the task."

"What about dessert?"

"We aren't serving dessert tonight."

"As you say, Mr. Richard." Eyes wide, the cook hustled over to a large serving tray and began to load it up with platters, muttering as she did so. "You'll take the beef, chicken, and turkey in, while Miss Lucinda brings in the remaining platter."

Lucinda lifted the lid off her dish. "This smells quite ripe. Whatever is it?"

"Spitchcocked eels over rice. One of the master's favorites. I bought them off the docks only yesterday."

A smell much like curdled eggs in bile wafted from the dish. Lucinda averted her nose. This was one dish she wouldn't even attempt to eat.

"Well, are you ready?" Richard asked, a smile playing about his lips. "One final course to go and we're done."

"I'm ready." She balanced the platter in her hands and followed him into the dining room.

Again they began their rounds. Lucinda's arms ached as she held her foul dish as far away from herself as possible. Richard didn't even bother to ask the diners if they wanted beef, turkey, or chicken; he simply slapped it onto their plates. Moisture breaking out on her brow, Lucinda dolloped gray spoonfuls of her eels with similar haste.

As they approached Sir James, he recommended that Richard avoid service of any type, as his demeanor lacked a certain respect. Richard replied not in words but in deed, pushing meat onto his father's plate in a careless manner and moving on without a backward glance.

Lucinda tried to show more decorum, but her arms ached. She feared she would shortly disgrace herself. She plopped a few eel pieces on top of Sir James' beef, noticing a button from his jacket on the floor. She kept the knowledge to herself and moved to Uncle George, and then on to the last diner, Squire Piggott.

Her face a study of dignity, she walked toward the Squire. Richard still hovered near him, evidently depositing meat on his plate. She, however, couldn't bear to wait a moment longer. She had to serve the Squire his eels immediately and rid herself of the platter or risk disaster.

She angled to the right, intending to circle around Richard and spoon the eels onto the Squire's plate. Richard finished serving his dish at precisely the same moment and bumped into her. With a muted gasp, she tipped the platter ever so slightly toward Squire Piggott. The spitchcocked eels teetered, almost righted themselves, and for one second Lucinda thought she would be saved.

Squire Piggott cried out, evidently sensing impending misfortune. The eels, as if startled by his cry, lost their battle to remain on the platter and tumbled down the front of his shirt. The serving dish clattered harmlessly to the floor.

He squealed and pushed back from the table, clawing at his shirt. "Good God!" He retched. "Miss Lucinda, look what you've done."

Sir James, fork in hand, jumped from his seat. "Dear sir, I'm so sorry."

Richard began to cough.

Faye looked from Squire Piggott to Sir James, and for one brief second Lucinda detected warmth in eyes usually so cold and measuring. Too quickly, however, the impression faded and Faye became her usual far-away self.

"Oh, Squire Piggott, I do apologize," Lucinda began, but Richard cut her off, his cough growing so violent that she feared he might choke. He grasped his platter and staggered from the dining room.

Carolly looked down at her plate. Her shoulders began to shake, and her chest convulsed, and with a start Lucinda realized Carolly was silently laughing and doing her best to hide it.

A moment later Liz hurried in, her mouth an *O* of shock. "Dear heaven, 'tis just as I feared. A little thing like Lucinda could never manage such a large platter." She began to fuss around the Squire, trying to pick pieces of eel from his shirt, but he slapped her hands away.

"Liz, please have a footman attend Squire Piggott," Sir James ordered, "if you locate one unaffected by the four o'clock tea. Why don't you resume your seat, good Squire, and we'll finish dinner as best we are able."

Instinct suggested she would be better served by a quick exit than another stumbling apology. Her face growing bright red, Lucinda followed Richard's lurching course out of the dining room, stopping only once, to scoop Sir James' button off the floor and slip it into her pocket. She found Richard sitting at the kitchen table, his eyes streaming, shoulders shaking.

She plopped down next to him, her arms weak and stomach roiling, and glared at him. But his mirth was contagious, and soon they were both laughing like fools and leaning into each other. At the feel of him so close beside her, her heart began to thud against her ribs. For one precious moment nothing mattered—not Squire Piggott, not her vision, not even Faye—and she imagined a future stretching out before them, one filled with warmth and happiness.

She wondered if that future would ever be hers.

14

The day of Carolly's birthday dinner dawned with cloudless skies, promising not only pleasant weather but good fortune for the girl. Two weeks had passed since the disastrous dinner with Squire Piggott, fourteen short days in which Richard had slowly emerged from his cave of war thoughts like a bear emerging from hibernation. The north wing had improved apace with his temperament, but to her regret, they'd had little time together since Richard spent most of his time repairing his former prison.

Lucinda's breakfast with Sir James, Carolly, and Faye had been a hurried affair as all the servants were busy preparing for the party. Richard, as usual, had occupied himself with renovations and planned to take all his meals in the north wing. Lucinda promptly decided she'd bring him a picnic lunch and some reading material to distract him.

First, however, she had other business to attend to. Faye continued to cast her spells of illness, and Lucinda continued to cast her spells of health. They were deep in a silent, unacknowledged war of magic, and

Lucinda wondered how long it would continue. What exactly did Faye have in store for them?

Over the last few weeks, Lucinda had tried to corner Faye, but the witch never seemed to be alone. She suspected Faye surrounded herself with people as protection against the crystal dove, knowing Lucinda wouldn't use the statue and endanger others.

Lucinda went to her trunk, lifted the lid, and pulled out several jars of herbs and two empty blue cloth bags. In each bag, she placed a clove of garlic, a pinch of eucalyptus, two pinches of sage, one of saffron, and a few dried spearmint leaves.

As she sewed up the open ends of the bags, she visualized the faces of her uncle and Sir James, murmuring, "Heal his lungs and heart from pain, make his body well again."

Breathing evenly, she closed her eyes and let herself relax. The stone beneath her feet, the cool air of her bedchamber, the warmth of the sun angling through the windows . . . all these things she concentrated on until her mind began to drift toward the dark garden. She called upon its magic to help Sir James and Uncle George, and felt the magic's weak reply.

Sighing, she put those aside and laid Sir James' button and Uncle George's strand of hair on her bed. First, she thought, the button.

She selected a tiny needle and a piece of blue silk thread from her trunk, threaded the button and tied a knot around it.

"Wound and bound, his sickness dies, before these words of will it flies."

She tied another knot around the button. "Holding, binding sickness tight, it shrivels beneath magic's might."

She put the button onto a square of black velvet, pulled the edges together to form a bag, and tied the top with another piece of blue silk thread. Again she invoked her magic and noted its tentative response. The bag she placed at the very bottom of her trunk, right next to Richard's Victoria Cross.

She had one final spell to accomplish, that of disease transference for Uncle George. On her bed sat a platter of bread and butter, one she'd brought back with her from breakfast. She buttered the bread, placed Uncle George's hair on it, and folded the edges over. Mouth puckered in a moue of distaste, she put the bread into her pocket and went in search of Samson, the hound.

She'd cured warts by rubbing potatoes on them and burying the potato in the backyard, and dog-bite infections by obtaining a hair of the dog who'd bitten. Likewise, if she could induce Samson to eat the bread, Samson would cough once or twice and both the dog and Uncle George would end up perfectly healthy.

She descended the grand staircase and made her way to the kitchen, where Samson often lolled about, looking for scraps.

Inside, morning sunshine streamed through the kitchen windows, turning the copper pots to a blaze of orange and warming Lucinda's skin.

Liz stood near a pot of broth near the hearth. She dropped a pinch of herbs into the broth and moved toward the oven. Sweat had already begun to darken her chignon to gray. "Good morning, Miss Lucinda. What can I do for you?"

Lucinda selected a scone from the table and took a bite. "Two things, Liz. First, I need a picnic basket for later this afternoon. I'm going to bring it to the Captain. He's holed up in the north wing, renovating. I want to make sure he eats."

"Of course. I'll have it ready for, say, two o'clock?"

"That would be fine."

Liz overturned a pan fresh from the stove. Several golden scones fell onto the pine worktable. "I thought I saw Mr. Richard on the grounds a little while ago. He may have taken a break from his work."

Lucinda hoped he hadn't decided to take a walk with Samson. She needed the dog. "Have you seen Samson, Liz?"

The cook's brows drew together. "Out in the stables, I think. When he isn't in here begging for scraps, he's pestering the horses. Why Sir James tolerates that hound, I'll never know."

Lucinda glanced at all of the golden scones lying on the table and inspiration struck. "May I take a few of these scones, Liz? I'd like to have them in case I run into the Captain."

Liz nodded and piled a few into a checkered napkin. She tied the ends and handed the bundle to Lucinda. "I hope you find him. He'll be lucky if you do."

Lucinda fought back a grin and left the kitchen, bundle clutched in one arm. She found the path to the stables, a winding gravel roadway that led straight through a grove of trees, and started walking. Tall oaks swayed above her, stirred in the light summer breeze, and acorns littered the path beneath her feet. She breathed in the smell of freshly scythed grass and rich earth, and tried to imagine Richard's expression when he discovered her in the north wing again, this time with a lunch basket and *Goetia* in her arms.

In the distance, someone laughed.

Hearty male laughter coming from the stables.

And followed by girlish squeals.

Lucinda slowed her step.

The stables loomed ahead, their brick walls covered with ivy and wooden timbers sporting leather bridles, crops, and saddles in various states of polish. Wax and an old rag sat nearby. Hay puffed from one of the half doors.

She stemmed a surge of annoyance. Evidently one of the stablehands had tumbled a willing maidservant. She wished the couple had chosen someplace a little more private. How could she find Samson without interrupting their antics?

"Hello," she called out, hoping to alert them to her presence.

More giggling and laughter.

"Hello!"

The two in the stall suddenly became quiet. Then more laughter pealed out, even louder than before, followed by a "Shh."

She paused, wondering if she ought to choose another time, but then, within the depths of the building she espied Samson, rooting around in the straw. The sooner she coaxed the dog to eat the bread, the sooner Uncle George would feel better.

The memory of her uncle's gray pallor firmly fixed in her mind, she maneuvered her way into the stables, straw catching in her lace hem as she walked past the stalls. Horses whickered and blew at her through their nostrils. She ignored them, listening for the couple, wanting to avoid them while cornering Samson.

The dog, apparently sensing her approach, looked up from his snuffling. His tail began to wag. Her steps slowed, for the voices, although hushed, were nevertheless increasing in volume.

She made gestures to the dog, trying to induce him to follow her. Samson ignored her, instead slipping into a stall he apparently found much more interesting. She couldn't see inside the small cubicle. Even though the door—made of solid wood on the bottom and wooden bars on the top—stood partially open, it blocked her view. She sidled up to the entrance, worked up her nerve, and peeked around the stall door.

Carolly, her bodice gaping and her eyes as wide as a poached salmon's, huddled beneath the straw, while a stablehand tucked his shirt into his breeches, his face stark white. Samson lay nearby in the straw, his tongue hanging out of his mouth in a doggy smile.

Lucinda choked back a gasp.

"I thought 'twas Faye coming," Carolly whispered, peeking up at her. Dirt smudged her elfin features.

Lucinda narrowed her eyes. If Faye knew about Carolly's indiscretion, she must have promoted it as well. Anyone with Carolly's best interests at heart would have done their utmost to stop this relationship immediately.

"Carolly, I cannot begin to tell you how ill-advised your meetings with, er, Mr.—"

"Josh Smith," the lad supplied, his voice trembling.

"How ill-advised these assignations with Mr. Smith are," Lucinda finished. "Do you realize what you risk? You could be cut from polite society and shunned for the rest of your life. If either your father or brother were to discover this, their hearts would break; you would most definitely lose their respect. In short, Carolly, if word of your affair with Mr. Smith were to become public, you would be completely ruined."

She turned to the stablehand. "And you, sir, are beyond contempt, luring an innocent young girl into such doings. What have you to say for yourself?"

"I love her," he croaked.

Lucinda sighed.

Carolly angled to her feet, her gaze darting from left to right. Lucinda noted she didn't make a similar declaration. "Are you going to tell Father?"

"Please, Miss," the stablehand said, his eyes as dark as bruises, "don't tell the master. He'll sack me for sure and my mum and sisters will go hungry."

"If you're worried about your mum and sisters, why were you embracing your employer's daughter?"

The lad rubbed his eyes. Lucinda thought he looked ready to cry.

"Rearrange yourself, Carolly," she ordered. She spared a severe glance for the stablehand. "You as well. And see that you leave Miss Clairmont alone."

The lad scuttled away.

Lucinda advanced on Carolly and began to pull the straw from her hair and smooth her skirts.

Carolly fussed with her bodice, returning it to order. "I'm so sorry, Lucinda."

"Are you?" A hundred criticisms rushed to her lips, but she kept her mouth firmly closed until the stablehand had disappeared from sight.

"Well, if Father hadn't canceled my tour of the Continent and taken away every last bit of joy from my life—"

"Carolly! Your father canceled your tour because he wanted you to know he considered your carriage race a very serious transgression. Evidently you're bent on additional ruination despite the lessons of that day."

"Who are you to scold me, Lucinda?"

"I'm not scolding you," she began, then took a deep breath and started over. "Well, yes, I'm scolding you, but only because I want you to be happy, Carolly. You're too young to spoil yourself without experiencing more of the world."

"Father treats me like a child. I don't think he'll ever change. He won't even let me drink champagne!"

Lucinda stifled a sigh. The girl wanted to grow up too quickly without realizing that adulthood brought responsibilities which her childlike shoulders couldn't yet bear. "Hasn't he allowed Faye to provide you with a new wardrobe?"

"Yes, yes, but he picks the most demure of styles. I'll still appear the schoolgirl."

"I thought your gowns tasteful."

"I think them stodgy."

"Well, we'll go over them again and see if we can give them a bit more polish."

Carolly's eyes brightened. "I would like that very much."

"If you can just hold on for another few weeks," Lucinda urged, "things will change drastically, I assure you. You'll be presented at Court, and men will begin to call, and if you play your cards right you'll soon have some rich duke sprawled at your feet, begging for your hand in marriage. But first I must ask you a delicate question. Have you and Mr. Smith . . . that is, did you and he . . ."

"Did we make love?" the girl asked. "No, not yet."

"Not *ever*." Lucinda gripped her arm. "Not ever, Carolly."

A large form blotted out the light streaming from the door.

Richard strode in, elegantly clad in a navy riding coat and breeches, his stock snowy white against tanned skin, his waistcoat sporting blue embroidery. Samson frolicked to his side, apparently anticipating a walk in the woods.

Hands encased in brown kidskin gloves, he plucked a strand of hay from Carolly's hair and flashed Lucinda a curious glance. "What have you two been doing?"

Carolly frowned, then looked toward Lucinda, a silent plea in her eyes.

He examined them closely. "Well?"

"We're . . ." Lucinda hesitated, lower lip caught between her teeth. Carolly's transgression was serious indeed. If she told Richard what she'd learned, he'd likely banish the girl to the schoolroom for months to come. Such actions were guaranteed to alienate Carolly further and encourage more grievous misdeeds.

Lucinda shifted her attention to Carolly. The girl frowned, her hackles already rising in anticipation of a tussle. In that instant, she decided to protect her, just this once. If she could persuade the Clairmont men to treat their ward in a more adult fashion, she might prevent further trouble.

"We were looking for Samson," Lucinda finished.

Carolly slumped. Small beads of moisture had formed on her brow. She withdrew a handkerchief from her pocket, and, her hand trembling, she blotted them away.

Richard ruffled his sister's hair. "That dog has a way of disappearing. But why does she have so much straw in her hair?"

A pregnant pause ensued. Carolly dropped the handkerchief and scrambled to pick it up.

Richard's eyebrows rose as he examined both of them. When neither of them spoke, his eyes narrowed. "Well?"

Lucinda regarded the straw at her feet, searching for a likely excuse. "She . . . I . . ."

"One of the grooms, not realizing we'd entered the stables, tossed some hay over my head," Carolly invented.

He rested one hand on his hip. "I see. Where is this groom? I'd like to speak to him."

Carolly's face took on a gray cast.

"I don't know." Lucinda made a show of peering around the stables. "Maybe he's gone on to another task."

Richard turned and strode toward the front of the stables, his back stiff. Lucinda followed at a quick pace, and Carolly scurried behind her. When they reached the front, they found the area deserted.

"Your groom seems to have disappeared." His voice had an edge to it. "Maybe he was never here at all. What are you two hiding?"

"Nothing," Lucinda insisted. " 'Tis as we've said."

Richard pointed at the hound. "Here's Samson. What were you going to do, walk with him?"

"Yes. To the glen."

"Well, I won't delay your walk a moment longer." He eyed them both suspiciously before turning on his heel. "Good morning."

They watched him stride off, gratitude softening Carolly's gaze. "Thank you, Lucinda."

"It seems we must walk," Lucinda said.

Carolly linked her arm through Lucinda's. "Then we walk."

The two started off, Samson lingering in the stables.

"I don't think the dog wants to come," the younger girl said.

"Oh, he'll come." Lucinda handed the bundle of scones to Carolly and pulled the piece of buttered bread from her pocket. "Come on, boy, I have a treat for you." She held the bread out. The dog trotted over, sniffed the sandwich, and ate it in two bites.

Abruptly, Samson grew still. His eyes began to water. With a loud woof he coughed once, twice, and then licked his chops.

Lucinda kneeled down and looked him in the eyes, rubbing his ears as she did so. "What a good boy. Samson, you're such a fine dog."

Samson looked at her with narrowed doggy eyes, as if he'd suddenly realized she'd put one over on him.

" 'Twas for Uncle George."

He vigorously shook his ruff.

"I'll make it up to you," she promised. "I'll save you a big chunk of meat from dinner tonight."

He placed his head on his paws and gazed at her, looking for all the world like a poor, lost soul.

"And when I return from London," she added, "I'll save you a chunk of meat from dinner for an entire week."

He woofed once and bounded into the woods before them.

"Don't fuss so over him. He's a big, slobbering hole-digger," Carolly accused.

"He's a gem."

Raising her gaze heavenward, Carolly clucked a little as they made their way through the trees. Lady's slippers, violets, and forget-me-nots put on a show alongside the trail they followed, drawing delighted comments from the girl.

Lucinda thought her a bit *too* delighted. "Carolly, we need to talk. There are other things that have puzzled me."

"Can we not just walk?"

"No."

"What do you want to know?"

"Well, how this . . . relationship with Mr. Smith began, for one."

"I met him one day about three weeks ago, almost immediately after you joined us at Clairmont Hall. Faye and I had been planning an outing, and we came down to the stables to fetch a gig." Carolly shrugged. "Josh fetched the gig and drove for us, and things, well, just happened."

"Things don't 'just happen.' Didn't Faye do anything to discourage you two?"

"Faye understands how lonely I feel. She knows how Father frustrates me by treating me like a child. *She* thinks I should grow up a bit, especially before we go to London. I need to know how to handle the gentlemen there, you know. They're very fast."

Lucinda nodded, her attention on Faye's role in all this. "Faye promoted this relationship between you and Mr. Smith?"

"She thought the experience would prove helpful. You're not angry with her, are you, Lucinda?"

"No," Lucinda said, although inside, she seethed. She felt certain Faye had deliberately set out to ruin Carolly, just as she sought to weaken Uncle George and Sir James with illness. "Although I don't agree with her."

"Please, Lucinda, don't tell her that you know about my relationship with Mr. Smith. She made me promise not to speak of it to anyone, and if she finds out you know, she'll think I'm trying to send trouble her way. She might tell Father everything, to have revenge on me!"

Privately Lucinda speculated Faye was indeed having her revenge on all of them, but aloud she promised to remain silent on this matter of Mr. Smith.

"So, Carolly, all these weeks we've been together, you've looked for ways to bore me silly so I'd give you free time—time to see Mr. Smith."

Carolly's cheeks grew pink. "I don't really like painting and embroidery. I suggested them because I knew you hated them and would fly at the first opportunity."

"And the strange tea that felled the staff during Squire Piggott's dinner? Was that you, too?"

The girl nodded, her countenance glum. "I put saltpeter into the batter for the scones when Liz wasn't looking. Everyone tried one. Indeed, they thought Liz's scones uncommonly good that day and complimented her endlessly."

"*My* saltpeter. From my trunk. You stole it the day you unpacked my clothes for me."

"Yes," she whispered.

"Do you know how many people you made ill?"

" 'Twas a harmless purgative."

" 'Tis also the primary ingredient in gunpowder," Lucinda said.

"Josh Smith wanted to meet that night." The girl looked at her with wide, moist eyes. "We hadn't met for almost a week, and with that awful Squire Piggott coming to dine, I couldn't resist. Faye reassured me that the saltpeter would do no lasting damage."

Lucinda shook her head.

"I know. I was wrong." A few tears ran down her cheeks. "I'm sorry, Lucinda. I truly am."

Lucinda pulled a handkerchief from her pocket and gave it to Carolly. She heard the sincerity of her words and linked her arm through the girl's. "Well, it's over and done with. We had best put it behind us with the promise to never do anything similar again. Let's go home and decide upon something for you to wear tonight."

A tremulous smile curved Carolly's lips. She wiped her tears away and placed her hand over Lucinda's. "Lucinda, may I ask you a question?"

"Go ahead."

"Why did you bring saltpeter with you to Clairmont Hall? And the rest of those pouches in your trunk, what did they contain?"

"That's two questions," Lucinda said, drawing a sigh from Carolly. "But I'll answer them both. Saltpeter is not just a purgative. 'Tis also quite flammable when mixed with the proper ingredients. The pouches contain herbs and flowers, and I intended to mix them with the saltpeter to form an incense."

"You wanted to burn incense?"

"Well, yes." Lucinda and Carolly emerged onto the grounds surrounding Clairmont Hall. "Your home is an old one, Carolly, and old homes are often musty. I didn't know what sort of room I'd have here, but I came prepared to drive off the smell if I needed to."

The girl smiled. "Faye told me you were a witch."

Lucinda stilled. Her stomach took a giant leap before settling down into an uncomfortable coil. "A witch?"

"A dried-up old spinster who liked to spoil other people's fun. I, however, think you're quite nice."

"Thank goodness for that," Lucinda said, fighting the urge to fan herself.

At two o'clock in the afternoon Lucinda collected her picnic basket from Cook. *Goetia* tucked under her free arm, she went to the ground-floor staircase that led directly to the north wing. She raced up the steps, basket swinging, noting the lack of cobwebs and dust.

251

In record time she reached the oaken door which led into Richard's apartments.

She pushed it open with the slightest bit of trepidation and peered inside. The foliate masks decorating the stone wall had received a dusting, and now their smiles seemed to reflect simple good humor rather than leering contempt. A heap of rotting drapes sat near the door. Richard had evidently torn them from the windows, flooding the hallway with light and banishing its previous feeling of doom.

She stepped into the hall and began to walk toward his bedchamber. Muffled oaths and the sound of creaking furniture filled the air. Smiling, she followed the noise, finding his bedchamber door propped open by the statue missing both arms and its head.

She peered around the doorway, lips curved upward. "Hello, Richard."

Cursing, he straightened and stepped from behind a large mahogany wardrobe he'd been pushing.

Lucinda stared at him, lips parted. He had dressed simply in a linen shirt and trousers, his shirt loose and flowing, the top open two buttons. A fine web of black hairs at the base of his neck teased her with thoughts of an even thicker mat on his chest. Dirt spotted his trousers, obviously an older pair, but instead of appearing disheveled, he looked vital and undeniably male, without society's trappings or its rules of conduct.

He assessed her with an insolent stare which touched her everywhere and seemed to bare all her secrets. "Why are you here?"

"I've brought you lunch and a good book." She lifted the basket and shook it, and then dropped *Goetia* onto his bureau.

He glanced at the spellbook, his gaze hardening. "Didn't I warn you not to trespass in my apartments?"

"But I thought you might be hungry."

"I am hungry," he said, his attention not focusing even once on her basket.

She placed the basket onto his bed. "Richard, what's wrong?"

"Why don't you tell me what you and Carolly were doing in the stables today?" he challenged. "I'm not an idiot, Lucinda. I don't believe that a groom threw hay into Carolly's hair. If you ask me, you and Carolly were throwing something of a more fragrant variety with your explanations."

"What does it matter?"

"You lied to me. That matters."

She sighed impatiently, unable to draw the lie out even more. "Carolly confided something to me of a very intimate nature, and I can't repeat it to you. I told a small fib to prevent you from learning the nature of her confidence. Consider it women-talk, if you must."

"Why were you taking Carolly to your magic glen? Are you trying to teach her how to cast spells?"

"Carolly and I sought privacy in the woods to speak about this problem of hers."

"I recall how uncomfortable Carolly seemed the evening Squire Piggott ate dinner with us, and how eager you were to end Squire Piggott's distasteful courtship. I can't help but wonder if you and Carolly were somehow involved in the poisonous tea that made the staff ill."

"I was *not*," she insisted, giving him a half-truth that made her voice tremble. Carolly had indeed been involved.

A low growl erupted from his throat. With one easy flick of his wrist, he captured her hand and pulled her against his chest. "Did you put something in the tea to send Squire Piggott on his way before he could bother you further? Or did you have Carolly poison the tea?"

"Neither, I assure you." Her throat tightened and she tried to edge away, but he would have none of it and held her firmly.

For one prolonged second—it seemed like an eternity—he stared at her, eyes narrowed, mouth twisted in a frown. "You lie."

"Believe what you wish," she murmured.

He released her with a snort. "I'll have the truth from you, Lucinda. One way or another."

"Exactly *what* are you going to do? Put me in leg irons?"

"Nothing so dramatic as that," he said, reckless vitality gleaming in his hazel eyes. "I told you what happens to women who trespass in men's bedchambers."

"So you're going to . . . kiss the truth out of me."

His attention dropped to her lips. "Would you like that?"

A peculiar giddiness whirled in her stomach at the sharpness of his gaze, the suggestion of hungers barely satisfied. She wanted to surrender to that hunger, one that gnawed on both of them, and extract every morsel of enjoyment from the moment rather than worry about their future.

"I should go," she murmured.

"Then go." He smiled, a toe-curling grin that heated her blood and set her heart to thumping at a crazy pace. "On the contrary, perhaps you should stay. We *are* to become lovers. Why resist Fate any longer?"

§15§

$\mathcal{T}$rembling, Lucinda thrust the basket toward Richard. She wanted him terribly, and yet, the cool self-assurance in his eyes suggested he thought he'd already conquered her. She lifted her chin. She had her pride.

"Do you expect me to fall into your arms because destiny has declared us lovers? I want you to love me for who I am, not because I'm convenient."

As soon as the words left her mouth, she wished she could take them back. Warmth drained from her face as the word *love* echoed in her head. "I don't want your love," she babbled. "I didn't mean it quite that way . . ."

He stared at her, his eyes wide, clearly shocked.

"I must leave," she gasped.

He stepped in front of her, blocking her exit. His face had become shuttered, his eyelids half-closed and masking his expression. "No. Stay. We'll eat."

Her throat tight, she nodded. Tears gathered at the corners of her eyes. By God, she was an idiot to say such a thing. Where had the words come from? She

255

didn't want to fall in love with Richard Clairmont, and didn't want him to fall in love with her.

Did she?

Her heart lurched in her chest.

Richard placed the picnic basket on the bed, snapped its wicker top open, yanked out a blue checkered blanket, and handed her two corners. Silently they spread the cloth on the ground. He selected a few pillows from his bed and spread them around the blanket. Lucinda sat down amid the pillows, her cheeks now flaming with heat. Her back stiff, she looked toward the windows and blinked away her tears.

He pulled a bottle of wine from the basket and set it aside with two wineglasses. " 'Tis a bit early in the day for this."

"Cook must have packed it," she mumbled.

Quiet settled between them as he pulled cheese, bread, leftover chicken, two ripe peaches, and deviled eggs from the basket. He selected a piece of chicken and waved toward the spread. "Aren't you going to eat?"

"My appetite has evaporated, Captain Clairmont. I ought to leave."

"Why this return to formality?"

"We aren't kin. We're acquaintances who've known each other for less than a month. Formality seems appropriate in our circumstance."

"If you expect me to call you Miss Drakewyck, you'll find yourself disappointed. And I won't answer to Captain Clairmont."

A hesitant smile played about his mouth. It took every ounce of strength she possessed not to smile back at him.

After a moment, he shrugged and took a bite of chicken. "I believe we must have some sort of conversation. I might remark upon the weather, and you upon your plans for the day."

Her lips twitched unwillingly. He was throwing her own words back in her face. Admiring his wit, she played along. "What purpose would such idle conversation serve?"

"It would aid in digestion. If you scowl at me throughout lunch, I fear my stomach will become quite upset."

She nodded. "All right. You've won. What would you like to talk about?"

Richard stretched against the pillows, drawing her attention to his wide, powerful shoulders and unusual height. He was a big man, yet he possessed the grace of a warrior who'd learned to move silently and avoid the enemy.

"Something has puzzled me for many weeks," he said. "Why did you call me Lancelot that night I found you in the glen?"

"Well, you looked strong, and you rescued me, and I've always had an interest in Lancelot."

"Tell me about him."

Relieved to move on to a neutral subject, she gladly took up his suggestion. "I've always thought Lancelot a study of contrasts. He was the strongest knight in the realm; and yet, his forbidden desire for Guinevere made him the most vulnerable."

"I see. So I'm your Lancelot, your damaged warrior."

Nodding, she plucked a peach from the hamper and took a bite. Soft and ripe, the fruit nearly burst with juice, filling her mouth with the taste of summer.

His attention slipped lower, to her lips. She detected a sharpness deep within his eyes, one that made her insides coil tight.

257

"Guinevere made Lancelot weak," he murmured.

Peach raised for another bite, she paused. A tremor ran through her. "Many would agree with you. I, however, cannot blame a woman for a fault in a man's character. 'Twas Lancelot's own longing for something he could not have that weakened him."

With a toss of her head, she lifted the peach to her lips and took a hearty bite. Juice threatened to drip down her chin. She felt for her handkerchief and abruptly remembered she'd given it to Carolly. She could lick the moisture away, but he observed her in such a fixed manner that she didn't quite dare. Her cheeks warming, she wiped the corner of her mouth with her thumb.

"Lancelot loved his king, but desired the Queen more," she continued, trying to sound casual. " 'Tis a classic war between the good and evil we all hold within."

"Every apple may hold a worm at its core," he agreed.

Involuntarily she glanced at the peach she held in her hand. "Why, yes. Lancelot did indeed have a worm at his core. He coveted another man's wife. But if you remember, his love for his king, the goodness in him, triumphed in the end."

She hoped he understood what she was saying . . . that by trusting himself and trusting in love, even a damaged warrior could overcome his past.

"You've quite a rosy view of life, Lucinda."

"And you are uncommonly cynical."

"Perhaps I've seen more of the world than you. I assure you, good has lost to evil many times in my experience."

A breeze blew through the terrace doors and rustled the drapes. Errant rays of light splashed through the room. Sunlight and shadows played across his face, but as the breeze died down, the shadows gained mastery.

The war still had its hold on him, she mused. The poor man had known a difficult time, and here she was, invading his bedchamber again, telling half-truths, and waving her spellbook beneath his nose. An overwhelming urge to confess all to him grabbed hold of her.

"There's another reason Lancelot interests me," she said, her voice low. "I spoke of it once before, right before we stopped at St. Paul's Church. Do you remember when I said that I'd seen you before we'd ever met?"

He nodded.

"When the magic in my dark garden showed you to me, I had a sense that you would be my Lancelot. That you would save me from harm."

"I'm not certain I understand." He shifted against the pillows, his posture becoming stiff. Eyes narrowed and unreadable, he measured her with a single glance.

"I knew you were damaged, just as Lancelot was damaged. I knew only you could save me."

"Save you? From what?"

"Not what. *Who.*" Lucinda drew in a breath.

"Who will I save you from? Squire Piggott is the only one who's been threatening you, and his threats don't require a savior, but rather a firm *no*. Are you suggesting that I marry you to save you from Squire Piggott?"

She gasped. "No! The thought never crossed my mind."

"I have no plans to marry." He stood, walked toward the latticework doors, and surveyed the grounds. "I'm not ready to marry. Not now. Perhaps not ever." His gaze swept the rolling hills and trees. "I still watch my men die in my dreams. I can hear their widows crying at their funerals."

She followed him to the doors. "I don't want to marry you. Indeed, you're the last man I would marry, and I'll tell you why. Marriage between us could lead to love; and love, to certain death for us both."

He swung around and stared at her, eyebrows nearly touching his hairline. "Love leads to death? That's a novel concept. How so?"

"It has to do with the things my dark garden showed me. When I saw you, I knew we would become lovers, and I knew you would always try to protect me, but I also understood that any love that grew between us would force us to forfeit both our lives."

"You aren't answering any of my questions. How would love lead to death? And who am I saving you from, if not Squire Piggott?"

"You need to look at *Goetia.*" She clasped his arm and drew him to the spellbook, which she'd placed on a bureau. Breath coming quickly, she lifted the cover and pointed to Edward Drakewyck's entry.

His voice filled with condescension, he read aloud.

> Somerton, the 31st of October, 1593
> *Let this be a warning to all who will come.*
> *Herewith lies a record of Morgana Fey, witch unrepentant and bringer of evil to the village of Somerton. Let me not justify my actions here, for her crimes were many, but simply say I was persuaded there could be no other end for her.*
> *The events that occurred on the eve of Samhain,*

in the year of our Lord 1593, concern the safety of the Drakewyck and Clairmont families. I thought it my duty to acquaint all who will come with the particulars of her final moments.

He paused, one eyebrow raised. "This is the entry you were talking about a few weeks ago when we stopped at St. Paul's Church."

Lucinda nodded. "Read on."

As Morgana Fey was put to rest, she called upon witchcraft to curse our families and predict our end. "When the world is older and you are dead," sang she, "and I am sleeping in my bed, a Drakewyck witch and Clairmont knave will awaken me from my lonely grave. They will love and the dove will be mine, and utter destruction will be thine."

You, my ancestor, will know her by her wheat-blonde hair, beautiful, lustrous, and begging for touch; by her ice-blue eyes whose shifting patterns conceal something darker, more fluid, and dangerous; by the gold filigree locket she wears around her neck. I pray to God she never appears, but if she does, only the dove can destroy her.

> *I am, with all duty and respect,*
> *Your most humble servant*
> *Edward Drakewyck*

Richard closed the book with a snap and stepped away from it. "So this witch Morgana Fey is the one I am to save you from. Are you sure Edward Drakewyck penned this, or are you trying to pull off an elaborate hoax?"

"Why?"

He snorted. "The entry might as well have Faye Morgan's portrait painted beneath it. Edward Drakewyck's description sounds exactly like her."

"It isn't a hoax, Richard."

His gaze became quizzical.

"Morgana Fey and Faye Morgan are one and the same person," Lucinda whispered. "She's returned to wreak vengeance on us all."

A laugh burst out of him, the sound more a disgusted rumble than an expression of mirth.

"'Tis true," Lucinda insisted, growing hot with embarrassment at how crazy her claim sounded. Still, he *had* to believe, or they both were lost.

"But if Faye Morgan were the ancient witch, that would make her over two hundred years old. She doesn't look a day over thirty."

"Edward Drakewyck preserved her in some manner."

"That's an utter contradiction of nature."

"There is no such thing as a contradiction of nature. There are only contradictions to what we *know* of nature."

He shook his head stubbornly.

"Can't you see it, Richard? Look at your father. Ever since Faye arrived, either his leg or his lungs have been paining him. My uncle, too, has become ill with some chance disease. And Carolly. My God, Richard, Faye almost—"

She broke off, aware that she'd nearly betrayed Carolly's confidence. If Richard found out his sister had lain in the stable with a groom, he'd lock the girl in a tower for the next twenty years.

"I knew my father felt ill, but not your uncle. What about Carolly?" he asked, his tone clipped.

"Nothing. I misspoke."

"Ah, we're back to lying." Scowling, he began to shove the remnants of their picnic back in the basket. "I agree. All of these illnesses surfacing at once sounds suspicious. They coincide with *your* arrival as well as Faye's."

"I don't make people ill with my magic. I cure them."

"And how do you cure them? Do you give them a little tincture? You are not qualified to practice medicine. For all I know, you've been causing the illnesses you wish to blame on Faye Morgan."

She stiffened. "You insult me."

"I'm trying to talk some sense into you." The disapproving tone left his voice, replaced by an intensity she could feel as well as hear. It seemed to vibrate across the air to her. "You believe in witchcraft. You cast spells rather than make an honest effort. I don't want to hurt you, Lucinda. But I won't lie, either. I'll not allow you to cast your healing spells on those who live in Clairmont Hall."

"Magic is a part of me. I breathe it, I live it. It makes me who I am." Her stomach turning slow, sour flips, she clutched his sleeve. "If you cannot accept my magic, then you do not accept me, either."

He looked at her, his gaze fierce. "If you wish to stay on, you must abide by that one simple rule. Otherwise I'll insist my father return you to Drakewyck Grange."

She drew a deep, shuddering breath. Tears gathered behind her eyes. Her lower lip trembled.

"You're a fire," he murmured, his voice husky, "and like the veriest fool, I continually hop into your flames and burn myself. But no more."

"Fire brings warmth." She held herself still, praying the tears wouldn't spill but knowing she was lost. "Fire brings light on the darkest of nights."

"Fire burns," he prodded. "Do I have your word on this?"

She pressed her lips together and looked away.

"Lucinda? You would defy me after all these illnesses have felled those we care about?"

At her continued silence, he turned his back to her. She searched his tall, muscular form for a sign of compromise.

"I'll send someone to pack your trunks." His voice shook slightly.

She closed her eyes. Dizziness washed over her. He was going to force her to leave Clairmont Hall. She would live each day without him, without his smile, his touch, his warmth. Suddenly Faye and her plans for revenge didn't matter nearly as much as the years stretched out before her, bleak and gray, filled with the dust of old tomes and loneliness.

Tears began to spill at last, down her cheeks to settle against her neck. Almost sick with regret, she choked back a sob.

Stiffening, he spun around. "Promise me, damn you!"

Lips parted, she stared at him. A bitter sort of wonder coursed through her and made her tremble harder. She hadn't realized how deeply his feelings ran; but what did it matter? He simply wouldn't accept her as she was.

He placed his hands on her cheeks and cupped her face. "Is it not worth the peace it will bring us?"

"Such a promise will bring us no peace." His closeness stirred something tremulous inside her. Like a feather it tickled and teased, urging her onward into

264

disaster. "You ask me to disown myself. Would you have me lie and pretend to be the woman you wish for?"

He wiped at her tears with soft fingers. "And yet you cry."

"I wish things were different."

"We are at an impasse, then," he said, his voice soft. "I, too, must remain faithful to my beliefs, or become something intolerable."

He turned abruptly and moved to the wine. It glistened like liquid berries in the sunlight. With a neat twist, he pulled the cork, poured two glasses, and handed one to her. "Perhaps it *isn't* too early for this."

Her hand trembled as she accepted the glass. Liquor sloshed over the rim.

Eyes half-hidden by heavy, drooping lids, he placed his hand over hers to steady her. "This obsession for you, it scares me. I don't want to give my soul to a witch."

"I don't want your soul."

"You want my heart."

"I want neither." She took a hearty sip of wine and wished he wouldn't stand so near. Her head was so muddled, she could hardly think.

Unexpectedly he smiled. "One thing is certain. You know how to make me laugh."

"Wonderful. Shall I wear a jester's cap and bells, too?"

His smile became an unrepentant chuckle. "You and your magic dove, your nonsensical rhymes and spell casting, your penchant for trouble, they all combined to make my life miserable at first. I can't begin to tell you all the plans I devised to send you away— the farther, the better. But at some point I realized I was smiling through it all."

"At least my misfortunes brought someone pleasure."

"You bring me more than pleasure."

She looked away. Why did he say such things to her? He was cruel, giving her hope when she knew there was none.

Another gulp of wine rolled down her throat, tart and burning, joining the bitterness already pooled in her stomach. She knew she had probably damned herself by remaining in his bedchamber, but this husky, sleepy-eyed man had left her bereft of words. She could only gape at him and the promise in his eyes that drew them still closer.

He put both hands on her shoulders and lightly kneaded them. "Your future stretches out before you, and although magic remains a sore point between us, you might find a gentleman without my . . . prejudices. Indeed, you deserve better than me, a soldier who dug his best friend's grave with his bare, bleeding hands."

"Stop blaming yourself—"

He placed a finger against her lips. "The last time we kissed, your good sense came to our rescue. This time, 'tis my turn. I want you very badly, Lucinda, but I don't want to marry. If we make love, honor and duty will force me to marry you. So leave now, before my resolve gives out entirely and we find ourselves leg-shackled to each other, until death do us part."

She stared at him, her heart taking a giant leap in her chest before settling down to an uncomfortable throb. She knew the consequences of staying with him; indeed, she'd just lectured Carolly on this very situation. Still, Carolly had a rosy future stretching before her, while she had nothing but the possibility of an early death.

"I want to stay," she said, her cheeks instantly flushing with warmth. If the ancient witch ended her life, she'd die knowing the pleasure of Richard's most intimate embrace.

"Lucinda, you can't possibly know—"

"I'm quite certain. I have no expectations of marriage." She looked up and touched his hair with one small hand, recklessly caressing him, tracing his ear. "Don't send me away."

"Go, Lucinda," he demanded. "Now."

"You don't want me?"

"Deuce take it, use your head." He clenched his jaw. "I can offer you nothing. What if I strip off your clothes and we're discovered? What if I get you with child? You deserve better than me."

"That doesn't matter to me, not now." She pressed her face against his neck, breathing his scent in as she did so, every nerve in her body strung tight with hope.

She felt him stiffen. His eyes darkened and he seemed to wrestle with some inner demon. Knowing that he teetered on the edge of surrender, she pressed a tentative kiss against his lips. Nostrils flaring, he groaned low in his throat and wrapped his arms around her, enfolding her with their warmth, crushing his mouth to hers. Tiny explosions of sensation ripped through her as he slipped his fingers beneath the edge of her bodice and rubbed her skin.

"I want you so terribly," she whispered against his lips.

"I've thought of nothing but you since the first day we met." Swiftly he turned her around and began to undo the tiny pearl buttons down the back of her dress. She heard a few pop as he pushed the fabric apart and kissed the skin at the nape of her neck.

A violent tremor shook her. "Show me, Richard. Show me what it means to make love—"

"Shh." He lifted the dress over her head, giving her time to slide her arms through the sleeves, and tossed it aside. Breath hot against her neck, he worked the petticoat strings around her waist until they, too, gave way, revealing her corset.

He muffled an exclamation and turned her around. Eyes hooded, he buried his face in her breasts, which surged upward in a startling display of flesh and cleavage. Hesitantly she stroked his hair, and as one they moved backward until her calves pressed against the bed. He propped one knee against the mattress, trapping her between his thigh and the bedpost, and popped each one of the fasteners on her corset.

At last, the device fell away in a heap of stiff fabric and whalebone. Freedom had never felt so wonderful. She stretched, forcing blood back into her cramped midsection.

He drew in a swift breath, his gaze running from her curls, down to her drawers, and back again. "You have no idea how many times I've thought about these drawers," he murmured, slipping his fingers beneath the waistband to slide them down her thighs, dragging his fingers along her skin as he did so.

She trembled and fought an instinct to cover her breasts, barely concealed by a cotton chemise as thin as tissue paper. Slow warmth invaded her cheeks when he hooked his fingers in her chemise straps and pulled them down her arms, revealing her skin inch by inch until the chemise pooled in a puddle of white cotton at her feet.

The tiny explosions which had warmed her blood strengthened, yet they didn't satisfy, not quite. Clad only in silk stockings and garters, she threw back her head and closed her eyes, baring the column of her throat to him, not knowing what she wanted but wanting it desperately.

He kissed her just beneath her chin, his lips skimming the surface of her flesh, his palms cupping her breasts then sliding down to her waist. She wanted to cling to him but he stepped away, taking a moment to look at her.

"My God, you're beautiful," he said, his voice harsh. "Beautiful." In one hasty movement he slipped his arms beneath her knees and laid her on the bed. Then, his gaze lingering upon her, he stepped away. After a short battle his empty boots struck the floor. Seconds later, his shirt and trousers followed.

He straightened, completely naked. For one precious moment he stood before her, his body a study of sunlight and shadows. Her breathing grew shallow as she contemplated his arousal and in that moment, she realized her power over him, one far stronger than any magic spell might impart.

She wanted to laugh aloud, but settled on a smile. Boldness heated her blood, mingling with the fever he'd stirred and making her almost queasy with anticipation. She snuggled against the counterpane and savored the sight of him, his naked chest, the black curly hair between his legs, and his erection nudging upward, urging her to look, to touch.

When he came close, she clasped his damaged hand and pulled him onto the mattress. Ropes squeaked as their bodies tangled, hot flesh against soft, full curves. Moist summer air brushed against her back as she gazed into his eyes, hooded no longer but staring with an intensity that saw directly into her soul.

"Lucinda . . ." His voice was rough, raw. He kissed her softly on her cheek and touched the back of her neck, then removed her garter belt and stockings until she lay naked upon the bed. Suddenly embarrassed, she shielded her breasts and the curls between her legs with her hands. Gently he pushed her hands away and, with a groan, she surrendered to the fire between them.

His lips were warm and moist, his fingers deft, and his movements tender yet assured as he tutored her. He stroked and pulled at her nipples, and when they grew unbearably hard he wetted them with his tongue and blew on them. The sudden cold sharpened her craving until she moaned and begged him to take them into his mouth, which he did, one by one, his hot, silken tongue rubbing and exploring, making her skin flush with sweet torment. When he'd finished with them he gently gathered her breasts in his hands and kissed them, his worship drawing a long, shuddering sigh from her.

He trailed kisses down from her breasts to her navel, and she twisted against him, the flesh between her legs swelling, moisture slicking the core of her. His palm was very strong and hot as he held her steady, and with his free hand he tormented her, gliding his fingers up inner thighs, brushing across her swollen flesh, and then gliding back down again, his touch as light as a butterfly's wings. Over and over he did this, his face resting against her belly, until her tortured flesh brimmed with wetness and she cried out, maddened.

He chuckled deep in his throat.

"Please, Richard," she pleaded, but he would have none of it and moved upward to kiss her quickly, harshly, silencing her even as he found the source of her torment and began to rub in a lazy circular motion.

Lucinda closed her eyes. She had become a being of pure sensuality, her body involuntarily arching as he pushed back the folds of flesh between her thighs and touched her directly, yet so lightly she nearly sobbed with pleasure. He didn't slow the pace, nor quicken it; he simply stroked the most tender piece of flesh she possessed with soft pressure, and dreamily she realized his fingers now dropped lower, too, probing her gently, as if testing the moisture that seeped from her. She lifted her hips to meet him, for her need had almost become too great to bear, but still he denied her, evidently waiting for some sign only he would recognize.

Her chest caught at the feel of his arousal pushing against her thigh. She trailed her fingers downward and curled her palm around him, liking the feel of his hard, hot length in her hand, wondering at its silkiness and the wetness at its tip. He pushed into her hand a little, and she felt her power again, the command she had over him just as he commanded her. Audaciously she slipped her palm around to cup his sac, then tested its weight before gliding one finger along the skin behind it. She felt him groan and knew he wanted more. Learning from his movements, she curled her fingers around his erection and began to pull on him as he'd pulled and stroked her nipples, feeling the length of him growing even harder and hotter, watching his lips part and his eyes close and his face become sharp with the same unbearable ache that tormented her.

She wondered what it would be like to kiss him there, just as he'd kissed her breasts. Drinking in his musky male scent, she dragged her lips across his torso and down past his navel, feeling his body stiffen, perhaps in shock but she didn't care. Beyond anything but a need to increase the pleasure they both felt, she rubbed her face against the fine network of black hair covering his lower belly and flicked her tongue against the base of his arousal.

He jerked and his chest began to heave, igniting a new spark within her. Recklessly she ran kisses up to the tip of his erection, in the same way he'd trailed his lips across her breasts. She pressed his soft tip against her mouth and felt salty moisture wet her lips.

Rejoicing in the need she'd aroused in him, she laughed.

"Little witch," he muttered. He drew her up to him and then he was on top of her, all the master now, his lips forcing hers apart as he took what he wanted from her. He probed her boldly between her legs with his finger and she strained against him, wanting more of him inside her, wanting him to feel the same taut pleasure that threatened to overwhelm her. Her body felt as though it had swelled, ready to explode, and the flesh he'd teased and tormented began to convulse around his finger.

"Easy, love," he breathed. He pulled away and poised his weight over her. She clung to him, ran her palms along his muscles, trying to draw him down to her. He was stronger than she, however, and took his time, evidently savoring the moment, his hazel eyes looking deep into hers. Fevered, she kissed his arm, his shoulder, any spot of skin on him that was within her reach.

A low groan rumbled in his chest. He slipped his knees between hers and urged her thighs apart, his breath rasping in his throat. Eagerly she complied, a thousand sensations rippling through her—anticipation of blinding pleasure, relief that the overwhelming need he'd aroused would soon be assuaged, a gut-wrenching hunger for him to fill the emptiness inside her.

"Kiss me," she whispered, and he crushed her lips with his, his arousal pushing against her inner thighs, hard and hot and moist. She felt his silken tip brush against her swollen flesh, teasing more moisture from her, seeking entry. Seconds stretched out between them, and abruptly, some of the dreaminess left as she realized she was about to become a woman, in the truest sense of the word.

A bolt of instinctive panic made her stiffen, but before she could make a sound, she heard his muttered apology as he thrust forward and stopped, and then thrust again, harder, deeper, slicing into her flesh and filling her with a knife-like pain that cut through all the longing. A sticky wetness coated her thighs, and the counterpane suddenly seemed to smother her. She tried to cry out, but his mouth was on hers, kissing her, and he was moving inside her, and the pain became a blissful ache. The fever returned even hotter than before and ravaged her as he drove deeper, faster, his eyes closed and back arched, his chest shuddering; she wound her legs around his waist and drew him in even closer.

Without warning, his entire body grew taut and he gasped her name before thrusting forward one last time, touching some secret part of her deep within. Tremors rocked him, and at the same time the fever ravaging her body burst in a final explosion. Crying out, she clutched his back and pressed her face against his neck, breathless, utterly shocked and humbled, her innocence lost forever.

16

$\mathcal{R}$ichard cradled Lucinda in his arms as she trembled in the aftermath of pleasure, her slender fingers tangled in his hair. He fell back against the pillows, his body hot and feverish, his limbs sapped of strength, his chest still heaving.

"Lucinda . . ." This time, his voice was soft and full of regret, not for making love to her as he'd so longed to do, but for the disgrace he'd brought her this afternoon with his touch.

She raised herself on one elbow and looked at him, her brown-gold eyes drowsy with their lovemaking, her hair a mass of chocolate curls spread around her shoulders and draping over her breasts. He caressed her soft pink nipples, swollen from his kisses, his gaze traveling along the gentle curve of her belly and down to the glistening thatch of curls between her legs. He felt himself stir again. She was so beautiful and so very responsive that he wondered if he could ever have enough of her.

His throat tight, he pressed a hungry kiss against her lips, her mouth opening easily under his, her tongue teasing him, sparring with him, even. He broke away and clasped her to him and rubbed his forehead against the top of her head, her hair tickling his nose with its sweet scent.

"What are we to do, Richard?"

He kissed the tip of her nose. "Marry. Tomorrow." He said it matter-of-factly, for he'd taken her maidenhead and lain with her.

"I thought you weren't ready for marriage."

"Duty and honor demand I make an honest woman of you," he insisted. Secretly he cherished the thought of having her by his side, growing old together, sharing the laughter that life offered while comforting each other through its sadnesses. He knew he was selfish, unbearably so, for by marrying her he'd be saddling her with a man who could never believe in her magic nor forget the war memories that still made him writhe.

She pushed away from him, her eyes losing that sleepy quality. "I won't marry you."

Icy fingers gripped his heart. His mouth turned downward in a grim line. So, she refused to have him, a damaged man both inside and out, even if the alternative was possible ruination. He could hardly blame her. Still, they no longer had a choice.

His gaze flickered across the spots of blood dotting his sheets. "I've taken your virginity, Lucinda. I've spilled my seed into you. Even now, you could be carrying my child. You *will* marry me."

"We cannot marry. We cannot love! My God, you mustn't fall in love with me, even if I already love you—" She clapped a hand across her mouth and stared at him with a stricken gaze.

Her words echoed in his head. She'd said she loved him. How was that possible?

"Lucinda, I . . ."

He trailed off, unable to find the right thing to say. He felt an overpowering urge to tell her he loved her, too, if only to spare her hurt. But he wasn't certain. Did he love her? Was it possible for a man like him, someone so utterly damaged, to love? He cast his mind back over the times they'd spent together, the way she'd teased him from his black thoughts, his desire to possess her now, and tomorrow, and every day beyond that. Was that love?

He just didn't know. A sense of helplessness and confusion brought an ache to his temples. Only one thing became clear to him. Whatever his feelings, he wouldn't tell her he loved her just to spare her hurt. She deserved honesty from him, at least.

"I . . . don't know if I love you," he finally admitted.

"Thank God," she said, her words at odds with the sudden shadow in her eyes, the slight pull at her mouth that suggested pain. She slipped out of bed, her limbs white and glowing in the sunlight, and pulled her chemise over her head.

He keenly felt the loss of her soft warmth next to him. He almost called her back, but his confusion was growing, and with it frustration that she continued to mutter dire warnings without giving him the full story. "Stop talking in riddles, Lucinda, and tell me why love between us is so dangerous."

"Love will make us vulnerable." She found her petticoats and tied them around her waist. Recognizing the practicality of her actions, he grabbed his trousers and shrugged them on.

"How?"

"I haven't figured that part out yet. It has to do with my vision and the entry in my spellbook."

"Let's start from the beginning, then. To make things easier, I'll assume magic exists."

She nodded and bent over to sweep her stockings and garter belt off the floor. Her gaze locked on something beneath his bed and she paused. Lower lip caught between her teeth, she reached beneath his bed and retrieved a small wooden box, one he'd never seen before.

"Is this yours?" She traced the strange runes decorating its sides with her finger.

"No." He took the box from her and slid the top open. Inside, rose petals and pine cones nestled against a black velvet bag. Salt crusted its wooden interior. "What in damnation . . ."

"A spell box," she murmured. "Roses for love, pine cones for fertility, and this black velvet bag holds tokens from the two lovers."

Her fingers shaking, she untied the cord which held the bag closed. A tiny piece of lint and a string lay upon the velvet, but nothing more. "Someone has cast a love spell upon us, Richard, and I'm quite certain I know who did."

"Did you cast the spell?" he couldn't help asking.

"Of course not. I don't want to love you."

"Who cast it, then?"

She walked to the terrace, emptied the box's contents onto the stone floor, and scattered it with her bare foot. "Faye Morgan. She's determined that we will love."

Again, Richard had that sense that crucial details were getting away from him, that soon he'd find himself completely out to sea, without a hope of understanding what went on in that head of hers.

"Let's start from the beginning," he repeated, his voice firm. "First of all, Edward Drakewyck cast some sort of magic spell on Morgana Fey for reasons unknown, and laid her to rest, but not permanently. She didn't die, but merely slept, to be later awakened by you and me. Am I correct?"

Lucinda brought the spell box back into his room and laid it on his bureau. "Yes. Henry Clairmont evidently helped Edward silence Morgana, and then they both allowed her husband, Christopher Fey, to take responsibility for Morgana's disappearance. Christopher was accused of murdering his wife and died a warlock's death."

"All right. That's easy enough to follow." He gathered Lucinda's dress, lifted it over her head and pulled it downward. He stepped behind her and fastened her pearl buttons, all the while eyeing the tender skin at the nape of her neck. He wanted to kiss her but held himself back. He had a sinking feeling he'd need all his wits about him. "Before she died, Morgana vowed to have revenge on the Drakewyck and Clairmont descendents. Edward's entry also explained, if memory serves me correctly, that she'd regain her dove. What dove does he speak of?"

Lucinda brushed her skirts and adjusted her bodice, then slipped her hand into her pocket to pull out a crystal dove. He remembered the statue from that night in the glen, weeks ago, when her bonfire had burned out of control.

She held it out to him and he grasped it, its surface smooth and cool in his palm. The magic bird had its head turned to the side and its wings folded, and a ruby heart lay nestled in its depths.

He turned it this way and that, studying the ruby, then returned it to her. "The statue could be worth a fortune, if that ruby's real. Is that why Morgana wants the dove?"

"I don't think so." She slipped the statue back into her pocket. "The crystal dove is a magical icon, passed down through the centuries. It absorbs magic from those who use it, and as it grew old it became truly powerful. Faye covets the dove's power, not its monetary value."

"Couldn't Faye Morgan be a descendent of Morgana Fey? That might explain why she looks so much like the woman described in your spellbook," he gently suggested. "Faye Morgan might have read of the crystal dove in an entry in her own family Bible, realized its value, and returned to Somerton to claim it."

"She isn't a descendent or a look-alike," Lucinda insisted, brows knit together. "The timing of her arrival in Somerton, right after yours, is too coincidental, too perfectly in line with my vision."

He sighed. Apparently she wouldn't be swayed from her belief that a two-hundred-year-old woman walked the streets. "So Morgana Fey wants two things: revenge and the dove. If Faye Morgan is this ancient witch, then you and I must have awakened her. When and how did we do this?"

"The night you joined me in the glen. I lost my dove, and we both searched for it and touched it at the same time. Do you remember the magic that spewed forth from the crystal? How your hand tingled? I think we inadvertently called upon the power of the dove to awaken Morgana."

"And the very next night, you and Carolly ran her over in my gig," Richard said.

"I believe she jumped in front of the gig. Her clever maneuver provided a convenient excuse for her lack of money, clothes, and family, and put her safely in the home of her enemy, where she might work her evil magic."

He snorted. "We finally have an explanation for Faye's mysterious past, even if it is a wild one."

"Think, Richard," she urged. "Do you remember her strange speech when she first awoke from that bump on her head? Do you recall how your own father described her gown as antiquated?"

He nodded, unwillingly. "I can see where you might believe Faye Morgan is Morgana Fey, particularly with your imagination. The events you've described even follow a strange sort of logic. Even so, I insist a more rational explanation will be found with patience.

"But let's move on rather than argue. I know you consider me your Lancelot, your damaged warrior who might save you as Lancelot fought for Guinevere. You also claim love between us will ruin us, just as the forbidden love between Lancelot and Guinevere destroyed Camelot. The question is: why?"

" 'Tis clear Faye wants us to love," she murmured, brow furrowed. She paced over to the terrace doors. "But I don't know how love between us will lead to our destruction."

"You say she wants this dove." He jabbed his shirt-tails into his waistband and pulled on his boots. "Why doesn't she just take it from you?"

"Because she's afraid I'll call upon its magic to stop her before she ever touches it."

"I see." Unbidden, memories of those last moments with John Burke at Balaclava surfaced in his mind. The Cossack pressing a pistol against John's midsection. He, Richard, wanting to fire but knowing he couldn't without risking John's life. In the end, losing John and blowing his own damned hand off.

He smiled and shook his head. The answer was so simple he wondered if she tested him in some obscure way. "I can tell you why love is so dangerous between us. If Faye threatens me, and you love me, you'll give in to her rather than destroy her; and then *she* will destroy you."

Lucinda turned from the terrace to face him, her lips parted. "Explain this to me."

"When I was on the battlefield with my friend John Burke, and the Cossack grabbed him, I had a chance to fire at the Cossack and kill him. In doing so, however, I would have forfeited John's life. Instead, I hesitated, and the Cossack killed him." He drew on his jacket, shaking his head. "Similarly, if Faye wants this dove, what better way to ensure she gets it than to threaten someone you love?"

"Why did she not threaten Uncle George, then?"

"We know Edward Drakewyck and Henry Clairmont killed her husband. Perhaps she wanted to make the circumstances of our downfall similar to her own. An eye for an eye, a husband for a husband."

Her features taut, Lucinda walked up to him and placed a hand on his arm. "She wants us married, so she can kill my husband, just as Edward killed hers. So you see, we can't possibly marry."

Richard played along, just out of curiosity. "And if she held a pistol on me and demanded the dove? What would you do?"

"If I refused to give the dove over, she would kill you," Lucinda said, her face growing very pale. "But then I could finish her off with the magic in the dove. You would die so I might live."

"And if you gave her the dove?"

"She'd use the magic in the dove to kill us both. Thus, love leads us to forfeit both our lives."

He smiled. "Well, it seems either I must go, or we both go. In that case, let her kill me, Lucinda, and then finish her off with the dove."

"You would sacrifice yourself for me," she whispered. "Just like Lancelot would have for Guinevere."

Sighing deeply, he pulled her into his arms. "Your arguments have an odd sort of rationality to them. Still, they're based on the assumption that magic exists, and I've already told you that I don't believe in magic. So where does that leave us? Intimate and unmarried, a circumstance I intend to change."

Eyes narrowed, she forced him to loosen his embrace and, with a neat twist, escaped him. "You think I'm a fool. You're indulging me."

"Why would I indulge you?" His gaze dropped to her lips.

"Because when I'm finished recounting my tale, you're . . . going to kiss me again."

"A capital suggestion. I much prefer kissing you to listening to your tales of witchcraft."

"You must take me seriously!"

"I simply wish to take you."

Scowling, she stepped around him and headed for the door. "Mark my words, Richard Clairmont. You will see the truth in my explanation, and when you do, you'll wish you believed sooner."

Sighing heavily, Lucinda made a final inspection of herself in the cheval glass. Her cinnamon-colored silk gown curved around her bosom and hugged her waist before puffing out into a four-foot bell. Ivory tulle formed decorative straps that kept the gown from slipping off her shoulders, while large ivory bows festooned the hem of each of her three silk skirts.

A maidservant had parted Lucinda's hair in the middle and drawn it into soft waves that framed her face. Cinnamon-colored roses danced in her hair. Her cheeks glowed with a bit of pink powder, but her eyes were still somber, her mouth drawn, her skin too white. Perhaps she wouldn't dazzle anyone tonight at Carolly's seventeenth birthday party, but she wouldn't embarrass herself, either.

Carolly stood at her side, her elfin face wreathed in a smile. "You'll draw the attention of every gentleman there."

"This I doubt very much. I believe you'll hold that distinction."

She inspected Carolly's gown of glimmering white satin embroidered with blue quilled ribbons. She'd helped embroider the ribbons herself, but at the time she hadn't realized how low Faye had cut the bodice or how voluptuous Carolly had grown. The satin seemed to cling to the girl's every curve, hinting at slender hips and long legs, while her cleavage nearly overflowed the heart-shaped neckline.

A necklace of sapphires and pearls dipped across Carolly's bosom, and Lucinda wondered if it wasn't too worldly for her. Still, this was Carolly's first entrée into society as a woman full grown, and Lucinda didn't want to spoil the night.

She hoped Faye didn't plan to spoil the night, either. Faye's first attempt to destroy Carolly by encouraging her affair with a stablehand had failed. Tonight the entire town of Somerton was coming to see the girl, and if Faye wanted to ruin Carolly forever, tonight would prove the perfect opportunity. Lucinda silently prayed the night wouldn't feature a repeat of the stables incident but on a grander scale.

"I daresay I can scarce believe the transformation," Lucinda murmured. "You're a beautiful woman, Carolly."

"My insides are quaking. I'm not certain I can descend the grand staircase."

Neither am I, Lucinda thought. Hours had passed since she'd made love to Richard and her limbs still felt weak, her mind still reeled with the unimaginable pleasure he'd given her. But their lovemaking had done little to resolve the differences between them. Indeed, it had only made the situation worse.

Richard now insisted upon marrying her for the sake of duty, but he'd already made it clear how distasteful he'd find their union. She, after all, was a spell caster who made a habit of dosing those she loved with ill-prepared tinctures.

She, for her part, wanted a husband who loved her despite her "faults."

Then again, did any of it really matter? She *wasn't* going to marry him.

"Together, we'll descend the staircase," Lucinda soothed. She moved across the room to pull a silk and gold fan from her trunk, half-packed with gowns she wished to bring to London. "Remember, not too much ratafia. Keep the gentlemen at arm's length, and for heaven's sake, do nothing to aggravate your father."

"I'll be very careful. We're leaving for London in two days and I want nothing to prevent the trip. I'm afraid one more provocation would convince Father to keep me home forever."

Lucinda imagined Faye slipping some sort of mood-altering substance into Carolly's glass of lemonade. "Watch your drinks, too."

"My drinks? Whatever for?"

"Just don't leave them lying about," Lucinda insisted.

"All right." Shrugging, Carolly opened a flacon of perfume and dabbed it on her wrists and between her breasts. Lucinda watched with a bit of dismay, noting Carolly's hair, drawn back in a sleek French chignon that accentuated her high cheekbones and clear hazel eyes. Here, before her, stood a gorgeous woman, seductive yet unspoiled. How would Sir James react to seeing his daughter all grown up?

"I have something for you," Carolly said, her smile becoming mischievous. She pulled a small velvet bag from a pocket hidden within her skirt and moved to stand behind Lucinda. "Close your eyes."

"Carolly—"

"Close them."

Lucinda sighed and sealed her lids tight. She felt some fumbling at the back of her neck, and suddenly, the press of cold smoothness against her bosom.

"All right, you may look."

Slowly, she opened her eyes, her focus settling directly upon the large topaz pendant, set in a delicate filigree of gold, that nestled on her breasts. She sucked in a breath. "Carolly, where did this come from?"

" 'Twas Mother's. Look, Lucinda, how it matches your eyes."

"A wonderful piece," Lucinda agreed. "And perfect for my gown, too." The smoky jewel brought a sheen of gold to her brown eyes and lent an unmistakable glamour to her ensemble. " 'Tis lovely, and very thoughtful. But you can't expect me to keep it." She grasped one of Carolly's hands and squeezed.

Carolly squeezed back and then let go. "I'm afraid I have to return it to Mother's room tomorrow. I wish

I could do more. You've done so much for me, and when I remember how I treated you at first—"

The girl paused and sucked in a breath, her hand pressed against her midsection.

"Carolly, what's wrong?"

"Nothing. Just a little twitch in my side."

Lucinda studied her for a moment. "Are you sure?"

"Quite. Will you hold my hand?"

An unwilling smile crossed Lucinda's lips. "Yes, of course. Take a deep breath, now. Have courage." *For both of us,* she silently added.

She clasped Carolly's hand. Together they stepped through the doorway, Carolly no doubt thinking of the men she would conquer this eve, Lucinda thinking of the man she could never allow herself to love.

"Lucinda, I'll look like a fool on the dance floor. It's been three years since I received those lessons from Monsieur Luchard." Carolly looked at her with wide, frightened eyes.

"Nonsense. I've seen you practicing. You're perfectly in mode, I assure you." She patted Carolly's hand and avoided mentioning she was far from knowledgeable on the subject.

They walked through a long hallway, heading toward the staircase which descended into the grand hall. Outside, beyond the bank of windows, torch bearers littered the drive, two per carriage as they escorted vehicles to the front door. Lucinda couldn't count all the torches, and held Carolly's hand tighter.

On the whole, she didn't enjoy balls, always felt a little outmoded, a bit gauche, a woman more accomplished in scholarship than dance. Small groups of people appealed to her, were more manageable. Carolly's birthday party, however, seemed to have drawn the entire town of Somerton.

Pulse pounding in her throat, Lucinda reached the top of the staircase. Carolly paused beside her, and together they stared out over the sea of people, old and young, seated and dancing, many still arriving. Gowns of silk and satin and lace, some shot with jewels that sparkled beneath hundreds of candles, warred for attention with the men's superfine evening coats. Fans fluttered and glasses of wine sloshed onto the marble floor. Music, a soft, lilting piece, drifted up the staircase, and the luscious fragrance of roses competed with the delicious smell of a buffet spanning several tables against the far wall.

Lucinda grasped the railing with her free hand and began her descent, feeling for each step before placing her weight. Carolly remained at her side. Their skirts rustled and swelled around them, silk against satin, and the heels of their slippers clicked against stone, and Carolly's hand trembled within hers. Lucinda set the pace, her slow entrance more an effort to keep from falling than a coy attempt at garnering attention. Nevertheless, by the tenth step, conversation had dampened and all eyes had focused their way.

"Who are those lovely gels?" someone asked.

Lucinda's step slowed even more, and Carolly hesitated beside her. She ceased to breathe. She stared blindly across the ballroom, her tongue pasted to the roof of her mouth. So many faces . . .

Abruptly her gaze locked onto the man standing near the front entrance. Richard bowed to an elderly dame and then paused, brows drawn together, perhaps feeling the weight of her stare. He turned, his smile fading as he scanned the room, seeking and finding her, his eyes dark and intent.

He whispered to Sir James, who stood at his side.

Sir James looked over his shoulder at them. He smiled and nodded before returning to the task of greeting their guests.

Richard strode toward Lucinda and Carolly, lips slightly parted. "Good evening, ladies. I see you've created quite a sensation."

His voice, deep and husky, flowed over Lucinda, thawing her limbs. She released Carolly's hand and looked at him. His tall boots gleamed like black onyx. Black trousers accentuated the strength and size of his thighs. Silk scrollwork danced across his white velvet waistcoat, and his double-breasted evening coat embraced his broad chest and shoulders with the devotion of a lover. But it was the admiration in his eyes—admiration for her alone—that made her quiver, that forced her to drop her gaze.

"Miss Drakewyck," he murmured, and drew her gloved hand from her side. His fingers pressed into her palm, firm and warm, and a whisper of air brushed across her face as he bowed over it.

She dropped a curtsey and looked at him from beneath her lashes. "Good evening, Captain Clairmont."

His attention slid to her breasts before returning to her eyes, the shift so quick and practiced she might not have noticed it if she weren't so aware of him. A slow smile spread across his face, and the sensual curve to his lip grew more pronounced, leaving little doubt where his thoughts lay.

He swiveled to Carolly and acknowledged her with a nod. "Will you join us in the receiving line?"

The girl gave him a shaky smile. "If I must."

"You must." He returned to Lucinda. "Enjoy yourself, Miss Drakewyck. Save a dance for me." With a formal bow in her direction, he grasped Carolly's arm and drew her toward Sir James.

A tiny breath escaped her as she watched him go. Her attention never straying very far from him, she moved to an alcove near the staircase. Several bejeweled guests cast curious looks in her direction. She didn't know for certain if Squire Piggott had spread the word that she'd become a paid companion, but suspected his jaws had flapped nonstop over the matter. She shifted uncomfortably on her feet, silently cursing the man, reminding herself that the revelation had produced at least one positive result—she no longer had to fight off the Squire's advances.

Faye, her skirt flaring out like a giant pink bell and a flush on her face, had a bevy of admirers surrounding her. Positioned near the fireplace, she paid only partial attention to the men who fought for her regard, her attention resting solely on Carolly. A secret, enigmatic smile curled her lips as she toyed with the filigree locket at her throat.

The witch reminded Lucinda of the pink roses that spilled from vases scattered throughout the room. Lush, overripe. Burdening the air with their scent. When Faye's gaze sought and captured hers, a finger of dismay crept down her spine. Even from across the room she saw Faye tighten her lips and give a little nod, as if recognizing an enemy. The witch, Lucinda thought, had something special in store for Carolly this evening. Perhaps for all of them.

Her inner temperature plummeted a few degrees.

Women gathered in a crowd nearby suddenly parted, and Uncle George emerged to stand at her side. He leaned forward to hug her. "My dear Lucinda."

"Uncle George." She returned his hug, giving him an extra squeeze, and smiled. "I'm so happy to see you."

He started to reply, but a vicious cough grabbed hold of him. He bent over with the force of it, his glasses falling out of his pocket.

Lucinda bent over and retrieved his glasses. She noticed dirt marring the lenses and rubbed them against her skirt before returning them to him. Her joy at seeing him became deep concern as she noticed his pallid complexion and red-rimmed eyes. His cravat, she thought, sat askew on his neck; and although her uncle hadn't much fashion sense, he'd never been slovenly. "Uncle, how long have you been ill?"

His eyes watering, he wiped his mouth with a square of linen. "For a few weeks at least."

"Two weeks ago, when you came to Clairmont Hall, you looked ill. Have you seen any signs of improvement?" she asked, thinking of the spells she'd cast.

"I've rallied once or twice, but this pleurisy seems to have gone deep into my chest."

She put an arm around him and tried to usher him toward a chair pushed up against the wall.

"Pshaw! Unhand me, gel, I'm not in the grave yet." He pushed her arm away and stood his ground, his eyes stark blue in a pale face.

"Have you seen Dr. Bennet?"

"Twice. He's going to kill me with his elixirs." His voice dropped and he stared across the ballroom. "We both know medicines won't help me."

She followed the direction of his gaze and saw Faye, her blue eyes wide, emotionless, yet sharp, somehow.

"I've cast a few healing spells on your behalf," she whispered. "But in a war of magic, I can't beat her. I'm not as strong as I used to be. Not since I used the dove."

Uncle George's eyes widened. "How much of your magic did the dove absorb? I always thought it claimed a negligible amount. Otherwise, no one would ever dare use the thing."

"Unfortunately, in my case it took quite a bit." She settled her hand on his sleeve. She needed to touch him. "I'm frightened for you, Uncle. I don't now how to stop her."

"I have a confession to make, gel. I've dusted off my spellbooks and tried casting a few spells, not only to heal myself but to protect you. She's strong, this Faye Morgan. I haven't been able to slow her down, let alone stop her."

Wonder filled her at the thought of Uncle George invoking the magic he'd sworn he'd never use again. Abruptly their situation took on an even more dangerous cast. If he'd resorted to magic, things must be bad, indeed. "What are we to do?"

Eyes closed, he rubbed his brow. "I don't know. But I must admit I still don't like you living under the same roof with her."

"So far I've never been alone with Faye. Someone is always around when I'm in a room with her: Carolly, Sir James, Richard, a servant. In these situations she seems preoccupied and keeps up her pretense of amnesia."

"Don't underestimate her, gel. She's had two hundred years to think about having her revenge on us. I wish we knew what exactly she planned to do." He paused to nod and smile at a woman who glided past, a magenta ostrich feather sticking out of her coiffure.

"I have a few ideas about that," she told him. "Richard and I have investigated her and we've come up with a few interesting facts."

"Richard, is it? Not Captain Clairmont?"

Heat flooded her cheeks. "I've gotten to know him better, Uncle, and he's not half so bad."

"You've gotten to know him too well, I'll wager." Uncle George eyed her closely. "Tell me what you and Richard have unearthed."

Quietly, but with as much intensity as she could muster, she explained how they'd found Morgana's entry in the parish register, and their discovery that her husband had been accused of her murder and executed for it, all through Edward Drakewyck's and Henry Clairmont's machinations. She went on to explain Richard's theory on how Faye planned to force the dove from her, and why Faye waited—because she wanted Lucinda and Richard married.

Uncle George listened to her tale in silence. When she'd finished, he nodded thoughtfully. "I can see why she'd want revenge. I even feel a little sympathy for her, God help me. What interests me even more are Captain Clairmont's thoughts on this. He accepts your explanation of events?"

"No, not at all. He doesn't believe in magic. He thinks my version has a lot in common with a fairy tale. He also suggested Faye Morgan is a descendant of Morgana Fey, out to claim the dove because of its monetary value." A little throb made her voice waver, and she looked away, hoping he hadn't noticed any telltale emotion in her eyes.

"Exactly how are things between you and Captain Clairmont?"

Unbidden, memories of Richard's faced pressed against her breasts surfaced. She swallowed, her face growing even hotter than before. Uncle George had the unnerving ability to read her mind.

He grasped her chin and forced her to look at him. "Lucinda, you must tell me. Has he disgraced you in any manner?"

"No," she answered too quickly.

A red flush crept into his face. "You may be my niece by birth, but in all other ways you are my daughter. I'll allow no one, not even Richard Clairmont, to toy with your affections."

"Uncle," she breathed, "you're too loud. People are looking in our direction." Conversation had ceased in a knot of women who stood about ten feet away.

He took a deep breath and pulled at his cravat. "Promise me, gel. Promise me you'll stay away from Richard Clairmont. Don't disgrace us."

She looked down at the carpet. "According to my vision, he is the only one who can save me from Faye. Without him, I have no future. I'll do what I must."

17

*C*arriages continued to crunch up the drive, unloading more guests until Clairmont Hall seemed near to bursting. Matrons gathered in small groups to chat, while the elderly sought chairs and games of chance. Reverend Wood and Squire Piggott conversed near the front door, the Squire preening as he studied several unattached women.

Carolly's birthday party, Lucinda thought, had attracted almost everyone in Somerton, and the notion that Faye planned a final, devastating blow to the girl's reputation continued to dog her. A sick, bubbly feeling gathered in her stomach, forcing her to sit in a chair, one centrally placed where she might observe the entire assemblage.

Servants circulated among the crowd, offering glasses of the finest champagne and ratafia; the stronger stuff remained bottled on a side table, where a group of seasoned men had clustered. Fruits and cheeses and meats of every variety overflowed linen tablecloths, and an Oriental Buddha—carved in ice— offered Russian caviar between his two fat hands.

At length, everyone had arrived and the Clairmont family began to wander among their guests. Carolly, Lucinda noted, had acquired a bevy of admirers, all laughing and joking and doing their best to impress. The girl wore a flirtatious grin, exciting Lucinda's uneasiness yet again, but her father seemed unaffected, even bestowing an occasional smile upon Carolly.

After Sir James had greeted most of his guests, he approached the musicians, who promptly discarded their country dance for a little flourish that drew everyone's attention. His face serious, he waved his hands, asking the crowd to become quiet.

" 'Tis my pleasure," he said as silence fell across the room, "to announce my daughter Carolly Clairmont's seventeenth birthday."

All eyes turned toward Carolly, who steadied herself with a hand on Richard's arm and brushed the other across her perfect coiffure. People began to clap while several women clustered around Carolly. Richard smiled easily, endured a few slaps on the back, and left Carolly to her admirers. His smile quickly fading, he made his way to a waiter bearing glasses of whiskey.

Parties were hard on him, too.

Sir James nodded and waved to the musicians, who struck up another country dance. Lucinda sidled toward the fireplace and caught Sir James' glance. Smiling, he walked in her direction.

" 'Tis a fine gathering, no?" He watched his daughter, a smile curving his lips.

"Very fine indeed. You set a bountiful table."

"I only wish I were young enough to make merry. I fear I'm already looking forward to my bed." He glanced up at a picture above the fireplace.

She took a step away from the fire and examined the picture. Of a young Sir James, the portrait emphasized how very much the man had aged. His thick black hair had become gray and sparse, and his assured stance had changed to one that was stooped and weak. Indeed, he seemed much worse now than when she'd arrived at Clairmont Hall.

Her thoughts darted to Faye. She suspected the witch had stepped up her efforts to bring Sir James to his knees. Her insides tightened with frustration. She knew she'd have to cast another spell on his behalf and wished its effect would last a bit longer. They were all growing tired of suffering under Faye's hand.

"Painted almost fifteen years ago." Sir James chuckled, the sound dissolving into a discreet cough. "The artist gave me such a grand appearance, I've never been satisfied with myself since."

She forced a smile to her lips. "Ah, Sir James, you're far too hard on yourself."

"Perhaps I am. I know I've been too hard on Carolly." His grip on his cane tightened. "She resembles my wife so closely, and after Elizabeth died, I was afraid to let her grow up because I thought I might lose her, too."

They both looked across the hall at Carolly, who stood near the entrance to the ballroom. Perhaps it was the tightly coiled hair, which gave her a sleek stylishness, maybe it was the relaxed way she held her fan; but somehow, she managed to look both bored and worldly, despite the young men who hovered around her. Carolly, Lucinda mused, ought to try her hand on Drury Lane.

"But now that I see her as polished and beautiful as any jewel, I realize how wrong I've been. I've wasted too many years fighting with her when we could have been enjoying each other's company."

Lucinda touched his arm, moved by the regret in his voice. "She loves you, you know."

They both fell silent, and around them, party manners gave way to high spirits as people began to move into the ballroom. Sir James offered her an arm, and together, they followed the crowd. As soon as they entered the ballroom, Lucinda sucked in a breath, for she felt quite sure she'd never seen such a luxurious spectacle.

No less than three chandeliers hung overhead, each sporting crystal drops that glittered in the light of hundreds of candles. Greek columns supported an arched ceiling painted in gold and sky blue, and heavy damask drapes formed ivory frames around each window. But the Chinese pagoda set into the far wall was by far the most spectacular element. Black veined marble, intricate jade scrollwork, and gold trim combined to form a fashionable reminder of the Orient.

"This room quite takes my breath away," she admitted, remembering only dust, darkness, and white shapes the last time she'd visited the ballroom.

Sir James patted her hand. "I had Hilton remove the shrouds from the furniture and pagoda only last week."

At that moment, the musicians struck up a stately melody suited to a quadrille. Sir James left her side and joined Carolly on the dance floor, along with three other couples. With much flute-playing and horn-blowing, the orchestra guided the dancers through the quadrille, the bored expressions on two ladies' faces suggesting they thought the opening dance a chore to be borne. Carolly alone looked animated, her head held high and her clasp on her father's hand firm as she walked through the figures.

Everyone, Lucinda knew, was waiting for a waltz, the true pleasure, to begin. She watched the couples finish their dance and disperse, looking between their coiffed heads for a dark-haired man. She found him near the garden doors, his gaze fixed upon her. Even from a distance she noted the sensual thrust to his full lower lip and shivered.

She broke eye contact, warmth seeping through her limbs to settle between her legs, the place he'd explored so intimately mere hours before. She began to ache, the sensation making thoughts of propriety difficult. Her face felt hot; moisture beaded her brow. Swallowing, she dabbed it away.

Sir James passed by her as he left the dance floor and paused to pat her arm in a fatherly gesture. Like a papal blessing, Sir James' gesture encouraged others—particularly those in trousers—to approach her. Someone shoved a glass of champagne in her hand, and another pulled her onto the dance floor, and soon she found herself laughing with a uniformed soldier who swung her gaily about the ballroom. Relieved to have her thoughts occupied by someone other than Richard, at least for the moment, she smiled up at him.

He blinked, as if dazed.

When the song ended, the soldier escorted her from the dance floor, but lingered nearby until an elderly gent took his place. His manner courtly, the older man flirted with her, and in vain she tried to remember his name. Dillard? Spartus? Why could she recall several passages from *Le Morte D'Arthur* within seconds, but forget that most important of social necessities? She shook her head and grimaced, her attention falling on Richard.

He no longer stood at his post by the garden doors. He seemed to have disappeared. She craned her neck, searching for him, when suddenly he appeared at her side.

"A waltz, Miss Drakewyck," he said, his countenance a pattern card for civility, despite the fact that he'd taken her virginity mere hours before. "Care to join me?"

She examined him from beneath her lashes. He was so large and male and utterly potent in black, and at least a foot taller than any other man there. With a sigh she laid her hand on his arm. How could she do otherwise? "You've kept me waiting quite a long time."

" 'Twas my duty to satisfy certain obligations." He covered the hand she'd placed on his arm with his free one, reminding her of how safe and warm she had felt on his bed, cradled beneath him. "Now I have time for pleasure."

She paused, struck by his sensual tone. Uncle George's stern visage shimmered in her mind. Her own arguments against their relationship repeated themselves in quick succession. Helplessly she dismissed them all. She'd already sipped the wine and savored its lush flavor and delicious sting. Without Richard, that wine became mere water, completely bland and unsatisfying.

"And I am your willing partner."

His hazel eyes smoldering with unspoken promises, he led her onto the dance floor. He slipped his arm around her back, held her hand next to his chest, and began to swing her around in a three-step pattern, each movement executed with lithe animal grace. She clung to him, silently damning herself for her weakness, feeling as though they'd already begun to make love again.

Richard could scarce keep his hands where propriety demanded they remain. He felt her surrender in the way she clutched his arms and threw back her head, in her quick breaths that made her breasts shiver, in the pink color that tinted her cheeks. Clenching his jaw, he appeased himself by studying every adorable inch of her.

Her hair swept back from her forehead in rich coppery brown waves, and her eyes burned gold with sultry impudence, enough to tempt a saint. Her neckline was far too low and trimmed with a tissue-thin ivory tulle that rubbed against her bosom, provoking him to touch, to taste as he had before. Her gown narrowed to a point at her small waist, then belled out, mimicking the sweet curve of her hips and teasing him with its rustling and swishing against her silken pantaloons and garters.

Bloody hell, he wanted to have her all to himself, to undress her beneath the noontime sun and examine every satiny curve, to possess her and marry her and be done with it once and for all.

"I trust you're enjoying yourself," he managed.

"Far too much. I fear my feet will ache in the morning and I won't be able to take a step."

"Why not use a broomstick?"

She loosened her grip and examined him with narrowed eyes. "Are you calling me a witch, sir?"

"You are indeed," he murmured softly, so only she could hear. "I can think of nothing but you."

She laughed, a soft little sound that went straight to his head. "We had better talk about something more neutral, before we shock Sir James' guests."

"I don't care if they're shocked. By tomorrow night we'll be married."

A little sigh escaped her. "Why must you persist in demanding I marry you?"

"For God's sake, Lucinda, I took your virginity," he muttered, his voice audible only to her. " 'Tis my duty to marry you. How could you turn down an honest offer in favor of intrigue?"

"Intrigue?"

"I want to make love to you again. I want to spend days in a bedchamber learning every sweet curve of your body." He drew a deep, shuddering breath and barely squashed the urge to crush her against his chest. "If we don't marry, I cannot promise to leave you alone."

Her cheeks grew bright red. "I don't want a husband who marries out of duty. Besides, Faye wants us married, and I refuse to put us both in danger by bowing to her wishes."

"So you choose intrigue."

She lowered her lashes. "I do."

Lips tight, he nodded. Silently he vowed to drag her to the altar if he had to. He would not make a mistress of her, even if, in her innocence, she wished it so.

Music curled around them, carrying them around the room in a bubbling wave. The lively dance required a good deal of exertion, and other dancers bumped against them, the smell of perfume and body odor and roses mingling in an unpleasant medley.

"We travel to London in two days," she murmured. "Will you be joining us?"

"Have I any choice?"

"I see you're unhappy about the prospect."

"I returned to Somerton to find relief from society and its reminders of war. I don't relish the idea of wallowing in war stories and squiring females to and from London's social engagements."

She raised an eyebrow. "Why not allow your father to escort us around? We're more than satisfied with his company."

"My father hasn't the stamina for such an endeavor. Indeed, I'm certain Carolly's coming-out will tax us more than a six-month fox hunt would."

A rueful smile curved her lips.

He stared at her, struck anew by the rich luster of her hair beneath the chandelier, by the strange combination of innocence and wisdom in her eyes. He dipped his head closer to hers, totally engrossed in the woman he held. Their steps matched perfectly as they spun about the ballroom more slowly than the other couples.

Suddenly, Lucinda sighed deeply, as if she'd drawn it from the depths of her soul. "I wish I'd never set eyes on Faye Morgan."

"I agree. Particularly since, in your view, she stands in the way of our marriage." He loosened his hold on her, allowing her to drift away a few inches. The action brought little relief. His loins tightened with every glance downward, at her hair, her pert nose, her eminently kissable mouth.

"You'll never believe in magic. You'll never believe in me," she blurted, and pressed her lips together, but not before he noticed them trembling.

His only answer was one she didn't wish to hear, so he remained silent.

Lucinda turned in his arms and looked over his shoulder. "Tell me, what is Faye doing now, pray?"

He glanced at the blonde, who stood with a round willow basket. Guests were placing personal objects in the basket—hair, fabric, and other items—all snipped with scissors she'd placed on a side table.

"She has a parlor game she wishes to play, something about wearing a blindfold and identifying an item by touch. Carolly spoke to me about it earlier. What do *you* suppose she's doing?"

Lucinda lowered her voice. "Just as Cook stocks her pantry for certain favorite recipes, Faye is stocking her pantry for various nasty spells."

He snorted, the sound gaining the attention of an elderly gent who had bumped them three times previously, and swung her toward the outskirts of the dance floor.

She edged away from him. "You're so stubbornly entrenched in your own beliefs you can't see beyond the end of your nose."

Stung, he frowned. "Are you saying I'm narrow-minded?"

"I am."

"Impertinent chit."

"Obstinate mule."

They glared at one another for a moment, but then a smile twitched her lips, and Richard found himself fighting off an answering grin.

"I'm going to prove everything to you, Richard," she said, her voice casual. "I hope I convince you soon enough for you to avoid whatever net she's set for you."

At that moment, the music ended. He steered her toward the edge of the dance floor, released her gently, and bowed. This, he thought, would be their only dance. He didn't dare torture himself with another.

"You've already netted me, Lucinda. I would not worry overmuch about Faye."

Eyebrow raised, she curtseyed and left him.

Bereft, he watched a red-coated soldier—a youth whose sideburns hadn't quite grown in—claim her hand and draw her to a refreshment table. She drank the champagne the soldier procured and then followed him onto the dance floor for another waltz. Richard's stomach turned slow, sour flips as Lucinda smiled at her partner. The soldier hustled her around the floor, his enthusiasm that of a man whose future stretched before him with rosy promise.

Now there, Richard thought, was the perfect husband: a man who had scars on neither his body nor his soul. He bore the youth no ill will, but couldn't stop himself from wishing he'd sprain an ankle, if only to release Lucinda from his too-eager embrace.

For the next two hours he watched a parade of perfect husbands hold her hand for a country dance or embrace her in a waltz, and sought solace in a glass of whiskey—the only stuff in the room strong enough to make him forget how much he'd like to silence her refusals with a few well-placed kisses.

Finally, near the stroke of midnight, he could take it no longer and slouched off toward the library. He rounded a corner and bumped his shin against a chair, scraping it across the wooden floor. Gently he pushed the furniture against the wall and eyed it with dissatisfaction. Damned silly place to put a chair, he thought, and worked his way around it. The door to his library, he noted, was partly open. He entered the temporary sanctuary and shut the door against all intruders.

Smiling, Morgana marked Richard's exit.

Soon she would see their faces crying. Soon she'd witness their pain. She nodded absently to one of the

304

fools who swarmed around her, his words of flattery
doing little to penetrate her concentration.

Edward Drakewyck and Henry Clairmont, she
thought, had shattered her wings, but still she flew,
higher and stronger than she ever had before.
Throughout those long centuries buried beneath sti-
fling earth, her spirit had never let go. It had cleaved
to her, filling her with determination that only hatred
could bring. Now, each day brought her closer to the
revenge she longed for more fervently than a desert
wanderer yearned for a drop of moisture against his
lips.

She chuckled, recalling the waltz between the witch
and the knave. She'd thought they might couple on
the dance floor, so close had they cleaved together, so
intent were their gazes on each other. Listening to the
whispers around her, she knew she wasn't the only
one who had drawn such a conclusion. George Drakewyck glared at everyone and everything in his path
and Sir James Clairmont's eyebrows had drawn together in evident concern.

In a way, she almost felt sorry for the knave and
witch. They'd brought back memories of Christopher's courtship. Discovering the sweet wonder of his
love, feeling his touch for the first time . . . they'd
been wondrous experiences that had left her giddy
with pleasure. And after they'd married, their love
had only grown stronger, deeper.

Until Edward Drakewyck had decided to destroy
her utterly.

Hot blood surged through her veins, but then that
strange voice in the back of her mind began speaking,
and confusion tempered her rage.

She frowned.

Who spoke to her, and for what purpose? She simply couldn't hear the words clearly enough. The voice teased her from the edge of her consciousness, spouting tangled words that asked her to remember.

To forgive.

She stiffened. No! Never.

Never, she vowed.

With a nod of her head, she called Carolly over to her.

The younger woman looked pristine yet sophisticated with her white dress and sleek dark hair. Too bad, she thought, that the Drakewyck witch had spoiled her plans for Carolly. Still, the poppet she'd created in Carolly's image ought to put a bit of suffering into her evening. Indeed, the girl had already begun to limp.

"Carolly," Morgana said, "I just saw your brother enter the library, looking quite dejected. Thoughts of war are likely bothering him again. Perhaps you ought to go and comfort him."

Her cheeks flushed, Carolly looked helplessly at her little circle of admirers. "But I can't leave now, Faye. Mr. Pierce has my hand for the next dance, and the orchestra is already preparing to start."

As they spoke, the trilling melody of a flute clashed with a violin's whiny notes.

"Is there someone else who might comfort him?"

Carolly's gaze fell directly on the Drakewyck witch as Faye had known it would. "I'll find someone. Thank you, Faye, for pointing out Richard's difficulty to me. I would not like to think him unhappy at my party."

Faye nodded graciously. "Enjoy yourself, dear."

Carolly gave her a brilliant smile and nearly skipped over to her admirers. She looked young and happy and utterly untouched by the evil that brewed around her.

Remorse whispered at the corners of Morgana's mind, surprising her.

Remember, the voice said.

Remember what we'd had.

Relentlessly Morgana shut the voice out.

She set her sights on Sir James. She'd give the witch ten minutes alone with her lover in the library, and then bring a few people along to spoil their pleasure. Human nature as it was, she had no doubts that by tomorrow evening, the witch and the knave would be fast wed.

Morgana had a sense of events coming to pass, of plans reaching fruition. She tried to force another smile to her lips and failed. Helplessly she wondered why the notion didn't bring the pleasure she'd expected it would.

18

"Lucinda, you must go after Richard."

Lucinda felt a tugging on her arm. She smiled at the middle-aged man who chatted with her and turned to find Carolly at her side. The girl's words registered and Lucinda thought, *Faye's gotten to him.* Dread instantly curled through her insides.

Carolly's attention had strayed to a young gentleman who stood by himself, about ten feet away.

Lucinda clasped the girl's hand. "Where is Richard? What's happened?"

The first notes of a waltz trilled through the ballroom. Blinking, Carolly refocused on her. "Oh, he's all right. He just seems a bit morose. Perhaps memories of the war are bothering him. Whatever the case, he's closeted himself in the library. Would you go and cheer him up? You seem quite good at that, you know."

"Of course." Lucinda sighed, the sound shaky.

"I'd go myself, but I've promised to dance with Mr. Pierce."

"Go ahead, dance. 'Tis your birthday party. You deserve to enjoy yourself. But Carolly, remember my warnings. Be careful with the gentlemen; don't do anything that might upset your father. Watch your drinks, and don't go anywhere unchaperoned."

Carolly pressed a quick kiss against her cheek. "You're a dear to worry so much about me."

Her heart still fluttering, Lucinda watched as Carolly took Mr. Pierce's arm and began to dance with him. She'd been concentrating almost entirely on Carolly, and now realized she'd neglected Richard. He needed a spell of protection, not only to help keep him safe from Faye, but to ease her worry. At her first opportunity she'd procure something personal from him. A snippet of his hair would work best.

Smoothing her skirts, she started toward the library. She skirted the edges of the dance floor and noticed Faye near the garden doors, listening but not responding to one of Somerton's elderly gents. The witch's gaze, ever restless, swept the room, and paused for a moment to linger on Lucinda before moving on. A tiny, secretive smile formed on Faye's lips.

Lucinda hurried out of the ballroom and away from Faye's malevolent presence with the silent vow to return quickly and watch over Carolly. When she reached the library, she tried the doorknob but found it locked.

She rapped sharply on the oak.

"Who is it?"

" 'Tis I, Lucinda."

The sound of a key turning in a lock squeaked in her ears. A moment later, the door swung open. She stepped inside and studied Richard. His jacket rumpled and his cravat loose, he bumped into the tripod that supported his globe. The stack of books he clutched for balance promptly fell to his feet, kicking up a cloud of dust and forcing him to stumble again. Cursing, he stomped to the mantelpiece and turned up the oil lamp, throwing more light into the room, but not enough to dispel the shadows.

Having wreaked enough havoc, he slouched into a chair and stared into the fire. Whiskey fumes lingered in the air.

Hand on her hips, Lucinda regarded him. "Richard, are you foxed?"

"A bit."

She advanced into the room. Carolly had been right to call on her. Memories of the war must have set him to drinking. "You have to stop. You'll make a spectacle of yourself."

"I'm not returning to the ballroom. I'm staying here for the rest of the evening."

"I'm staying with you until you change your mind."

"Silly wench, must you constantly encourage trouble?"

"How am I encouraging trouble by offering comfort when memories of the Crimea have obviously gotten the better of you?"

He snorted. " 'Tis your comfort I need, that's for certain."

Eyeing him suspiciously, she found his glass of whiskey and drained it in a potted palm.

"You're acting like a wife," he observed. "And yet, you refuse to become one in reality."

She hid a smile and plopped onto a jade settee next to him. "You don't sound like a man caught up in memories of bloodshed and death."

"I'm not, by God. Something far worse than that is plaguing me, and it takes the shape of a luscious little witch who begs me with her eyes to kiss her."

"I beg for nothing." Eyebrow raised, she stretched her feet toward the embers which glowed in the fireplace and slouched back against the settee. She felt his gaze burn across her breasts, and realized her hunched position had urged her breasts upward until they seemed ready to spill from their silken cage. He probably thought she was deliberately tempting him.

She didn't change her position.

"Do you want *me* to beg, then?" he asked. "On second thought, don't answer. I just might say to hell with my pride, get down on my hands and knees, and hate myself in the morning." He reached for a decanter of brandy that sat on a side table.

She moved more quickly and swept it away.

He groaned and rubbed his eyes.

Now, she thought, was the perfect time to clip that piece of his hair. Whiskey had him befuddled. He'd never notice the loss. She moved to his desk and rifled through the top drawer until she found a pair of shears, wincing at the scraping sound she'd made.

"What are you doing?" he asked, not bothering to look at her.

She froze. "Organizing my thoughts."

"Well, spare my desk your organizing. I've already placed things where I wish them to be. In fact, we ought to move to a more . . . pleasant occupation. A little intrigue, maybe?"

She choked back a snort at his shameless offer, crept up behind him, and snipped a tiny piece of his black hair.

He spun around. "What in hell?"

So much, she mused, for his whiskey-fuddled thoughts. Shears in one hand, a lock of his hair in the other, she smiled apologetically. "You don't mind, do you?"

"Good God, woman!" He sprang to his feet, snatched the shears from her hand, and slammed them against his desk. "You've cut my hair."

"I needed something personal from you."

He grabbed her arm and pulled her against him. "So, you want to play Faye's game? Where is your willow basket?"

"What use have I for a basket? I play only with you."

She relished the way her breasts flattened against his chest, pushing upward, taunting him even more; relished the twist to his mouth that was something close to pain. She'd provoked him deliberately and wished that the ropes of propriety that bound him would snap and free them both.

The barest of smiles touching his lips, he dipped his hand into her bodice, his palm cupping her breast, his fingers gentle as he rubbed one nipple. Her soft gasp, more a moan than an outcry, was the sound of feminine satisfaction. A shiver swept through her until her whole body was quaking.

"Tell me," he murmured, "what do I have in my hand?"

She met his gaze, the trembling unabated, until suddenly a husky laugh burst from her throat. "You are a rogue," she breathed, her eyes watering.

He grinned. "Only with you."

Eyes closed, she leaned into his hand, filling his palm with her flesh, wishing the merrymakers in the ballroom into another county. Heavy footsteps pounded past the door, accompanied by giggling. Lucinda grew still and cast a worried glance at Richard.

Richard withdrew his hand. "You should return to the ballroom."

She tapped him playfully on the arm. Inside, however, she shivered at her own boldness. "Why are you always telling me to go?"

"Someone has to look out for you. You obviously haven't the sense to look out for yourself."

Swallowing, she walked over to the library door. The key still remained in the lock. She turned it. Carolly, she thought, could take care of herself for a little while, at least. "Aren't you going to ask me why I cut your hair?"

A dark flush spread across his face. "I don't need to. You plan to cast a spell over me, and my hair is a vital ingredient." He moved to her side and leaned close until his breath warmed her cheek. "I encourage you to try. Indeed, tell me the nature of your spell, and I'll report if it achieves the desired effect."

" 'Tis a love spell, of course," she lied, then tilted her head up to peek at him through her lashes.

Without warning he swooped down to kiss her upturned mouth, opening it and thrusting his tongue deep inside her. Weakness invaded her every limb and she held on to him, tight, lest she collapse beneath the bold plunder of his tongue. She felt none of the shyness that had beset her during their picnic when she'd opened to him for the first time. Rather, anticipation created a hot shiver that started in her breasts and crept downward to settle between her legs. Her sensitive flesh had already begun to grow moist and she strained against him, yearning to feel again the searing jolts of pleasure which only he could bring.

"We must not, not here," he groaned, but she ignored him, reaching back to feel his trousers and the firm muscles of his buttocks beneath.

He gasped aloud and held her tighter, his kiss becoming more urgent. They twisted against each other, his lips parting with hers only to settle on her breasts, his tongue dipping into her cleavage. She held his head between her palms, refusing to free him from her heated flesh, which he licked and rubbed so patiently.

When her breasts began to throb and the ache between her thighs became painful, she released him and ran her fingers through his hair, across his powerful shoulders and down to the waistband of his trousers to slip beneath and caress his naked skin. She felt hot, feverish, nearly frantic with need for him. Their earlier lovemaking had introduced her to sensations she hadn't known possible, and now she wanted to revel in every sensual delight he thought to teach her.

"My God, Lucinda . . ." His breath coming in soft pants, he put his arm around her shoulders and urged her backward until she pressed against the library wall, her voluminous skirts a starched-cotton barrier between them. He began to kiss her again, crushing her against the wall with his powerful body, his thigh between her legs, urging them apart. She rubbed against his knee, needing desperately to feel him inside her, not against her.

Suddenly he was fishing through her skirts and petticoats, trying to find her drawers, and dragging the fabric up around her waist. She took her skirts from him and held them bunched at her waist as he knelt before her, found her drawers, and pulled them down around her ankles. She kicked them off, glad to be rid of them, and felt his palms on her thighs, spreading her wider. A warm breath blew across the place between her legs, and then he was kissing her, his tongue gentle yet insistent as he licked the center of her pleasure.

At first, she stiffened at the thought of him right there, looking at her, the light from an oil lamp illuminating her most secret parts. Heat scalded her face. But with each delicate stroke of his tongue, violent jolts radiated through her, bringing her closer to total deliverance. Her embarrassment dissolved beneath a torrent of desire and she cried out.

At the sound he instantly straightened and pressed his mouth against hers, quieting her, gentling her. His trouser-clad knee pressed against her moist folds of flesh, keeping her legs parted, the fabric maddening her as she helplessly rubbed against it, no longer a propriety-bound lady but a creature of pure sensuality.

He moaned, the sound torn from somewhere deep inside him, and broke away to unfasten his trousers. Giddy anticipation made breathing difficult. She let her head roll back against the wall, aware that soon he would soothe the ache that nearly brought sobs to her throat.

Her breasts flushed and tingling, she watched as he pushed his trousers down around his hips and bared himself to her admiring gaze. His arousal thrust at her, the hard tip pushing against her leg, and she twisted until it nuzzled against her moistness.

"Richard, please," she whispered against his ear. "I need you now. I don't care if you think me without an ounce of virtue."

"Shhh. You're perfect. Perfect."

His caresses had forced her breasts upward until her nipples grazed the edge of her bodice. He paused to kiss each throbbing peak, his features sharp and eyes nearly black with passion. Unwilling to suffer any more delay, she wound her fingers through his hair and pulled his head upward until his lips brushed hers. She locked her mouth against his and kissed him frantically.

Her skirts bunched between them, he grasped her naked buttocks, lifted her until her feet no longer touched the carpet, and pressed her against the wall. She wrapped her legs around his waist and her arms around his neck and clung to him as he drove into her, bringing no pain this time, filling her completely.

He held her there for a moment, thoroughly possessed, before he began to thrust, lifting her a little and then impaling her on the full length of his arousal. He cradled the back of her head with his hand and drove his tongue between her lips, claiming her mouth while he rode her, thrusting ever faster.

Weightless, she felt nothing but the hard wall at her back and the scorching pleasure of him as he emptied her and filled her, over and over again, her hips bumping against the wall in frenzied cadence. As if from far away, she heard a voice, but dismissed it as revelers who'd strayed from the ballroom. The delicious feel of him deep inside her, touching her innermost core, drove out all other thoughts.

"Oh, Lucinda . . ." His chest shuddered. He buried his face in her neck and, his breath coming in gasps, he quickened his movements until the pleasure tormenting her reached an unbearable apex and her thigh muscles tightened and indescribable sensations washed through her in a wave. She surrendered to that shattering delight, her moistness convulsing on him as he stilled, the full length of him inside her, his gaze fastened on her face.

She closed her eyes and collapsed against him.

With a low groan he began to ride her very quickly, thrusting forward, his body straining as he reached his climax and emptied himself into her. She felt warmth flush through her most tender parts and sighed in utter contentment.

Three determined knocks sounded at the library door.

"Richard, Lucinda, are you all right?" Sir James' voice drifted through the door to settle on her ears. She jerked upright.

Lucinda grew still. Disbelief turned her veins to ice.

"By God, open this door!" Uncle George pounded on the oak, making it rattle in its frame.

"One moment," Richard called out. The flush in his face gave way to a whitish pallor. He withdrew from her and allowed her to slide to the floor, his gaze on the door, his mouth pulled into a grimace. "Bloody *hell*," he muttered. "We're found out. Hurry, fix your dress."

Lucinda tried to force her skirts into the proper bell-shaped position, but her numerous petticoats made her so ungainly she hadn't the slightest success. As she struggled, she marveled at how deftly Faye had outmaneuvered her. She'd been waiting all night for a replay of the stables incident, and Faye had delivered, although she'd caught Lucinda and Richard in her net, not Carolly.

He pushed his erection back into his trousers; but rather than fix himself further he pulled her skirts downward like a deranged lady's maid, fluffing and arranging even though he obviously hadn't the slightest idea what he was about.

Lucinda heard the unmistakable sound of a key turning in the lock. She clasped her breasts in panicked hands and tried to fit them properly into her bodice. Her heart was racing and her cheeks burned so hot she thought they must have turned scarlet. Abruptly their lovemaking seemed tawdry, where once it had been a passionate expression of love.

"I'd rather they find me in a state of disarray than you," he muttered, just as the door swung open.

Sir James, Uncle George, Faye, and Carolly pushed into the library. Uncle George took one look at them and turned white, while Sir James, his gaze dropping to Richard's trousers, flushed a perfect red. Carolly's eyes were circles of shock. Faye, for her part, had a wide smile on her lips. Lucinda had once seen a similar smile on a cat; a bird's leg had protruded from its mouth.

Richard moved in front of her, shielding her from their view, his back straight and proud.

Sir James turned to Carolly and Faye. "Ladies, I ask you to leave, now, and say nothing of this to anyone."

Nodding, Faye and Carolly left the room, their gazes remaining on Lucinda and Richard until they'd stepped out of view.

"And I ask you to leave as well," Richard demanded, "and give us a moment."

His hand clenched on his cane, Sir James turned to leave.

"By God, I wish I had a shotgun," Uncle George muttered, his attention locking on her abandoned drawers.

Sir James placed a hand on her uncle's sleeve. "Now, George, I know it's bad, but I'm certain Richard will marry her."

"Immediately," Richard confirmed.

Uncle George examined the elder Clairmont through a narrowed gaze. Suddenly he took a step backward, his lips parted, eyes wide. "You're happy about this, man. Admit it. I can see it in your face."

Sir James made placating gestures with his hands. "I'm not happy. I'm highly annoyed that my son would take advantage of Lucinda. Still, I don't think his intent wicked; indeed, their marriage, in my opinion, was inevitable."

Her uncle nodded his gray-haired head and smothered a cough with his fist. "Yes, I suppose it was."

"I will admit to thinking Richard's taste in women unsurpassed." Sir James, pausing to give Lucinda a comforting smile, led Uncle George away. "We'll be waiting," he said, and pulled the door shut.

Richard heaved a deep sigh. His gaze sought hers, his lids heavy, this time clearly with remorse. After a moment, he pulled her into his arms and rested his chin on the top of her head. "Lucinda, I cannot tell you how sorry I am for this. I'm older. I know more of the world. I should have stopped before risking your reputation."

She huddled against his broad chest and drew comfort from his closeness. "We're both at fault. You wanted to stop. You gave the appropriate warnings. Still, I craved the pleasure you bring me and would have done anything to kiss you again, to feel your lips, well, everywhere." She lowered her lashes, hoping he wouldn't think her completely gauche.

He kissed her forehead. "Well, 'tis no matter, for we'll marry tomorrow."

"You *are* persistent." Cheek pressed against him, Lucinda considered her position. Now the people closest to her, the people whose respect she needed the most, knew she'd fallen from grace. Her sins had become public and marriage was the only possible atonement. If she continued to refuse marriage, she'd suffer humiliation beneath the gazes of those she loved, but she'd also remain safe from Faye and free from a loveless marriage. "Richard, I can't marry you—"

"Hush," he said. "I know your reasons for refusing to marry me. You're afraid we'll remove the last barrier that stands between us and Faye's revenge, and you don't think I could become a good husband. But your refusals, Lucinda, sound like defeat rather than defiance. Marriage between us would be a gesture of hope—hope that we might survive Faye, hope that you and I might someday come to terms. I never thought you the kind to choose defeat over hope."

Without waiting for her answer, he retrieved her drawers and helped her put them on. Eyes wide, she slanted a curious glance his way as he finished rearranging her skirts, then fixed his trousers. By God, she mused, he'd made good sense. Who was the optimist here, and who the war-torn soldier?

The door opened and Sir James entered, trailed by Uncle George. Richard's father paused at a side table and poured four brandies. Her uncle walked around him to her side, his frame shaking, his shoulders stooped. Suddenly he looked very, very old.

"My God, gel, you've allowed him to disgrace you. Didn't I tell you to stay away from him?"

While Lucinda hung her head, Uncle George turned toward Richard and shook a finger at him. "Impudent dog. How could you take her innocence like that?"

His face cold, his lips tight, Richard drew himself up and towered over her uncle. "Lucinda and I are marrying."

She clasped his hand in hers. "Tomorrow, in fact."

Richard focused on her with a wide-eyed gaze.

A hesitant smile curled her lips. "You've convinced me," she murmured, and the look of happiness that transformed his features convinced her she'd made the right decision. Faye, she reasoned, would come for her eventually, married or not.

Sir James took a sip of brandy and held a snifter out to each of them. She and her uncle turned them down, while Richard, his jaw clenched, tossed off the snifter's entire contents.

"I'll obtain a license for you." Sir James regarded his son with a clear gaze. "Reverend Wood should be in the ballroom somewhere. I'll tell him that you and Lucinda have been secretly engaged. We'll pretend you're concerned that the Queen might soon call you back into service, and you wish to marry Lucinda now, in case you are forced to leave Somerton. 'Tis a complete fabrication, of course, but we should disguise our need for haste."

"I quite agree." Richard put his arm around Lucinda's waist and drew her close to his side. His voice, when he spoke, was husky. "You need not fear for Lucinda, either of you. She is very precious to me, more so than my own life. I will make her happy."

Lucinda froze in his arms and looked up at him, shocked at the raw emotion in his voice, and saw that his jaw had clenched with the force of his vow.

He met her gaze, his hazel eyes bright, his black hair gleaming in the candlelight. Almost dizzy with the implications of his words, Lucinda felt her heart turn over in her breast. He had, indeed, become her Lancelot, willing to sacrifice even himself for her. The thought brought a warm glow to every inch of her body.

And yet, deep inside, she knew that they'd pushed past another notch on the wheel of Fortune, bringing them that much closer to their ultimate destiny. Faye could attack at any time after they wed tomorrow.

Sir James studied them with a faint smile on his lips. "I suggest Lucinda retire and get some sleep before the ceremony tomorrow. Richard and I will make the necessary preparations for their marriage. George, can you meet us at St. Paul's Church at, say, eleven o'clock tomorrow morning?"

Uncle George grunted. "I'll be there."

"Good. Until tomorrow then."

Lucinda's uncle escorted her from the room, leaving Richard alone with his father. Richard's shoulders drooped and he rubbed his eyes. "I cannot believe the mess I've made of things."

"It'll straighten out," Sir James predicted. "I didn't dare admit this before George Drakewyck, but I'm damned happy you're going to marry her, Richard. I can't think of anyone I'd want more for a daughter-in-law. And she's good for you. She's turned you around and made you forget the war."

"I love her." Richard shrugged, the statement so simple and obvious he couldn't understand why he hadn't seen it before. Her smiles and sweet laughter and gentle, loving presence had become necessary to his very survival.

"I know you do. And I believe she loves you, too."

"She may love me, but she regrets it. Until we were compromised, she'd absolutely refused to marry me. I suspect she resents being forced into a marriage with a man scarred as I am."

"You're underestimating her."

"With time, I hope to prove myself to her," he said, and knew it as the truth. He would work harder than a laborer in the fields to protect her and love her and keep her satisfied in all ways.

"Well, first we've got to get you married." Sir James removed several guineas from a velvet bag in his desk and slipped them into his pocket. "I'll find Reverend Wood. You must ask someone to stand up for you. Afterward, get some sleep, and we'll meet early in the morning to make final plans."

"I hope this won't affect your desire to leave for London on Monday."

"No, but you raise an important point. I must ask you to delay your bridal tour until the Queen has given Carolly her blessings. We should attend as a family to witness what will no doubt prove a definitive moment in her life."

Richard nodded. "Of course. I would have it no other way, and I'm certain Lucinda will agree."

Sir James swirled the brandy around in his snifter, his lips curved in a smile as he gazed at the dark, velvety liquid. A comfortable silence grew between them.

At length, the older man took a sip and regarded Richard quizzically. "Who are you going to ask to stand up for you?"

"I haven't many acquaintances available on such short notice," Richard admitted. A sudden thought struck him. "But I am quite certain I know of one who would be glad to stand up for me."

"Who?"

"Squire Piggott."

"Indeed." His father didn't look convinced.

"Lucinda has already turned down his marriage proposal," Richard revealed, "and I assure you, he'll find my 'secret engagement' to Lucinda quite a balm to his wounded pride. Besides, the Squire never turns away from an opportunity to associate himself with Lady Rothfield, and participating in Lucinda's wedding would prove a perfect reason for several visits to the lady's estate, if only to gossip."

"Sounds reasonable to me." Sir James placed his glass on a side table. "I'll see if I can find the reverend."

They both walked toward the door. Richard paused in the entryway, a thought occurring to him. "Why did you come looking for Lucinda and me, and how did you know where to find us?"

"Why, Faye told me. She said you seemed morose and had disappeared into the library, and Lucinda had followed. When almost an hour passed since she saw you enter, she grew concerned and alerted both myself and George Drakewyck."

"We weren't together anywhere near an hour," he muttered. "The woman hasn't an ounce of discretion."

"She meant well," his father insisted, but Richard wasn't so sure.

Some of his elation at marrying Lucinda fizzled away. He remembered that Lucinda had insisted Faye wanted them married. Evidently she'd been quite correct.

Cool fingers of dismay crept along the back of his neck.

Perhaps there was more to her vision and the strange entry written in that spellbook of hers. He didn't think for a moment that Faye was an ancient witch risen from the dead; still, the prophecy seemed to be coming true with Faye and Lucinda at the center of it.

He wondered if Faye had somehow found out about both the spellbook entry and the ruby heart that lay in the core of Lucinda's crystal dove. Maybe the blonde was playing on Lucinda's fears, making it seem as though the prophecy were coming true so Lucinda would believe her an ancient witch capable of killing him with a wave of her hand.

In that case, he reasoned, when Faye finally demanded the dove, Lucinda would be so sure of her evil intentions that she'd hand the statue over without thought, to save both him and herself. Laughing at the tremendous joke she'd played upon poor, gullible Lucinda, Faye could then trot off to a London jeweler and sell the ruby heart for a tidy sum.

His gut bubbled at the thought.

But would Faye stoop to poisoning the rest of the family members, bringing on illnesses just to make it appear as if the spellbook entry were coming true?

He remembered accusing Lucinda of harming her uncle and his father with her "tinctures." She'd hotly denied it, and now he wondered if he'd made a terrible mistake in blaming her in the first place.

He examined his father with a critical gaze. "You're not feeling any better, are you?"

"Don't worry about me, Richard. We have more important issues to concern us right now."

"Have you eaten anything odd lately? Has your food tasted as it should?"

"I haven't got indigestion, just a touch of pleurisy."

Richard frowned. He wasn't certain if a poison to induce lung complaints existed. While his father was speaking to Reverend Wood, he'd go and talk to Dr. Bennet. Later, he'd speak to both Cook and the Drakewycks' housekeeper to make sure their food wasn't poisoned again.

First, however, he planned to have a little chat with Faye.

19

$\mathcal{A}$ maidservant roused Lucinda just after eight o'clock in the morning and brought her a tray of hot chocolate and croissants. Yawning, she sat up in bed. Something nagged at her, something wonderful yet frightening, and for one second she sat there, wondering what it was, but then the maidservant dimpled and congratulated her and she remembered everything.

She was marrying Richard today.

Carolly sailed into the room, her hazel eyes bright, her face wreathed in a smile. "Good morning, Lucinda. Or should I say 'sister.'" She jumped onto the bed, making the mattress bounce. "You are a sly one. I never knew for a moment that you and my brother had formed a tendre."

Lucinda floundered for an answer. "We're very private," she finally said. By marrying Richard, she was embracing the future, and for the first time since the vision had come to her she felt hope. But what if she'd chosen incorrectly? What if Faye killed them slowly, or her life with Richard remained loveless?

Nothing truly worthwhile, she told herself, comes without risk.

Carolly narrowed her eyes in mock annoyance. "And here I thought you'd marry Squire Piggott."

"I'll leave him for you."

The girl swatted her playfully. "I would prefer to test the waters in London. Are you going with me to town tomorrow? I'd understand if you told me no, as you and Richard are marrying this morning, but I would so love to know you're there, supporting me."

"Of course we'll come," Lucinda said. "Your happiness is very important to us both."

She clasped Lucinda's hand. "I think I'll enjoy very much having you for a sister."

Lucinda wondered how long they'd be sisters, how long their happiness would last with Faye around. "Will Faye be attending the wedding?"

"How odd that you would mention her. I haven't seen her since my party last night. I honestly do not know if she's even heard a wedding is planned."

Lucinda sat up straight in bed. She didn't like the sound of Faye's disappearance. A sense of wheels turning, of plans falling into place, made the skin at the back of her neck tingle.

"Why, Lucinda, you're suddenly very pale." Carolly patted her hand. "Don't worry about Faye. She'll turn up. At any rate, you're going to be so busy over the next few hours that you'll hardly have a chance to worry. Indeed, we must start right away. I've taken the liberty of selecting one of my new gowns for your wedding dress and recruited every maidservant in the house. Between all of us, we'll have your gown properly altered within an hour. May I show you the gown?"

"Of course. You're very generous, Carolly. Thank you."

Carolly jumped off the bed and rushed out the door. In a few minutes she'd returned, an ivory satin creation lying across her arm. "We'll put some more lace on it, and sew a few satin rosettes for the bodice, and the gardener is already putting a long, cascading bouquet together for you."

" 'Tis beautiful," Lucinda murmured, looking at the dress.

Grinning, the girl pulled out an ivory satin sack that she'd hidden beneath the gown, opened it, and withdrew a gold tiara studded with pearls. "I thought you could wear this in your hair. We'll drip some lace from the back of it."

Lips parted, Lucinda touched it with gentle figures. "I'm overcome."

" 'Twas my mother's," Carolly confided. "I hope to wear it when I marry—" Without warning, the girl bent over and groaned, a hand pressed against her side. The tiara fell to the floor.

"Carolly!" Lucinda flung back the counterpane and hurried to her side. She held Carolly's shoulders while the girl continued to groan.

"Fire in my side," Carolly gritted. "Lord, it hurts."

Lucinda cast a frantic glance toward the door. "Sit down and I'll get help."

"No, no, it's easing." Her lips pressed together, Carolly grasped the tiara, straightened, and laughed shakily. "It goes as quickly as it comes. You must not worry about me, not today."

Lucinda studied her, her forehead creased with concern. "Have you noticed any redness or swelling around the spot that hurts?"

"No, none at all. In fact, between the pains I feel perfectly fine. There's no lingering ache, just a sudden stab which disappears."

"How long have you had these pains?"

"They started about two weeks ago."

"After you and Mr. Smith had ceased meeting?"

"Yes, although I hadn't thought of it that way before."

Faye, Lucinda thought. The witch had tried to ruin the girl's reputation and failed; now she'd obviously resorted to a direct attack.

"Why didn't you tell me sooner about them?"

"They were mild at first. Hardly anything to talk about. But last night they got worse."

"Do you experience the pains in the same place every time?"

"No. They seem to have no preference. Last night, I even felt one on the bottom of my foot. I attributed it to a cramp."

Lucinda frowned. These pains weren't the symptoms of a lingering illness Faye had foisted upon the girl. The witch must have made a poppet in Carolly's image and now stuck thorns into it. She could imagine Faye trying to spoil Carolly's pleasure in her first adult party by making her feet ache. "Did Faye ever take anything of a personal nature from you?"

Carolly thought for a moment, then shook her head. "Not that I'm aware of. Why?"

"Did she ever show you a tiny waxen doll that looked like you?"

"No. Lucinda, what odd questions."

Lucinda rubbed her temples. She still felt certain Faye had created a poppet of Carolly. Carolly's ignorance of the doll was a point in their favor. If the

victim didn't know about the poppet, the thorns
thrust into the doll seemed to lose potency.

"I'm all right, I swear it," Carolly said, evidently
reading something in Lucinda's expression. "Let me
call for a bath for you. You have to get ready for your
wedding. 'Tis almost eight-thirty; we have only two
hours before you must leave for St. Paul's Church."

Lucinda nodded. The wedding came first.

Faye would come next.

In the time remaining before she had to leave, Lucinda bathed in water scented with lavender blossoms
and washed her hair until it nearly squeaked with
cleanliness. A maidservant dried her hair with a towel
and helped her put on a snow-white chemise with
tiny little straps and inset lace. Lucinda blushed at the
scrap of fabric, knowing it was the sort of thing a
bride might wear to tempt her husband. The maidservant lowered her gaze and giggled.

Carolly, who had left during her bath to supervise
the wedding gown's alterations, rejoined her. She'd
taken the time to dress in a powder blue silk gown,
and now she and the maidservant fastened Lucinda
into a corset, drawing the strings tight but leaving her
room to breathe. Next came the petticoats, six ivory
layers of them, and before she knew it Lucinda was
dressed in the ivory wedding gown, the tiara fixed on
her shining brown curls, her cheeks pale and her eyes
dark shadows in her face.

Throughout it all, she tried to feel excited about the
thought of marrying Richard but too many worries
weighed on her.

Faye had disappeared. Carolly, Uncle George, and
Sir James were all feeling the effects of malignant
witchcraft. She and Richard were getting married, and
in doing so they would remove the last of Faye's bar-

riers. The witch would have no reason to delay her quest for revenge any longer.

"Come see yourself," Carolly urged.

Lucinda moved to stand before the cheval glass.

Carolly put a hand on her arm. "You are beautiful, sister."

A tremulous smile curling her lips, Lucinda nodded. She forced herself to consider the girl in the cheval glass. She'd never thought of herself as a beauty, but in this gown she had to admit she looked gorgeous. The rich fabric accentuated her creamy complexion and the red highlights in her brown hair, and whispered around her as she turned this way and that.

And yet, the sight of herself in that traditional wedding gown began to stir even deeper feelings that she couldn't quite name. Her throat grew tight and, for a moment, she thought she would cry. Carolly, too, had tears in her eyes. Even the maidservant sniffled.

" 'Tis time," Carolly said with a glance at the clock. She wiped her eyes and drew Lucinda to the door. "We must bring you downstairs."

Her steps hesitant, Lucinda began to follow, then stopped, remembering something she'd wanted to take with her. She opened her trunk and reached inside, retrieving not only the crystal dove but also Richard's Victoria Cross. Both she placed in a concealed dress pocket.

At last she felt ready. She followed Carolly through the hall and down the stairs, pausing upon the first rise when she saw Uncle George, dressed up in the finest jacket and trousers he owned.

He strode forward and took her arm. "When I allowed you to go to Clairmont Hall, I didn't realize I'd lose you forever."

Lucinda leaned into him. "You haven't lost me forever. Clairmont Hall is only a few miles away from Drakewyck Grange. Richard and I will make a habit of visiting you every day. Indeed, you'll become tired of seeing us."

He cleared his throat, his eyes becoming suspiciously moist. "Let's go, gel. Your husband waits for you at St. Paul's."

With Uncle George beside her and Carolly bringing up the rear, Lucinda climbed into the Drakewyck's barouche. She scooted to the side and made space for her new sister and uncle, who joined her. The three of them set off for the church and, in Lucinda's opinion, reached the building far too quickly. As they'd traveled over Somerton's bumpy roads, anxiety had continued to dog her and now reached a fever pitch. Her heart thudded and she knew she was no longer pale but pink with color.

Squire Piggott's chaise and the reverend's landau were parked outside the church. Wondering at the Squire's presence, Lucinda allowed Uncle George to lead her into St. Paul's Church. The reverend had lit candles in deference to their marriage and placed a brazier of sweet-smelling incense on the altar. Lucinda gazed at the jeweled windows which blazed colors into the church. They dappled the benches with patterns of light, giving the cavernous interior a magical feel.

She drew in a breath, then let it out slowly.

"Miss Lucinda!"

Squire Piggott rushed to her side, kissing her hand with his usual excess flattery, and bombarded her with a torrent of words.

"I give you my very best congratulations," he said, hands pressed together, "and wishes for your eternal happiness. I understand everything now. If only you had been at liberty to tell me you were already engaged when I proposed to you!

"And that nonsense about you accepting wages from the Clairmonts fooled me entirely. I had thought you'd stepped into permanent ruin but instead you courted the finest man in all of Somerton. When Captain Clairmont asked me to stand up for him, I agreed in an instant, thrilled beyond words to hear that your character was saved."

Lucinda smiled. Richard had shown a deft touch, indeed, when he'd asked the Squire to participate in their wedding. "Squire, I do apologize if I abused your feelings—"

"No, no, not at all."

"Will you do me a favor, Squire?"

"Anything, Miss Lucinda."

"Please inform my aunt, Lady Rothfield, of the details of my wedding. Newly married as I am, I may not have the time to write her immediately."

The Squire bowed low. "That would be my particular pleasure."

She made her way past the Squire, her gaze seeking and finding Richard. He stood near Reverend Wood at the altar, his tailored black jacket and trousers of wool superfine emphasizing his unusual height and powerful shoulders while his white waistcoat and cravat tempered his commanding presence with an air of purity.

A perfect knight, Lucinda thought.

Sir James stood at Richard's left, garbed in a similar outfit. He regarded the reverend with a benevolent smile.

Reverend Wood motioned to Uncle George. "Will the bride approach, please?"

Carolly shoved a cascade of flowers into her hands. Uncle George took her arm, and in silence they walked to the front of the church. Her uncle released her as they reached Richard's side, and Lucinda moved to stand next to him. Carolly remained a few paces behind her, and Squire Piggott, a few behind Richard.

Beneath her lashes, she cast a glance at Richard. He must have sensed her regard for he looked back, his hazel eyes solemn yet soft, his lips curled in a warm smile.

The reverend cleared his throat and intoned in that basso voice of his, beginning the ceremony that joined man to woman until death parted them. Lucinda felt the potency of the words he spoke, like a spell that had built up tremendous power by virtue of its frequent use. When her turn came, she gave the proper answers and listened to Richard's deep voice as he pledged himself to her, as well. Finally, Reverend Wood turned to Richard and asked him to place a ring on her finger.

He slipped his hand into his pocket and brought out a beautifully wrought ring of gold filigree set with a large ruby. Tiny diamonds clustered around the ruby, their depths sparkling in the sunlight that filtered through the church windows. Wonder and delight bubbled within her as he slipped it onto her ring finger. It felt a little loose but not loose enough to fall off easily.

By God, she was married.

"Richard, it's beautiful," she murmured.

" 'Twas my mother's."

"I have something for you, too." She reached into her dress pocket until she felt the hard, pointed corners of his Victoria Cross, and clasped it in her palm.

"Wear this for me." She drew the cross out and fumbled with the catch at the back.

He grew still. "My medal," he whispered, his voice shaking. "You still have it."

"Of course I do." She glanced up at him while she pinned it to his lapel. "Don't you realize that I've always believed in you?"

He lowered his head, hiding his expression, and for a moment she thought he might cry. But then he looked at her with fierce hazel eyes and before the reverend could even direct him to do so he kissed her, his lips soft, questing, with none of the passion she'd learned to expect from him. He seemed to draw her very soul from her body and she sank against him, relishing the feel of his hard form against hers, returning his kiss with all the acceptance and love she could muster.

"Ahem." Reverend Wood cleared his throat.

Richard lifted his lips from hers and smiled, a new fire burning in his eyes, one that seared her insides and left her giddy with anticipation.

The reverend took their hands and drew them to the altar. "Please sign the parish register, so we might know for all time that you have joined in love and honor."

Richard affixed his signature to the paper with a strong, upright scrawl. Her hand trembling, Lucinda tried to do the same and ended up with something illegible.

"Go in peace," the reverend said. "May the years bring you nothing but happiness."

Richard clasped her hand and hurried her down the aisle. Behind them, Sir James invited all concerned back to Clairmont Hall for a wedding breakfast. Lucinda could only think of another sort of hunger as she climbed into the barouche with Richard. As soon as he had her to himself he drew her onto his lap and held her close, neither of them speaking as the conveyance rattled its way back to Clairmont Hall. Nothing needed to be said. Their kisses would say it all later.

Clairmont Hall, she realized, had gone through some changes since she'd left for her wedding ceremony. She walked into the great hall with Richard by her side and gazed about in amazement. Roses and lilies festooned the walls and staircase, framing the hall which had been rearranged to accommodate several buffet tables. Servants had piled the tables high with boiled and buttered eggs, bacon, grilled trout, cutlets, beef chops, roast woodcock, chicken, and a dizzying display of pastries. People milled about, some of them acquaintances of Lucinda's, others townfolk she nodded to but didn't really know. When Richard and Lucinda entered, they applauded, and some of the men shouted congratulations. Blushing, she followed Richard into the crowd and visited their guests, one by one.

The rest of their wedding breakfast passed in a haze for Lucinda. Ever aware of the smoldering promise in Richard's eyes, she nodded and smiled to the well-wishers who sat near them. She barely tasted the food she pushed past her lips. When a three-piece musical ensemble struck up a melody, she allowed Richard to lead her onto the floor for a quadrille. She knew only him as they performed the steps and received rousing applause once they'd finished.

The partying went on and on, and Lucinda grew tired of waiting to have her husband alone. Richard also cast increasingly frequent glances toward the tall case clock that ticked away the minutes, and when the hour approached three in the afternoon, he announced to all that he was claiming his wife for himself. Amid frequent backslaps and much ribbing, he picked Lucinda up and carried her to the north wing.

In short order Lucinda found herself deposited on his four-poster bed. He neither talked nor wasted time; he simply began to undress her. And when she lay on the sheets before him, completely naked, he stripped himself of his own clothes and enfolded her with his body. Several minutes passed as he held her that way, the silence between them charged with emotion.

With a groan, as if he could stand their closeness no longer without caressing her, he began to press little kisses against her, trailing his lips along her collarbone and down to her breasts. She cupped her breasts in her palms and lifted them in silent offering, and he flushed darkly and worshipped them one by one. He stroked and licked until she cried out, then dipped his head lower, his lips working downward to the place she ached the most, bringing her the same exquisite pleasure she'd known in the library.

She arched against him and, as if sensing the pleasure that built too quickly in her, he broke away. He evidently would not allow her deliverance so easily this time. Sighing, she curled her palm around his hard, hot length and felt the wetness at the tip. She caressed his arousal with her fingers, stopping now and then to grasp him firmly, drawing a groan from him, kissing him deeply all the while.

Tremors continued to build within her as they pleasured one another, their caresses marked by none of their earlier urgency. She found this slow pace intriguing, and when at last he filled her and began to drive into her with a softer, easier rhythm, she nearly purred with contentment and clung to him, her body warm, languid, gradually expanding with pleasure she knew would burst in gut-wrenching sensation.

Just as the pleasure became too much to bear, it peaked, flooding her with delirious warmth. She shuddered, moaning his name. His gaze mellow, he looked into her eyes, and then he was quivering too, thrusting deep into her one final time before he pressed against her, satiated.

Much, much later, after the sun had disappeared beneath the horizon, she whispered to him of her worst fears.

"Richard, now that we're married, Faye will pursue her revenge against us. I'm frightened."

Eyes closed, he snuggled her against his side. "Can we discuss Faye in the morning?"

"If I'm to sleep at all, we must discuss her now."

He pressed a gentle kiss against her ear. "All right, what do you propose?"

"I have no solutions, just worries. My uncle and your father grow more ill with each day, and even Carolly is feeling pains now."

He pushed himself up on one elbow. Moonlight streamed through the windows, revealing his furrowed brow. "Damn. Carolly too, now? If only I'd had a chance to talk to Faye before she disappeared. I might have stopped her sooner."

"Stopped her sooner?" Lucinda couldn't keep the surprise from her voice. "You agree with me that Faye would see us dead?"

"Faye sent your uncle and my father to us when we were making love inside the library. As you suspected, she wanted us married. Although the logic is twisted, evidence supports your claim. Faye will stop at nothing to acquire your crystal dove."

"So you finally believe in magic."

"I didn't say that." Richard draped an arm across her hip. "I believe Faye is pretending to be the ancient witch Edward Drakewyck described in your spellbook to lure the dove from you. Once she's convinced you she's Morgana Fey, she assumes you'll be so paralyzed with fear that you'll turn the dove over to her instantly. She'll then take it to London and sell the ruby at its core for a tidy sum."

"But Faye hasn't seen the spellbook."

"She must have at some point."

"How do you explain all of these illnesses that are felling the household?"

" 'Tis clear to me Faye has somehow poisoned their food. Not the entire supply, for in that case the servants would also grow sick, but just Sir James' and your uncle's plates. Obviously she must have gotten to Carolly too."

He paused as a sudden wind whistled through the eaves and bits of chaff tapped against the windows. A storm had gathered on the horizon, and judging by that wind, Lucinda guessed it would prove quite formidable.

"How Faye is effecting this I'm not certain," he continued. "I've alerted Cook and your uncle's housekeeper. They've promised to watch every morsel of food prepared for those two. Also, I asked Dr. Bennet to visit your uncle and my father. He examined them and claims the poison Faye used must have been mild and will soon pass through them with no lasting damage."

"Magic, not poison, is the culprit," she insisted.

He sighed deeply. "As always, magic remains a sore spot between us."

"We must go to London tomorrow for Carolly's presentation," she reminded him. "But once the Queen has bestowed her blessings on Carolly, I suggest we return to Somerton and visit Donald Mallory. Langford mentioned him when he learned we were hunting for lore about Morgana. A visit to Mr. Mallory may not have been urgent a few weeks ago, but now, I fear we have little time left. We should listen to what he says."

"To what purpose?"

"He may have the proof you need to convince you of Morgana Fey's reincarnation as Faye Morgan."

"And if he doesn't?"

"We'll go to the graveyard and find Morgana's grave," Lucinda said.

"And do what, dig her up?"

"I don't know." She turned her face away. "Somehow, I must make you believe."

"Shhh," he said, stroking her hair. "We'll go and visit Mr. Mallory if you wish to. And when you've heard what he has to say, and have seen Morgana's grave, perhaps your mind will ease and magic will cease to come between us."

She peered at him, trying to read his expression, to see if he patronized her or was just seeking a compromise between them. Storm clouds had all but obscured the moon, leaving their chamber in utter darkness. She decided to take his statement at face value. "Thank you," she whispered. "My mind is already eased."

Wind blew through the small glen nestled in the woods between Clairmont Hall and Drakewyck Grange. Her grave mere feet away, Morgana stood near the Drakewyck witch's fire ring and lifted her arms high into the sky, a staff of oak clenched in her hand. She swirled the tip of it around in tiny circles.

"Great power of the east," she cried, "come to me now. I call upon thee, ruler of storm and whirlwind, of tempest and cyclone and Prince of Air. I call to thee!"

She threw her head back, the sleeves of her black robe pooling around her elbows, and closed her eyes, calling into mind all the howling, blustering winds she'd ever encountered and projecting them into the air around her. She turned her staff in ever-larger circles. The air near its tip became mist and swirled much like a dollop of cream placed in the middle of chocolate and stirred with a spoon to make whorls of white amidst brown.

She laughed, elation filling her. She was going to raise the worst storm Somerton had ever seen. The witch and the knave wouldn't dare leave for London, not in this weather.

Her moment had come.

The air around her emitted a low-pitched humming noise and the wind grew stronger, blowing small twigs and leaves into the air, making her hair dance and twist, filling the glen with her fury.

"Great power of the south," she shouted, "come to me now. I call upon thee, ruler of lightning and thunder, of sunlight and heat and Prince of Fire. I call to thee!"

In her mind she saw a brilliant bolt of lightning forking through the sky to strike the south end of her glen. Small sparks began to shoot from the tip of her wand even as the mist swirled around it, and when she opened her eyes she saw thick, dark storm clouds gathered on the horizon. They rushed toward her with preternatural speed. The great ruler of the south had heard her. Fire was coming.

"Great power of the west," she screamed, "come to me now. I call upon thee, ruler of the deep abyss and bitter sea, of moisture and fog and Prince of Water. I call to thee!"

The circles she spun with her staff grew wider and more agitated until steam poured from its tip, as water touched fire, and mixed with the mist. A giant cloud was forming above the tip of her wand, and with a savage thrust she pointed the wand at the heavens, and the cloud she'd created bounced upward to join the others, enlarging as it touched them, encompassing the others with her will.

Storm clouds raced overhead. Lightning sparked within them, illuminating their dark surfaces with a ghastly luster. A low rumble of thunder reverberated through the heavens and grew in pitch until it crashed right above her, making the earth tremble. Rain began to pour down on her, whipping her in its frenzy, and she let the water roll down her bare head, washing her clean, stinging her skin, purifying her, readying her for the confrontation to come.

She dropped the staff from nerveless fingers. From within her cloak she withdrew a leather cord and tied a knot into it, murmuring tonelessly all the while.

"Prince of Air, I bind thee now. Here must you stay until the knot is loosed. So mote it be."

The wind blew at her and lifted her skirts as if enraged at being trapped. Morgana laughed and tied another knot. "Prince of Fire, I bind thee now. Here must you stay until the knot is loosed. So mote it be."

Lightning cracked the heavens open and sizzled the ground to her left, filling the air with the smell of burnt grass. The witch ignored it and tied another knot. "Prince of Water, I bind thee now. Here must you stay until the knot is loosed. So mote it be."

She clenched the cord in her fist and shook it at the sky. The clouds churned above her, the mass of them far too black and unsettled. A primitive instinct sent a shiver across her skin. Grinning, Morgana slipped the cord into her cloak and retrieved her poppet of Carolly. Thorn clasped between her fingers, she poked the tip into the wax doll and settled down to wait for the witch and the knave. If the weather wasn't enough to deter them from leaving for London, Carolly's incessant pain certainly would.

A strange golden glow flickered against the tree trunks in front of her as though someone crept behind her with a lantern. Beneath the fury of the storm she heard the voice that had dogged her every waking hour, the soft voice which begged her at such a low volume that the words slurred together and became a hum.

She spun around and scanned the trees, the woods, the brush. The hairs at the back of her neck prickled.

Nothing.

Still the glow flickered, hesitantly now, soft golden motes of light which almost seemed to want to coalesce. Head tilted, eyes narrowed, she stared into the cloud of luminescence, watching the motes cling in certain places, forming a strong nose, a square chin . . .

An itch built in the back of her mind. She *knew* this person. Without quite realizing it, she reached out to the glow, her fingers long and pale in the darkness of the night.

Radiance danced across her skin, but the sensation was fleeting, incorporeal. Although her mind registered warmth, her skin remained cold. The face also remained elusive, refusing to gain shape any further.

Morgana, someone whispered in her mind.

Remember.

Forgive.

"Who are you?" she cried out, maddened, and jammed her fists against her temples, trying to shut it out. But she couldn't dismiss it, not any longer. It had nagged her too thoroughly for her to pretend it didn't exist.

The voice seemed to sigh, *I love you,* then faded away.

"Leave me alone," she whimpered, eyes closed, and felt her throat grow tight with sobs she couldn't shed. Christopher was dead. There was nothing left for her but revenge.

20

 loud rapping on the bedchamber door woke Richard up. He felt Lucinda's soft form cuddled against him and groaned. They were supposed to leave for London today, he thought. A maidservant had probably brought a tray, ostensibly bearing tea and scones but in truth ready to roust them out of bed and get them on the road to London.

"One moment," he mumbled.

He cast a bleary glance toward the windows. Rain streamed down the panes, wind rattled through the eaves, and black clouds obscured the sky. Low-pitched thunder rumbled in the distance. This was the kind of day for staying in bed, particularly when the bed held someone as delectable as his wife. Annoyed, he slipped from beneath the bedclothes, waking Lucinda in the process. He yanked on his trousers while she dove under the blankets, and he opened the door.

Sir James stood without, his mouth drawn in a white line. "Something has happened to Carolly."

Richard stilled. His father had the pallor of a man condemned. "What's wrong?"

"She has a terrific pain in her midsection. She cannot rise."

Lucinda's muted gasp reached them both. Richard caught a sudden flurry of activity out of the corner of his eye as she jumped out of bed, a blanket wrapped around her.

"Have you called the physician?"

"Of course." Sir James clenched his hands into fists until his knuckles shone white. "He diagnosed an abscess, possibly of the appendix. He says an operation is her only hope."

Richard felt the blood drain from his face. He remembered all too well the fate of those with abdomen wounds in the Crimea. In most cases, the operation and its resultant gangrene killed the man, not the wound itself. "A person laid on the operating table is exposed to more chances of death than an English soldier on the field of Balaclava."

Sir James nodded. "I'm fully aware of the risks we take but I have no choice. I'm going to give Dr. Bennet my permission to operate. I just wanted you to know."

Lucinda appeared behind Richard, her brown curls mussed. Concern sharpened her gaze. "How much longer does she have before the abscess becomes critical?"

" 'Tis critical now."

"Will Dr. Bennet operate right away?"

"No, not until later this afternoon, possibly this evening. He's sent for one of his colleagues from London, a surgeon by the name of Lamton who's had some experience with abdominal abscesses. As soon as that gentleman arrives they plan to move Carolly to Dr. Bennet's house for surgery."

"Good. We have some time yet," she said. "And Faye, has she returned to Clairmont Hall?"

Sir James rubbed his temples. "With the urgency surrounding Carolly I hadn't thought of Faye, but now that you mention it, I haven't seen her since Carolly's birthday party two nights ago. But what has this to do with my daughter's illness?"

"Faye may have a lot to do with it."

The elder Clairmont turned a surprised gaze on Lucinda. "Faye? Whatever do you mean?"

" 'Tis too complicated to go into now, Father," Richard said. "Is Dr. Bennet certain about his diagnosis?"

"Oddly enough, he said the abscess wasn't displaying the usual symptoms, such as fever. As you know, fever always accompanies an infection. Still, he insisted the pain Carolly described could come from nothing else."

Silently Richard cursed. Despite all of his precautions, Faye must have slipped his sister a new dose of poison. They had to find Faye, convince her to tell them what type of poison she'd used, and procure an antidote. "Try to hold the surgeon off for as long as possible. Lucinda and I may be able to find an alternative to surgery."

"But . . . why . . . who . . ." Sir James protested as Richard pushed him firmly out the door.

"We haven't much time. I'll explain all later," Richard promised, shutting the door on his father.

He pressed a quick kiss against Lucinda's forehead. "You'll stay at Clairmont Hall while I go out and look for Faye."

Without waiting for a reply, he turned away and shrugged into his shirt.

She, too, launched into action, pulling on a chemise and a single petticoat. "I'm not going to stay here and let you face Faye alone. She's dangerous, Richard."

"Precisely. That's why I want you to remain at Clairmont Hall."

"Without me, you haven't a chance against Faye."

"Don't be silly. I'm a great deal stronger and extremely determined."

"You're nothing when compared to her magic. She'll decimate you."

"Lucinda, can we please stop pretending she's Morgana Fey, at least for the moment? The situation is far too perilous. I can't play along with you anymore."

"And how do you explain Carolly's illness? Poison again?"

"There is no other explanation."

She shoved a gown into his hands and lifted her arms over her head. "Help me dress. I haven't the time to wait for a lady's maid."

Sighing impatiently, he complied, wasting precious minutes fumbling with the buttons at the back of her gown. At last, he'd fastened them, and made as if to leave.

She held on to his arm. "Richard, wait. You must listen to me for a moment. I have read extensively and received an education from George Drakewyck, a scholar in his own right. I'm not the sort to be overcome by superstition or believe in things frivolously."

She paused and took a deep breath. Her grip on his arm tightened.

"I'm your wife now. If you have any regard for me at all, you'll open your mind, just a crack, to the fact that I might be right about magic, and allow me to come along with you. If I'm correct, Faye is no ordinary creature. Only the crystal dove will save us."

She faced him, small lines of worry gathered around her mouth. Richard gazed into her brownish-gold eyes, calm and rational eyes that had turned his life around, and admitted he could do no less than she asked. He didn't believe in magic but would allow the possibility that he was completely wrong.

"All right, come with me. And bring your dove. We may need it."

The smile she gave him went straight to his head. He knew at that moment he'd made the right decision.

She hurried to her wedding dress which hung over the back of a chair, drew the crystal dove from the ivory satin and shoved it into her gown.

Hand in hand, they left the north wing and stopped to check on Carolly. He'd always felt out of place in her bedchamber, a frilly room stuffed near to bursting with delicate Chippendale furniture. This morning, however, he looked at the furnishings with raw fear. The bedchamber embodied his sister's frilly delicacy and, as his attention drifted from the perfumes and brushes to the flowered wallpaper, it made him realize how much her loss would devastate him.

Carolly looked tiny in her huge bed, her complexion far too pale, almost gray. A maidservant sat next to her bed, a water-filled basin in her lap, and continually sponged her brow.

Lucinda rushed to her side and took the cloth from the maidservant. She sponged Carolly's forehead herself. "Carolly, dear, how are you feeling? Have the pains gotten any worse?"

"They've settled into a constant throbbing," she murmured, her voice weak. "Oh, Lucinda, make it stop."

"We will," Richard said. "Just as soon as we can." He ran his hand over Carolly's forehead, noting her cool skin. As he'd suspected, poison was at work. He blamed himself for this. He should have paid more attention to Lucinda's worries about Faye.

The girl appeared to drift off to sleep.

"She's resting comfortably for the moment," Lucinda whispered. "We'd better go."

Richard took her arm and together they descended to the great hall. Outside, thunder cracked the heavens open and rain continued to gush downward, a flood that never seemed to end.

Lucinda studied the skies beyond the window with a critical glance. "Something doesn't feel right about this storm. Thunderstorms, even the worst of them, pass within an hour. This one has lingered since last night."

"Are you suggesting Faye has whipped up a storm?"

"Perhaps she wants to make sure we don't leave for London."

"I would have thought the hex she placed on Carolly enough to stop us."

"I'm almost certain Faye has used a poppet against Carolly. A poppet," she explained, her expression earnest, "is a tiny waxen doll made in the victim's image, one that a witch will stick thorns or pins into to generate great pain. They're most effective when the victim is aware of their existence, putting her in a receptive state of mind."

Lucinda paused, as if gauging his reaction. He nodded and tried to look thoughtful, but in truth was simply humoring her.

"Carolly," she forged on, "hasn't mentioned anything of a waxen doll, even when I questioned her about it, so Faye might be concerned about the poppet's effectiveness and raised a storm as added insurance. We must find Faye and convince her to release Carolly from the poppet's spell."

"Can you not remove the spell?"

"Only the one who created the poppet can destroy it."

"We share the same purpose then: Find Faye and convince her to release Carolly from her illness." He grasped her hand and yelled for Hilton to have the groom, Mack, bring a carriage around front.

In short order they'd piled into the carriage and set off for Somerton at a fast clip. Lucinda kept her gaze fixed upon the passing scenery and pleated her skirt with trembling fingers. He drew her onto his lap and held her there, stroking her hair until they reached the main street through town.

Richard asked the driver to pull the carriage over, and went over the likely places Faye might hide in his mind.

"Where shall we look?" she asked.

His gaze slid past the Tempest Tavern, the Old Guildhall, St. Paul's Church, and Langford's Book Shop. "She'll probably want to confront us privately. The church is usually quiet on a Monday afternoon. We'll try there. Other than that, I can't think of anywhere she might conceal herself. What else do we know about her?"

"She's a seamstress," Lucinda offered. "But as she's from a century long past, she has no friends, no relatives, no place to hide here in town."

Richard allowed her magical assessment of Faye to slide by. "Damn. We really don't know anything about her, do we? So we can't possibly know where she might go." He had to admit trying to find Faye in a town as big as Somerton would be akin to finding one small stone buried in a mountain of rock.

"We may not know much about Faye Morgan, but Morgana Fey isn't as much a mystery."

"You're right. If Faye is pretending to be Morgana Fey, then she might be hiding where Morgana Fey would have hid. Let's review the facts about Morgana."

Lucinda frowned. "The facts are sparse. We know only that Edward put an end to her and executed her husband for practicing witchcraft."

Richard nodded, excitement nevertheless stirring in his gut. This line of thought had real possibility. "Where did Morgana live? Where, indeed, is her grave?"

"I'm not certain. But Donald Mallory might know."

"We'll visit him first."

"What about St. Paul's Church?"

"Your idea, my love, has much greater merit." He swooped down to plant a swift kiss on her lips and told the groom to drive on to Donald Mallory's.

Lucinda stood on a small porch that sheltered her from the rain and rapped on the door to Donald Mallory's house with a heavy fist.

A new idea was churning inside her, one she'd thought of on the carriage ride over. Faye, she thought, wanted revenge on the families who had destroyed her. If the men who had murdered her were exposed to all of England for their crime, albeit posthumously, perhaps Faye's desire for revenge would ease.

Richard, at her side, raised an eyebrow. "Are you trying to break down the door?"

"He's hard of hearing," she explained. "He has a hearing-horn but doesn't use it when he's alone."

She lifted her hand to knock even harder when suddenly the door swung open and the squint-eyed codger stuck his head out into the afternoon downpour.

"Eh? Miss Lucinda!"

Lucinda curtseyed. "Good afternoon, Mr. Mallory. Captain Clairmont and I have come to chat."

"Tea, you say?" He bent his head closer to her.

"We'd love to join you for tea. May we come in?"

He shuffled back from the door and waved them in.

Lucinda stepped into his kitchen, which also served as a parlor. Richard bowed to Mr. Mallory, exchanged a few words of greeting with him, then removed Lucinda's cloak and hung it on a pegboard near the door. His own cloak joined hers.

A fireplace dominated the far wall, the hearth large enough to accommodate cooking implements as well as an old rocker. A kettle boiled over the open fire. Mr. Mallory, she thought, had yet to give way to the pleasures of a stove. And yet, the wooden floor shone with beeswax and a blue enameled screen hid the less desirable aspects of the kitchen from view. He'd even hung a piece of lace over his mantelpiece and decorated the windows with striped curtains. For a man, she mused, and particularly for a scholar, he showed a delicate taste.

"I'll retrieve your horn, Mr. Mallory," she offered. "Please sit."

The old man willingly complied. She fetched his horn first, a black, cone-shaped contrivance he stuck in one ear to amplify sound. His chipped tea set followed, the teapot filled with the water he'd boiled.

An arrangement of sugar, clotted cream, and spoons followed.

Richard leaned toward Mr. Mallory. "We hope we haven't inconvenienced you, but we'd like to ask you what you know about Morgana Fey."

"Eh? A rainy day, you said?"

Lucinda laid a restraining arm on Richard. "Mr. Mallory. Your hearing-horn."

"Don't usually need the thing," he grumbled, loud enough to make her ears ring. "But since you've always been so soft-spoken, I suppose I'll have to use it." He stuck the black horn in his ear.

"How have you been, Mr. Mallory?" she said into the horn. "My uncle and I have missed you at Drakewyck Grange."

"Haven't you moved to Clairmont Hall?" the old man asked.

"Why, yes. Captain Clairmont and I married only yesterday."

Donald looked at Richard, his eyes wide, then crinkling at the corners as a smile curled his lips. "Congratulations! Your uncle is going to miss you plenty. That old rascal still burying his nose in the books?"

She smiled. "I rarely see him any other way."

"Eh?"

She spoke directly into the horn. "The books are *stuck* to his nose."

A chuckle rasped in his throat. "Always were."

"And you? I understand you and Doctor Bennet have struck up quite a friendship."

"When he's not bleeding me with leeches, he's plying me with whiskey." He coughed, the phlegm-clogged sound making her wince.

"You need a solid course of rest and food. I'll have the cook at Clairmont Hall send some dinner over."

She put her teacup down. "But I confess our visit is more than a social one. Captain Clairmont and I are pursuing the solution to a difficult puzzle."

A light sparkled in Donald's eyes. "A puzzle. Always enjoy 'em."

"You may be able to help me solve this one, at least in part. You're a descendent of Christopher Fey's, no?"

"Indeed I am. My bloodlines go way back into the fifteen hundreds. Not many folks in this town can claim likewise."

"Mr. Langford mentioned that you'd researched the legend of Morgana Fey, a witch who lived in the sixteenth century." Her spine began to tingle at the very mention of her name.

He grew somber and pushed back from the table. "And why would you bother yourself with such a dreadful tale?"

She debated telling him the truth—that she suspected Morgana had returned to Somerton—and decided against it. She had neither the time nor the inclination to convince him, and didn't have the patience to withstand another doubting Thomas' snorts of disbelief.

"Simple curiosity. I found an entry in the Drakewyck family Bible, written by the vicar Edward Drakewyck, also from the sixteenth century. He claims to have . . . well, disposed of Morgana Fey."

Quickly, she explained in general the substance of Edward's entry and the corroborating evidence in the parish register. She also told him how they'd connected the Drakewycks and Clairmonts in friendship through that old portrait of Henry Clairmont, found in the Clairmont Hall attic.

"Our curiosity is piqued," she finished, "and I believe I speak for Captain Clairmont as well when I say I feel a sense of responsibility. Our ancestors committed a heinous sin but died without ever seeing justice." With a sideways glance at Richard, she mentioned her newest idea. "We'd like to discover as much as we can, with the possibility of publishing our findings in the *London Evening Star*."

Richard's eyes widened, but she couldn't tell if admiration or outrage had prompted him.

Donald Mallory nodded. " 'Tis a fine gesture."

"We'll discuss this later," her husband muttered into her ear.

Outrage, Lucinda thought.

Richard leaned toward Donald's hearing-horn. "What do you know about Morgana, Mr. Mallory?"

"I found Christopher Fey's journal in an old trunk some thirty years ago." Donald paused and cleared his throat. Lucinda guessed he wanted to wring the last drop of suspense from the moment. He'd always had a flair for drama.

"His is a sad tale indeed," the old man continued. "He fell in love with Morgana and married her. They planned a family. But Morgana Duchard possessed a crystal dove, a statue that Edward Drakewyck"—he paused to level a stare at Lucinda—"coveted so much he murdered her for it."

"What was it about this dove that made it so desirable?" Richard asked.

" 'Twas a magical icon," the old man replied, "filled with the spirit of the old ones, able to perform miracles, according to my ancestor. Now, it doesn't matter whether or not you believe in magic; the point is, they did."

Lucinda shot a significant glance toward Richard.

"According to Christopher, Edward Drakewyck was a warlock, and Morgana a witch. Edward wanted the crystal dove, so he murdered Morgana and took it." Donald shook his head, as if disgusted by his own tale. "Henry Clairmont helped him. And to keep Christopher quiet, the pair accused him of Morgana's murder, searched his house, found Morgana's magical supplies, and had him accused of witchcraft. They tried and executed him, but not before he was able to pen this tale in his journal."

Lucinda swallowed against a lump in her throat. Somehow, hearing the story from Donald Mallory, as told in Christopher Fey's journal, made it undeniably real for her. She felt truly embarrassed—horrified, even—that Edward Drakewyck's blood flowed through her veins. She remembered Uncle George's words: *magic corrupts*. For the first time in her life, the thought of casting a spell left a sour taste in her mouth.

"I have the locket Morgana gave to Christopher on the eve of his wedding," the old man revealed. "Would you like to see it?"

Lucinda nodded. "Very much."

"I'll get it for you." Shuffling, Donald made his way out of the room. Moments later, he returned.

"Here you are, Miss Lucinda."

She took the proffered locket, her grasp clammy. Christopher's locket was made of gold filigree, an exact duplicate of the one Faye Morgan had worn from the first moment Lucinda had laid eyes on her.

Fingers trembling, she opened the clasp.

Faye Morgan stared up at her, her ice-blue eyes yellowed with age, her wheat-blonde hair cracked, a tiny gold filigree locket fixed securely around her neck. A small beauty mark graced the corner of her mouth. Lucinda stared at the picture, sucked in a breath, and shoved it into Richard's hand.

He took one look at the miniature and muffled an exclamation.

"Miss Lucinda?" Donald Mallory placed a hand on her shoulder. "You look quite pale."

Weak inside, as if her insides had turned to water, she fanned herself with her hand. "The last few days have been rather hectic. I'm fine."

Richard's hands shook as he handed the locket back to Donald Mallory. "Do you know where Morgana lived in Somerton?"

"Oh, their house has long since been demolished. I believe the Old Guildhall now sits on the property."

"How about her grave? In his journal, did Christopher mention where Edward and Henry buried her?"

"Edward Drakewyck, evidently in a fit of gloating, mentioned a secret glen in the woodlands, near a hunter's cottage. Christopher had no idea as to the exact location, however."

Lucinda grew still. She knew the precise location of that glen. At the sound of Richard's indrawn breath, she realized he knew, too.

They both stood simultaneously.

"We have to go, Donald," Lucinda said, shivering from excitement, not weakness. But it was a sick sort of excitement, the kind that brought nightmares. "I promise to inform you when the piece on Morgana and Christopher Fey is to appear in the *London Evening Star*. Indeed, I'll purchase a copy of the newspaper for you."

"Capital, Miss Lucinda, but why the rush? You've only just arrived."

"Nevertheless, we must go." Richard took her arm and hustled her to the door. He pulled her cloak around her shoulders and donned his own before they gave Donald their final farewells. They left him muttering about young folks always being in a rush, and hurried through the pouring rain to their barouche.

Once inside its musty interior, Lucinda clasped Richard's hand. His skin, she noted, felt unusually cold. "We must go directly to my glen. 'Tis there she waits for us. I know it."

His face white, Richard spared her a quick glance before asking their driver to head down Covington Road and stop by the woodlands that separated Drakewyck Grange from Clairmont Hall. When he returned his attention to her, his eyes seemed shadowed. Haunted. He'd pressed his lips into a grim line and when he spoke, his voice trembled. "The resemblance between the woman in Donald Mallory's locket and Faye Morgan is quite startling. They look exactly the same, right down to the beauty mark at the corner of their mouths."

She squeezed his hand once, for reassurance. "You *know* why."

"I know what my gut is telling me," he whispered, a bead of moisture forming on his brow. "But my mind cannot believe it."

"Faye Morgan *is* Morgana Fey."

"But that would mean . . . all this time I've derided you for believing in magic . . . how can I ignore such a weight of evidence?" He broke off and looked out the window, clearly adrift in some private torment.

"Richard, listen to me. I blame you for nothing. You were simply behaving in a way your nature demands you behave. I would change you for nothing. Indeed, you're a dose of rationality that I sorely needed. At the same time, you must allow yourself to believe in magic, to believe in hope . . . to believe in love."

"This dark garden of yours. It really exists."

"Yes, it does."

"And the soldiers who died in the Crimea . . . my men. Perhaps they walk through this dark garden."

"I'm certain they do."

Chills chased down her spine at the look of wonder on his face. Suddenly, his lips curved in a smile that broke through the gloom around them to lighten her heart as sunshine banishes the darkest clouds. He had, she thought, finally forgiven himself for surviving the war.

21

$\mathcal{R}$ichard pressed tiny kisses all over her face, then caught her lips with his and gently stroked the inside of her mouth with his tongue until she could hardly breathe. At last he broke away to stare deep into her eyes, his own shining with moisture. "Lucinda . . . I love you."

She rubbed her cheek against his. "And I love you, so much that my heart aches. My God, Richard, I never knew love would feel this way, painful and delirious and utterly fulfilling."

They held each other close. So far, she mused, everything in her vision and Edward Drakewyck's entry had come true. Only the prophecy of their utter destruction remained. She glanced at the passing woodlands, wondering if by walking into the glen she was walking into the arms of Death. Probably. But what good would it do to run, to hide? Faye would eventually find her. Fate would eventually catch up with her. And a life spent worrying about what might be wasn't a life worth living. She had to make her stand now.

The carriage ground to a halt and the driver announced that they had reached the stretch of woodlands separating Drakewyck Grange and Clairmont Hall.

Richard ran his fingers across her features as though trying to commit them to memory before clasping her hands in his. "I want you to remain in the carriage. I won't see you endangered."

"I can't stay. Fate has declared that we see this through together."

"If you die, Lucinda, my own life will be over."

She thought of the vision; how her Lancelot would sacrifice himself for her. *No.* She wouldn't surrender to Fate. They *would* prove the vision wrong.

"I'm not going to die," she insisted, "and neither are you. I plan to tell Faye about the piece we're going to publish in the *London Evening Star*. It might appease some of her rage if she realizes her murderers will be exposed."

Richard nodded, his face tight. "When you first mentioned it, I could only think of my wife's name in a newspaper read by all of England, linked to a crazy story about witchcraft and an ancient crime. But now I think it's as good a plan as any. Will these help, do you suppose?" He pulled two silver pistols from a little drawer beneath his seat.

"Perhaps. Bring them along," she agreed. Still, the sight of the pistols gave her little comfort. Faye likely had enough power at her command to defeat two cannons, let alone two pistols.

He shoved them into his waistband. "Let's go."

As soon as he opened the carriage door, a strong wind assaulted them and ripped at their clothes. The rain, however, had abated somewhat, and for that Lucinda was thankful. Their driver had stopped at the midway point between Drakewyck Grange and Clairmont Hall, and she knew the glen was less than a ten-minute walk into the trees.

"What if Faye isn't here?" she suddenly asked.

"She will be."

Frowning, Lucinda clasped his hand. Together they began their trek into the woodlands, weaving between gnarled tree trunks and treacherous, exposed roots. Brambles pulled at her cloak and hood, seeking to poke at her skin, tangle her brown hair. But the warmth of Richard's palm and the strength of his fingers gave her courage, and she trudged onward, aware that beneath the trees the rain had ceased almost entirely.

At length they grew closer to the glen and Lucinda's steps lagged. When the hunter's cottage, dilapidated and nearly hidden by ivy, came into view, she stopped walking altogether. Richard paused by her side.

A black-cloaked figure stood within the doorway to the hunter's cottage.

"Faye," Lucinda whispered. Her heart froze in her chest, then began to beat with rapid, hollow strokes.

Richard moved in front of her, shielding her with his form. "Faye Morgan," he called out. His good hand, Lucinda noted, clenched around the handle of his pistol.

The air around them seemed to grow several degrees colder.

Motionless, the black-cloaked figure watched them.

His damaged hand gripping hers, he began to walk toward Faye. Lucinda lagged behind him, her muscles weak and rebelling against further steps toward the witch. She drew the dove from her pocket. It burned against her palm and glowed with white fire. How much death and destruction would Faye wring from the statue if Lucinda surrendered it to her?

At the appearance of the dove, Lucinda sensed a change in Faye, a sudden stiffening that suggested a heightened awareness.

Her throat tight, Lucinda rubbed its back as though it were a real bird. The ruby in its depths seemed to pulsate. "I've brought the dove."

"Good," the witch said, her voice deep, almost masculine in timber, reverberating through the small glen like an echo of thunder. She threw back her hood. Water had plastered her blonde hair to her head and her ice-blue eyes looked harder and colder than marble. "Bring it here."

"We both know it's not that easy," Richard said, hand still clasped around the pistol grip.

"Oh, yes, it *is* that easy." Faye raised a hand and waved it negligently.

Lucinda felt power gather in the air around her. The witch, she saw, had fixed a gimlet stare on Richard. Faye's lips moved but no sound emerged.

"Richard, watch out," Lucinda cried.

Faye slipped her hand into her pocket and retrieved a small black pouch. She began to chant, her eerie words floating across the clearing, and clenched her hand around the pouch, forming a fist. "With spiderwebs I bind him tight. I break his legs and stop his sight. He cannot hear or speak or fight."

Richard gasped, his hands clutched around his midsection. He stumbled toward Faye, panting, a low, keening moan erupting from his throat.

A binding spell, Lucinda thought. Her legs suddenly felt rubbery. She held on to a tree trunk for support. Her tongue had glued itself to the roof of her mouth and resisted her efforts to shout. Finally she worked up some moisture and her tongue began to flap. "Release him, I will not allow you to hurt him, he means too much to me."

The witch's lips stretched in a feral grin.

"Stop!" Lucinda screamed, hand clenched around the dove.

Faye opened her fist and dangled the pouch from two fingers. Richard dropped to the ground like a stone and lay there, panting.

"Aren't you going to use the dove against me?" Faye asked.

"Please, let us go," Lucinda babbled. Her chest had tightened to the point of pain, and her limbs had grown even weaker. "Stop this bid for vengeance. I know my ancestors committed an unspeakable atrocity against you. I wish they would have been punished in life, for surely they deserved it. But they're dead, and beyond your reach. Still, I vow I'll reveal their crime for the world to see. They'll not go unpunished in this time."

"They buried me deep to cover my sins, dear. Nothing you do will compensate me for years spent in a grave, sleeping yet aware. Horribly aware."

"I'll give you anything you want. Just let us go."

"Will you give me the crystal dove?"

"Will you release us if I do?"

Faye shrugged. "Of course."

Lucinda heard the lie in her voice. Cold, moist fear embraced her, raising bumps on her skin. Her heart writhed in her chest like a trapped rabbit.

Faye suddenly dropped to her haunches, a dagger clutched in her palm. She positioned the blade against Richard's throat. Utterly helpless, he remained prone, his gaze fixed upon Lucinda, pleading, beseeching . . .

Save yourself, he silently begged. *Let her kill me.*

A thin trickle of blood ran from his nostrils.

"My God," Lucinda breathed, strings of panic tightening through her at Faye's brutality. He'd suffered more than a mere binding spell. "What have you done to him?"

"I've attacked him spiritually, just as Edward Drakewyck attacked me." She slid the knife along Richard's throat, drawing a thin trickle of blood. "What have you to say, knave?"

Wild-eyed, he stared at her. Blood pooled at the top of his shirt and streamed down his chin as well.

Lucinda's vision narrowed. Blackness fuzzed her thoughts. The world began to spin. *I'm going to swoon,* she thought.

"Tell me, Lucinda," Faye cackled, "how does it feel to watch your beloved tormented so relentlessly? I know. I watched my husband suffer, and awoke in your time only to learn he'd been executed by Edward Drakewyck and Henry Clairmont for my murder."

Lucinda clenched her fists so tight that her fingernails dug into her palms. The pain kept her in the present.

"I've known nothing but anguish since I first saw you," she cried. "I've lived for months with the knowledge that my death is near. I've worried about the illnesses my loved ones have endured and now I see my beloved writhing beneath your hatred. We've all felt the pain of your wrath. My God, Faye, must you take our lives, too? We've been punished, and we didn't even commit the crime!"

"I made a promise to Edward Drakewyck," Faye said, her eyes dark pools in her face, "and I always keep my promises."

Lucinda eyed Faye closely. Had her voice wavered?

"Hatred has made you forget how to feel," Lucinda said, strength flowing back into her veins. Her voice ran clear and true. "At one time you were a young woman, anticipating the joys of creating a family. Don't you remember how much your husband loved you? Try to remember, Faye. For just as you loved Christopher, I love Richard. I'm not 'the other.' Our common humanity binds us together."

Faye's eyes grew unfocused, and inside, Lucinda felt a surge of triumph. Perhaps she'd gotten through to the woman who had once loved.

"What will murdering Richard and me prove?" Lucinda pressed. "Is satisfaction enough to release you from the torment you now suffer, or will our murder heap more crimes upon your head, and lengthen your torment?"

The witch shook her head back and forth, slowly, as if trying to wake up from a dream.

Lucinda softened her tone. "What must you do to truly release yourself from the hell Edward Drakewyck has created for you?"

"Forgive," Faye whispered, her voice detached, as though from far away. But then the witch's gaze hardened and she looked at Lucinda as though Lucinda had pulled some nasty trick on her.

"Forgiveness is for the weak." She squeezed the black pouch, and Richard began to writhe again, his booted feet scrabbling against the earth. "Come, our destinies are inextricably entwined. You can't escape, so don't take too long to decide. What shall it be? Will you give me the dove and die with your husband, or will you use the dove against me and force me to kill him?"

"Let her kill me," Richard croaked, then began to shudder at the effort his plea had cost him.

"How will you feel, witch, living through the years knowing your lover is dead, never to return?" Faye asked. "I understand this feeling intimately. Use the dove against me and find out for yourself."

Lucinda stared at her clenched hands. Evidently her arguments had convinced Faye of nothing. Her knuckles white, she began to tremble. She didn't want to live without Richard. How could she survive a lifetime of years knowing he'd died to spare her life? And yet, what choice did she have?

Death for them both.

And endless walks together in the dark garden.

Her body shaking, her limbs wracked with chills, she ran her fingers along the dove's cool, smooth contours. It seemed to grow warm in her hands. Tears beginning to roll down her cheeks, she lifted it toward Faye.

"No, Lucinda, don't give it to her," he suddenly choked out. "The darkness in her soul is pitch-black and impenetrable. Stop her while you still can."

Lucinda froze, her arm outstretched. Richard's plea hadn't given her pause; rather, something strange was happening behind the witch. She dropped the dove to her side and stared at the motes of gold that spun in a cloud behind Faye like tiny flames, sparse at first but growing thicker with every moment. A figure was forming in the cloud, a face she didn't recognize, and yet, even as it tried to coalesce, some of the motes swirled in open rebellion.

Chills raced up and down her limbs. Excitement made her stomach clench. On the edge of her awareness, she heard a man's voice, crying for help. He could be the answer she'd been waiting for, another choice to offer Faye, the only way to thwart Fate.

Magic, she thought. Her own magic combined with the power in the dove would strengthen him.

She surrounded the dove with both her hands and called to it with a desperation born of pure love. She concentrated every ounce of her will and imagined the magic within the statue's heart was within *her* heart.

The crystal dove began to glow with a pure white light.

"Ah nal nath rac," she chanted, *"uth vas bethad, do-chiel dienve."*

Her heart began to beat faster, her blood thinning and flowing more quickly through her veins. A ball of energy formed in her midsection. With each chant it expanded until it became a hot catapult of magic capable of great goodness. Or great destruction.

The ruby heart inside the dove began to pulsate faster. Sparkling bands of color exploded from its crystal interior, reflecting across Faye's face and spraying the glen with light. Faye cried out. The hand she held the dagger with twitched. And yet, she paused, sparing Richard.

Hoping her instinct would prove true, Lucinda sent every last bit of magic she possessed toward the figure trying to emerge from the glowing cloud.

Morgana stiffened, her grip on the dagger loosening.

The voice had returned, that strange buzz on the edge of her consciousness which demanded she listen, the one she couldn't dismiss, despite the fact that she stood on the brink of triumph.

What if the voice belonged to Christopher?

She closed her eyes, released the binding-bag, and let the voice come to her. It washed over her slowly from somewhere behind her, growing more clear as the words penetrated her brain, their deep, rough comfort so familiar that she froze.

No, it couldn't be.

Shocked, her insides suddenly churning, she spun around. A golden cloud of stardust was coalescing behind her, the magic in it potent, good, cleansing; she breathed it in and felt it purify her lungs, driving out the hatred, making her want, making her need, making her hope . . .

Someone was forming in the golden cloud, and without warning she saw a shimmering image of Christopher, as though his face had for a second surged through. She trembled. Was it true? Or was it a trick of the storm-induced twilight? A trick of her desperate mind?

Tears dropped one by one onto her cloak.

She wanted so much to believe . . .

A warm wind not of her making swept through the glen, stirring the hair at her temples and slapping her cloak against her legs. The air was charged, somehow, as though another thunderstorm were approaching, this one much stronger, much more powerful. Each tiny hair on her arms stood on end.

Suddenly she had the sense of something coming, something close, swooping down at her. It had a benevolent feeling, as though it meant her no harm. A bird. No, an eagle. Involuntarily she scanned the skies immediately above her. Something strong, proud.

She couldn't see anything, but it was directly above her.

Sensation enveloped her.

Her eyes widened. She stiffened. She gasped.

Christopher had just swept through her.

Tremors weakened her legs and she staggered.

370

She could smell him everywhere, in the weave of her cloak, on her hands, in her hair; she could feel him, the light touch of his kiss, a comforting hand on her shoulder, a deep, permanent love that strengthened her and made her yearn for more.

A cry burst from her lips. Her husband had returned for her. He hadn't turned his back on her all those centuries ago when Edward Drakewyck had destroyed them both. Their love would never be destroyed, not by anyone.

Abruptly she heard his voice, caressing her ears, the wisdom in it making her tremble. "Forgive them, Morgana. Their suffering will also be yours, forever. Forgive them and come with me, my love. I've waited long for you."

A river of light was forming behind the golden motes, and with a sudden burst of longing she realized the storm clouds had parted to allow a ray of sunlight to strike the earth near her feet. She turned to Lucinda, seeing not a witch but a young woman in love with her husband as she and Christopher loved. She would free them to love as destiny had decreed.

The woman still had the dove outstretched toward her. Her touch gentle, Morgana took the dove and lifted it high into the air. *"Ah nal nath rac,"* she began to chant, *"uth vas bethad, dochiel dienve."*

The dove's magic filled her and began to bubble in her veins, contracting them painlessly, making her light-headed, dimming her vision even as Christopher's face grew clearer. He was smiling, she saw, and holding his hand out to her.

"Ah nal nath rac, uth vas bethad, dochiel dienve."

Her body began to shimmer around her. She felt weightless. She was dying, she knew, but her death was long overdue. The place of magic, of voices young and old, of past, present, and future awaited her.

Christopher awaited her.

Magic swirled around her, enveloping her in its soft, enchanted embrace. She became a mere wisp of what had been, but she wasn't afraid. She would not fear, not with her husband so near, his hand outstretched. As she became incorporeal her grasp on the dove loosened. Smiling, she watched it tumble toward the earth, head over wing, around and around, its fall from grace seeming to last an eternity, until at last it struck a rock embedded in the earth squarely.

Light exploded from the dove, white light that forced the woman to hide her eyes, that released the man from his thrall of magic, then became the light of a thousand rainbows that died down into a soft glow. Shards of tiny crystal points rained down on the trees, on the brush, on the woman's and man's clothes.

But Morgana didn't feel them. She dove into the river of light, her hand clasped tight in Christopher's, his loving presence setting her soul free.

Lucinda stood outside of Clairmont Hall, Richard at her side, their trunks being strapped to a caravan of phaetons and barouches ready to set out for London. She smothered a grin at Richard's harried expression as he tried to herd his sister into a carriage. She dawdled about, checking her reticule, then running back in the house to go through the things she'd left in her bedchamber, then returning to consult with her lady's maid.

Carolly, without a doubt, had recovered from Faye's spell.

Indeed, as Faye had disappeared into the river of light, her cloak and clothes had dropped from her body. Immediately Lucinda had checked Faye's gown and found the poppet, melted and totally harmless.

What had happened to Faye? Lucinda wasn't certain. After she'd strengthened the golden mist with the last of her magic, the cloud had seemed to envelop Faye; and then, Faye had called upon the magic in the dove and become a being of golden dust herself. Lucinda had sensed a warm presence in the mist, a loving sensation that had enveloped her even as it must have enveloped Faye. Privately she hoped the presence had been Faye's husband Christopher, returning to claim Faye and bring her peace.

Sir James had informed the constable of Faye's disappearance and, as they were due in London, had placed the matter in the constable's able hands. Lucinda knew Faye was a mystery they'd never solve. Whatever the case, she knew nothing but relief and joy that they'd thwarted Fate. She put her arm around Richard and snuggled next to him.

He placed a distracted kiss on her hair. "You smell good."

" 'Tis the lavender soap you gave me. I feel very clean. I must admit, I've never taken an hour-long bath, but last night, you persuaded me of its pleasures."

He placed his hands on her shoulders and turned her to face him, heedless of the footmen who smiled behind their hands. She drank him in for a moment, her attention lingering on his strong, square chin, shadowed by a day's beard growth; his warm hazel eyes, accented by laugh lines at the corners; his full, sensual mouth which had taught her about another kind of enchantment.

Her heart thumped mightily before settling down into an even rhythm. "I love you, Richard."

His only answer was a kiss, a kiss that told her far better than words how fervently he returned her love. She clung to him, savoring the moment, thinking about the lifetime of similar moments that stretched before her.

Behind them, someone cleared his throat.

They broke away from each other. Lucinda felt her cheeks grow warm. She turned to find Uncle George smiling at her, a glow of health replacing his former pallor.

"I've come to see you off," he said. "I'm glad you're going to London, and even more pleased you've already caught your husband."

His smile widened to include Richard.

"We'll be back in a fortnight," Richard promised, "as soon as the Queen has given Carolly her blessing. Thereafter, we'll both be in your backyard so often I'm sure you'll get tired of us."

"I hope you keep your promise." The sounds of horses' hooves striking the earth and rattling harnesses reached them. Uncle George turned to look down the carriageway. "Isn't that Squire Piggott's chaise?"

Lucinda stifled a groan. "He must be coming to wish us goodbye."

Carolly stopped to join their small group, her gaze alighting on the Squire. Her groan was more lively. "Oh, Lord, not the Squire. He'll regale us with tales of Lady Rothfield's noble estate for hours." She ran for the carriage and climbed in.

"I'll have to thank the Squire for one thing," Richard remarked. "He's finally convinced Carolly to get into the carriage."

Uncle George and Lucinda laughed.

374

Wiping his eyes, her uncle refocused on their caravan. "So you're staying in London for a fortnight, until Carolly is presented. And what of Sir James?"

"He'll stay in London with her the entire time. He plans to squire her to and from the endless parties she'll attend," Lucinda confided just as Sir James emerged from Clairmont Hall and stepped onto the drive. His attitude seemed more lively too, now that Faye had ceased to work her magic on him.

"Really? I did not think him the type to make merry. He hasn't done so since his wife died all those years ago."

She slanted a glance at her husband beneath her lashes. "Richard and I are both hoping he finds a . . . companion in London, one closer to his own age. Indeed, we both think he's ready. When he saw Carolly on the night of her birthday party, a change seemed to come over him. He had a sense of time passing that he could have better used. We hope he finds happiness."

"And you, gel. Are you happy?"

"Very."

Richard smiled down at her, then ran a hand through his hair, obviously distracted. "Pardon me while I make certain we're ready to leave." He walked to his father's side and consulted with him, their heads bent together.

Lucinda fished through her pocket and brought out the heart of the dove, her only reminder of how love and forgiveness had triumphed over hatred and vengeance. The ruby sparkled and glowed against her palm as though full of magic, and indeed, if any magic were to be found in the vicinity, the heart of the dove was the place to look. Lucinda had used the last of her magic during her confrontation with Faye.

She was now an ordinary person and rather liked the feel of it.

"It's over, Uncle," she murmured.

"I know." He put an arm around her shoulders. "Every witch and warlock in England marked your confrontation with Faye. Indeed, when the dove shattered, I saw such a blaze of light in my mind that my temples ached for hours. I'm proud of you, gel. You came through it well."

He curled his fingers around hers, enfolding the ruby heart with both of their hands. "I hope you're going to keep the heart as a token of remembrance. Why not have it set and wear it? It matches your wedding ring rather well."

" 'Tis my intention. After all, the heart of the dove," she began, smiling.

"Is a heart of love," he finished for her, and they both chuckled.

Richard returned to her side and cast an apologetic glance at Uncle George. "We had better leave. The skies on the horizon this morning were pink. You know that old rhyme, pink in the morn, sailors be warned. I, for one, would prefer to avoid another storm like the one we had yesterday."

Lucinda and Uncle George exchanged a smile at his serious tone before she poked Richard in the ribs. "I see you've become a superstitious old fool like the rest of us."

He gave her a mock frown. "Beware, madam, that I don't cast a love spell over you."

Ignoring Uncle George's amused gaze, she brushed a lock of hair back from his forehead. "I'm afraid you've already worked your magic on me."

He rested his head upon hers, his voice throbbing with emotion. "Today, we begin a new journey."

"Yes, one filled with happiness. Shall we celebrate . . . again?"

"For the rest of our lives." He leaned down to finish the kiss they'd started, in full view of every eye that cared to look their way. Sighing, Lucinda surrendered to the magic that only genuine love can bring.

Let

Andrea Kane

romance you tonight!

Dream Castle 73585 -3/$5.99

My Heart's Desire 73584 -5/$5.50

Masque of Betrayal 75532 -3/$4.99

Echoes In the Mist 75533 -1/$5.99

Samantha 86507 -2/$5.50

The Last Duke 86508 -0/$5.99

Emerald Garden 86509 -9/$5.99

Wishes In the Wind 53483 -1/$5.99

Legacy of the Diamond 53485 -8/$5.99

The Black Diamond 53482 -3/$5.99

The Music Box 53484 -X/$6.50

The Theft 01887 -6/$6.50

Available from Pocket Books

**POCKET BOOKS
PROUDLY PRESENTS**

Forbidden Garden
Tracy Fobes

**Coming soon in paperback
from Sonnet Books**

**The following is a preview of
Forbidden Garden. . . .**

The Wicklow Mountains,
Ireland, 1860

Anne Sherwood brushed the grass off her traveling gown, smoothed a hand over her hair, and fought for calm. Her nighttime walk down the road to the village of Balkilly had proven less than enjoyable, but with the stagecoach sitting askew on three wheels, she'd had little choice. If she hadn't walked the rest of the way to the village, she would have spent the evening in the stagecoach with two drunken, snoring drivers.

She glanced up at the sign above her: BALKILLY ARMS. Muffled voices and low-pitched male laughter from the inn helped banish the shadows which fell beyond the lantern's glow. Suddenly, she didn't feel quite so alone. Squaring her shoulders, she lifted her chin, walked to the door, and pushed it open.

Conversation spilled out into the night. Swallowing, she stepped into the foyer and squinted through the whiskey fumes clogging the air. The door had opened on the inn's dining room. A rectangular pine table stretched nearly the length of the room. Near the center of the table, a group of men clustered. They were a rough bunch, their frieze coats tattered and bespeaking lean times. She wondered what had drawn their attention so thoroughly. A game of cards perhaps?

Wood burned in an open-hearth fireplace. The flames warmed her but didn't cast enough light to dispel the pocket of darkness near the door. Her entrance went unmarked. She navigated around a peasant, whose drunken snores drowned out the men's conversation, and scanned the crowd for the innkeeper. When she didn't find a likely candidate, she decided to pick out the least threatening man and ask for assistance. She wasn't the kind of woman who demanded comforts at every turn, but the thought of a warm bed that didn't rock back and forth was extremely tempting after days of journeying.

Nevertheless, as the seconds passed, she felt so completely out of her element—among men whose behavior she couldn't even begin to fathom after a lifetime of proper English gentlemen—that she couldn't find the nerve to push into the crowd and ask for the innkeeper. At least not yet.

The men continued to focus on something in the middle of the table. Between their huddled bodies, she caught a glimpse of ivory and pink and white. *Fabric,* she suddenly realized. They had satins and silks, for heaven's sake. Since when did a bunch of Irishmen find fabric so interesting?

One of them sat apart from the others. He was a big man, his legs stretched out casually, his shoulders broad and powerful, easily spanning the captain's chair he had folded his frame into. His hair was dark and shaggy, his skin swarthy, and his nose had evidently been broken more than once. A small gold loop sparkled in his left ear.

She found herself unable to look away.

He was different from the others in some ineffable way. Alone, he watched but didn't participate. Her attention slid lower, to his mud-spotted trousers and boots. His frieze coat, she thought, appeared filthy, and she wrinkled her nose in distaste. It wasn't the dirt that bothered her. During her years at Kew Gardens, she'd learned to respect the gardeners who tended the plants; they usually wore a coating of earth on their clothes. Rather, she disliked the way it looked on him. The dirt lent him a dangerous air, conjuring images of brawls on hard-packed earth. Obviously, the man was one of County Wicklow's rowdier peasants.

At that moment, as she stood there with her nose scrunched and her aversion to him obvious, he glanced up and saw her. She quickly tried to school her features into a more pleasant expression, but it was too late. His full lips twitched in a half-smile, and she realized he didn't give a damn what she thought of him. Warmth crept into her cheeks at the realization he'd caught her in such an ill-mannered display.

He scraped back his chair, stood, and set a tankard of ale on the table with a subdued thump. His gaze upon her was intense as he walked to her side, his eyes the color of a lough on a stormy day—blue, flecked liberally with gray.

A peculiar giddiness curled in her stomach. She shrank backward a few steps before pride took over and insisted she hold her ground.

"Good evening to you, my lady." He bent a full smile upon her, blasting her with Irish charm. " 'Tis certain the fairies have deposited you on the doorstep. Where else could you have come from?"

She cleared her throat once, twice, finding it difficult to speak. Most of the men she knew were scholarly types. Their fine breeding, gentleness, and preoccupation with cerebral matters sometimes made her forget they were men. Even her late husband had been gentle with her, giving her carnal knowledge while teaching her nothing of pleasure. But this dark Irishman had a certain vitality, a primitive earthiness she'd never encountered before.

His smile grew broader. "From the fairies, then. They've been good to us tonight." He motioned to a weary-looking innkeeper who had appeared behind the counter to serve up pints of ale. "Some water, Patrick, for the lady. I'll not have her telling her tale with a dry throat. And an ale for me."

She frowned. "I'm Mrs. Sherwood. I've been traveling by stagecoach—"

"So, you're not from the fairies, but from England. Michael McEvoy, at your service." He sketched her a bow, his gaze flickering across her lips and breasts, the shift so quick and practiced she might not have noticed it if she hadn't been watching him so carefully. "And Mr. Sherwood? Will he be coming along, too?"

"I'm a widow." Her breath coming faster, she narrowed her eyes. *Michael McEvoy.* She remembered the name well. Lord Connock had employed him as a naturalist who traveled to foreign lands for rare plants.

An adventurer.

"Mr. McEvoy," she began crisply, "I appreciate your fine Irish hospitality, but I'm afraid—"

A sudden burst of whistling cut her off. They both looked toward the clustered men. One of the Irishmen had a wispy piece of ivory silk in his hands.

Anne narrowed her eyes. That ivory silk looked familiar . . .

"The stagecoach was late tonight," Michael McEvoy said as he grabbed the two tankards the innkeeper pushed toward him. He handed one to her, somehow managing to brush his fingertips across her wrist. "I'm assuming your bags are outside. How did you enjoy your journey, and who are you here to visit?"

"I didn't enjoy my journey at all." She raised the tankard to her lips and, expecting water, gulped warm Irish beer instead. Immediately she broke into a fit of coughing as the bitters assaulted her tongue.

He grinned and switched their drinks. "I beg your pardon. Wrong tankard."

Anne eyed him closely. She told herself his earthiness was no more fetching than that of a pig in a sty. "Mr. McEvoy," she began in her most forbidding tone, "I am from England. I'm also tired and hungry. If you'll be silent for a moment and allow me to 'tell my tale,' as you put it, perhaps I might seek my bed before too much longer."

"My mouth is closed, ma'am."

"You're a man with sense, I see. A rare breed."

Her retort startled a grunt out of him. His eyes glinted with male appreciation before his lids dropped half-mast. It was a look designed to draw a response from her and respond she did, helplessly, her heart quickening in her chest. He was, quite simply, the most masculine male she'd ever met, and the woman in her could not dismiss him.

She clasped her hands together and took a few steps toward the men clustered around the pine table. She had to put some distance between herself and this dark Irishman. Words didn't come easily with him standing so nearby. "Obviously you didn't recognize my name, but I know yours. I've come from London to work for Lord Connock as a botanical illustrator. And you are Lord Connock's naturalist."

His dark eyebrows twitched upward. "By all that's holy, Lord Connock never told me he hired a woman. I was expecting a man to arrive tomorrow."

She could see he possessed not a jot of forward thinking. Obviously, he thought her gender better suited for gentler pursuits. And what sort of gentle pursuits might he value most? Anne thought she knew. Judging by the way his gaze had burned across her a moment before, he liked his women in his bed.

Her cheeks flamed. "I did not want to spend the night in Dublin, so I bought a seat on the next stage-coach bound for the Wicklow Mountains."

"Why such a need for haste?"

"I . . . didn't like the city," she confided, remembering the squalor and poverty.

"I'm a Connaught man myself. 'Tis the fairest country in the land. Still, if you saw Dublin on a good day, with sunlight turning the mountains to an emerald green while a soft Irish rain misted down upon the avenues and the sailboats in Dublin Bay, you might change your mind."

Brow furrowed, Anne tilted her head. "I saw only the poor."

"No man's poor who lives in Ireland."

"I must have missed something."

"That you have, ma'am."

Her expression smoothed out and she grew silent., his words resonating within her. She'd known Michael McEvoy for no more than a few minutes; yet, how easily he'd pointed out the one thing that had been bothering her most these past years. She was missing something. She had forgotten something.

She understood endings better than beginnings.

"Will you be wanting me to take you to Glendale Hall?" he asked, breaking into her thoughts.

"I wouldn't disturb Lord Connock at such an hour. A room in this inn will do fine for now."

"And your baggage . . . 'tis outside?"

She began to tell him that her baggage was two miles away, strapped to a broken-down stagecoach. Hoots from the men around the table drowned her out. She caught a glimpse of sky-blue satin edged with ivory lace in a set of hammy fingers and froze. Her insides clenched into a knot.

By God, they had her underwear.

How it had happened, she couldn't guess, but these papist heretics had her underwear. Lord, the whole village was going to know her little secret, her weakness for fancy underwear. The flush that had kept her cheeks warm while she'd talked to Michael abruptly drained away.

"Mrs. Sherwood? Are you ill?" He placed a hand on her arm, his palm warm and gentle, and in a distracted way she recognized how very good it felt.

She gestured toward the man. "What, exactly, are they pawing through?"

"A trunk. Paddy found it several miles away, just sitting in the middle of the road. Said his horse almost tripped over it."

She remembered that odd thump she'd experienced as the stagecoach had passed through Sally Gap and felt her inner temperature plummet several degrees. "What does the trunk contain?"

"Lady's underwear." He grinned. "And not just any lady's underwear. No stiff, starched bloomers for our lassie. All silks and satins in colors that this village has never seen the like of. Old Paddy thought he'd died and gone to heaven when he opened it."

"Mr. McEvoy . . ." She paused, searching for words, her cheeks filling with heat again, the heat spreading down to the tops of her breasts. "Those lady's unmentionables are . . . mine."

"Yours?" He stared down at her brown serge traveling gown, one even she thought of as pure ugliness. His look of shock would have been comical in any other circumstance.

She pressed a hand against her forehead. "Our driver was drinking poteen. The stagecoach shimmied from one side of the road to the other. When we passed through Sally Gap, I heard a bump, and now I realize one of my trunks must have fallen off—"

"Mother of God," he murmured. He left her side and pushed toward the men, his attention fastening on a rose-colored chemise embroidered with tiny flowers along the bodice. "Lads, I'm afraid you can't be looking at these anymore."

"Why not?" a grizzled man asked, his gray hair topped by a felt hat that had seen better days.

Michael slid a glance her way before facing his cronies again. "Because I'm going to buy them from you, that's why, and I don't want them damaged."

Anne took a deep breath and let it out slowly. Evidently, Michael McEvoy was gentleman enough to spare her further embarrassment. Her estimation of him went up a notch or two.

"What if I don't want to sell 'em?" the old man asked.

"Come on, Paddy, who're you going to give them to? Your wife, Moira? She'll give you the beating of your life for visiting a fancy woman."

Amid a chorus of guffaws, Michael touched the chemise, his fingers running reverently along the embroidery before he picked it up with gentle fingers and placed it back in the trunk. A pair of her ivory silk hose followed, the wisps of fabric draping across his arm as he set them next to the chemise.

Paddy grumbled good-naturedly. "I guess I can buy Moira something nice, maybe earn myself a smile. What are *you* going to do with 'em, McEvoy?"

"Give them to the poor."

Hearty laughter broke out around the table.

Anne could hardly bear to watch; still, she knew if she didn't watch, her imagination would torture her even worse. She forced herself to keep her attention on the dark Irishman and squinted with embarrassment at the red flush that had risen in his cheeks.

He grasped her sky-blue drawers and slipped them into the trunk, but, rather than withdraw his hand, he paused, his eyes growing wider. "Holy Mother of God," he murmured again.

The grizzled man's eyebrows climbed. "What did you find?"

"Come on, McEvoy, show us," a man with a brutally scarred face shouted.

Michael withdraw his hand, slowly, as if he couldn't help himself. She saw scarlet silk between his fingers and let out a low moan.

He had found the corset.

He didn't remove it entirely, but just enough so he might examine it himself, fully, the red flush creeping down to his neck.

"A scarlet corset," one male voice whispered.

"With black lace and black ties," another said with hushed reverence.

Anne closed her eyes. She wondered if a person could die from shame. She only wore the corset on days when she was feeling particularly dismal, and it never failed to brighten her mood. Surely that wasn't a crime?

When she opened her eyes she found Michael staring at her, his expression curious, his gaze very warm. She shivered. Somehow she managed to raise her chin.

He dropped the corset and closed the trunk. "I'll be by with a purse tomorrow, Paddy. Do you mind if I take the trunk tonight?"

Still grumbling, the old man nodded his assent.

Now that the trunk ceased to be the center of attention, the men dispersed, and the scarred man saw her. He jumped in surprise and pointed; soon they'd all eyed her up.

Anne pressed a hand against her throat. She wondered if any of them suspected she owned the scandalous underwear.

Michael returned to her side, but angled himself so he stood partially in front of her, shielding her from the other Irishmen's eyes. "I want you all to meet Mrs. Sherwood, from London," he said. "She's here as Lord Connock's guest and will be staying at the inn for the night. Patrick, can you fix her a room?"

The innkeeper smiled. "We'll have you in a warm bed in no time, Mrs. Sherwood."

Tugging on his felt hat, Paddy nodded. "Pleased to meet you, ma'am."

For the first time, Anne noticed an odd growth on the side of Paddy's head, a deformity of some sort on the skin beneath his ear. Her scientific curiosity piqued, she wondered at its origin.

A chorus of greetings followed Paddy's, and then the men dispersed, two of them sidling up to the bar, the others stomping out the door. Some, she noted, had deformities similar to the old Irishman's. Silently, she decided that the people of Balkilly must have suffered greatly during the potato famine. Their poor nutrition had obviously produced visible effects on their children.

Anne let out a sigh. "Mr. McEvoy, I still haven't finished telling you what happened on the way from Dublin."

He guided her over to a chair. "Sit down, Mrs. Sherwood, and finish your tale."

She collapsed gratefully, and Michael settled into another chair by her side.

"The stagecoach driver grew so drunk," she finally told him, "that he steered the carriage into a ditch and the wheel broke. He and his companion are lying on the side of the road, some two miles back. I can't say they're waiting for rescue, however. They probably won't even remember the accident."

Michael thumped his palm against his forehead. "Why didn't you tell me sooner that you'd been in an accident?"

"You didn't allow me to."

"And *you* let me fold underwear, knowing you'd just had a nasty shock." He shook his head in evident disgust. "What else haven't you told me?"

Anne frowned. First he made love to her with his gaze, then he badgered her with reprimands; what would he do next? Her patience, already stretched to a thread, suddenly snapped. "What haven't I told you? Well, I didn't tell you about my fright when we crashed, and my horrific walk down the road, and the peculiar rustling in the woods, and the ivy that tripped me—" She broke off and drew a breath, her chest heaving. "Nor about the oak tree in the yard. which is ready to topple upon this lovely little establishment!"

She could see his surprise in the way he stiffened, but he recovered quickly. When he spoke, his voice was gentle. "Easy, easy. I can see you've had a bad time of it. We'll get you into bed."

"I'll get myself into bed," she informed him.

An unwilling smile twitched his lips. "Tomorrow, I'll bring you to Glendale Hall. Once you're settled in, we'll start our work."

"*Our* work?"

The dark Irishman raised one eyebrow. "Didn't Lord Connock tell you he'd asked me to assist you in whatever manner necessary?"

"No, he most certainly didn't."

"Mrs. Sherwood, tomorrow we embark on what I'm certain will be a long and fruitful relationship." He winked at her. "I'll return your underwear then."

Look for
FORBIDDEN GARDEN
**Wherever Books
Are Sold
Coming Soon
in Paperback from
Sonnet Books**